The Rocks Of Valpré

by

ETHEL M. DELL

The rocks of valpré
by ETHEL M. DELL

ISBN: 978-93-63056-64-0

Published by

DOUBLE 9 BOOKS

2/13-B, Ansari Road
Daryaganj, New Delhi – 110002
info@double9books.com
www.double9books.com
Tel. 011-40042856

ABOUT THE AUTHOR

From 1911 to 1939, Ethel May Dell Savage, better known by her pen name Ethel M. Dell, was a British writer of more than 30 bestselling romance novels and several short tales. Dell was born on August 2, 1881, to a middle-class family in Streatham, a London neighborhood. Her father was a clerk in the City of London, and she has an older sister and brother. Dell began writing stories at a young age, and many of them have been published in popular journals. Her stories were primarily romantic in nature, set in the British Raj and other former British colonial territories. Some thought her stories were too sexual. Dell worked on her first novel, The Way of an Eagle, for several years before releasing it with T. Fisher Unwin after being rejected by eight other publishers. The book was part of Unwin's First Novel Library, a series that celebrated a writer's first novel. The Way of an Eagle was first published in 1911 and went through thirty printings by 1915. In 1922, Ethel married Lieutenant-Colonel Gerald Tahourdin Savage, who resigned his service at the time of their marriage, leaving Dell as the family's sole support. Despite negative reviews from reviewers, she built a loyal fan base and earned between £20,000 and £30,000 per year. Her husband was loyal to her and zealously protected her privacy.

CONTENTS

I
Dedicate This Book To MY MOTHER

AS A VERY SMALL TOKEN OF THAT LOVE WHICH NO WORDS CAN EXPRESS

"Love is indestructible:
Its holy flame for ever burneth,
From Heaven it came, to Heaven returneth;
  Too oft on Earth a troubled guest,
  At times deceived, at times opprest,
  It here is tried and purified,
  Then hath in Heaven its perfect rest:
It soweth here with toil and care,
Bat the harvest-time of Love is there."

The Curse of Kehama—Robert Southey.

PROLOGUE

CHAPTER I
THE KNIGHT OF THE MAGIC CAVE

When Cinders began to dig a hole no power on earth, except brute force, could ever stop him till he sank exhausted. Not even the sight of a crab could divert his thoughts from this entrancing occupation, much less his mistress's shrill whistle; and this was strange, for on all other occasions it was his custom to display the most exemplary obedience.

Of a cheerful disposition was Cinders, deeply interested in all things living, despising nothing however trivial, constantly seeking, and very often finding, treasures of supreme value in his own estimation. It was probably this passion for investigation that induced him to dig with such energy and perseverance, but he was not an interesting companion when the digging mood was upon him. It was, in fact, advisable to keep at a distance, for he created a miniature sand-storm in his immediate vicinity that spoiled the amusement of all except himself and successfully checked all intrusive sympathy.

"It really is too bad of him," said Chris, as she sat on a rock at twelve yards' distance and dried her feet in melancholy preoccupation. "It's the third day running, and I'm so tired of having nobody to talk to and nothing to do—not even a crab-hunt."

There was some pleasure to be extracted from crab-hunting under Cinders' ardent leadership, but alone it held no fascinations. It really was just a little selfish of Cinders.

She glanced towards him, and saw that the sand-storm had temporarily abated. He was working away the heap that had collected beneath him in preparation for more extensive operations.

"Cinders!" she called, in the forlorn hope of attracting his attention. "Cinders!" Then, with a sudden spurt of animation, "Cinders darling, just come and see what I've found!"

But Cinders was not so easily deceived. He stood a moment with his stubby little body tensely poised, then plunged afresh with feverish eagerness to his task.

The sand-storm recommenced, and Chris turned with a sigh to contemplate the blue horizon. A large steamer was travelling slowly across it. She watched it enviously.

"Lucky people!" she said. "Lucky, lucky people!"

The wind caught her red-brown hair and blew it out like a cloak behind her. It was still damp, for she had been bathing, and when the wind had passed it settled again in long, gleaming ripples upon her shoulders. She pushed it away from her face with an impatient hand.

"Cinders," she said, "if you don't come soon I shall go and find the Knight of the Magic Cave all by myself."

But even this threat did not move the enthusiastic Cinders. All that could be seen of him was a pair of sturdy hind-legs firmly planted amid a whirl of sand. Quite plainly it was nothing to him what steps his young mistress might see fit to take to relieve her boredom.

"All right!" said Chris, springing to her feet with a flourish of her towel. "Then good-bye!"

She shook the hair back from her face, slipped her bare feet into sandals, slung the towel across her shoulders, and turned her face to the cliffs.

They frowned above the rock-strewn beach to a height of two hundred feet, tunnelled here and there by the sea, scored here and there by springs, rising mass upon mass, in some places almost perpendicular, in others overhanging.

They possessed an immense fascination for Chris Wyndham, these cliffs. There was a species of dreadful romance about them that attracted even while it awed her. She longed to explore them, and yet deep in the most private recesses of her soul she was half-afraid. So many terrible stories were told of this particular corner of the rocky coast. So many ships were wrecked, so many lives were lost, so many hopes were quenched forever between the cliffs and the sea.

But these facts did not prevent her weaving romances about those wonderful caves. For instance, there was the Magic Cave, for which she was bound now, the entrance to which was only accessible at low tide. There was something particularly imposing about this entrance, something palatial, that stirred the girl's quick fancy. She had never before quite reached it on account of the difficulty of the approach; but she had promised herself that she would do so sooner or later, when time and tide should permit.

Both chanced to be favourable on this particular afternoon, and she set forth light-footed upon the adventure, leaving Cinders to his monotonous but all-engrossing pastime. A wide line of rocks stretched between her and her goal, which was dimly discernible in the deep shadow of the cliff—a mysterious opening that had the appearance of a low Gothic archway.

"I'm sure it's haunted," said Chris, and fell forthwith to dreaming as she stepped along the sunlit sand.

Of course she would find an enchanted hall, peopled by crabs that were not crabs at all, but the afore-mentioned knight and his retinue, all bound by the same wicked spell. "And I shall have to find out what it is and set him free," said Chris, with a sigh of pleasurable anticipation. "And then, I suppose, he will begin to jabber French, and I shall wish to goodness I hadn't. I expect he will want to marry me, poor thing! And I shall have to explain—in French, ugh!—that as he is only a foreigner I couldn't possibly, under any circumstances, entertain such a preposterous notion for a single instant. No, I am afraid that would sound rather rude. How else could I put it?"

Chris's brow wrinkled over the problem. She had reached the outlying rocks of the belt she had to cross, and was picking her way between the pools in deep abstraction.

"I wonder!" she murmured to herself. "I wonder!"

Then suddenly her rapt expression broke into a merry smile. "I know! Of course! Absurdly easy! I shall tell him that I am under a spell too—bound beyond all chance of escape to marry an Englishman." The sweet face dimpled over the inspiration. "That ought to settle him, unless he is very persevering; in which case of course I should have to tell him—quite kindly—that I really didn't think I could. Fancy marrying a crab—and a French crab too!"

She began to laugh, gaily, irrepressibly, light-heartedly, and skipped on to the first weed-covered rock that obstructed her path. It was an exceedingly slippery perch. She poised herself with arms outspread, with a butterfly grace as airy as her visions.

Away in the distance Cinders, nearing exhaustion, leaned on one elbow and scratched spasmodically with his free paw.

"Good-bye, Cinders!" she called to him in her high young voice. "I'm never coming back any more."

Lightly she waved her hand and sprang for another rock. But her feet slipped on the seaweed, and she splashed down into a pool ankle-deep.

"Bother!" she said, with vehemence. "It's these silly sandals. I'll leave them here till I come back."

She scrambled out again and pulled them off. "If I really don't come back I shan't want them," she reflected, with her merry little smile.

She arranged sandals and towel on the flat surface of a rock and pursued her pilgrimage unhampered.

She certainly managed better without the sandals, but even as it was she slipped and slid a good deal on the treacherous seaweed. It took her considerably longer than she had anticipated to cross that belt of rocks. It was much farther than it looked. Moreover, the pools were so full of interest that she had to stop and investigate them as she went. Anemones, green and red, clung to the shining rocks, and crabs of all sizes scuttled away at her approach.

"What a lot of retainers he must have!" said Chris.

She was nearing the Gothic archway, and her heart began to beat fast in anticipation. What she really expected to find she could not have said. But undoubtedly this particular cave was many degrees more mysterious and more eerie than any other she had ever explored. It was very lonely, and the cliff that frowned above her was very black. The afternoon sun shone genially upon all things, however, and this gave her courage.

The waves foamed among the rocks but a few yards from the jutting headland. Already the tide was turning. That meant that her time was short.

"I won't go beyond the entrance to-day," said Chris. "But to-morrow I'll start earlier and go right in. P'raps Cinders will come too. It wouldn't be so lonely with Cinders."

The rocks all about her lay scattered like gigantic ruins. She stood upon a high boulder and peered around her. There was certainly something awe-inspiring about the place, the bright sun notwithstanding. It seemed to lie beneath a spell. She wondered if she would come across any bits of wreckage, and suppressed a shudder. The Gothic archway looked very dark and vault-like from where she stood. Should she, after all, go any nearer?

Should she wait till Cinders would deign to accompany her? The tide was undoubtedly rising. In any case she would have to turn back within the next few minutes.

Slowly she pivoted round and looked again from the smiling horizon whereon no ship was visible to the Magic Cave that yawned in the face of the cliff. The next instant she jumped so violently that she missed her footing and fell from her perch in sheer amazement. Something—someone—was moving just within the deep shadow where the sunlight could not penetrate!

It was not a big drop, but she came to earth with a cry of pain among a mass of fallen stones, whereon she subsided, tightly clasping one foot between her hands. She had stumbled upon wreckage to her cost; a piece of rusty iron at her side and the blood that ran out between her locked fingers testified to that.

"Oh, dear! Oh, dear!" she wailed, rocking herself, and then glanced nervously over her shoulder, remembering the mysterious cause of the disaster.

The next moment swiftly she released the injured foot and sprang up. A man, attired in white linen, had emerged from the Magic Cave.

He stood a second looking at her, then came bounding towards her over the rocks.

Chris shrank back against her boulder. She was feeling dizzy and rather sick, and the apparition frightened her.

As he drew near she waved a desperate hand to stay his approach. "Oh, please go away!" she cried in English. "I—I don't want any help. I'm only looking for crabs."

He paid no attention whatever to her gesture or to her words. Only, reaching her, he bowed very low, beginning with some formality, "*Mais, mademoiselle; permettez-moi, je vous prie,*" and ending in tones of quick compassion, "*Ah, pauvre petite! Pauvre petite!*"

Before she knew his intention he was on his knees before her, and had taken the cut foot very gently into his hands.

Chris leaned back, clinging to the boulder. The sunlight danced giddily in her eyes. She felt as if she were slipping over the edge of the world.

"I can't—stand," she faltered weakly.

"No, no, *petite!* But naturally!" came the reassuring reply. "Be seated, I beg. Permit me to assist you!"

Chris, being quite incapable of doing otherwise, yielded herself to the gentle insistence of an arm that encircled her. She had an impression—fleeting at the time but returning to her later—of friendly dark eyes that looked for an instant into hers; and then, exactly how it happened she knew not, she was sitting propped against the rock, while all the world swam dizzily around her, and someone with sure, steady hands wound a bandage tightly and ever more tightly around her wounded foot.

"It hurts!" she murmured piteously.

"Have patience, mademoiselle! It will be better in a moment," came the quick reply. "I shall not hurt you more than is necessary. It is to arrest the bleeding, this. Mademoiselle will endure the pain like a brave child, yes?"

Chris swallowed a little shudder. The dizziness was passing. She was beginning to see more clearly, and her gaze travelled with dawning criticism over the neat white figure that ministered so confidently to her need.

"I knew he'd be French," she whispered half aloud.

"But I speak English, mademoiselle," he returned, without raising his black head,

"Yes," she said, with a sigh of relief. "I'm very glad of that. Must you pull it any tighter? I—I can bear it, of course, but I'd much rather you didn't if—if you don't mind."

She spoke gaspingly. Her eyes were full of tears, though she kept them resolutely from falling.

"Poor little one!" he said. "But you are very brave. Once more—so—and we will not do it again. The pain is not so bad now, no?"

He looked up at her with a smile so kindly that Chris nearly broke down altogether. She made a desperate grab after her self-control, and by dint of biting her lower lip very hard just saved herself from this calamity.

It was a very pleasing face that looked into her own, olive-hued, with brows as delicate as a woman's. A thin line of black moustache outlined a mouth that was something over-sensitive. He was certainly quite a captivating fairy prince.

Chris shook the thick hair back upon her shoulders and surveyed him with interest. "It's getting better," she said. "It was a horrid cut, wasn't it? You don't know how it hurt."

"But I can imagine it," he declared. "I saw immediately that it was serious. Mademoiselle cannot attempt to walk."

"Oh, but I must indeed!" protested Chris in dismay. "I shall be drowned if I stay here."

He shook his head. "Ah no, no! You shall not stay here. If you will accept my assistance, all will be well."

"But you can't—carry me!" gasped Chris.

He rose to his feet, still smiling. "And why not, little one? Because you think that I have not the strength?"

Chris looked up at him speculatively. She felt no shyness; he was not the sort of person with whom she could feel shy. He was too kindly, too protecting, too altogether charming, for that. But he was of slender build, and she could not help entertaining a very decided doubt as to his physical powers.

"I am much heavier—and much older—than you think," she remarked at length.

He laughed boyishly, as if she had made a joke. "*Mais c'est drôle, cela*! Me, I have no thoughts upon the subject, mademoiselle. I believe what I see, and I assure you that I am well capable of carrying you across the rocks to Valpré. You lodge at Valpré?"

Chris nodded. "And you? No," hastily checking herself, "don't tell me! You live in the Magic Cave, of course. I knew you were there. It was why I came."

"You knew, mademoiselle?" His eyes interrogated her.

She nodded again in answer. "You have lived there for hundreds of years. You were under a spell, and I came and broke it. If I hadn't cut my foot, you would have been there still. Do you really think you can lift me? And what shall you do when you come to cross the rocks? They are much too slippery to walk on."

He stooped to raise her, still smiling. "Have no fear, mademoiselle! I know these rocks by heart."

She laughed with a child's pure merriment. "Oh, I am not afraid, *preux chevalier*. But if you find me too heavy—"

"If I cannot carry the queen of the fairies," he interrupted, "I am not worthy of the name."

He had her in his arms with the words, holding her lightly and easily, as if she had been an infant. His eyes smiled reassuringly into hers.

"So, mademoiselle! We depart for Valpré!"

"What fun!" said Chris.

It seemed she was to enjoy her adventure after all, adverse circumstances notwithstanding. Her foot throbbed and burned, but she put this fact resolutely away from her. She had found the knight, and, albeit he was French, she was very pleased with him. He was the prettiest toy that had ever yet come her way.

Possibly in this respect the knight's sentiments resembled hers. For she was very enchanting, this English girl, fresh as a rose and gay as a butterfly, with a face that none called beautiful but which most paused to admire. It was the vividness, the entrancing vitality of her, that caught the attention. People smiled almost unwittingly when little Chris Wyndham turned her laughing eyes their way; they were so clear, so blue, so confidingly merry. There was a rare sweetness about her, a spontaneous charm irresistibly winning. She loved everybody without effort, as naturally as she loved life, with an absence of self-consciousness so entire that perhaps it was not surprising that she was loved in return.

"You are much stronger than you look, *preux chevalier*," she remarked presently. "But wouldn't you like to set me down while you go and fetch my sandals? They are over there on the rocks. It would be a pity for them to get washed away, and I might manage to walk with them on."

He had brought her safely over the most difficult part of the way. He seated her at once upon a flat rock, and stooped to assure himself as to the success of his bandage.

"It gives you not so much of pain, no?" he asked.

"It scarcely hurts at all," she assured him. "You will be quick now, won't you, because I ought to be getting back. If you see Cinders, you might bring him too."

"Cinders?" he questioned, pausing.

"My dog," she explained. "But he doesn't talk French, so I don't suppose he will follow you."

He received the information with a smile. "But I speak English, mademoiselle," he protested for the second time.

"Ah yes, you do—after a fashion," admitted Chris. "But I don't suppose Cinders would understand it. It's not very English English."

He raised his shoulders in a gesture that was purely French. "*La belle dame sans merci!*" he murmured ruefully. "*Bien!* I will do my possible."

"Splendid!" laughed Chris. "No one could do more."

She watched him go with eyes that sparkled with merriment. The trim, slight figure was quite good to look upon. He went bounding over the rocks with the sure-footed grace of a chamois.

"I wonder who he really is," said Chris, "and where he comes from."

CHAPTER II
DESTINY

Over the rocks went the stranger with the careless speed of youth, humming to himself in a soft tenor, his brown face turned to the sun. The pleasant smile was still upon it. He had the look of one in whose eyes all things are good.

Ahead of him gleamed the towel with the sandals upon it, sandals that might have been fashioned for fairy feet. He quickened his pace at sight of them. But she was charming, this English child! He had never before seen anyone quite so dainty. And of a courage unique in one so young!

He was nearing the sandals now, but the sun was in his eyes, and he saw only the towel spread like a tablecloth over the rock. He sprang lightly down on to a heap of shingle, and reached for it, still humming the *chanson* that the little English girl had somehow put into his head.

The next instant a deep growl arrested him, and sharply he drew back. There was something more than a pair of sandals on the towel above him, something that crouched in an attitude of tense hostility, daring him to approach. It was only a small creature that thus challenged him, only a weird black terrier of doubtful extraction, but he bristled from end to end with animosity. Quite plainly he regarded the sandals as his responsibility. With glaring eyes and gleaming teeth he crouched, prepared to defend them.

The young Frenchman's discomfiture was but momentary. In an instant he had taken in the situation and the humour of it.

"But it is the good Cinders!" he said aloud, and extended a fearless hand. "So, my friend, so! The little mistress waits."

Cinders' growl became a snarl. He sucked up his breath in furious protest, threatening murder. But the stranger's hand was not withdrawn. On the contrary it advanced upon him with the utmost deliberation till Cinders was compelled to jerk backwards to avoid it.

So jerking, he missed his footing as his mistress had before him, lost his balance, and rolled, cursing, clinging, and clambering, over the edge of the rock.

Had the Frenchman laughed at that moment he would have made an enemy for life. But most fortunately he did not regard an antagonist's downfall as a fit subject for mirth. In fact, being of a chivalrous turn, he grabbed at the luckless Cinders, clutched his collar, and dragged him up again. And—perhaps it was the generosity of the action, perhaps only its obvious fearlessness—he won Cinders' heart from that instant. His hostility merged into sudden ardent friendship. He set his paws on the young man's chest, and licked his face.

Thenceforth he was more than welcome to sandals and towel and even the effusive Cinders himself, who leaped around him barking in high delight, and accompanied him with giddy circlings upon his return journey.

Chris, who had viewed the encounter from afar with much interest, clapped her hands at their approach.

"And you weren't a bit afraid!" she laughed. "I couldn't think what you would do. Cinders looked so fierce. But any one can see you understand dogs—even English dogs."

"It is possible that at heart the English and the French resemble each other more than we think, mademoiselle," observed the Frenchman. "One can never tell."

He bent again over the injured foot with the sandal in his hand.

"It's very good of you to take all this trouble," said Chris abruptly.

He flashed her a quick smile. "But no, mademoiselle! It gives me pleasure to be of service to you."

"I'm sure I don't know what I should have done without you," she rejoined. "Ah, that is much better. I shall be able to walk now."

"You think it?" He looked at her doubtfully.

She nodded. "If you will take me as far as the sand, I shall do splendidly then. You see, I can't let you come into Valpré with me because—because—"

"Because, mademoiselle—?" Up went the black brows questioningly.

She flushed a little, but her clear eyes met his with absolute candour. "We have a French governess," she explained, "who was brought up in a convent, so she is very easily shocked. If she knew that I had spoken to a stranger, and a man"—she raised her hands with a merry gesture—"she would have a fit—several fits. I couldn't risk it. Poor mademoiselle! She doesn't understand our English ways a bit. Why, she wouldn't even let me paddle if she could help it. I shall have to keep very quiet about this foot of mine, or it will be '*Jamais encore!*' and '*Encore jamais!*' for the rest of my natural life. And, after all," pathetically, "there can be no great harm in dipping one's feet in sea-water, can there?"

But the Frenchman looked grave. "You will show your foot to the doctor, will you not?" he said.

"Dear me, no!" said Chris.

"*Mais, mademoiselle*—"

She checked him with her quick, winning smile.

"Please don't talk French. I like English so much the best. Besides, it's holiday-time."

"But, mademoiselle," he persisted, "if it should become serious!"

"Oh, it won't," she said lightly. "I shall be all right. Nothing ever happens to me."

"Nothing?" he questioned, with an answering smile.

She was hobbling over the stones with his assistance. "Nothing interesting, I assure you," she said.

"Except when mademoiselle goes to the cavern of the fairies to look for the magic knight?" he suggested.

She threw him a merry glance. "To be sure! I will come and see you again some day when the tide is low. Is there a dragon in the cave?"

"He is there only when the tide is high, mademoiselle, a beast enormous with eyes of fire."

"And a princess?" asked the English girl, keenly interested.

"No, there is no princess."

"Only you and the dragon?"

"Generally only me, mademoiselle."

"Whatever do you do there?" she asked curiously.

His smile was bafflingly direct. "Me? I make magic, mademoiselle."

"What sort of magic?"

"What sort? That is a difficult question."

"May I come and see it?" asked Chris eagerly, scenting a mystery.

He hesitated.

"I'll come all by myself," she assured him.

"*Mais la gouvernante—*"

"As if I should bring her! No, no! I'll come alone—with Cinders."

"*Mais, mademoiselle—*"

"If you say that again I shall be cross," announced Chris.

"But—pardon me, mademoiselle—the governess, might she not object?"

"Absurd!" said Chris. "I am not a French girl, and I won't behave like one."

He laughed at that, plainly because he could not help it. "Mademoiselle pleases herself!" he observed.

"Of course I do," returned Chris vigorously. "I always have. I may come then?"

"But certainly."

"When?"

"When you will, mademoiselle."

Chris considered. They had reached the firm sand, and she stood still. "I can't come to-morrow because of my foot, and the day after the tide will be too late. I shall have to wait nearly a fortnight. How dull!"

"In a fortnight, then!" said the Frenchman.

"In a fortnight, *preux chevalier!*" Her eyes laughed up at him. "But I dare say we shall meet before then. I hope we shall."

"I hope it also, mademoiselle." He bowed courteously.

She held out her hand. "I shall come on the tenth of the month—it's my birthday. I'll bring some cakes, and we'll have a party, and invite the dragon." Her eyes danced. "We will have some fun, shall we?"

"I think that we shall not want the dragon," he smiled back.

"No? Perhaps not. Well, I'll bring Cinders instead."

"Ah, the good Cinders! He is different."

"And we will go exploring," she said eagerly. "I shan't be a bit afraid of anything with you there. The tenth, then! Don't forget! Good-bye, and thank you ever so much! You won't fail me, will you?"

He bent low over the impetuous little hand. "I shall not fail you, mademoiselle. *Adieu!*"

"*Au revoir!*" she laughed back. "Come along, Cinders! We shall be late for tea."

He stood motionless on the sunlit sand and watched her go.

She was limping, but she moved quickly notwithstanding. Cinders trotted soberly by her side.

As she reached the little *plage*, she turned as if aware of his watching eyes and nonchalantly waved the towel that dangled on her arm. The sunlight had turned her hair to burnished copper. It made her for the moment wonderful, and a gleam of swift admiration shot across the Frenchman's face.

"*Merveilleux!*" he whispered to himself, and half-aloud, "Good-bye, little bird of Paradise!"

With a courteous gesture of farewell, he turned away. When he looked again, the child, with her glorious, radiant hair, had passed from sight.

He went back, springing over the rocks, to the Gothic archway that had fired her curiosity. The tide was rising fast. Already the white foam raced up to the rocky entrance. He splashed through it, and went within as one on business bent.

He was absent for some seconds, and soon a large wave broke with a long roar and rushed swirling into the cave. As the gleaming water ran out again, he emerged.

A single glance was sufficient to show him that retreat by way of the beach was already cut off. He recognized the fact with a rueful grimace. The long green waves tumbling along the rocks were rising higher every instant.

With a quick glance around him, the young man sprang for an upstanding rock, reached it in safety, and paused, keenly studying the black face of the cliff.

It frowned above him like a rampart, gloomy, terrible, impregnable. He shrugged his shoulders with another grimace, then, as the foam splashed up over his feet, leaped lightly onto another rock higher than the first, whence it was possible to reach a great buttress that jutted outwards from the cliff itself.

Once upon this, he began to climb diagonally, clambering like a monkey, availing himself of every inch that offered foothold. A slip would have meant instant disaster, but this fact did not apparently occur to him, or if it did he was not dismayed thereby. He even presently, as he cautiously worked his way upwards, began to hum again in gay snatches the song that a child's clear eyes had set running in his brain that afternoon.

It was a progress that waxed more perilous as he proceeded. The waves dashed themselves to cataracts below him. Return was impossible, and many would have deemed advance equally so. But he struggled on, maintaining his zigzag course upwards, with nerve unfailing and spirits unimpaired.

Gulls flew out above his head and circled about him with indignant protests. He looked somewhat like a gigantic gull himself, his slim white figure outlined against the darkness of the cliff. He cried back to the startled birds reassuringly in their own language, but the commotion continued; and presently, finding precarious foothold on a narrow ledge halfway up, he stopped to wipe his forehead and laugh with merriment unfeigned. He was plainly in love with life—one in whose eyes all things were good, but yet who loved the hazard of them even better.

The ledge did not permit of much comfort. Nevertheless he managed to turn upon it and to lean back against the cliff, with his brown face to sky and sea. He even, after a moment, took out a cigarette and lighted it. The sun shone full in his eyes, and he seemed to revel in it. A sun-worshipper also, apparently!

He smoked his cigarette to the end very deliberately, flicking the ash from time to time towards the raging water below. When he had quite finished, he stretched his arms wide with a gesture of sublime self-confidence, faced about, and very composedly continued his climb.

It grew more and more arduous as he neared the frowning summit. He had to feel his way with the utmost caution. Once he missed his footing, and slipped several feet before he could recover himself, and after this experience he took a clasp-knife from his pocket and notched himself footholds where none offered. It was a very lengthy business, and the sun was dipping downwards to the sea ere he came within reach of his goal. The top of the cliff overhung where he first approached it, and he had to work a devious course below it till he came to a more favourable place.

Reaching a gap at length, he braced himself for the final effort. The surface of the cliff here was loose, and the stones rattled continually from beneath his feet; but he clung like a limpet, nothing daunted, and at last his hands were gripped in the coarse grass that fringed the summit. Sheer depth was below him, and the inward-curving cliff offered no possibility of foothold.

He stood, gathering his strength for a last stupendous effort. It was a supreme moment. It meant abandoning the support on which he stood and depending entirely upon the strength of his arms to attain to safety. The risk was desperate. He stood bracing himself to take it.

Finally, with an upward fling of the head, as of one who diced with the gods, he gripped that perilous edge and dared the final throw. Slowly, with stupendous effort, he hoisted himself up. It was the work of an expert athlete; none other would have attempted it.

Up he went and up, steadily, strongly; his head came level with his hands; he peered over the edge of the cliff. The strain was terrific. The careless smile was gone from his lips. In that instant he no longer ignored what lay behind him; he knew the suspense of the gambler who pauses after he has thrown before he lifts the dice-box to read his fate.

Up, and still up! The grass was beginning to yield in his clutching fingers; he dug them into the earth below. Now his shoulders were above the edge; his chest also, heaving with strenuous effort. To lower himself again was impossible. His feet dangled over space. And the surging of the water below him was as the roaring of an angry monster cheated of its prey.

He set his teeth. He was nearing the end of his strength. Had he, after all, attempted the impossible, flung the dice too recklessly, dared his fate too far? If so, he would pay the penalty swiftly, swiftly, down among the cruel rocks where many another had perished before him.

The surging sounded louder. It seemed to be in his brain. It bewildered him, deprived him of the power to think. A great many voices seemed to clamour around him, but only one could be clearly heard; only one, and that the voice of a child close to him—or was that also an illusion born of the racking strain that had driven all the blood to his head?

"You won't fail me, will you?" it said.

Surely his grasp was slackening, his powers were passing, when like a flashlight those words illuminated his brain. He was as one in deep waters, swamped and sinking; but that voice called him back.

He opened his eyes, he drew a great breath. He flung his whole soul into one last great effort. He remembered suddenly that the little English girl, the child with the glorious hair and laughing eyes, his acquaintance of an hour, would be looking for him exactly two weeks from that moment. He was sure she would look, and—she would be disappointed if she looked in vain. One must not disappoint a child.

The memory of her went through him, vivid, enchanting, compelling. It nerved his sinking heart. It renewed his grip on life. It urged him upwards.

Only a child! Only a child! But yet—

"I shall not—shall not—fail you!" he gasped, and with the words his knees reached the top of the cliff.

His strength collapsed instantly, like the snapping of a fiddle-string. He fell forward on his face, and lay prone...

A little later he worked the whole of his body into security, rolled over on his back with closed eyes to the sky, and waited while his heart slowed down to its normal rhythmic beat.

At last, quite suddenly, he sat up and looked around him. The laughter flashed back into his eyes. He sprang to his feet, mud-stained, dishevelled, yet exultant.

He clicked his heels together and faced the sinking sun, slim and upright, one stiff hand to his head. He had diced with the gods, and he had won.

"*Destinée! Je te salue!*" he said, and the next instant whizzed smartly round with a soldier's precision of movement and marched away towards the fortress that crowned the hill above the rocks of Valpré.

CHAPTER III
A ROPE OF SAND

Undoubtedly Mademoiselle Gautier was querulous, and equally without doubt she had good reason to be so; but it made it a little dull for Chris. Accidents would happen, wherever one went, and what was the good of making a fuss?

Of course, every allowance had to be made for poor Mademoiselle in consideration of the fact that she was torn in pieces by the valiant attempt to keep her attention focussed upon three children at once. The effort had not so far been a brilliant success, and Mademoiselle, conscious within herself of her inability to cope adequately with her threefold responsibility, being moreover worn out by her gallant struggle to do so, was inclined to shortness of temper and a severity of judgment that bordered upon injustice.

If Chris would persist in flying about the shore in that wild fashion with her hair loose—that flaming hair which Mademoiselle considered in itself to be almost indecent—what could be expected but that some *contretemps* must of necessity arrive? It was useless for Chris to protest that it was not her hair that had got her into difficulties, that she had only left it loose to dry it after her bathe, that there had been no one to see—at least, no one that mattered—and that the cut on her foot was solely due to the fact that she had taken off her sand-shoes to climb over the rocks. Mademoiselle only shook her head with pursed lips. Chris *était méchante—très méchante,* and no amount of arguing would make her change her opinion upon that point.

So Chris abandoned argument while the worried little Frenchwoman bathed and bandaged her foot anew. She would not be able to bathe again for at least a week, and this fact was of itself sufficient to depress her into silence. Yet, after a little, when Mademoiselle was gone, a cheery little tune rose to her lips. It was not her nature to be depressed for long.

Mademoiselle Gautier would have been something less than human if she had not yielded now and then under the perpetual strain in which, for many days past, she had lived. She had come to Valpré in charge of

Chris and her two young brothers, both of whom had developed diphtheria within a day or two of their arrival. The children's father was absent in India; his only sister, upon whom the cares of his family were supposed to rest, was entertaining Royalty, and was far too important a personage in the social world to be spared at short notice. And so the whole burden had devolved upon poor Mademoiselle Gautier, who had been near her wits' end with anxiety, but had nobly grappled with her task.

The worst of the business, speaking in a physical sense, was now over. Both her patients—Maxwell, who was Chris's twin, and little Noel, the youngest of the family, aged twelve—had turned the corner and were progressing towards convalescence. Over the latter she still had qualms of uneasiness, but the elder boy was rapidly picking up his strength and giving more trouble than he had ever given before in the process.

By inexorable decree Chris was kept away from the two over whom Mademoiselle, aided by a convent nurse, still watched with unremitting care; and it did seem a little hard in the opinion of the harassed Frenchwoman that her one sound charge could not be trusted to conduct herself with circumspection during her days of enforced solitude. Chris Wyndham, however, had been a tomboy all her life, and she could scarcely be expected to reform at such a juncture. She was not accustomed to solitude, and her restless spirit chafed after distraction.

The conventions had never troubled her. Brought up as she had been with three unruly boys, running wild with them during the whole of her childhood, it was scarcely to be wondered at if her outlook on life was more that of a boy than a girl. She had been in Mademoiselle Gautier's charge during the past three years, but somehow that had not sobered her very materially. She was spoilt by all except her aunt, who was wont to remark with some acidity that if she didn't come to grief one way or another, this would probably continue to be the case for the term of her natural life. But it was quite plain that Aunt Philippa expected her to come to grief. Girls like Chris, unless they married out of the schoolroom, usually played with fire until they burnt their fingers. The fact of the matter was Chris was far too attractive, and though as yet sublimely unconscious of the fact, Aunt Philippa knew that sooner or later it was bound to dawn upon her. She did not relish the prospect of steering this giddy little barque through the shoals and quicksands of society, being shrewdly suspicious that the task might well prove too much for her. For with all her sweetness, Chris was undeniably wilful, a princess who expected to have her own way; and Aunt Philippa had a daughter of her own, Chris's senior by three years, as well as a son in the Guards, to consider.

No, she did not approve of Chris, or indeed of any of the family, including her own brother, who was its head. She had not approved of his gay young wife, Irish and volatile, who had died at the birth of little Noel. She doubted the stability of each one of them in turn, and plainly told her brother that he must attend to the launching of his children for himself. She was willing to do her best for them as children, but as grown-ups she declined the responsibility.

His answer to this had been that they must remain children until he could spare the time to attend to them. The eldest boy, Rupert, was now at Sandhurst, Maxwell was being educated at Marlborough, and Noel, who was never very strong, was at present with Chris in Mademoiselle Gautier's care. The summer holiday at Valpré had been Mademoiselle's suggestion, and bitterly had she lived to regret it.

Chris had regretted it, too, for a time, but now that her two brothers were well on the road to recovery it seemed absurd not to extract such enjoyment as she could from the situation. Of course, it was lonely, but there was always Cinders to fall back upon for comfort. She was thankful that she had insisted upon bringing him, though Mademoiselle had protested most emphatically against this addition to the party. How she was to get him back again she had not begun to consider. Doubtless, however, Jack would manage it somehow. Jack was the aforementioned cousin in the Guards, a young man of much kindness and resource, upon whom Chris was wont to rely as a sort of superior elder brother. He would think nothing of running over to fetch them home and to assist in the smuggling of Cinders back into his native land. In fact, if the truth were told, he would probably rather enjoy it.

In the meantime, here was she, stranded with a damaged foot, and all the delights of the sea temporarily denied to her. Perhaps not quite all, when she came to think of it. She could not paddle, but she might manage to hobble down to the shore, and sit on the sun-baked rocks. Even Mademoiselle could surely find no fault with this. And she might possibly find someone to talk to. She was so fond of talking, and it was a perpetual regret to her that she could not understand the speech of the Breton fishermen.

It was on the morning of the second day after her accident that this idea presented itself. All the previous day she had sat soberly in a corner of the little garden that overlooked the little *plage* where none but *bonnes* and their charges ever passed. Nothing had happened all day long, and she had been bored almost to tears. The beaming smiles of Mademoiselle, who was thankful to have her within sight, had been no sort of consolation to her, and on the second day she came rapidly to the conclusion that she would die of *ennui* if she attempted to endure it any longer.

She did not arouse Mademoiselle's voluble protests by announcing her decision. Mademoiselle was busy with the boys, and what was the good? She was her own mistress, and felt in no way called upon to ask her governess's leave.

Her foot was much better. The nurse had strapped it for her, and, beyond some slight stiffness in walking, it caused her no pain. Her hair was tied discreetly back with a black ribbon. It ought to have been plaited, but as Mademoiselle had no time to bestow upon it and Chris herself couldn't be bothered, it hung in glory below the confining ribbon to her waist.

Whistling to Cinders, who was lying in the sunshine snapping at flies, she rose from her chair in the shade, dropped the crochet with which Mademoiselle had supplied her on the grass, and limped to the gate that opened on to the *plage*.

At this juncture a rhythmical, unmistakable sound made her pause. A quick gleam of pleasure shone in her blue eyes. She turned her head eagerly. A troop of soldiers were approaching along the *plage*.

Sheer fun flashed into the girl's face. With a sudden swoop she caught up the lazy Cinders.

"Now you are not to say anything," she cautioned him. "Only when I tell you, you are to salute. And mind you do it properly!"

Cinders licked the animated face so near his own. When not drawn by his one particular vice, he was always ready to enter into any little game that his mistress might devise. He watched the oncoming soldiers with interest, a slight frown between his brows.

The soldiers were interested also. Chris of the merry eyes was not a spectacle to pass unheeding. She smiled upon them—there were about forty of them—with the simplicity of a child.

Rhythmically the blue and red uniforms began to swing past. Their wearers stared and grinned at the smiling little *Anglaise* who was so naively pleased to see them.

She raised an imperious hand. "Cinders, salute!" And into Cinders' ear she whispered, "They are only French, chappie, but you mustn't mind."

And Cinders, quite unconcerned, obeyed his mistress's behest and lifted a rigid paw to his head.

A murmur of appreciation ran through the ranks. The grins widened. One boy, with bold admiration for the *petite Anglaise* in his black eyes, raised his hand abruptly and saluted in return. Every man who followed did likewise, and Chris was enchanted. Mademoiselle Gautier would have been horrified had she seen her frank nods of acknowledgment, but mercifully Fate spared her this.

Behind the last line of marching men came a trim young officer. His sword clanked at his heels. He swung along with a free swagger, head up, shoulders back, eyes fixed straight before him. A gallant specimen was he, for though of inconsiderable height, he was well made and obviously of athletic build. His thoughts were evidently far away, his handsome, boyish face so preoccupied that it had the look of a face in a picture, patrician, aloof, immobile.

But a sudden glimpse of the girl at the gate—the child with the shining hair—brought him back in a fraction of time, transformed him utterly. Recognition, vivid surprise, undoubted pleasure, flashed over his face. With an eager smile, he paused, clicked his heels together, saluted.

She extended an eager hand—her left; Cinders monopolized her right.

"Oh," she exclaimed, "you! I didn't know you were a soldier!"

He took the hand over the gate, stooped and kissed it. "But I am delighted, mademoiselle!" he said.

Cinders was also delighted, and struggled with yelps of welcome to reach him. He stood up, laughing, and patted the little creature's head.

"And the foot?" he questioned.

"Much better," said Chris. "I am going down to the shore presently. I wish you could come too."

He smiled and shook his head, with a glance after his men retreating up the hill towards the fort. "I wish it also, mademoiselle, but—"

"Couldn't you?" begged Chris. "This afternoon! Just for a little while! There's only Cinders and me."

"*Et Mademoiselle la gouvernante—*"

"She is looking after the boys, and they are ill," Chris explained cheerfully. "You might come. I'm wanting someone to talk to rather badly."

The young officer hesitated. The blue eyes were very persuasive.

"I would ask you to come in to tea afterwards," she said, "only Mademoiselle is so silly—quite cracked, in fact, on some points. But that needn't prevent your coming down to the shore for a little to play with Cinders and me. You will, won't you? Say you will!"

"I will, mademoiselle." His surrender was abrupt, and quite decisive.

She beamed upon him. "We will play at sand-pictures. You know that game, I expect. One draws and the other has to guess what it's meant for. I shall look out for you, then. Good-bye!"

She waved a careless hand, and he, still smiling, saluted again and hastened after his men.

She was certainly unconventional, this English girl, quite superbly so. She was also sublimely and completely irresistible.

Did she guess of the power that was hers as she turned back into the little garden? Did some dim suggestion of a spell yet dormant present itself as she stood thus on the threshold of her woman's kingdom? Possibly, for her face was thoughtful, and remained so for quite ten seconds after her new playmate's departure.

At the end of the ten seconds she kissed Cinders, with the remark, "Chappie, that little Frenchman is a trump. I'm sure Jack would think so." She and Jack Forest generally saw things in the same light, which may have been the reason that Chris valued his opinion so highly.

She postponed her visit to the shore till the afternoon in consideration of the fact that her sense of boredom had completely evaporated. After all, what was there to be bored about? Life was quite interesting again.

The tide was on the ebb when she finally set forth. She directed her steps towards a little patch of firm sand which she regarded as peculiarly her own. The shore was deserted as usual. The *bonnes* preferred the *plage*.

Would he be there before her, she wondered? Yes; almost at once she spied him in the distance. He had discarded his uniform, in favour of white linen. She regretted his preference somewhat, but admitted to herself that linen might be cooler.

He was very busy with a swagger-cane, drawing in the sand, far too intent to note her approach, and as he drew he hummed a madrigal in his soft voice.

Noiselessly Chris drew near, a dancing imp of mischief in her eyes. She wanted to get a glimpse of the work of art that he was elaborating with such care before he discovered her. But his sensibilities were too subtle for her. Quite suddenly he became aware of her and whizzed round.

He made her a low bow, but Chris waived the ceremony of greeting with impatient curiosity. "I want to see what you are doing. I may look?"

"But certainly, mademoiselle."

She came eagerly forward and looked.

"Oh," she said, "is that the dragon? What an awesome creature! Is he really like that? How splendidly you have done his scales! And what frightful claws! Why"—she turned upon him—"you are an artist!"•

He shrugged his shoulders, with his ready smile. "I am whatever mademoiselle desires."

"How nice!" said Chris. "Well, go on being an artist, please. Draw something else!"

"I think it is your turn now, mademoiselle," he said.

"Oh, but I'm no good at it," she protested. "I can't compete. You are much too clever."

He laughed at that and began again.

She seated herself on a rock and watched him, deeply interested.

"How quick you are!" she murmured presently. "Whatever is it, I wonder? A horse with a man on it! Ah, yes! St. George killing the dragon!

Excellent!" She clapped her hands. "It is a real picture. What a pity for it to be washed away!"

"The destiny of all things, mademoiselle," he remarked, still elaborating his work.

"Not all things!" she exclaimed. "Look at the Sphinx, and Cleopatra's Needle, and—and a host of other things!"

"You think that they will endure for ever?" he said.

"For a very, very long while," she maintained.

"But for ever, mademoiselle?" He turned round to her, quite serious for once. "There is only one thing that endures for ever," he said.

Chris frowned. "I don't want to think about it. It makes me feel giddy," she said. "Please go on drawing. The tide won't be up yet."

He turned back again instantly, looking quizzical. "*Alors*, shall we build a barrier of stones and arrest the sea?" he suggested.

"Or weave a rope of sand," amended Chris.

CHAPTER IV
THE DIVINE MAGIC

When Chris went bathing it was her custom to slip a mackintosh over her bathing costume and to run down to the shore thus equipped, discarding the mackintosh before entering the water and leaving it in the charge of Cinders.

Cinders never went treasure-hunting on these occasions, but invariably sat bolt upright, brimful of importance, watching his mistress's proceedings from afar with eager eyes and quivering nose. He would never be persuaded to follow her, owing to a rooted objection to wetting his feet. He was, as a rule, very patient; but if she kept him waiting beyond the bounds of patience he howled in a heartrending fashion that always brought her back.

Chris was a good swimmer, and had a boy's healthy love of the sea. Great was her joy when her injured foot healed sufficiently for her to resume the morning bathe. Mademoiselle Gautier's pleasure was not so keen, but then—poor Mademoiselle!—who could expect it? Besides, what could she know of the exquisite enjoyment of floating on a summer sea with the summer sun in one's eyes and wave after gentle wave rocking one to drowsy content?

The only drawback was the impossibility of diving, Chris longed for a dive on that brilliant morning, longed for the headlong rush through water, the greenness of it below the surface, the sparkling spray above. If only she could have commandeered a boat! But that would have entailed a boatman, and Mademoiselle would have been scandalized at the bare suggestion.

"She would make me bathe in a coat and skirt and a hat if she could," reflected Chris, shaking the wet hair out of her eyes.

It was still early, not nine o'clock. The sea lay calm and empty all about her. Was she really the only person in Valpré, she wondered, who cared for a morning dip? She had swum some way from the little town, and now found herself nearing the point where the rocks jutted far out to the sea. The Magic Cave was at no great distance. She saw the darkness of it and the water foaming white against the cliffs. Even in the morning light it was an awesome spot, and she remembered how her friend had told her that the dragon was there when the tide was up. With a timidity half-actual, half-assumed, she began to swim back to her starting-point.

Half-way back, feeling tired, she allowed herself a rest in consideration of the fact that this was the longest swim that she had ever undertaken. Serenely she lay on the water with her hair floating about her. The morning was perfect, the sea like a lake. Overhead sailed a gull with no flap of wings. She wondered how he did it, and longed to do the same. It must be very nice to be a gull.

Regretfully at length—for she was still feeling a little weary—she resumed her leisurely journey towards the shore. As she did so she caught the sound of oars grating in rowlocks. She turned her head, saw a boat cutting through the water at a prodigious rate not twenty strokes from her, caught a glimpse of its one rower, and without a second's hesitation flung up an imperious arm.

"Stop!" she cried. "It's me!"

He ceased to row on the instant, but the boat shot on. She saw the concern in his face as he brought it back. His black head shone wet in the sunlight. He was evidently returning from a bathe himself.

"It's all right," smiled Chris. "Are you in a great hurry? I wondered if you would tow me a little way. I've come too far, and I'm just a tiny bit tired."

He brought the boat near, and shipped his oars. "I will row you to the shore with pleasure, mademoiselle," he said.

"No, no," she said. "Just throw me a rope, that's all."

"But I have no rope, mademoiselle."

He leaned down to her as she swam alongside; but Chris still hung back, with laughing eyes upraised. "You will capsize in a minute, and that won't help either of us. Really, I don't think I will come out."

But she gave him her hand, nevertheless.

His fingers closed upon it in a warm clasp that seemed very sure of itself. He smiled down at her. "I think otherwise, mademoiselle."

She found it impossible to resist him, and so yielded with characteristic briskness of decision. "Very well, if you will let me dive from the boat afterwards. Hold tight, *preux chevalier*! One—two—three!"

She came up to him out of the sea like a bird rising from the waves. A moment he had her slim young body between his hands. Then she stepped lightly upon the thwart, and he let her go.

And in that instant something happened: something that was like the kindling of spirit into flame ran between them—a transforming magic that only one knew for the Divine Miracle that changes the face of the whole earth.

To the girl, with her wet hair all around her and her face of baby-like innocence, it only meant that the sun shone more brightly and the sea was more blue for the coming of her *preux chevalier*. And she sang, without knowing why.

To the man it meant the sudden, primal tumult of all the deepest forces of his nature; it meant the awakening of his soul, the birth of his manhood.

He was young, barely twenty-two. Very early Ambition had called to him, and he had followed with a single heart. He had never greatly cared for social pleasures; he had been too absorbed to enjoy them. But now—in a single moment—Ambition was dethroned. At the time, though his eyes were open, he scarcely realized that the old supremacy had passed. Only long afterwards did he ask himself if the death-knell of his success had begun to toll on that golden morning; because a man cannot serve two masters.

"A penny for your thoughts!" laughed the elf in the stern, and he came to himself to wonder how old she was. "No, never mind!" she added. "I daresay they are not worth it, and I couldn't pay if they were."

Her eyes dwelt approvingly upon him as, with sleeves rolled above his elbows, he began to pull at the oars. He was certainly very handsome. She wondered that she had not noticed it before.

"Mademoiselle will not swim so far again all alone?" he suggested gently, after a few steady strokes.

She looked at him frowningly. There was no faintest tinge of dignity about her, only the careless effrontery of childhood and the grace that is childhood's heritage.

"I am going to swim as far as the skyline some day," she announced lightly, "and look over the edge of the world."

"*Mais, mademoiselle—*"

She held up an imperious hand. "That is one of the things you are not allowed to say. You are never to talk French to me. It is holiday-time when I am with you, and I never talk French in the holidays, except to Mademoiselle, who won't listen to English. And won't you call me Chris? Everyone else does."

"Chris?" he repeated after her very softly, his eyes upon her, tenderly indulgent. "Ah! let it be Christine. I may call you that?"

"Of course," she returned practically. "My actual name is Christina, but that's a detail. You can call me Christine if you like it best."

"I have another name for you," he said, with slight hesitation.

"Have you?" she asked with interest. "What is it? Do tell me!"

But he still hesitated. "It will not vex you? No?"

She flashed him her merriest smile. "Of course not. Why should it?"

He smiled back upon her, but there was the light of something deeper than mirth in his eyes. "I call you my bird of Paradise," he said.

"How pretty!" said Chris. "Quite poetical, *preux chevalier*! You may go on calling me that if you like, but it's too long for general use. And what shall I call you? Tell me your Christian name."

"Bertrand, mademoiselle."

She held up an admonitory finger. "Chris!"

"Christine," he said, with his friendly smile.

She nodded. "Now don't forget! I think I shall call you Bertie because it sounds more English. I'm going to dive now, so don't row any farther."

She sprang to her feet and stepped on to the thwart, where she stood balancing, her arms above her head.

He waited motionless to see her go. But she remained poised for several seconds, the sunlight full upon her slim, straight figure and bare, upraised arms. Her hair, that had begun to dry, fluttered a little in the breeze. The splendour of it almost dazzled the onlooker. He sat with bated breath. She was like a young goddess, invoking the spirit of the morning.

Suddenly she turned a laughing face over her shoulder. "Bertie!"

He pulled himself together. "Christine!" he answered, with a quick smile.

She laughed a little more. "Well done! I wondered if you would remember. Will you do something for me?"

"All that you wish," he said.

"Well, when you come to tea with me in the Magic Cave on the tenth bring a lantern. Will you?"

"But certainly," he said.

"I want to explore," said Chris. "I want to find out all the secrets there are."

She turned back to contemplate the deep blue water at her feet, paused a moment longer; then, "Good-bye, Bertie!" she cried, and was gone.

He saw the curve of her young body in the sunshine before she disappeared, felt the spray splash upwards on his face; but he continued to gaze at the spot where she had stood as a man spellbound, while every pulse and every nerve throbbed with the thought of her and the mad, sweet exultation that she had stirred to life within him. Child she might be, but in that amazing moment he worshipped her as man was made to worship woman in the beginning of the world.

CHAPTER V
THE BIRTHDAY TREAT

It was her birthday, and Chris scampered over the sands with Cinders tugging at her skirt, singing as she ran. She had three good reasons for being particularly happy that day—the first and foremost of these being the long-anticipated adventure that lay before her; the second that her two young brothers had improved so greatly in health that the tedious hours of her solitude were very nearly over; and the third that a letter from Jack, cousin and comrade, was tucked up her sleeve.

Jack's letters were infrequent and ever delightful. He always struck the right note. He had written for her birthday to tell her that he had bought a present for her to celebrate the memorable occasion, but that he was reserving to himself the pleasure of offering it in person when they should meet again, which happy event would, he believed, take place at no distant date. In fact, Chris might see him any day now, since the privilege of escorting her and her following back to England was to be his, and he understood that the ruling power had decreed that their return should not be postponed much longer.

She was by no means anxious to go; in fact, when the time came she would be sorry. But she was not thinking of that to-day. It was not her custom to dwell upon unwelcome things, and Jack had, moreover, made the prospect attractive by the suggestion that they might possibly spend two or three days in Paris on their return. Paris under Jack's auspices would be paradise in Chris's estimation. She could imagine nothing more enchanting.

So she and Cinders were in high spirits and prepared to enjoy the birthday treat to the uttermost. She carried a small—very small—bag of cakes which Mademoiselle had packed for her picnic—poor Mademoiselle, who could not understand how any *demoiselle* could prefer to eat her food upon the beach. In fact, Chris had only carried the point because it was her birthday, and naturally Mademoiselle had not been informed that she had invited a guest to the meagre feast.

Chris, however, was quite content. With the serenity of childhood she was sure there would be enough. She even told herself privately that it would be the best birthday-party she had ever had. And Cinders was apparently of the same opinion.

They raced nearly all the way to the rocks, spurred by the sight of a familiar white figure awaiting them there. He came to meet them with his customary courtesy, bare-headed, with shining eyes.

"Will you accept my good wishes?" he said, as he bent over her hand.

She laughed and thanked him. "I'm getting horribly old. Do you know I'm seventeen? I shall have to put up my hair next year."

"I grieve to hear it," he protested.

"Never mind. It isn't next year yet. Have you remembered the lantern? Where is it? No, I don't want any help, thank you. I balance best alone."

She was already skipping over the rocks with arms extended. He followed her lightly, ready to give his hand at a moment's notice. But Chris was very sure-footed, and though she allowed him to take her parcel, she would not accept his assistance.

"I haven't brought anything to drink," she remarked presently, "I hope you don't mind."

No, he minded nothing. Like herself, he was enjoying the treat to the uttermost. He had not forgotten the lantern. It was waiting by the Magic Cave. He begged that she would not hasten. The tide would not turn yet.

But Chris was in an impetuous mood. She wanted to start upon her adventure without delay. Should they not explore first and have tea after? It should be exactly as she wished, he assured her. Was it not her *fête*?

But when at length she reached the shingle under the cliffs, she found a surprise in store for her that made her change her mind.

A white napkin was spread daintily upon a flat-topped rock, and on this were set a large pink and white cake and a box of *fondants*.

"Goodness!" ejaculated Chris.

"*Merveilleux!*" exclaimed the Frenchman.

She turned upon him. "Now, Bertie, you needn't pretend you are not at the bottom of it, for I am old enough to know better. No," as he shrugged his shoulders and spread out his hands, "it's not a bit of good doing that. It doesn't deceive me in the least. I know you did it, and you're a perfect dear, and it was sweet of you to think of it. It's the best picnic I ever went to. And you even thought of tea," catching sight of a small spirit-kettle that sang in a sheltered corner. "Let's have some at once, shall we? I'm so thirsty."

He had forgotten nothing. From a basket he produced cups, saucers, plates, knives, and arranged them on his improvised table.

Chris surveyed the cake with frank satisfaction. "What a mercy the gulls didn't seize it while your back was turned! Do cut it, quick!"

"No, no! You will perform that ceremony," smiled Bertrand.

"Shall I? Oh, very well. I expect I shall do it very badly. What lovely sweets! Did they come out of the Magic Cave? I hope they won't vanish before we come to eat them."

"I thought that my bird of Paradise would like them," he said softly.

"Your bird of Paradise loves them," promptly returned Chris. "In fact, if you ask me, I think she is inclined to be rather greedy. Please take the kettle off. It's spluttering. You must make the tea if I'm to cut the cake. And let's be quick, shall we? I believe it's going to rain!"

They were not very quick, however, for, as Chris herself presently remarked, one couldn't scramble over such a cake as that. And the rain came down in a sharp shower before they had finished, and drove them into the Magic Cave for shelter.

The girl's young laughter echoed weirdly along the rocky walls as she entered, and she turned with a slightly startled expression to make sure that her companion was close to her.

He had paused to rescue the remains of the feast. "Quick!" she called to him. "You will be drenched."

"*Je viens vite—vite,*" he called back, and in a few seconds was at her side.

"*Comment!*" he said. "You are afraid, no?"

"No," said Chris, colouring under his look of inquiry. "But it's horribly eerie. Where is Cinders?"

A muffled bark from the depths of the cave answered her. Cinders was obviously exploring on his own account, and believed himself to be on the track of some quarry.

"Light the lantern—quick!" commanded Chris, her misgivings diverted into another channel. "We mustn't lose him. Isn't it cold!"

She shivered in her light dress, but turned inwards resolutely.

"Tenez!" exclaimed the Frenchman, quick to catch her mood. "I will go to find the good Cinders. He is not far."

"And leave me!" said Chris quickly.

"Eh bien! Let us remain here."

"And leave Cinders!" said Chris.

He smiled and shrugged his shoulders, then stooped without further words and kindled his lamp.

The rain was still beating in fierce grey gusts over the sea and pattering heavily upon the shingle. The waves broke with a sullen roaring. Evidently a gale was rising.

Chris, with her face to the darkness of the cave, shivered again. Somehow her spirit of adventure was dashed.

The flame of Bertrand's lamp shone vaguely inwards, revealing a narrow passage that wound between rugged cliff-walls into darkness. The rock gleamed black and shiny on all sides. Underfoot were stones of all shapes and sizes, worn smooth by the sea.

"What a ghastly place!" whispered Chris, and something seemed to catch the whisper and repeat it sibilantly a great many times as if learning it off by heart.

"Permit me to precede you," said Bertrand. "You will find it not so narrow in a moment. If you look behind you, you will see the sea as in the frame of a picture. It is beautiful, is it not?"

His soft voice and casual words reassured her. She looked and admired, though the sea was grey and the shore all blurred with rain.

"There will be a rainbow soon," he said. "See! It grows more light already."

But he was looking at her as he spoke, though his glance fell directly she turned towards him.

"Do you come here often?" she asked.

"But very often," he said.

"And what do you do here?"

"I will show you by and bye."

"Very well," she said eagerly. "Then we won't go any farther when we have found Cinders."

But this last suggestion was not so easy of accomplishment. The darkness had swallowed Cinders as completely as though the jaws of the dragon had closed upon him.

"Where can he be?" said Chris, a quiver of distress in her voice.

"Have no fear! We will find him," Bertrand assured her.

He moved forward, holding the lantern to guide her. She kept very close to him, especially when a curve in the passage hid the entrance behind her. Her fancy for exploring was rapidly dwindling.

As he had told her, the passage soon widened. They emerged into a cave of some size and considerable height.

"He will be here," announced Bertrand, with conviction.

But he was mistaken; Cinders was nowhere to be seen.

Chris looked around her wonderingly. This chamber in the rock was unlike anything she had ever seen before. The very atmosphere seemed ominous, like the air of a dungeon.

"And you come here often!" she said again incredulously.

He smiled, and, raising his lantern, pointed to a crevice just above his head. "That is where I keep my magic."

Chris stood on tiptoe, and peered curiously. He reached up with his free hand, and drew forward something that gave back dully the flare of the lamp. She saw a black tin box that looked like a miniature safe.

He looked at her with a smile. "It contains my treasures—my black arts," he said, "and my future." He pushed it back again and turned. "Come! we will find the naughty Cinders."

Chris was on the point of asking eager questions regarding this new mystery, but before she could begin to utter them a long and piteous howl—the howl of a lost dog—sent them helter-skelter from her mind.

"Oh, listen!" she cried. "That's Cinders!"

She sprang forward while the miserable sound was still echoing all about them. "Oh, isn't it dreadful?" she gasped. "Do you think he is hurt?"

"No, no!" Bertrand hastened to reassure her. "He is only afraid. We will go to him."

He stretched out a hand to her, and she put hers into it as naturally as a child. Her chin was quivering, and her voice, when she tried to call to the dog, broke down upon a sob.

"He will never know where we are because of the echoes," she said.

"He is not far," declared the Frenchman consolingly. "See, here is the passage. They say that it was made by the contrabandists, but it leads to nowhere; it has been blocked since many years. Do not fall on the stones; they are very slippery."

A passage, even narrower than the first, led from the cave in which they had been standing. Bertrand went first, his hand stretched out behind him, still holding hers.

They had scrambled in this order about a dozen yards when again they heard Cinders' cry for help—a pathetic yelping considerably farther away than it had been before. The unlucky wanderer seemed to have lost his head in the darkness and to be running hither and thither in wild dismay.

"What shall we do?" said Chris in tears. "I've never heard him cry like that before."

Bertrand paused to listen. "The passage divides near here," he said. "Courage, little one! We may find him at any moment. Will you then wait while I search a little farther? I will leave you the lantern. I have some matches."

"Oh, please don't leave me!" entreated Chris. "Why can't I come too?"

"It is too rough for you," he said. "And there are two passages. If I do not find him in the one, without doubt he will return by the other to you."

"You—you'd better take the lantern then," said Chris, with a gulp. "If I am only going to stand still, I—I shan't want it."

"No, no—" he began.

But she insisted. "Yes, really. You will want it. I will wait for you here, if you think it best. Only you will promise not to be long?"

"I promise," he said.

"Then be quick and go," she urged, drawing her hand from his. "We must find him—we must."

But when his back was turned, and she saw him receding from her with the light, she covered her face and trembled. It was the most horrible adventure she had ever experienced.

For a long time she heard his footsteps echoing weirdly, but when they died away at last and she stood alone in the utter, vault-like darkness, her heart failed her. What if he also lost his way?

The darkness was terrible. It seemed to press upon her, to hurt her. Through it came the faint sounds of trickling water from all directions like tiny voices whispering together. Now and then something moved with a small rustling. It might have been a lizard, a crab, or even a bat. But Chris thought of snakes and stiffened to rigidity, scarcely daring to breathe. The roar of the sea sounded remote and far, yet insistent also as though it held a threat. And, above all, thick and hard and agitatingly distinct, arose the throbbing of her frightened heart.

All the horrors she had ever heard or dreamt of passed through her brain as she waited there, yet with a certain desperate courage she kept herself from panic. Cinders might run against her at any moment—at any moment. And even if not, even if she were indeed quite alone in that awful place, she had heard it said that God was nearer to people in the dark.

"O God," she whispered, "I am so frightened. Do bring them both back soon."

After the small prayer she felt reassured. She touched the clammy wall on each side of her, and essayed a tremulous whistle. It was a brave little tune; she knew not whence it came till it suddenly flashed upon her that she had heard it on Bertrand's lips on the day that he had drawn his pictures in the sand. And that also renewed her courage. After all, what had she to fear?

Over and over again she whistled it with growing confidence, improving her memory each time, till suddenly in the middle of a bar there came the rush and patter of feet, a yelp of sheer, exuberant delight, and Cinders, the wanderer, wet, ecstatic, and quite shameless, leaped into her arms.

CHAPTER VI
THE SPELL

She hugged him to her heart in the darkness, all her fears swept away in the immensity of her joy at his recovery.

"But, Cinders, how could you? How could you?" was the utmost reproof she could find it in her heart to bestow upon the delinquent.

Cinders explained in his moist, eager way that it had been quite unintentional, and that he was every whit as thankful to be back safe and sound in her loving arms as she was to have him there. They discussed the subject at length and forgave each other with considerable effusion, eventually arriving at the conclusion that no blame attached to either.

And upon this arose the question, What of the Frenchman, Chris's *preux chevalier*, who had so nobly adventured himself upon a fruitless quest?

"He promised he wouldn't be long," she reflected hopefully. "We shall just have to wait till he turns up, that's all."

She would not suffer her rescued favourite to leave her arms again, and they wiled away some time in the joy of reunion. But the minutes began to drag more and more slowly, till at length anxiety came uppermost again.

Chris began to grow seriously uneasy. What could have happened to him? Had he really lost his way? And if so what could she do?

Plainly nothing, but wait—wait—wait! And she was so tired of the darkness; her eyes ached with it.

Her fears mustered afresh, fantastic fears this time. She began to see green eyes glaring at her, to hear stealthy footfalls above the long, deep roar of the sea, to feel the clammy presence of creatures unknown and hostile. Cinders, too, weary of inaction, began to whimper, to lick her face persuasively, and to suggest a move.

But Chris would not be persuaded. She could without doubt have groped her way back to the cave where Bertrand kept his magic, and even thence to the shore. But she did not for a moment contemplate such a proceeding. She would have felt like a soldier deserting his post. Sooner or later Bertrand would return and look for her here, and here he must find her.

But her fears were growing more vivid every moment, and when Cinders, infected thereby, began to growl below his breath and to bristle under her hand she became almost terrified.

Desperately she grappled with her trepidation and flung it from her, chid Cinders for his foolish cowardice, and fell again to whistling Bertrand's melody with all her might.

Clear and flutelike it echoed through the desolate tunnels, startlingly distinct to her strained nerves. Sometimes the echoes seemed to mock her, but she would not be dismayed. It might be a help to Bertrand, and it certainly helped herself.

A long time passed, how long she had not the vaguest notion. Cinders, grown tired of his own impatience, rested his chin on her shoulder and went phlegmatically to sleep, secure in her assurance that there was nothing whatever to be afraid of. Small creature though he was, her arms ached from holding him, yet she would not let him go, he was too precious for that; and each minute that passed, so she told herself, brought the end of her vigil nearer.

Her heart was like lead within her, but she would not give way to despair. He was bound to come in the end.

And come in the end he did, but not till her hopes had sunk so low that when she heard the first faint sound of his returning feet she would not believe her ears. But when Cinders heard it also, and raised his head to growl, she suffered herself to be convinced. He really was coming at last.

His progress was very slow, maddeningly slow it seemed to Chris. She watched eagerly for the first sign of light from his lantern, but she watched in vain. No faintest ray came to illumine the darkness. Surely it was he; it could be none other!

Nearer and nearer came the footsteps, slow and groping. She listened till she could bear it no longer; then "Bertrand!" she cried wildly. "Bertie! Oh, is it you! Do speak!"

Instantly his voice came to her out of the darkness. "Yes, yes. It is me, little one. I have had—an accident. I am desolated—afflicted; there are no words that can say. And you awaiting me still, my little bird of Paradise, singing so bravely in the darkness!"

"Whistling," corrected Chris; "I can't sing. What on earth has happened? Are you hurt?"

"No, no! It is nothing—a *bagatelle*. Ah, but you have found the good Cinders! I am rejoiced indeed!"

"Yes, he came to me—ages ago. It is you I have been waiting for all this time. I thought you were never coming. At least, of course, I knew you would come; but oh"—with a great sigh—"it has been a long time!"

"Ah, pardon me!" he said. "But why did you wait?"

"Of course I waited," said Chris. "I said I would."

"And you were not afraid? No?"

He was standing close to her now, and Cinders was wriggling to reach and welcome him.

"Yes, a little," Chris admitted. "That's why I whistled. But it's all right now. Do let us get out."

"Ah!" he said. "But I fear—"

"What?" she asked, with sudden misgiving.

He hesitated a moment, then, "The tide," he said.

"Bertie!" For the first time Chris's bravely sustained courage broke down. She thrust out a clinging hand and clutched his arm. "Are we going to be drowned—here—in the dark?" she said, gasping.

"No, no, no!" His reply was instant and reassuring. He took her hand and held it. "It is not that. The water will not reach us. It is only that we cannot return until the tide permit."

"Oh, well!" Chris's relief eclipsed her dismay. "That doesn't matter so much," she said. "Let us get out of this horrid little tunnel, anyhow. Oh, darling Cinders! He wants to kiss you. Do you mind?"

Bertrand laughed involuntarily. But she was droll, this English child! Was it possible that she did not realize the seriousness of the dilemma in which she found herself? Well, if not—he shrugged his shoulders—it was not for him to enlighten her. As comrades in trouble they would endure their incarceration as bravely as they might.

The Rocks Of Valpré | 49

There was a faint spice of enjoyment in Chris's next remark: "Well, we are all together, that's one thing, and we've got the cake for supper, if we can only find it. Will you go first, please, so that I can hold on to you. It will be nice to see the light again. What happened to the lantern? Did you drop it?"

"I fell," he said. "I thought that I heard the good Cinders in front of me, and I ran. I tripped and struck my head. It stunned me. *Après cela*, I lay—*depuis longtemps*—insensible till I awoke and heard you singing so far—so far away."

"Whistling," said Chris.

"I thought it was a bird at the dawn," he said, "flying high in the sky. And I lay and listened."

"My dear *chevalier*, you wanted shaking," she interposed, with pardonable severity. "Are you sure you are awake now? Oh, look! There is a ray of light! How heavenly! But why didn't you relight the lantern?"

"It was broken," he said, "and useless. Also I found that I had only three matches."

"I hope it will be a lesson to you," she rejoined, breathing a sigh of relief as they emerged into the dim twilight of the cave. "Oh, isn't it nice to see again! I feel as if I have been blindfolded for years."

"Poor little one!" he said. "Can you ever pardon me?"

They stood together in the deep gloom. They could hear the water lapping the sides of the passage that led inwards from the shore.

"It must be knee-deep round the bend," said Chris. "Yes, I'll forgive you, Bertie. I daresay it wasn't altogether your fault, and I expect your head aches, doesn't it? I hope it isn't very bad. Is there a very big lump? Let me feel."

She passed her hand over his forehead till her fingers encountered the excrescence they sought.

"Oh, you poor boy, it's enormous!" she exclaimed. "Why didn't you tell me before? We must bathe it at once."

But Bertrand laughed and gently drew her hand away. "No—no! It is only a *bagatelle*. Think no more of it, I beg. I merited it for my negligence. Now, while there is still light, let us decide where you can with the greatest convenience pass the night."

He was prepared for some measure of dismay, as he thus presented to her the worst aspect of the catastrophe. But Chris remained serene. She was rapidly recovering her spirits.

"Oh, yes," she said. "And poor Cinders too! We must find him a nice comfy corner. He can lie on my skirt and keep me warm. Oh, do you know, I heard such a funny story the other day about this very cave. I'll tell you about it presently. But do find the cake first. I'm so hungry. We needn't go to bed yet, need we? It must be quite early. What time do you think the tide will let us get out? Poor Mademoiselle will think I'm drowned."

Chris's awe of the Magic Cave had evidently evaporated. The picnic mood had returned to take its place, and Bertrand knew not whether to be more astounded or relieved. He began to feel about for the basket containing the remnants of their feast, while Chris with much volubility and not a little merriment explained the situation to Cinders.

He calculated that they would be at liberty in the early hours of the morning unless he tempted Fate a second time by climbing the cliff. But Chris would not for a moment consider this proposition, and he was too shaken by his recent fall to feel assured of success if he persisted. Moreover, he seriously doubted if any boat could be brought within reach of her while the tide remained high.

Plainly his only course was to follow her lead and make the best of things. If she managed to extract any enjoyment from a most difficult situation, so much the better. He could but do his utmost to encourage this enviable frame of mind.

Chris, munching cheerfully in the twilight, had evidently quite forgotten her woes. They went down the passage later as far as the bend, and looked at the seething water, all green in the evening light, that held them captive.

"I wish it wasn't going to be quite dark," she said when they returned. "But if we hold hands and talk I shan't mind. That was a lovely cake of yours, Bertie, I shall never forget it."

They found a ledge to sit on, Chris with her feet curled up; and Cinders, grown sleepy after a generous meal, pressed against her. She protested when Bertrand took off his coat and wrapped it round her, but he would take no refusal. There was a penetrating dampness about the place that he feared for her.

"If you sleep, you will feel it," he said.

"But I'm not going to sleep," declared Chris. "I never felt more wide-awake in my life. I often do at bedtime. I hope you are not feeling sleepy either, for I want to talk all night long."

Bertrand professed himself quite willing to listen. "You were going to tell me something about this cave," he reminded her.

"Oh, yes." Chris swooped upon the subject eagerly. "Manon, the little maid-of-all-work, was telling me. She said that no one ever comes here because it is haunted. That's what made Cinders and me call it the Magic Cave. She said that it was well known that no one ever came out the same as they went in even in the daytime, and if any one were to spend the night here they would be under a spell for the rest of their lives. Just think of that, Bertie! Do you think we shall be? She didn't tell me what the spell was. I expect it was something too bad to repeat. That's how Cinders and I came to make up about the knight and the dragon. I hope the dragon won't find us, don't you?"

She drew a little nearer to him and slipped a hand inside his arm. He pressed it close to him,

"Have no fear, *chérie*. No evil can touch you while I am here."

"I should be terrified if you weren't," she told him frankly. "Did you ever hear about the spell? Do you know what it means?"

"Yes," he said slowly; "I have heard. That was in part why I came here at first, because I knew that I should be alone. I had need of solitude in order to accomplish that which I had begun."

"Your magic?" queried Chris eagerly.

"Yes, little one, my magic. But"—he was smiling—"I have never remained here for the night. And the charm, you say, is not so potent during the day."

"You may be under it already," she said. "I wonder if you are."

"Ah!" Bertrand's tone was suddenly grave. "That also is possible."

"I wonder," she said again. "That may be what made you knock your head. One never knows. But tell me about your magic. What is it? What do you do?"

"I think," he said, "I calculate. And I build."

"What do you build?"

"It is a secret," he said.

"But you will tell me!"

"Why, Christine?"

"Because I do so want to know," she urged coaxingly. "And I can keep secrets really. All English people can. Try me!" She thrust forward the little finger of the hand that his arm held. "You must pinch it," she explained, "as hard as you can. And if I don't even squeak you will know I am to be trusted."

He took the finger thus heroically proffered, hesitated a second, then put it softly to his lips. "I would trust you with my life," he said, "with my honour, with all that I possess. Christine, I am an inventor, and I am at the edge of a great discovery—a discovery that will make the French artillery the greatest in the world."

"Goodness!" said Chris, with a gasp; then in haste, "Not—not greater than ours surely!"

He turned to her impetuously in the darkness, her hands caught into his. "Ah, you say that because you are English! And the English—*il faut que les anglais soient toujours, toujours les premiers*—is it not so—always and in all things? Yet consider! What is it—this national rivalry—this strife for the supremacy? We laugh at it, you and I. We know what it is worth."

But Chris was too young to laugh. "I don't quite like it," she said. "I'm very sorry. Shall we talk of something else?"

But he still held her hands closely clasped. "Listen, Christine, my little one! These things they pass. They are as a dream in the midst of a great Reality. They are not the materials of which we weave our life. Envy, ambition, success—what are they? Only a procession that marches under the windows, and we look out above them, you and I, to the great heaven and the sun; and"—something more than eagerness thrilled suddenly in his voice—"we know that that is our life—the Spark Eternal that nothing can ever quench."

He ceased abruptly. Cinders had stirred in his sleep, and she had drawn away one of her hands to fondle him.

There fell short silence. Then, her voice a little doubtful, she spoke—

"You are not ambitious, then?"

He threw himself back against the rock, and with the movement a certain tension went out of the atmosphere—a tension of which she had been vaguely aware almost without knowing it.

"Ah, yes, I am ambitious," he said. "I am a builder. I have my work to do. And I shall succeed. I shall make that which all the world will envy. I shall be famous." He broke off to laugh exultantly. "Oh, it will be good—good!" he said. "One does not often reach the summit while one is yet young. There are times when it seems too wonderful to be true; and yet I know—I know!"

"Is it a gun?" said Chris.

"Yes, *mignonne*, a gun! It is also a secret—thine and mine."

She uttered a faint sigh. "I wish it wasn't a gun, Bertie. If it were only an aeroplane, or something that didn't hurt anyone! Of course, you are a soldier and a Frenchman. I couldn't expect you to understand."

He laughed rather ruefully. "But I understand all. And you do not love the French? No?"

"Not so very much," said Chris honestly. "Of course, I'm not being personal. I liked you from the first."

"Ah! But really?" he said.

"Yes, really; and so did Cinders. He always knows when people are nice. We shall miss you quite a lot when we go home."

"Quite a lot!" Bertrand repeated the phrase musingly as if questioning with himself how much it might mean.

"Yes," she went on, "we were so lonely till you came." She broke off to yawn. "Do you know, I'm beginning to get sleepy. Is it the spell, do you think, or only the dark?"

"It is not the spell," he said, with conviction.

"No?" She moved uneasily. "I'm not very comfy," she remarked. "I wish I were like Cinders. He can sleep in any position. It must be so convenient."

"Will you, then, lean on my shoulder?" Bertrand suggested, with a touch of diffidence.

She accepted the offer with alacrity. "Oh, yes, if you don't mind. It would be better than nodding one's head off, as if one were in church, wouldn't it? But what of you? Aren't you sleepy at all?"

"I have no desire to sleep," he told her gravely.

"Haven't you?" Chris's head descended promptly upon his shoulder. "I've never been up all night before," she said. "It feels so funny. How the sea roars! I wish it wouldn't. Bertie, you're sure there isn't such a thing as a dragon really, aren't you?"

His hand closed fast upon hers. "I am quite sure, *chérie*."

"Thank you. That's nice," she murmured. "I haven't said my prayers. Do you think it matters as I'm not going to bed? I really am tired."

"No, dear," he said. "*Le bon Dieu* understands."

She moved her head a little. "Are you going to say yours, Bertie?"

"Perhaps, little one."

"Oh, that's all right," she said comfortably. "Good-night!"

"Good-night, *chérie!*"

His lips were close, so close to her forehead. He could even feel her hair blow lightly against his face. But he remained rigid as a sentry—watchful and silent and still.

Once during that long night she stirred in her sleep—stirred and nestled closer to him with an inarticulate murmur; and he turned, moving for the first time, and gathered her into his arms, holding her there like an infant against his breast. Thereafter she slept a calm, unbroken slumber, serenely unconscious of him and serenely content.

And the man sat motionless, with eyes wide to the darkness, grave and reverent as the eyes of a warrior keeping his vigil on the eve of knighthood. But his heart throbbed all night long like the beat of a drum that calls men into action.

CHAPTER VII
IN THE CAUSE OF A WOMAN

To say that Mademoiselle Gautier was extremely anxious over her young charge's disappearance would be to state the case with ludicrous mildness. She was frantic, she was frenzied with anxiety.

All the evening and half the night she was literally dancing with suspense, intermingled with fits of despair that reduced her, while they lasted, to a state of absolute collapse. Before midnight all Valpré knew that the little English *demoiselle* was missing, and all Valpré scoured the shore for her in vain. Some of the fishermen put out in boats and continued the search by moonlight as near the rocks as it was possible to go. But all to no purpose.

When the moon went down, they abandoned the quest; but at dawn, when the tide was on the turn, they were out again, searching, searching for a white, drowned face and a mass of red-brown hair. But the sea only laughed in the sunlight and revealed no secrets.

Mademoiselle was quite prostrate by that time. She lay in a darkened room with her head swathed in a black shawl, and called upon all the holy saints to witness that she had always predicted this disaster.

Chris's two young brothers slept fitfully, waking now and then to assure each other uneasily that of course she would turn up sooner or later sound in wind and limb; she always did.

Noel, the younger, who was more or less in Chris's confidence, gave it as his opinion that she had eloped with someone, that officer-chap she met the other day, he'd lay a wager! But Maxwell poured contempt upon the bare suggestion. Chris—elope with a Frenchman! He could as easily see himself eloping with the Goat—a pet name that he and his brother had bestowed upon Mademoiselle Gautier, and which fitted her rather well upon occasion.

Three hours after sunrise the prodigal returned, lightfooted, gay of mien. She was alone when she arrived, having firmly refused Bertrand's escort farther then the end of the *plage*, lest poor Mademoiselle, who hated men, should have hysterics. But the tale of her adventures had preceded her. All Valpré knew what had happened, and watched her with furtive curiosity. All Valpré knew that the *petite Anglaise* had spent the night in a cave with one of the officers from the fortress, and all Valpré waited with bated breath, prepared to be duly scandalized.

But Chris was sublimely unconscious of this. Of course, she knew that Mademoiselle would be shocked, but then Mademoiselle's feelings were so extremely sensitive upon all points moral that it was almost impossible to spend an hour in her company without in some fashion doing violence to them. One simply tumbled over them, as it were, at every turn.

She expected and encountered the usual storm of reproach, but when Mademoiselle proceeded to inform her that she was ruined for life, she opened her blue eyes wide and barely suppressed a chuckle. She professed penitence and even asked forgiveness for all the anxiety she had caused, but she could not see that what had happened possessed the tragic importance that Mademoiselle assigned to it. According to her distracted governess, she had almost better have been drowned. For the life of her, Chris couldn't see why.

When the tempest had somewhat spent itself, she retreated to her brothers, to whom she poured out a full and animated account of the night's happenings. They all agreed that Mademoiselle must have rats in the upper story to make such a pother over the adventure, though Maxwell, who held himself to be approaching years of discretion, gave it as his opinion that the whole thing was a piece of bad luck and an experiment not to be repeated.

"It's over anyhow," said Chris. "And we are none the worse, are we, Cinders? So all's well that ends well, and now I'm going to get something to eat."

For the next two days, Mademoiselle continuing to be hysterical at intervals, Chris was exemplary in her behaviour. Perhaps even she had had a surfeit of adventure for the time being. She certainly had no further urgent desire to explore caves, magic or otherwise. She was also a little tired, and inclined, after her excitement, to feel proportionately slack. But early on the morning of the third day her strenuous nature reasserted itself.

The sea and the sunshine awoke her together and she arose and dressed, eager to revel in them both. She wondered if Bertrand were out in his boat, and rather hoped she might encounter him.

Bertrand, however, was nowhere to be seen, and she proceeded to enjoy her morning bathe in solitude. It was an enchanting day, and his absence did not depress her. The tide was low, and she had to wade out a considerable distance through the rippling waves; but she reached deep water at last and proceeded forthwith to enjoy herself to her utmost capacity.

She spent a delicious half-hour thus, and it was with regret that she finally returned to the shallows and began to wade back to the point where Cinders, with her mackintosh, awaited her.

Just beyond this spot was a fair stretch of sand, and she was surprised as she drew nearer to the shore to hear voices and to see a group of men in the blue and red uniform of the garrison gathered upon what she had come to regard as her own particular playground. She peered at them for some seconds from beneath her hand, for the sun was in her eyes; and suddenly a queer little thrill, that was not quite fear and not solely excitement, ran through her. For all in a moment, ringing on the still air of early morning, there came to her ears the clash of steel meeting steel.

"Good gracious!" she said aloud. "It's a duel!"

A duel it undoubtedly was. She had a clear view of the whole scene, distant but distinct, could even see the flash of the swords, the rapid movements of the two combatants. It impressed her like a scene in a theatre. She did not wholly grasp the reality of it, though her heart was beating very fast.

Knee-deep, she stood in the sparkling water, outlined against the blue of sky and sea, watching. Several seconds passed, during which they seemed to be fighting with some ferocity. Then, obeying an impulse of which she was scarcely aware, she moved on through the swishing waves, drawing nearer at every step, hearing every instant more distinctly the ominous clashing of the swords.

When only ankle-deep, she paused again. Perhaps, after all, it was only a game—a fencing-match, a trial of skill! Of course, that must be it! Was it in the least likely to be anything more serious? And yet something within told her very decidedly that this was not so. A trial of skill it might be, but it was being conducted in grim earnest.

She said to herself that she would slip on her mackintosh and go. But an overwhelming desire to investigate a little further kept her dallying. She had an ardent longing to see the faces of the antagonists. Later she marvelled at her own temerity, but at the time this overmastering desire was the only thing she knew.

She came out of the sea, reached her faithful attendant Cinders, slipped on the mackintosh, and advanced nearer still to the little group of officers upon the beach, buttoning it mechanically as she went.

Ah, she could see them now! One faced her—a mean-visaged man, fierce, ferret-like, with glaring eyes and evil mouth. She hated him at sight, instinctively, without question.

He was thrusting savagely at his opponent, whose back was towards her—a slim, straight back familiar to her, so familiar that she recognized him beyond all doubting, no longer needing to see his face. And yet, involuntarily it seemed, she drew nearer.

He was fencing without impetuosity, yet with a precision that even to her untrained perception expressed a most deadly concentration. Lithe and active, supremely confident, he parried his enemy's attack, and the grace of the man, combined with a certain mastery that was also in a fashion familiar to her, attracted her irresistibly, held her spellbound. There was nothing brutal about him, no hint of ferocity, only a finished antagonism as flawless as his chivalry, a strength of self-suppression that made him superb.

No one noticed Chris's proximity. All were too deeply engrossed with the matter in hand. But suddenly Cinders, who loved law and order in all things pertaining to the human race, scented combat in the air. It was enough. Cinders would permit no brawling among his betters if he could by any means prevent it. With tail cocked and every hair bristling, he rushed into the fray, barking aggressively.

With a cry of dismay Chris rushed after him, and in that instant the man facing her raised his eyes involuntarily and shifted his position. The next instant he lunged frantically to recover himself, failed, and with a violent exclamation received his adversary's point in his shoulder.

It all happened in a flash, so rapidly that it was over before either Chris or Cinders had quite reached the scene. Bertrand whirled round fiercely, sword in hand, anger turning to consternation in his eyes as he realized the nature of the interruption.

Chris had a confused impression that the whole party were talking at once and blaming her, while they buzzed round the wounded man, who lay back in the arms of one of them and cursed volubly, whether Bertrand, Cinders, or herself she never knew.

She had the presence of mind to snatch up her belligerent favourite, who was snapping at the prostrate officer's legs; and then, for the first time in her life, an overwhelming shyness descended upon her as the full horror of her position presented itself.

"I couldn't help it, Bertie! Oh, Bertie, I'm so sorry!" she exclaimed, in an agony of contrition.

There was a very odd expression on Bertrand's face. She did not understand it in the least, but thought he must be furious since he was undoubtedly frowning. If this were the case, however, he displayed admirable self-restraint, for he banished the frown almost immediately.

"Mademoiselle has been bathing, yes?" he questioned briskly. "But it is a splendid morning for a swim. And le bon Cinders also! How he is droll, ce bon Cinders!"

He snapped his fingers airily under the droll one's nose, and flashed his sudden smile into her face of distress.

"*Eh bien!*" he said. "*L'affaire est finie.* Let us go."

He stuck his weapon into the sand and left it there. Then, without waiting to don his coat, he turned and walked away with her with his light, elastic swagger that speedily widened the distance between himself and his vanquished foe.

Chris walked beside him in silence, Cinders still tucked under her arm. She knew not what to say, having no faintest clue to his real attitude towards her at that moment. He had ignored her apology so jauntily that she could not venture to renew it.

She glanced at him after a little to ascertain whether smile or frown had supervened. But both were gone. He looked back at her gravely, though without reproof.

"Poor little one!" he said. "It frightened you, no?"

She drew a deep breath. "Oh, Bertie, what were you doing?"

"I was fighting," he said.

"But why? You might—you might have killed him! Perhaps you have!"

He stiffened slightly, and twisted one end of his small moustache. "I think not," he said, faint regret in his voice.

Chris thought not too, judging by the clamour of invective which the injured man had managed to pour forth. But for some reason she pressed the point.

"But—just imagine—if you had!"

He shrugged his shoulders with extreme deliberation.

"*Alors*, Mademoiselle Christine, there would have been one *canaille* the less in the world."

She was a little shocked at the cool rejoinder, yet could not somehow feel that her *preux chevalier* could be in the wrong.

"He might have killed you," she remarked after a moment, determined to survey the matter from every standpoint. "I am sure he meant to."

He shrugged his shoulders again and laughed. "That is quite possible. And you would have been sorry—a little—no?"

She raised her clear eyes to his. "You know I should have been heart-broken," she said, with the utmost simplicity.

"But really?" he said.

"But really," she repeated, breaking into a smile. "Now do promise me that you will never fight that horrid man again."

He spread out his hands. "How can I promise you such a thing! It is not the fashion in France to suffer insults in silence."

"Did he insult you, then?"

Again he stiffened. "He insulted me—yes. And I, I struck him. *Après cela*—" again the expressive shrug, and no more.

"But how did he insult you?" persisted Chris. "Couldn't you have just turned your back, as one would in England?"

"No" Sternly he made reply. "I could not—turn my back."

"It's ever so much more dignified," she maintained.

The dark eyes flashed. "Pardon!" he said. "There are some insults upon which no man, English or French, can with honour turn the back."

That fired her curiosity. "It was something pretty bad, then? What was it, Bertie? Tell me!"

"I cannot tell you," he returned, quite courteously but with the utmost firmness.

She glanced at him again speculatively, then, with shrewdness: "When men fight duels," she said, "it's generally over either politics or—a woman. Was it—politics, Bertie?"

He stopped. "It was not politics, Christine," he said.

"Then—" She paused, expectant.

His face contracted slightly. "Yes, it was—a woman. But I say nothing more than that. We will speak of it—never again."

But this was very far from satisfying Chris. "Tell me at least about the woman," she urged. "Is it—is it the girl you are going to marry?"

But he stood silent, looking at her again with that expression in his eyes that had puzzled her before.

"Is it, Bertie?" she insisted.

"And if I tell you Yes?" he said at last.

She made a queer little gesture, the merest butterfly movement, and yet it had in it the faintest suggestion of hurt surprise.

"And you never told me about her," she said.

He leaned swiftly towards her. There was a sudden glow on his olive face that made him wonderfully handsome. "*Mignonne!*" he said eagerly, and then as swiftly checked himself. "Ah, no, I will not say it! You do not love the French."

"But I want to hear about your *fiancée*," she protested. "I can't think why you haven't told me."

He had straightened himself again, and there was something rather mournful in his look. "I have no *fiancée*, little one," he said.

"No?" Chris smiled all over her sunny face. She looked the merest child standing before him wrapped in the mackintosh that flapped about her bare ankles, the ruddy hair all loose about her back. "Then whatever made you pretend you had?" she said.

He smiled back, half against his will, with the eloquent shrug that generally served him where speech was awkward.

"And the woman you fought about?" she continued relentlessly.

"Mademoiselle Christine," he pleaded, "you ask of me the impossible. You do not know what you ask."

"Don't be silly," said Chris imperiously. The matter had somehow become of the first importance, and she had every intention of gaining her end. "It isn't fair not to tell me now, unless," with sudden doubt, "it's somebody whose acquaintance you are ashamed of."

He winced at that, and drew himself up so sharply that she thought for a moment that he was about to turn on his heel and walk away. Then very quietly he spoke.

"You will not understand, and yet you constrain me to speak. Mademoiselle, I am without shame in this matter. It is true that I fought in the cause of a woman, perhaps it would be more true if I said of a child— one who has given me no more than her *camaraderie*, her confidence, her friendship, so innocent and so amiable; but these things are very precious to me, and that is why I cannot lightly speak of them. You will not understand my words now, but perhaps some day it may be my privilege to teach you their signification."

He stopped. Chris was gazing at him in amazement, her young face deeply flushed.

"Do you mean me?" she asked at last. "You didn't—you couldn't— fight on my account!"

He made her a grave bow. "I have told you," he said, "because otherwise you would have thought ill of me. Now, with your permission, since there is no more to say upon the subject, I will return to my friends."

He would have left her with the words, but she put out an impulsive hand. "But, Bertie—"

He took the hand, looking straight into her eyes, all his formality vanished at a breath. "Ask me no more, little one," he said. "You have asked too much already. But you do not understand. Some day I will explain all. Run home to *Mademoiselle la gouvernante* now, and forget all this. To-morrow we will play again together on the shore, draw the pictures that you love, and weave anew our rope of sand."

He smiled as he said it, but the tenderness of his speech went deep into the girl's heart. She suffered him to take leave of her almost in silence. Those words of his had set vibrating in her some chord of womanhood that none had ever touched before. It was true that she did not understand, but she was nearer to understanding at that moment than she had ever been before.

CHAPTER VIII
THE ENGLISHMAN

Chris returned quite soberly to the little house on the *plage*. The morning's events had given her a good deal to think about. That any man should deem it worth his while to fight a duel for her sake was a novel idea that required a good deal of consideration. It was all very difficult to understand, and she wished that Bertrand had told her more. What could his adversary of the scowling brows have found to say about her, she wondered? She had never so much as seen the man before. How had he managed even to think anything unpleasant of her? Recalling Bertrand's fiery eyes, she reflected that it must have been something very objectionable indeed, and wondered how anyone could be so horrid.

These meditations lasted till she reached the garden gate, and here they were put to instant and unceremonious flight, for little Noel hailed her eagerly from the house with a cry of, "Hurry up, Chris! Hurry up! You're wanted!"

Chris hastened in, to be met by her young brother, who was evidently in a state of great excitement.

"Hurry up, I say!" he repeated. "My word, what a guy you look! We've just had a wire from Jack. He will be in Paris this evening, and we are to meet him there. We have got to catch the Paris express at Rennes, and the train leaves here in two hours."

This was news indeed. Chris found herself plunged forthwith into such a turmoil of preparation as drove all thought of the morning's events from her mind.

Her brothers were overjoyed at the prospect of immediate departure; Mademoiselle was scarcely less so; and Chris herself, infected by the general atmosphere of satisfaction, entered into the fun of the thing with a spirit fully equal to the occasion. The scramble to be ready was such that not one of the party stopped to breathe during those two hours. They bolted refreshments while they packed, talking at the tops of their voices, and thoroughly enjoying the unwonted excitement. Mademoiselle was more nearly genial than Chris had ever seen her. She did not even scold her for taking an early dip. At the time Chris was too busy to wonder at her forbearance; but she discovered the reason later, without the preliminary of wondering, when she came to know that it was Mademoiselle's urgent representations at headquarters regarding her own delinquencies that had impelled this sudden summons.

The thought of meeting her cousin added zest to the situation. Though ten years her senior, Jack Forest had long been the best chum she had—he was best chum to a good many people.

Only when by strenuous effort they had managed to catch the one and only train that could land them at Rennes in time for the Paris express, only when the cliffs and the dear blue shore where she had idled so many hours away were finally and completely left behind, did a sudden stab of realization pierce Chris, while the quick words that her playmate of the beach had uttered only that morning flashed torch-like through her brain.

Then and only then did she remember him, her *preux chevalier*, her faithful friend and comrade, whose name she had never heard, whom she had left without word or thought of farewell.

So crushing was her sense of loss, that for a few seconds she lost touch with her surroundings, and sat dazed, white-faced, stricken, not so much as asking herself what could be done. Then one of the boys shouted to her to come and look at something they were passing, and with an effort she jerked herself back to normal things.

Having recovered her balance, she managed to maintain a certain show of indifference during the hours that followed, but she looked back upon that journey to Paris later as one looks back upon a nightmare. It was her first acquaintance with suffering in any form.

Jack Forest, big, square, and reliable, was waiting for them at the terminus.

The two boys greeted him with much enthusiasm, but Chris suffered her own greeting to be of a less boisterous character. Dear as the sight of him was to her, it could not ease this new pain at her heart, and somehow she found it impossible to muster even a show of gaiety any longer.

"Tired?" queried Jack, with her hand in his.

And she answered, "Yes, dreadfully," with a feeling that if he asked anything further she would break down completely.

But Jack Forest was a young man of discretion. He smiled upon her and said something about cakes for tea, after which he transferred his attention to more pressing matters. Quite a strategist was Jack, though very few gave him credit for so being.

Later, he sat down beside his forlorn little cousin in the great buzzing vestibule of the hotel whither he had piloted the whole party, and gave her tea, while he plied the boys with questions. But he never noticed that she could not eat, or commented upon her evident weariness. Mademoiselle did both, but he did not hear.

Chris would have gladly escaped the ordeal of dining in the great *salle-à-manger* that night, but she could muster no excuse for so doing. At any other time it would have been an immense treat, and she dared not let Jack think that it was otherwise with her to-night.

So they dined at length and elaborately, to Mademoiselle's keen satisfaction, but she was aching all the while to slip away to bed and cry her heart out in the darkness. She could not shake free from the memory of the friend who would be waiting for her on the morrow, drawing his pictures in the sand for the playfellow who would never see them—who would never, in fact, be his playfellow again.

Returning to the vestibule after dinner to listen to the band was almost more than she could bear; but still she could not frame an excuse, and still Jack noticed nothing. He sent the boys to bed, but, as a matter of course, she remained with Mademoiselle.

They found a seat under some palms, and Jack ordered coffee. He got on very well with Mademoiselle as with the rest of the world, and there seemed small prospect of an early retirement. But at this juncture poor Chris began to get desperate. She had refused the coffee almost with vehemence, and was on the point of an almost tearful entreaty to be allowed to go to bed, when suddenly a quiet voice spoke close to her.

"Excuse me, Forest! I have been trying to catch your eye for the past ten minutes. May I have the pleasure of an introduction?"

Chris glanced quickly round at the first deliberate syllable, and saw a tall, grave-faced man of possibly thirty, standing at Jack's elbow.

Jack looked round too, and sprang impulsively to his feet. "You, Trevor! I thought you were on the other side of the world. My dear chap, why on earth didn't you speak before? You might have dined with us. Mademoiselle Gautier, may I present my friend, Mr. Mordaunt?"

Mademoiselle acknowledged the introduction stiffly. She had no liking for strange men.

But Chris looked at the new-comer with frank interest, forgetful for the moment of her trouble. His smooth, clean-cut face attracted her. His grey eyes were the most piercingly direct that she had ever encountered.

"My little cousin, Miss Wyndham," said Jack. "Chris, this is the greatest newspaper man of the age. Join us, Mordaunt, won't you? I wish you had come up sooner. Where were you hiding?"

Mordaunt smiled a little as he took a vacant chair by Chris's side. "I have been quite as conspicuous as usual during the whole evening," he said, "but you were too absorbed to notice me. Are you enjoying the music, Miss Wyndham, or only watching the crowd?"

Chris did not know quite what to answer, since she had been doing neither, but he passed on with the easy air of a man accustomed to fill in conversational gaps.

"I believe I saw you arrive this evening. Haven't you got a small dog with a turned-up nose? I thought so. Are you taking him for a holiday? How do you propose to get him home again?"

That opened her lips, and quite successfully diverted her thoughts. "He has had his holiday," she explained, "and we are taking him back. I don't know in the least how we shall do it. Jack will have to manage it somehow. Can you suggest anything? The authorities are so horribly strict about dogs, and I couldn't let him go into quarantine. He would break his heart long before he came out."

"A dog of character evidently!" The new acquaintance considered the matter gravely. "When are you crossing?" he asked.

"To-morrow," said Jack. "I'm sorry, Chris, but I came off in a hurry, as matters seemed urgent, and I have to be back by the end of the week."

"I wonder if you would care to entrust your dog to me," said Mordaunt. "I am fairly well known. I think I could be relied upon with safety to hoodwink the authorities."

He made the suggestion with a smile that warmed Chris's desolate heart. Not till long afterwards did she know that this man had crossed the Channel only that day, and that he proposed to re-cross it on the morrow because of the trouble in a child's eyes that had moved him to compassion.

They spent the next half-hour in an engrossing discussion as to the best means to be adopted for Cinders' safe transit, and when Chris went to bed at last she was so full of the scheme that she forgot after all to cry herself to sleep over the thought of her *preux chevalier* drawing his sand-pictures in solitude.

She dreamed instead that he and the Englishman with the level, grey eyes were fighting a duel that lasted interminably, neither giving ground, till suddenly Bertrand plunged his sword into the earth and abruptly walked away.

She tried to follow him, but could not, for something held her back. And so presently he passed out of her sight, and turning, she found that the Englishman had gone also, and she was alone.

Then she awoke, and knew it was a dream.

PART I

CHAPTER I
THE PRECIPICE

The angry yelling of a French mob rose outside the court—a low, ominous roar, pierced here and there with individual execrations, and the prisoner turned his head and listened. There was a suspicion of contempt on his face, drawn though it was. What did they care for justice? It was only the instinct to hunt the persecuted that urged them. Were he proved innocent ten times over, they would hardly be convinced or cease from their reviling.

But he knew that no proof of innocence would be forthcoming. He was hedged around too completely by adverse circumstances for that. Everything pointed to his guilt, and only he himself and one other knew him to be the victim of a deliberate plot devised to compass his destruction. He was too hopelessly enmeshed to extricate himself, and the other—the only man in the world who could establish his innocence—was the man who had set the snare.

Bertrand de Montville, gunner and genius, had faced this fact until he was in a measure used to it. There was to be no escape for him. He, who had dared to scale the heights of Olympus and had diced with the gods, was to be hurled into the mire to rise therefrom no more for ever. He had climbed so high; almost his feet had reached the summit. He had completed his invention, and it had surpassed even his most sanguine hopes of success. At four-and-twenty he had been acclaimed by his superiors as the greatest artillery engineer of his time. His genius had won him a footing that men more than twice his age, and far above him in military rank, might have envied. He had been honoured by the highest.

And then at the very zenith of his prosperity had come his downfall. His gun, the cherished invention that was to place the French artillery at the head of the list, the child of his brain, his own peculiar treasure, was discovered to have been purchased by another Government three months before he had offered it to his own.

None but himself—so it was believed, so it was ultimately to be proved to the satisfaction of impartial judges—had been in a position at that time to betray the secret, for none but himself had then possessed it. And a great storm of indignation went through the whole country over the revelation.

Passionately but uselessly he protested his innocence. There were a few, even among his judges, who secretly believed him; but the proof was incontestable. Inch by inch he had been forced down from the heights that he had so gallantly scaled, and now he was on the brink of the precipice, no longer fighting, only waiting with the unflinching courage of the French aristocrat to be hurled headlong into the abyss that yawned below.

The yelling of the crowd outside the court was only a detail of the bitter process that was gradually compassing his condemnation. He knew he was to be convicted. It was written in varying characters upon every face; pity, severity, disgust—he met them on every hand. And so on this the fifth and last day of his court-martial he confronted destiny—that destiny that he had once so gaily dared—with closed lips and eyes that revealed neither misery nor despair, only the indomitable pride of his race. Do what they would to him, they would never quench that while life remained. The worst indignity that man could inflict would provoke no outcry here. He had protested his innocence in vain, and he had no proof thereof to offer. It remained for him to face dishonour as an honourable man, steady and undismayed. Doubtless there were those who would deem his bearing brazen, but not his worst enemy should call him coward.

Across the court an Englishman, with keen grey eyes that took in every detail, sat and sketched him—sketched the proud, fearless pose of the man and the hard young face, with its faint, patrician smile. The sketch was little more than outline, a few bold strokes; but the people in England who saw it a couple of days later felt as if the artist had deliberately lifted a curtain and shown to them a man's wrung soul. And everyone who saw it said, "That man is innocent!"

Trevor Mordaunt said it himself many times that day before and after the making of the sketch. He knew, as well as did the prisoner himself, that there would be no acquittal. Almost from the commencement of the trial he had known it. But he knew also that two at least of the judges were disposed towards leniency, and upon this fact he based such slender hopes as he entertained on the prisoner's behalf. As a fellow-correspondent—a Frenchman—had remarked to him earlier in the trial, whatever the verdict, they would hardly martyrize the man lest at a later date further question as to his guilt should arise and all Europe be set bubbling anew upon that much-discussed topic—French justice.

Mordaunt was of the same opinion; but, as he watched the young officer throughout the whole of the day's proceedings, he came to the conclusion that the verdict was everything in this man's estimation and the sentence less than nothing. If he were condemned to be blown from his own gun, he would face the ordeal unshrinking, almost with indifference. Deprived of honour, what else was there in life?

So when the end came at last, and the inevitable verdict was pronounced, Mordaunt shut his note-book with a feeling that there was no more to be recorded.

As a matter of fact the sentence was not pronounced at the time, and only transpired two days later, when it was officially made public—expulsion from the army and incarceration in a French fortress for ten years.

"That, of course, will be commuted," said one who knew the probabilities of the case to Mordaunt when the sentence was made known. "They will release him *au secret* in a few years and banish him from the country on peril of arrest. They are bound to make an example of him, but they won't keep it up. The verdict was not unanimous. And, above all, they won't make a martyr of him now. The other *affaire* is too recent."

Mordaunt agreed as to the likelihood of this, but he did not find it particularly consolatory. He had seen the prisoner's face as he was guarded through the surging, hostile crowd; and he knew that for Bertrand de Montville the heavens had fallen.

An innocent man had been found guilty, and that was the end. He was beyond the reach of any lenient influence now that justice had failed him. They had pushed him over the edge of the precipice—this man who had dared to climb so high; and in the hissings and groanings of the crowd he heard the death-knell of his honour.

In silence he went down into the abyss. In silence he passed out of Trevor Mordaunt's life. Only as he went, for one strange second, as though drawn by some magnetic force, his eyes, dark and still, met those of the Englishman, with his level, unfaltering scrutiny. No word or outward sign passed between them. They were utter strangers; it was unlikely that they would ever meet again. Only for that one second something that was in the nature of a message went from one man's soul to the other's. For that instant they were in communion, subtle but curiously distinct.

And Bertrand de Montville went to his martyrdom with the knowledge that one man—an Englishman—believed in him, while Trevor Mordaunt was aware that he knew it, and was glad.

For he had studied human nature long enough to realize that even a stranger's faith may make a supreme difference in the hour of a man's most pressing need.

CHAPTER II
THE CONQUEST

It was a sunny morning in the end of June, and Chris was doing her hair in curls, for she was expecting a visitor. It took a very long time to do, for there was so much of it; and she looked very worried over the process. She would have liked to have borrowed Aunt Philippa's maid, but this was a prohibited luxury except on very exceptional occasions. And Hilda—dear, gentle Cousin Hilda—was away in Devon with her *fiancé's* people. So Chris had to wrestle with her difficulties in solitude.

It was the middle of her first season, and, with a few reservations, she was enjoying it immensely. The reservations were all directly or indirectly connected with Aunt Philippa, for whom Chris's feeling was that of an adventurous schoolboy for a somewhat severe headmaster. She was not exactly afraid of her, but she was instinctively wary in her presence. She knew quite well that Aunt Philippa had given her this season as her one and only chance in life, and had done it, moreover, more than half against her will, impelled thereto by the urgent representations of her son and daughter, who looked upon their merry little cousin as their joint *protégée*. She ought, doubtless, to have come out the previous year, but her aunt's ill-health had precluded this, and the whole summer had been spent in the country.

That excuse, however, would not serve Mrs. Forest this year. She had taken a house in town, and there was no other course open to her than to launch her brother's child into society, however sorely against her will. Her main anxiety had fortunately by that time ceased to exist. There was no likelihood of Chris, with her brilliant, vivacious ways, outshining her own daughter. For Hilda was engaged to Lord Percy Davenant, who plainly had eyes and thoughts for none other, and the marriage was to be one of the events of the season.

Chris was therefore accorded her chance upon the tacit understanding that she was to make the most of it, since Mrs. Forest still maintained her attitude of irresponsibility where her brother's children were concerned, although the said brother had drifted to Australia and died there, no one quite knew how, leaving next to nothing behind him.

His sons and Chris had been brought up upon their mother's fortune, a sum which had been set aside for their education by their father at her death, after which, beyond providing them with a home—the ramshackle inheritance that had come to him from his father—he had made little further provision for them. His eldest son, Rupert, was a subaltern in a line regiment. No one knew whether he lived on his pay or not, and no one inquired. The second son, who possessed undeniable brilliance, had earned a scholarship, and was studying medicine. And Noel, now aged sixteen, was still at school, distinguishing himself at sports and consistently neglecting all things that did not pertain thereto.

Undoubtedly they were a reckless and improvident family, as Mrs. Forest so often declared; but perhaps, all things considered, they had never had much opportunity of developing any other qualities, though it was certainly hard that she should be regarded as in any degree responsible for them. She and her brother had always been as far asunder as the poles in disposition, and neither had ever felt or so much as professed to feel the faintest affection for the other.

It vexed her that Jack and Hilda should take so lively an interest in Chris, who was bound to turn out badly. Had she not already shown herself to be incorrigibly flighty? But since it vexed her still more that anyone should regard her actions as blameworthy, she had yielded to their persuasions. And thus Chris had been given her chance.

She was thoroughly appreciating it. Everyone was being kind to her, and it was all extremely pleasant. She was looking forward keenly to the coming that morning of Trevor Mordaunt, who had been regarded as a privileged friend ever since he had smuggled Cinders back into England three years before, secreted in an immense pocket in the lining of a great motor-coat. Not that she had seen very much of him since that memorable occasion. In fact, until the present summer they had scarcely met again. He was a celebrated man in the literary world, and he travelled far and wide. He was also immensely wealthy. Men said of him that whatever he touched turned to gold. And fame, wealth, and a certain unobtrusive strength of personality had combined to make him popular wherever he went.

He was more often out of England than in it, and there were even some who suspected him of being an empire-builder, though their grounds for doing so were but slight.

It was, however, characteristic of Chris that she never forgot her friends, a characteristic which Trevor Mordaunt also possessed to a marked degree.

Therefore it was not surprising that soon after her first appearance in London society he had claimed and had been readily accorded the privileges of old acquaintanceship.

Since that day they had met casually at several functions, and people were beginning to wonder a little at Mordaunt's unusual energy in a social sense, for it was several years since he had brought himself to tread the mill of a London season.

Chris always hailed his appearance with obvious pleasure, though she was very far from connecting it in any sense with herself. He was always kind to her, always ready to make things go smoothly for her, and she never knew an awkward moment in his society. There were plenty of people who spoke of him with awe, but Chris was not one of these. She never found him in the least formidable.

And so it was with ingenuous pleasure that she anticipated his advent that morning. They had met at a dance on the previous evening, and her card had been full before his arrival. It had not occurred to her to save a dance for him.

"I never thought you would come," she had told him in distress. "I wish I had known!"

And then he had looked at her quietly for a moment with those intent grey eyes of his that never seemed to miss anything, and had asked her if he might call on the following morning, since he was to see nothing of her that night.

She had responded with a pressing invitation to do so, and he had simply thanked her and departed.

And so when the morning came Chris was still struggling with her hair when he arrived, having breakfasted in bed and finally arisen at a scandalously late hour. But that she knew Aunt Philippa to be also in bed, she would scarcely have ventured upon such a proceeding. Aunt Philippa knew nothing of the expected visitor. As a matter of fact Chris, in her airy fashion, had quite forgotten to mention the matter. Mrs. Forest, being still uncertain as to Mordaunt's state of mind, had discreetly foreborne to put the girl on her guard. She had at the beginning of things carefully instilled into her that it was essential that she should miss no opportunity of making a wealthy marriage, and she hoped that Chris would have the sense to bear this in mind.

Had she known of Mordaunt's coming she would probably have drilled her carefully beforehand, but luckily Chris's negligence spared her this. And so on that sunny summer morning she was sublimely unconscious of what was before her, and entered Mordaunt's presence at length almost at a run. Chris at twenty was very little older than Chris at seventeen.

"I'm so sorry to have kept you waiting," was her greeting. "Really I couldn't help it. I just couldn't get up this morning. You know how one feels after going to bed at four. It was very nice of you to come so early. Have you had any breakfast?"

All this was poured out while her hand lay in his, her gay young face uplifted, half-merry, half-confiding.

Yes, Mordaunt had breakfasted. He told her so with a faint smile. "And please don't apologize for being late," he added. "It is I who am early. I came early on purpose. I wanted to see you alone."

"Oh?" said Chris.

She looked at him interrogatively and then quite suddenly she knew what he had come to say, and turned white to the lips. For the first time she was afraid of him.

"Oh, please," she gasped rather incoherently, "please—"

"Shall we sit down?" he said gently. "I am not going to do or say anything that need frighten you. If you were a little older you would realize that I am at your mercy, not you at mine."

She looked at him wide-eyed, imploring. "Please, Mr. Mordaunt, can't we—can't we wait a little? I am afraid, I am so afraid of—of making a mistake."

The faint smile was still upon his face, though it did not reach his eyes. He laid a reassuring hand upon her shoulder.

"My dear little Chris," he said, "I won't let you do that."

That comforted her a little, though she still looked doubtful. She suffered him to lead her to a sofa and sit beside her, but she avoided his eyes. The crisis had come upon her so suddenly, she knew not how to deal with it.

"Has no one ever proposed to you before?" he said.

"No," she whispered.

"Well, it's all right," he said kindly. "Don't think I am going to trade on your inexperience. If you want to say 'No' to me, say it, and I'll go. I shall come back again, of course. I shall keep on coming back till you say 'Yes' either to me or to some other man. But I hope it won't be another man, Chris. I want you so badly myself."

"Do you?" she said. "How—how funny!"

"Why funny?" he asked.

She glanced at him speculatively; her panic was beginning to subside. "You must be ever so much older than I am," she said.

"I am thirty-five," he said.

"And I'm not quite twenty-one." A sudden dimple appeared in the cheek nearest to him. "Fancy me getting married!" said Chris, with a chuckle. "I can't imagine it, can you?"

"You will soon get used to the idea," he said. "Anyhow, there is nothing in it to frighten you—that is, if you marry the right man."

She nodded thoughtfully, her brief mirth gone. "But, Mr. Mordaunt, how is one to know?"

He leaned towards her. "I believe I can teach you," he said, "if you will let me try."

She slipped a shy hand into his. "But you won't ask me to marry you for a long while yet, will you?" she said pleadingly.

"Not until you have quite made up your mind to be engaged to me," said Mordaunt.

She looked at him quickly. "No, not then either. Not—not till I say you may."

He laughed a little; but there was something very protecting, infinitely reassuring, in his grasp. "And if I accept that condition," he said—"it's a very despotic one, by the way—but if I accept it, may I consider that you are engaged to me?"

Chris hesitated.

"Not if I tell you that I love you," he said, "that I want you more than anything else in life, that I would give the soul out of my body to make you happy?"

His voice was sunk very low. There was more of restraint than emotion in his utterance. He spoke as a man who knows himself to be upon holy ground.

And Chris was awed. The very quietness of the man made her tremble. She knew instinctively that here was something colossal, something that dominated her, albeit half against her will.

She closed her fingers very tightly upon his hand, but she said nothing.

He sat silent for several seconds, closely watching her, seeking to read her downcast eyes. But she would not raise them. Her heart was beating very quickly, and her breath came and went like the breath of a frightened bird.

At last very gently he moved, drew her to him, put his arm about her. "Are you afraid of me, Chris?"

She nestled to him with a little gesture that was curiously pathetic. With her face securely hidden against him, she whispered, "Yes."

"My darling, why?" he said very tenderly.

"I don't know why," murmured Chris.

"Surely not because I love you?" he said.

She nodded against his shoulder. "You ought not to love me like that. It's too much. I'm not good enough."

"My little girl," he said, "I am not worthy to hold your hand in mine."

His hand was on her hair, stroking, fondling, caressing. She nestled closer, without lifting her face.

"You don't know me in the least. I'm not a bit nice really. I get up to all sorts of pranks. I'm wild and flighty. Ask Aunt Philippa if you want to know."

"I know you better than Aunt Philippa, dear," he said.

"Oh no, you don't. You've only seen my good side. I'm always on my best behaviour with you."

"Another excellent reason for marrying me," said Mordaunt.

"Oh, but I shan't be always. That's just it. You—you will be quite shocked some day."

"I will take the risk," he said.

"I don't think you ought to," murmured Chris. "It doesn't seem quite fair."

His hand pressed her head very gently. "Meaning that you don't love me?" he said.

She made a vehement gesture of denial. "Of course not. I—I'd be a little beast if I didn't, specially after the way you helped me with Cinders long ago. I never forgot that—never! Only I do think—before you marry me—you ought to know how horrid I can be. It—it's buying a pig in a poke if you don't."

He laughed again at that in a fashion that emboldened Chris to raise her head.

"I am quite in earnest," she told him, in a tone that tried to be indignant. "You'll find me out presently. And when you do—"

She stopped with a gasp. His arms were about her, holding her as she sat. He looked straight down into the shining blue eyes. "When I do, Chris—" he said.

She met his look quite bravely. She was even smiling rather tremulously herself. "You will get a stick and beat me," she said. "I know. People who have eyes like steel never make allowances for those who haven't!"

She got no further, for quite suddenly Trevor Mordaunt dropped his self-restraint like an impeding cloak and caught her to his heart. For the fraction of a second her fear came back, she almost made as if she would resist him; and then in a moment it was gone, lost in a wonder that left no room for anything else. For he kissed her, once and once only, so passionately, so burningly, so possessively, that it seemed to Chris as if, without her own volition, even half against her will, she thereby became his own. He had dominated her, he had won her, almost before she had had time to realize that there was a stranger within her gates.

CHAPTER III
THE WARNING

"Well, all I have to say is, 'Bravo, young un!'" Rupert Wyndham stretched out a careless arm and encircled his sister's waist therewith. She was perched on the arm of his chair, and she tweaked his ear airily in response to this encouragement.

"Oh, you're pleased, are you?" she said. "That's very nice of you."

"Pleased is a term that does not express my feelings in the least," he declared. "I am transported with delight. You are the last person I should have expected to retrieve the family fortunes, but you have done it right nobly. I'm told the fellow is as rich as Croesus. It's to be hoped that he is quite resigned to the fact that he is going to have plenty of relations when he marries. By the way, hasn't he any of his own?"

"None that count—only cousins and things. Such a mercy!" said Chris. "And oh, Rupert, isn't it a blessing now that we never managed to sell Old Park, or even to let it? We shall be able to live there ourselves and turn it into a perfect paradise."

"He wants to buy it, eh?" Rupert glanced up keenly.

Chris nodded. "It's only in the clouds at present. He said something about giving it to me when we marry. But of course," rather hastily, "we're not going to be married for ever so long. It would have to belong to him till then. He is going to talk to you about it presently. You wouldn't object, would you? You are entitled to your share now, he says, and Max will come into his directly. But Noel's will have to go into trust till he is of age."

"An excellent idea!" declared Rupert. "I'm damnably hard up, as your worthy *fiancé* has probably divined. But why this notion of not getting married for ever so long? I don't quite follow the drift of that."

"Oh, don't be silly!" said Chris, colouring very deeply. "How could we possibly? Everyone would say I was marrying him for his money?"

"And that is not so?" questioned Rupert.

"Of course it isn't!" She spoke with a vehemence almost fiery. "I—I'm not such a pig as that!"

"No?" He leaned his head back upon the cushion and gazed up at her flushed face. "What are you marrying him for?" he asked.

Chris looked back at him with a hint of defiance in her blue eyes. "What do most people marry for?" she demanded.

He laughed carelessly. "Heaven knows! Generally because they're stupid asses. The men want housekeepers and the women want houses, and neither want to pay for such luxuries. Those are the two principal reasons, if you ask me."

Chris jumped off the arm of his chair with an abruptness that seemed to indicate some perturbation of spirit. She went to one of the long windows that looked across the quiet square.

"Those are not our reasons, anyhow," she said, after a moment, with her back to the cynic in the chair.

He turned his head at her words and smiled, a mischievous boyish smile that proclaimed their relationship on the instant.

"Ye gods!" he ejaculated. "Is it possible that you're in love with him?"

Chris was silent. She seemed to be watching something in the road below her with absorbing interest.

"You needn't trouble to keep your back turned," gibed the brotherly voice behind her. "I can see you are the colour of beetroot even at this distance. Curious, very! But I'm glad you are so becomingly modest. It's the first indication of the virtue that I have ever detected in you."

"You beast!" said Chris.

She whirled suddenly round, half-laughing, half-resentful, seized a book from a table near, and hurled it with accurate aim at her brother's head.

He flung up a dexterous hand and caught it just as the door opened to admit Mordaunt, who had been asked to dine to meet his future brother-in-law.

Rupert was on his feet in a moment. With the book pressed against his heart, he swept a low bow to the advancing stranger.

"You come in the nick of time," he observed, "to preserve me from my sister's fratricidal intentions. Perhaps you would like to arbitrate. The offence was that I accused her of being in love—with you, of course. She seems to think the assertion unwarrantable."

"Oh, Trevor, don't listen!" besought Chris. "He only goes on like that because he thinks it's clever. Do snub him as he deserves!"

"Pray do!" said Rupert. "Begin by asking him how old he is, and whether he knows his nine-times backwards yet. Also—"

"Also," broke in Mordaunt, with a smile, "if he can't find something more profitable to do than to tease his small sister." He extended a quiet hand. "I have been wanting to make your acquaintance for some time. In fact, I was contemplating running down to Sandacre for the purpose."

"Very good of you," said Rupert. He dropped his chaffing air and grasped the proffered hand with abrupt friendliness. There was something about this man that caught his fancy. "You would be very welcome at any time. It isn't much of a show down there, but if you don't mind that—"

"I shouldn't come for the sake of the show," said Mordaunt. "I'd sooner see a battalion at work than at play."

"Ah! Wouldn't I, too!" said Rupert, with sudden fire. "We hope to be ordered to India next year. That wouldn't be absolute stagnation, anyhow. I loathe home work."

Mordaunt looked at the straight young figure brimming with activity, and decided that the more work this boy had to do the better it would be for him morally and physically.

"Keeps you in training," he suggested.

"Oh, I don't know. One is apt to get unconscionably slack. It's a fool of a world. The work is all wrongly distributed; some fellows have to work like niggers and others that want to work never get a look in." Rupert broke off to laugh. "I'm a discontented beggar, I tell you frankly," he said. "But I don't expect any sympathy from you, because, being what you are, you wouldn't reasonably be expected to understand."

"My good fellow, I haven't always been prosperous," Mordaunt assured him. "I've had luck, I admit. It comes to most of us in some form if we are only sharp enough to recognize it. Perhaps it hasn't come your way yet."

"I'll be shot if it has!" said Rupert.

"But it will," Mordaunt maintained, "sooner or later."

"Oh, do you believe in luck?" broke in Chris eagerly. "Because there's the new moon coming up over the trees, and I've just seen it through glass. Don't look, Trevor, for goodness' sake! No, no, you shan't! Shut your eyes while I open the window. You shall see it from the balcony."

She sprang to the window, and Mordaunt followed with an indulgent smile.

Rupert scoffed openly. "Chris is mad on charms of every description. If she hears a dog howl in the night she thinks there is going to be an earthquake. You had better not encourage her, or there will be no end to it."

But Chris, with her *fiancé's* hand fast in hers, was already at the window.

"If you don't believe in it, don't come!" she threw back over her shoulder. "Now, Trevor, you've got to turn your money, bow three times, and wish. Do wish for something really good to make up for my bad luck!"

Mordaunt complied deliberately with her instructions, her hand still in his.

"I have wished," he announced at length.

"Have you? What was it? Yes, you may tell me as I'm not doing any. Quick, before Rupert comes!"

Her eager face was close to his. He looked into the clear eyes and paused. "I don't think I will tell you," he said finally.

"Oh, how mean! And you would have missed the opportunity but for me!"

He laughed quietly. "So I should. Then I shall owe it to you if it comes true. I will let you know if it does."

"You are sure to forget," she protested.

"No. I am sure to remember."

She regarded him speculatively. "I don't like secrets," she said.

"Haven't you any of your own?" he asked.

"No. At least—" she suddenly coloured vividly under his eyes—"none that matter."

He sat down upon the balustrade of the balcony, bringing his eyes on a level with hers. "None that you wouldn't tell me," he suggested, still faintly smiling.

She recovered from her confusion with a quick laugh. "I shouldn't dream of telling you—some things," she said.

Her hand moved a little in his as though it wanted to be free, but he held it still. He bent towards her, his grey eyes no longer searching, only very soft and tender.

"You will when we are married, dear," he said.

But Chris shook her head with much decision. "Oh, no! I couldn't possibly. You would disapprove far too much. As Aunt Philippa says, you would be 'pained beyond expression.'"

But Mordaunt only drew her nearer. "You—child!" he said.

She yielded, half-protesting. "Yes, but I'm not quite a baby. I think you ought to remember that. Shall we go back? I know Rupert is sniggering behind the curtain."

"I'll break his head if he is," said Mordaunt; but he let her go, as she evidently desired, and prepared to follow her in.

They met Rupert sauntering out "to pay his respects," as he termed it, though, if there were any luck going, he supposed that his future brother-in-law had secured it all.

"Thought you didn't believe in luck," observed Mordaunt.

"I believe in bad luck," returned Rupert pessimistically. "I only know the other sort by hearsay."

"Isn't he absurd?" laughed Chris. "He always talks like that. And there are crowds of people worse off than he is."

"Query," remarked her brother, with a shrug of the shoulders; but an instant later, aware of Mordaunt's look, he changed the subject.

They were a small party at dinner, for there remained but Hilda Forest to complete the number. She had only that afternoon returned to town. Mrs. Forest was dining out, to Chris's unfeigned relief. For Chris was in high spirits that night, and only in her aunt's absence could she give them full vent.

But, if gay, she was also provokingly elusive. Mordaunt had never seen her so effervescent, so sublimely inconsequent, or so naïvely bewitching as she was throughout the meal. Rupert, reckless and *débonnaire*, encouraged her wild mood. As his youngest brother expressed it, he and Chris 'generally ran amok' when they got together. And Hilda, the sedate, rather pensive daughter of the house, was far too gentle to restrain them.

It was impossible to hold aloof from such light-hearted merry-making, and Mordaunt went with the tide. Perhaps instinct warned him that it was the surest way to overcome that barrier of shyness, unacknowledged but none the less existent, that kept him still a stranger to his little *fiancée's* confidence. Her dainty daring notwithstanding, he was aware of the fact that she was yet half afraid of him, though when he came to seek the cause of this he was utterly at a loss.

When he and Rupert were left alone together after dinner, they were already far advanced upon the road to intimacy. It was the result of his deliberate intention; for though a girl might keep him outside her inner sanctuary, it seldom happened in the world of men that Trevor Mordaunt could not obtain a free pass whithersoever he cared to go.

Rupert tossed aside his gaiety with characteristic suddenness almost as soon as the door had closed upon his sister and cousin.

"I suppose you want to get to business," he said abruptly. "I'm ready when you are."

Mordaunt moved into an easy-chair. "Yes, I want to make a suggestion," he said deliberately. "But it is not a matter that you and I can carry through single-handed. I want to talk about it, that's all."

Rupert, his elbows on the table, nodded and stared rather gloomily into his coffee-cup. "I suppose it'll take about a year to fix it up. Anything with a lawyer in it does."

Mordaunt watched him through his cigarette smoke for a few seconds in silence, until in fact with a slight movement of impatience Rupert turned.

"I'm no good at fencing," he said, rather irritably. "You want Kellerton Old Park, Chris tells me. Have you seen it?"

"No."

"Then"—he sat back with a laugh that sounded rather forced—"that ends it," he declared. "The place has gone to rack and ruin. You can't walk up the avenue for the thistles. They are shoulder high. And as for the house, it's not much more than a rubbish-heap. It would cost more than it's worth to make it habitable. We have been trying to get rid of the place ever since my father's death, but it's no manner of use. People get let in by the agent's description and go and see it, but they all come away shuddering. You'll do the same."

"I shall certainly go and see it," Mordaunt said. "Perhaps I shall persuade Chris to motor down with me some day. But in any case, if you are selling—I'm buying."

Rupert jumped up suddenly. "I won't take you seriously till you've seen it," he declared.

"Oh yes, you will," Mordaunt returned imperturbably. "Because, you see, I am serious. But we haven't come to business yet. I want to know what price you are asking for this ancestral dwelling of yours."

"We would take almost anything," Rupert said.

He had begun to fidget about the room with a restlessness that was feverish. Mordaunt remained in his easy-chair, calmly smoking, obviously awaiting the information for which he had asked.

"Almost anything," Rupert repeated, halting at the table to drink some coffee.

The hand that held the cup was not over-steady. Mordaunt's eyes rested upon it thoughtfully.

"I should like to know," he said, after a moment.

Rupert gulped his coffee and looked down at him. "Murchison said ten thousand when my father died," he said. "He would probably begin by saying ten now, but he would end by taking five."

"Murchison is your solicitor?"

"And trustee up to a year ago."

"I see." Mordaunt reached for his own coffee. "And you? You think ten thousand would be a fair price?"

Rupert broke again into his uneasy laugh. "I think it would be an infernal swindle," he said.

"I will talk it over with Mr. Murchison," Mordaunt said quietly. "I only wanted to be sure that you were quite willing to sell before doing so."

Rupert took a turn up the room. He looked thoroughly ill-at-ease. Coming back, he halted by the mantelpiece and began to drum a difficult tattoo upon the marble.

"I don't want you to be let in by Murchison," he said suddenly. "You will find him damnably plausible. If he thinks you really want the place he will squeeze you like a sponge."

"Thanks for the warning!" There was a note of amusement in Mordaunt's voice. He finished his coffee and rose. "You have done your best to handicap your man of business, but I think he will get his price in spite of it. You see, I really do want the place."

"Without seeing it!"

"Yes."

Rupert whizzed round on his heels, and faced him. "Sounds rather—eccentric," he suggested.

Mordaunt smiled in his quiet, detached way. "I can afford to be eccentric," he said. "And now look here, Wyndham. You said something just now about having to wait a year to fix things up. I don't see the necessity for that, situated as we are. Since you are willing that I should buy Kellerton Old Park, and since we are agreed upon the price, I see no reason to delay payment. I will write you a cheque for your share to-night."

"What?" said Rupert.

He stood up very straight, staring at the man before him as if he were an entirely novel specimen of the human race.

"Is it a joke?" he asked at length.

Mordaunt flicked the ash from his cigarette without looking at him. Perhaps he felt that he had studied him long enough.

"No," he said. "I don't see any point in jokes of that sort. Of course, I know it's not business, but the arrangement is entirely between ourselves. I don't see why even Murchison should be let into it. We can settle it later without taking him into our confidence."

"It's a loan, then?" said Rupert quickly.

"If you like to call it so."

"May as well call it by its name," the boy returned bluntly. "You're deuced generous, Mr. Mordaunt."

"I know what it is to be hard up," Mordaunt answered. "And since we are to be brothers we may as well behave as such, eh—Rupert?"

Rupert's hand came out and gripped his impulsively. For a second he seemed to be at a loss for words, then burst into headlong speech.

"Look here! I think I ought to tell you, before you take us in hand to that extent, that we're a family of rotters. We're not one of us sound. Oh, I'm not talking about Chris. She's a girl. But the rest of us are below par, slackers. Our father was the same. There's bad blood somewhere. You are bound to find it out sooner or later, so you may as well know it now."

Mordaunt's grey eyes looked his full in the face. "Is that intended as a warning not to expect too much?" he asked.

Rupert's eyelids twitched a little under that direct look. "Yes," he said briefly.

"And if I don't listen to warnings of that description?"

"You will probably get let down."

Rupert spoke recklessly, yet almost as if he could not help it. Undoubtedly there was something magnetic about Trevor Mordaunt at times, something that compelled. He was conscious of relief when the steady eyes ceased to scrutinize him.

"Not by you, I think," Mordaunt said, with his quiet smile. "You may be a rotter, my boy, but you are not one of the crooked sort."

"I've never robbed anyone, if that's what you mean." Rupert's laugh had in it a note of bitterness that was unconsciously pathetic. "But I'm up to the eyes in debt and pretty desperate. If I could have persuaded Murchison to raise money on the estate, I'd have done it long ago. That's why this offer of yours seemed too good to be true."

Mordaunt nodded. "I thought so. It's foul work floundering in that sort of quagmire. I wonder now if you will allow me to have a look into your affairs, or if you prefer to go to the devil your own way."

Rupert coloured and threw back his shoulders, but he did not take offence. The leisurely proposal held none. "I'm not over keen on going to the devil," he said. "But neither am I going to let you pay my debts, thanks all the same."

Mordaunt glanced at him and smiled. "I think you will cancel that 'but,'" he said, "in view of our future relationship."

Rupert hesitated, obviously wavering. "It's jolly decent of you," he said boyishly. "You make it confoundedly difficult to refuse."

"You are not going to refuse," said Mordaunt. "No one knows better than I do that it's ten times pleasanter to give than to receive. But that—between friends—is not a point worth considering."

"I should think you have a good many friends," said Rupert.

"I believe I have."

"Well,"—the boy spoke with a tinge of feeling beneath his banter—"you've added to the list to-night, and I wish you joy of your acquisition! But don't say I didn't warn you."

"No," said Mordaunt quietly. "I won't say that." He added a moment later, as he dropped the end of his cigarette into his coffee-cup, "I believe in my friends, Rupert."

"Till they let you down," suggested Rupert.

"They never do."

"Then allow me to say that you are one of the luckiest fellows I have ever met."

"Perhaps."

"And the best," Rupert added impulsively.

There was a moment's silence, then, "Shall we join the ladies?" suggested Trevor Mordaunt, in a tone that sounded rather bored.

CHAPTER IV
DOUBTS

"He's nice, isn't he?" said Chris.

She was seated on a hassock close to her cousin's knee, a favourite position of hers.

Hilda's fingers fondled the sunny hair. Her eyes looked thoughtful. "I am so glad for you, dear," she said.

"I knew you would be," chuckled Chris. "Aunt Philippa is delighted too. It's the first time I've ever known her pleased with me. It feels so funny. Ah! There is my sweet Cinders! I must just let him in."

She sprang up to admit her favourite, whose imperious scratch at the door testified to the fact that he was not accustomed to being kept waiting. There ensued a tender if somewhat pointless conversation between himself and his mistress before she returned to her seat and her confidences.

"Did you ever refuse to marry anybody, Hilda?" she wanted to know then.

"Yes, dear."

"Many?"

"Three," said Hilda.

"Goodness!" Chris looked up with shining eyes of admiration. "How ever did you do it?"

"I wasn't in love with them," said Hilda simply.

"Oh! And you are in love with Percy?"

"Yes, dear." Again with the utmost simplicity the elder girl made answer.

"How nice!" said Chris. "But I can't think how you knew," she said, after a moment.

Hilda leaned forward to look into the clear eyes. A faint gleam of anxiety showed for a moment in her own. "But surely you know, Chris!" she said.

"I!" said Chris, with a gay shake of the head. "Oh, no, I don't. You know, I don't believe it's in me to fall in love in the ordinary way. I was quite angry with Rupert only this evening for jeering at me, as if I were. Oh, no, Hilda, I'm not in love like that."

"But, my dear—" Hilda looked down in grave perplexity, not unmixed with apprehension.

Chris leaned back against her quite unconcernedly, her hands clasped round her knees, and laughed like an elf. "Darling, don't look at me like that! It's too funny. Don't you know that it's only you staid, good people who ever fall in love properly? The rest of us only pretend. That's where the romance comes in."

"But, dear, Trevor Mordaunt is in love with you," Hilda reminded her gently.

"Oh yes," said Chris, "I know. That's why I had to accept him. I don't believe even you could have said No to him."

Hilda's face cleared a little. She pinched the soft cheek nearest to her. "After that, don't talk to me about not being in love!"

"Oh, but really I don't think I am," Chris assured her quite seriously. "I have only once in my life met anyone with whom I could possibly imagine myself falling in love. And he was not a bit like Trevor."

"What was he like?" asked Hilda. "A sort of fancy person? Or someone out of a book?"

"Oh no, he was quite real—the nicest man." A faraway look came into Chris's eyes; she suddenly spoke very softly as one in the presence of a vision. "I think—I am not sure—that he belonged to the old French *noblesse*. He was not tall, but beautifully made, just right in every way, and very handsome, with eyes that laughed—the sort of man one dreams of, but never meets."

"And yet he was real," Hilda said.

"Oh yes, he was real. But it was ages and ages ago. He may have changed by this time. He may even be dead—my *preux chevalier*." Chris came out of her dream with a shaky little laugh. "Ah, well, I've given up crying for him," she said. "Anyhow it was only a game. Let's talk of something else."

"It was the man at Valpré," said Hilda.

"Yes, it was the man at Valpré. I never told you about him, did I? I never told anyone. Somehow I couldn't. People made such a horrid fuss. But the very thought of him used to make me cry at one time. Wasn't it silly? But I missed him so. I couldn't help it. We won't talk about him any more. It makes me melancholy. Hilda, wouldn't it be a novel idea if your bridesmaids carried fans instead of Prayer Books? You could have the marriage service printed on them in gold with illuminated capitals. Would Aunt Philippa think it immoral, do you think?"

To anyone who did not know Chris this sudden change might have seemed bewildering; but Hilda was never taken unawares by her swift transitions. She did not even deem her flippant, as did her mother. For Chris was very dear to her. She knew and loved her in all her lightning moods. It was possible that even she did not wholly understand her, but she was nearer to doing so than any other in Chris's world just then.

When Chris danced across to the piano and began her favourite waltz to the accompaniment of muffled howls from Cinders, she knew that the hour for confidences was past. Nor had she any desire to prolong it, for it seemed better to her to leave the hero of Chris's girlhood in obscurity. She had not the smallest doubt that her young cousin invested him with all the glamour of a vivid imagination. He was fashioned of the substance of dreams, and she fancied that Chris herself was more than half aware of this.

But still her faint misgiving did not wholly die away. Though Trevor Mordaunt had secured for himself the girl of his choice, she could not suppress a grave doubt as to whether he had yet succeeded in winning her heart. He would ultimately win it; she felt convinced of that. He was a man who was bound sooner or later to rule supreme. And thus she strove to reassure herself; but still, in spite of her, the doubt remained. Chris was so young, so gay, so innocent. She could not bear to think of the troubles and perplexities of womanhood descending upon her. She was so essentially made for the joy of life.

She sat and watched her unperceived, the slim young figure in the shaded lamplight, the shining hair, the slender neck—all vivid, instinct with life; and she comprehended the witchery that had caught Mordaunt's heart. Of the man himself she knew but little. He was not expansive, and circumstances had not thrown them together. But what she knew of him she liked. She was aware that her brother valued his friendship very highly—a friendship begun on a South African battlefield; and though they had met but seldom since, the intimacy between them had remained unshaken.

Trevor Mordaunt was a man of many friends—friends in all ranks and of many nationalities. No one knew quite how he made them; no one ever saw his friendships in the making. But all over the world were men who hailed his coming with pleasure and saw him go with regret.

She supposed him capable of a vast sympathy, a wide understanding. It seemed the only explanation. But would he understand her little Chris? she wondered. Would he make full allowance for her dear caprices, her whimsical fancies, her butterfly temperament? Would he ever thread his way through these fairy defences to that hidden shrine where throbbed her woman's heart? And would he be the first to enter there? She hoped so; she prayed so.

"Hilda"—imperiously the gay voice broke through her reverie—"if Percy wants to know what sort of pendants to give the bridesmaids, be sure you say turquoise and pearl. It's most important."

She was still strumming her waltz, and did not hear Mordaunt enter behind her.

"I saw a most lovely thing to-day," she went on. "One of those heart-shaped things that are still hearts even if you turn them upside down."

"Is that an advantage?" asked Mordaunt.

She whizzed round on the music-stool. "Trevor! I wish you wouldn't make me jump. Of course it is an advantage if a thing never looks wrong way up. You will remember, won't you, Hilda? Turquoise and pearl."

"Are you going to be chief mourner?" asked Rupert.

"Don't be horrid! I'm going to be chief bridesmaid, if that's what you mean?"

"And turquoise and pearl is to be the order of the day?" queried Mordaunt.

"A white muslin frock and a blue sash, I suppose," supplemented Rupert. "Hair worn long and tied with a blue bow rather bigger than an ordinary-sized sunshade. No shoes and no stockings, but some pale blue sandals over white lace socks. Result—ravishing!"

Chris glanced round for a missile, found none, so decided to ignore him.

"Yes," she said to her *fiancé*, "and we are going to carry bouquets of wheat and cornflowers."

"Sounds like the ingredients of a pudding," said Rupert.

Chris rose from the piano in disgust, and her brother instantly slipped into her place. "I say, Hilda," he called, "come and sing! There's no one to listen to you but me; but that's a detail. Trevor and Christina, pray consider yourselves excused."

"We don't want to be excused," said Chris mutinously "Do stop, Rupert! Cinders doesn't like it."

Rupert, however, was already crashing through Mendelssohn's Wedding March, and turned a deaf ear. She picked the discontented one up to comfort him, and as she did so Trevor moved up to her. He stood beside her for a few seconds, stroking the dog's soft head.

Chris looked hot and uncomfortable, as if Rupert's music pounded on her nerves; but yet she would not make a move. She stood hushing Cinders as if he had been an infant.

"Shall we go outside?" Mordaunt said at last.

She shook her head.

"Come!" he said gently.

She turned without a word, laid the dog tenderly in a chair, whispered to him, kissed him, and went to the open window.

They stepped out together, and the curtains met behind them.

The moon had passed out of sight behind the houses, but the sky was alight with stars. A faint breeze trembled through the trees in the quiet square garden, and the faint, wonderful essence of summer came from them. From a distance sounded the roar of countless wheels—the deep chorus of London's traffic.

They stood side by side in silence while behind them Rupert played the Wedding March to a triumphant end. Then quiet descended, and there came a long pause.

Chris broke it at last, moved, and shyly spoke. "Trevor!"

"What is it, dear?"

She drew slightly towards him, and at once he put a quiet arm about her. "I want to tell you something," she said.

"Something serious?" he questioned.

"I—I don't know." A faint note of distress sounded in her voice. She laid her cheek suddenly against his shoulder with a very confiding gesture. "I'm not quite happy," she said.

He held her closer. "Tell me, Chris!" he said very tenderly.

She uttered a little laugh that had a sob in it. "It's only that—that I can't help feeling that you're making rather a bad bargain. You know, the other day—when—when you proposed to me—I didn't have time to think. I've been thinking since."

"Yes?" he said.

"Yes. And now and then—only now and then—I feel rather bad. I—I like fair play, Trevor. It isn't right for me to take so much and give—so little." Her voice quivered perceptibly, and she ceased to speak. He pressed her closer to him, but he remained silent for several seconds.

At last, "Chris," he said, "will it comfort you to know that what you call a little is to me the greatest thing on earth?"

His voice was deep and very quiet, yet a tremor went through her at his words.

"That's just what frightens me," she said.

"It shouldn't frighten you," he said. "It need not."

"But it does," said Chris.

He was silent for another space, still holding her closely. In the room behind them they could hear the cousins talking; but they were alone together, shut off, as it were, from ordinary converse, alone under the stars.

"Suppose," said Mordaunt gently, "you leave off thinking for a bit, and take things as they come."

"Yes?" she said rather dubiously.

He bent down to her. "Chris, I will never ask more of you than you are able to give."

She moved at that in her quick, impulsive way, reached up and clasped his neck. "Oh, Trevor, I do love you!" she said, with a catch in her voice. "I do want you to have—the best!"

Her face was raised to his. For the first time she offered him her lips. They were nearer to understanding each other at that moment than they had ever been before.

The Rocks Of Valpré | 95

But as he bent lower to kiss her the notes of the piano floated out to them again, this time in a soft melody, inexpressibly sweet, full of a subtle charm, the fairy gold of romance.

She kissed him indeed—and it was the first kiss she had ever given him; but he felt her stiffen in his hold even as she did it. And the next moment, almost with passion, she spoke—

"I wish Rupert wouldn't play that thing! He knows—he knows—that I can't bear it!"

"What is it?" Mordaunt asked in surprise.

She answered him with a laugh that did not ring quite true. "It is the 'Aubade à la Fiancée.' He is only playing it to torment us. Let us go in and stop him!"

She turned inwards with the words, disengaging herself from his arm as casually as she might have pushed aside a chair. Mordaunt followed her in silence. There were no further confidences between them that night.

CHAPTER V
DE PROFUNDIS

It was pouring with rain, and the man with the flute at the corner shivered and pulled his rags more closely about him. He had not been lucky that day, or, indeed, for many days, as the haggard eyes that stared out of his white face testified.

He had spent the past three nights in the open, but to-night—to-night was cruelly wet. He questioned with himself what he should do.

In his pocket was that which might procure a night's lodging or a meagre supper; but it would not supply both. He had to decide between the two, unless he elected to go on playing till midnight in the drenching rain on the chance of augmenting his scanty store.

Though it was June, he was chilled to the bone. In the intervals between his flute-playing his teeth chattered. He looked horribly ill, but no one had noticed that. Men who wander about the streets with musical instruments seldom have a prosperous appearance. Passers-by may fling them a copper if they have one handy, but otherwise they do not even look at them. There are so many of these luckless ones, and each looks more wretched than the last. Most of them look degraded also, but, save for his rags, this man did not. There was a foreign air about him, but he did not look the type of foreigner that lives upon English charity. There was nothing hang-dog about him. He only looked exhausted and miserable.

At the suggestion of a policeman he abandoned his corner. After all, he was doing no good there. It was not worth a protest. He turned and trudged up a side-street, with head bent to the rain.

It was growing late, high time to seek some shelter for the night if that were his intention. But he pressed on aimlessly with dragging feet. Perhaps he had not yet decided whether to perish from cold or hunger, or perhaps he regarded the choice as of small importance. Possibly even, he had forgotten that there was a choice to be made.

The street he travelled was deserted, but he heard the buzz of a motor at a cross-road, and mechanically almost he moved towards it. He was not quite master of himself or his sensations. He may have vaguely remembered that there is sometimes money to be earned by opening the door of a taxi, but it was not with this definite end in view that he took his way. For, as he went, he put his flute once more to his lips, and poured a sudden, silvery melody—the *"Aubade à la Fiancée"*—that a young French officer had onced hummed so gaily among the rocks of Valpré—into the rain and the darkness.

It began firm and sweet as the notes of a thrush, exquisitely delicate, with the high ecstasy that only music can express. It swelled into a positive paen of rejoicing, eager, wonderful, almost unearthly in its purity. It ended in a confused jumble like the glittering fragments of a beautiful thing shattered to atoms at a blow. And there fell a silence broken only by the throbbing of the taxi, and the drip, drip, drip, of the rain.

The taxi came to a stand close to the lamp-post against which the flute-player leaned, but he made no move to open the door. The light flared on his ashen face, showing it curiously apathetic. His instrument dangled from one nerveless hand.

A man in evening dress stepped from the taxi. His look fell upon the wretched figure that huddled against the lamppost. For a single instant their eyes met. Then abruptly the new-comer wheeled to pay his fare.

"He's in for a wet night by the looks of him," observed the chauffeur facetiously.

"The gentleman is a friend of mine," curtly responded the man in evening dress.

And the taxi-cab driver, being quite at a loss, shot away into the darkness to hide his discomfiture.

The flute-player straightened himself with a manifest effort and turned away. If he had heard the words, he had not comprehended them. His wits seemed to be wandering that night, but he would not even seem to beg an alms.

But a hand on his shoulder detained him. "Monsieur de Montville!" a quiet voice said.

He jerked round, bringing his heels together with instinctive precision. Again, in the glare of the lamp-post their eyes met.

"I have not—the pleasure," he muttered stiffly.

"My name is Mordaunt," the other told him gravely. "You will remember me presently, though not probably by name. Come in out of the rain. It is impossible to talk here."

He spoke with a certain insistence. His hand held the Frenchman's arm. It was obvious that he would listen to no refusal. And the man in rags attempted none. He went with him meekly, as if bewildered into docility. His single flash of pride had died out like the final flicker of a match.

With the Englishman's hand supporting him, he stumbled up a flight of steps that led to the door of one of the houses in the quiet street, waited till the turning of a latch-key opened the door, and again numbly yielded to the steady insistence that drew him within.

He stood on a mat under a glaring electric lamp. The wet streamed down him in rivulets; he was drenched to the skin.

Mechanically he pulled the cap from his head and tried to still his chattering teeth. His lips were blue.

"This way," said the quiet voice. "Take my arm."

"But I am so damp, monsieur," he protested shakily. "It will make you damp also."

"What of it? I daresay I shall survive it if you do." Very kindly the voice made answer. He could not see the speaker plainly, for his brain was in a whirl. He even wondered in a dull fashion if it were all a dream, and if he would wake in a moment from his uneasy slumber to hear the rain splashing down the gutters and the voice of a constable in his ear bidding him move on.

He went up a flight of stairs, moving almost without his own volition, the Englishman's arm around him, urging him upwards.

They came to the threshold of a room of which Mordaunt switched on the light at entering, and in a moment more the tottering Frenchman found himself pressed down into a chair. He covered his face with his hands and sat motionless, trying to still the confusion in his brain. He was shivering violently from head to foot.

There followed a pause of some duration, during which he must have been alone; then again his unknown friend touched him, patted his shoulder, spoke.

"Here's a hot drink. You will feel better when you have had it. Afterwards you shall go to bed."

He raised his head and stared about him. Mordaunt, holding a cup of steaming milk that gave out a strong aroma of brandy, was stooping over him. There was another man in the room, evidently a servant, engaged in kindling a fire.

Slowly the vagabond's gaze focussed itself upon Mordaunt's face. He saw it clearly for the first time and gave a slight start of recognition.

"I have seen you before," he muttered, frowning uncertainly. "Where? Where?"

"Never mind now," returned the Englishman gently. "Drink this. You need it."

He lifted a shaking hand and dropped it again. All the strength seemed to have gone out of him.

"Monsieur will pardon my feebleness," he murmured almost inarticulately. "I am—a little—fatigued. It is nothing. It will pass."

"Drink!" Mordaunt said insistently.

He held the rim of the cup against the trembling lips, and perforce the Frenchman drank, at first slowly, then with avidity, till at last he clasped the cup in both his quivering hands and drained it.

His eyes sought Mordaunt's apologetically as he gave it back. The apathy had gone out of them. They looked out of his pinched face with brightening intelligence. His lips were no longer blue.

"Ah!" he said, with a deep breath. "But how it was good, monsieur!"

He glanced downwards, discovered himself to be sitting in a chintz-covered chair, and blundered hastily to his feet.

"Tenez!" he exclaimed almost incoherently. "But how I forget! See, I have—I have—"

He groped out before him suddenly, words failing him, and only Mordaunt's promptitude spared him a headlong fall.

"Bit light-headed, sir?" suggested the servant, glancing round with an inscrutable countenance.

"No, he'll be all right. Go and turn on the hot water," said Mordaunt.

To the Frenchman as the man departed he spoke as to an equal. "Monsieur de Montville, I am offering you the hospitality of a friend, and I hope you will accept it. In the morning if you are well enough we will talk things over. But to-night you are not fit for anything beyond a hot bath and bed."

The Frenchman nodded. Certainly his senses were returning to him. His eyes were growing brighter every instant. "It is true," he said. "I was ill. But your—so great—kindness has revived me. I will not, then, trespass upon you longer, except to render to you a thousand thanks. I am well now. I will go."

"No," Mordaunt said gently. "You will stay here till morning. You are not well. You are feverish. And the sooner you get to bed the better. Come! We are not strangers. Need we behave as if we were?"

Again de Montville looked at him doubtfully. "I wish that I could recall—" he said.

"You will presently," Mordaunt assured him. "In the meantime, it really doesn't matter, and it is not the time for explanations. I am very glad to have met you. You surely will not refuse to be my guest for a few hours."

He spoke with the utmost kindness, but also with inflexible determination. The Frenchman still looked dubious, but quite obviously he did not feel equal to a battle of wills with his resolute host. He uttered a sigh and said no more.

He firmly declined the assistance of Mordaunt's man, however, and it was Mordaunt himself who waited upon him, ignoring protest, till his shivering *protégé* was safe in bed.

He seemed to resign himself to his fate then, being too exhausted to do otherwise. A heavy drowsiness came upon him, and he very soon fell into a doze.

Mordaunt sat in an adjoining room, opening and answering letters. His demeanour was quite serene. Save that he paused now and then and leaned back in his chair to listen, there was nothing about him to indicate that anything unusual had taken place.

It was nearing midnight when his man came softly in with a cup of beef-tea.

"All right, Holmes! I'll see to him. You can go to bed," he said then.

Holmes paused. "I've made up the bed in the spare-room, sir," he said.

"Oh, thanks! I shall not want it though. I will sleep on the sofa here."

"Very good, sir." Holmes still paused. He never expressed surprise at anything his master saw fit to do; he only did his utmost to give his proceedings as normal an aspect as possible. His acquaintance with Mordaunt also dated from a South African battlefield; they knew each other very well indeed.

"I was only thinking to myself," he said, in answer to Mordaunt's look, "I could just as easy attend to the gentleman as you could, sir. I'm more or less up in night duty, as you might say, and I'll guarantee as he wants for nothing if you'll put him in my charge."

Holmes had been a hospital orderly in his time, and Mordaunt knew him to be absolutely trustworthy in a responsible position. Nevertheless he declined the offer.

"Very good of you, Holmes! But I would rather you went to bed. I shouldn't be turning in yet in any case. I have work to do. I don't fancy he will give any trouble. If he does, I will call you."

Holmes withdrew without further argument, and a few minutes later Mordaunt, armed with the beef-tea, went to his guest's bedside.

He found him dozing, but he awoke at once, looking up with fever-bright eyes to greet him.

"Ah! but you are too good—too good," he said. "And I have no hunger now. I am only yet a little fatigued. I shall repose myself, and I shall find myself well."

"Yes, you will be better after a sleep," Mordaunt said. "You shall settle down when you have had this, and sleep the clock round."

He was aware once more of the Frenchman's puzzled eyes watching him as he submissively took the nourishment, but he paid no heed to them. It was not his intention to encourage any discussion just then.

Outside, the rain pattered incessantly, beating against the windows. At a sudden gust of hail de Montville shivered.

"Monsieur," he said, choosing his words with care, "your great kindness is such as I can never hope to repay, but permit me to assure you that my gratitude will constrain me to regard myself your debtor till death. If it is ever in my power to serve you, I will render that service, cost what it may. You have called me by my name. It appears that you know me?"

He paused for an answer.

"Yes, I know you," Mordaunt said.

"And for that you extend to me the hand of friendship?" questioned the Frenchman, his quick eyes still searching the Englishman's quiet face.

Mordaunt's eyes looked gravely back. "I also happen to believe in you," he said. "Otherwise I should probably have helped you because you needed it; but I most certainly should not have brought you here."

"Ah!" Sudden understanding flashed into de Montville's face; he leaned forward, stuttering with eagerness. "You—you—I know you now! I know you! You are the English journalist, the man who believed in me even against reason, against evidence—in spite of all! I remember you well—well! I remember your eyes. They sent me a message. They gave me courage. They told me that you knew—that you were my friend—the only friend, monsieur, that was not ashamed of me. And I thanked *le bon Dieu* that night—that terrible night—simply because I had looked into your eyes."

He broke off in quivering agitation. Trevor Mordaunt's hand was on his shoulder. "Easy—easy!" the quiet voice said. "You are exciting yourself, my dear fellow, and you mustn't. You must go to sleep. This matter will very well keep till morning."

De Montville's face was hidden in his shaking hands. "If I could thank you—if I could make you comprehend—" he murmured brokenly.

"I do comprehend. I comprehend perfectly." Mordaunt's voice was soothing now, almost motherly. He stroked the bent shoulders with a consoling touch. "Come, man! You are used up; you are ill. Lie down and rest."

He coaxed his forlorn guest down upon the pillows again and drew the bedclothes over him. Then for a space he sat beside him, divining that he would recover his self-command more quickly with him there than left to his own devices.

A nervous hand, bony as a skeleton's, came hesitatingly forth to him at length, and he gripped and held it for several quiet seconds more.

Finally he rose. "I'll leave you now. If you are wanting anything, you have only to ask for it. I shall be in the next room. Quite comfortable?"

Yes, he was quite comfortable. He assured him of this in unsteady tones, and begged that Mr. Mordaunt would give himself no further trouble on his account. He would sleep—he would sleep.

As the assurance was uttered somewhat incoherently, through lips half closed, Mordaunt judged that he could be trusted to carry out this intention, and so left him, to return to his writing-table in the adjoining room.

Ten minutes later he crept back noiselessly and found him in a deep sleep. He stood a moment to watch him, and noted with compassion a faint, pathetic smile that rested on the worn features.

But he did not guess that Bertrand de Montville had returned in his dreams to a land of enchantment, where the sun was always shining, and the sea was at peace, even that land where first he had forgotten the great goal of his ambition and had halted by the way to listen to a girl's light laughter while he drew for her his pictures in the sand.

CHAPTER VI
ENGAGED

"My dear Trevor, do let me warn you against making yourself in any way responsible for Chris's brothers."

Mrs. Forest spoke impressively. She was rather fond of warning people. It was in a fashion her attitude towards life.

"You will find," she continued, "that Chris herself will need a firm hand—a very firm hand. Though so young, she is not, I fear, very pliable. I have known her do the most unheard-of things, chiefly, I must admit, from excess of spirits. They all suffer from that upon occasion. It is a most difficult thing to cope with."

"But not a very serious failing," said Mordaunt, with his tolerant smile.

"It leads to very serious complications sometimes," said Mrs. Forest, in the tone of one who could reveal much were she so minded.

But Mordaunt did not seem to hear. His eyes had wandered to a light figure in the doorway—a girl with wonderful hair that shimmered like burnished copper, and eyes that were blue as a summer sea. It was a Sunday afternoon, and several people had dropped in to tea. The engagement had been announced the previous day, and Mordaunt had dropped in also to give his young *fiancée* the benefit of his support. Chris, however, was not, to judge by appearances, needing any support. She seemed, in fact, to be frankly enjoying herself. The high spirits which her aunt deplored were very much in evidence at that moment. Her gay laugh reached him where he sat. Being engaged was evidently the greatest fun.

"They are all like that," continued Mrs. Forest, with her air of one fulfilling an unpleasant duty—"all except Max, who is frankly objectionable. Gay, *débonnaire*, fascinating, I grant you, but so deplorably unstable. Those boys—well, I have never dared to encourage them here, for I know too well what it would mean. If you are really thinking of buying their old home for yourself and Chris, do be on your guard or you will never keep them at arms' length."

"Kellerton Old Park will be Chris's property exclusively," Mordaunt replied gravely. "If she cares to have her brothers there, she will be quite at liberty to do so."

"My dear Trevor, you are far too kind," protested Mrs. Forest. "I see you are going to spoil them right and left. They will simply live on you if you do that. You won't find yourself master in your own house."

"No?" said Mordaunt, with a smile.

Chris was coming towards him. He rose to meet her.

"Oh, Trevor," she said eagerly, "I can go down to Kellerton with you to-morrow, and Max has written to say he will join us there. I am so glad he can get away. I haven't seen him since Christmas."

"Isn't he coming to your birthday party?" asked Jack Forest, strolling up at that moment.

He addressed Chris, but he looked at his mother, who, after the briefest pause, made reply, "Of course Chris can ask whom she likes."

"Oh, can I?" exclaimed Chris. "How heavenly! Then I will get Rupert to come too. I wish Noel might, but I suppose he is out of the question."

She slipped a hand surreptitiously inside Jack's arm as her aunt moved away, and squeezed it. She knew quite well that the party itself had been of his devising—an informal dance to celebrate her twenty-first birthday, which was less than a fortnight away.

Jack smiled upon her indulgently. "Are you going to ask me to your birthday party, Chris?"

"No," said Chris. "I shall never ask you anywhere. You have a free pass always so far as I am concerned."

He made her a low bow. "You listening, Trevor? I'll bet she never said that to you."

But Chris turned swiftly away towards her *fiancé*. "There is no need to say anything of that sort to Trevor," she said, in her quick way. "He understands without."

"Thank you," said Trevor quietly.

Jack laughed. "One to you, my boy! I admit it frankly. By the way, I heard a funny story about you yesterday. Someone said you were turning your rooms in Clive Street into a home for sick organ-grinders. Is it true by any chance?"

"Not strictly," said Mordaunt.

"Nor strictly untrue either," commented Jack. "I know the sort of thing. You are always doing it. Was it a child or a woman or a monkey this time?"

"It was a man," said Mordaunt.

"A man! A friend of yours, I suppose?" Jack smiled over the phrase. He had heard it on Mordaunt's lips more than once.

"Exactly. A friend of mine." The tone of Mordaunt's reply did not encourage further inquiries.

Chris, glancing at him, saw a slight frown between his brows, and promptly changed the subject.

"It's really rather good of Aunt Philippa to let me have the boys here," she said later, when they were alone together for a moment just before he took his departure. "She never gets on with them, especially Max. Of course it's partly his fault. I hope you will like each other, Trevor."

By which sentence Trevor divined that this was her favourite brother.

"We shall get on all right," he said.

"It isn't everyone that likes Max," she said. "But he's tremendously nice really, and very clever. What time will you be here to-morrow? I must try not to keep you waiting."

But of course when the morning came she did keep him waiting. With the best intentions, Chris seldom managed to be ready for anything. And Mordaunt had nearly half an hour to wait before she joined him.

She raced down at last with airy apology. "I'm very sorry really. But it was Cinders' fault. We went to be photographed, and I couldn't get him to sit at the right angle. And then when I got back I had to dress, and everything went wrong."

She was carrying Cinders under her arm and evidently meant him to join their expedition. She did not look as if everything had gone wrong with her, neither did she look particularly penitent. She laughed up at him merrily, and he—because he could not help it—drew her to him and kissed her.

"Oh, but you should kiss Cinders too," she said. "I love kissing Cinders. He is like satin."

"If we don't start we shall never get there," observed Mordaunt.

"What an obvious remark!" laughed Chris. "Let's start at once. I hope you are going to scorch. Wouldn't it be funny if the motor broke down and we had to spend the night under a hedge? We should enjoy that, shouldn't we, Cinders? We would pretend we were gipsies or organ-grinders. Oh, Trevor, it is a sweet motor! Do let me drive!"

"While I sit behind with Cinders?" he said. "Thanks very much, but I'd rather not. Do you think we want Cinders, by the way?"

She opened her eyes wide in astonishment. Her motor-bonnet gave her a very babyish appearance. She hugged her favourite to her as she might have hugged a doll.

"Of course we want Cinders! Why, he has been looking forward to it for ever so long. Kellerton is home to him, you know."

"Oh, very well! Jump in," said Mordaunt, with resignation. "Are you going to sit beside me?"

"Of course we are. We can see better in front. Oh, Trevor, I am horrid. I quite forgot to thank you for that lovely, lovely ring. I'm wearing it round my neck, because I had to wash Cinders this morning, and I was afraid of hurting it. I've never worn a ring before. And it was so dear of you to remember that I liked turquoise and pearl. I was furious with Aunt Philippa because—" She broke off abruptly.

Mordaunt was starting the motor, but as they skimmed smoothly away he spoke. "Aunt Philippa thought it ought to have been diamonds, I suppose?"

"Well, yes," Chris admitted, turning very red. "But I—I didn't agree with her. Diamonds are not to be compared with pearls."

"You are not old enough for diamonds, dear," he said. "I will give you diamonds later."

"Oh, but I don't want any." Shyly her hand pressed his knee. "Please don't give me too much, Trevor," she said. "I shall never dare to ask for the things I really want if you do. Aunt Philippa thinks I'm getting horribly spoilt as it is."

"I don't," he said.

"How nice of you, Trevor! Do you know I'm so happy to-day, I want to sing."

"You may sing to your heart's content when we get out into the country," he said.

She laughed. "No, no! Cinders would howl. How cleverly you drive! You will teach me some day, won't you? Do you know, I dreamt I was driving your organ-grinder last night. Do tell me about him. Is he really a friend of yours?"

"Yes, really, Chris."

"How exciting!" said Chris, keenly interested. "And what are you going to do with him?"

"I haven't decided at present. He has had a pretty bad spell of starvation. I don't know yet what he is fit for."

"It must be dreadful to starve," said Chris soberly. "It's bad enough not to have any pocket-money. But to starve—Is he ill, then?"

"He has been. He is getting better."

"And you are taking care of him?"

"Yes, I'm housing him for the present."

"Trevor, it was good of you not to send him to the workhouse."

Mordaunt frowned. "It was not a case for the workhouse. He would probably have died before he came to that."

"Oh, how dreadful!" A shadow crossed her vivid face. "But—he won't die now, you think?"

"Not now, no!"

"And you won't let him go organ-grinding any more?"

"No."

"That's all right; though I don't think it would be at all bad on fine days in the country, if one had a nice little donkey to pull the organ."

"Nice little donkeys have to be fed," Mordaunt reminded her.

"Oh yes. But they eat grass and thistles and things. And they never die. Isn't that extraordinary? One would think the world would get overrun with them, wouldn't one?"

"So it is, more or less," observed Mordaunt.

"Trevor! What a disgusting insinuation!" The merry laugh pealed out. "I've a good mind to turn round and go straight back."

"If you think you could," he said.

"Of course I could!" Chris leaned forward and laid a daring hand on the wheel.

"Yes," he said. "But that won't do it, you know."

"But if I were in earnest?" she said, a quick note of pleading in her voice. "If I really wanted you to turn round?"

He kept his eyes fixed ahead. "Are you ever really in earnest, Chris?" he said.

"Of course I am!"

Mordaunt was silent. They were crossing a crowded thoroughfare, and his driving seemed to occupy his full attention.

Chris waited till he had extricated the car from the stream of traffic, then impulsively she spoke—

"Trevor, I didn't think you were like Aunt Philippa. I thought you understood."

She saw his grave face soften. "Believe me, I am not in the least like your Aunt Philippa," he said.

"No; but—"

"But, Chris?"

"I think you needn't have asked me that," she said, a little quiver in her voice. "Even Cinders knows me better than that."

"Cinders ought to know you better than anyone," remarked Mordaunt. "His opportunities are unlimited."

She laughed somewhat dubiously. "I knew you would think me horrid as soon as you began to see more of me."

He laughed also at that. "My dear, forgive me for saying so, but you are absurd—too absurd to be taken seriously, even if you are serious—which I doubt."

"But I am," she asserted. "I am. I—I am nearly always serious."

Mordaunt turned his head and looked at her with that in his eyes which she alone ever saw there, before which instinctively, almost fearfully, she veiled her own.

"You—child!" he said again softly.

And this time—perhaps because the words offered a way of escape of which she was not sorry to avail herself—Chris did not seek to contradict him. She pressed her cheek to Cinders' alert head, and said no more.

CHAPTER VII
THE SECOND WARNING

Rupert's description of Kellerton Old Park, though unflattering, was not far removed from the truth. The thistles in the drive that wound from the deserted lodge to the house itself certainly were abnormally high, so high that Mordaunt at once decided to abandon the car inside the great wrought-iron gates that had been the pride of the place for many years.

"That nice little donkey of yours would come in useful here," he observed, as he handed his *fiancée* to the ground.

She tucked her hand engagingly inside his arm. "Ah! but isn't the park lovely? And look at all those rabbits! No, no, Cinders! You mustn't! Trevor, you do like it?"

"I like it immensely," he answered.

His eyes looked out over the wide, rough stretch of ground before him that was more like common land than private property, dwelt upon a belt of trees that crowned a distant rise, scanned the overgrown carriage-road to where it ended before a grey turret that was half-hidden by a great cedar, finally came back to the sparkling face by his side.

"So this is to be our—home, Chris?" he said.

"Isn't it beautiful?" she said proudly. "Oh, Trevor, you don't know what it means to me to feel it isn't going to be sold after all."

He smiled. "I understood it was to be sold and presented to my wife for a wedding-gift."

She turned her face up to his. "Trevor, you don't think I'm ungrateful too, do you?"

"My darling," he said, "I think that gratitude between you and me is out of place at any time. Remember, though I give you this and a thousand other things, you are giving me—all you have."

She pressed his arm shyly. "It doesn't seem very much, does it?" she said.

He laid his hand upon hers. "You can make it much," he said very gently.

"How, Trevor?"

"By marrying me," he said.

"Oh!" Her eyes fell instantly, and he saw the hot colour rise and overspread her face. "Oh, but not yet!" she said, almost imploringly. "Please, not yet!"

His own face changed a little, hardened almost imperceptibly, but he gave no sign of impatience. "In your own time, dear," he said quietly. "Heaven knows I should be the last to persuade you against your will."

"Aunt Philippa is always worrying me about it," she told him, with a catch in her voice. "And I—I—after all, I'm only twenty-one."

"What does she worry you for?" he said, a hint of sternness in his voice.

She glanced at him nervously. "Because—because I've no money. She says—she says—"

"Well, dear, what does she say?"

"I don't want to tell you," whispered Chris.

"I think you had better," he said.

"Yes—I suppose so. She says that as I am bringing you nothing, I have no right to—to keep you waiting—that beggars can't be choosers, and—and things like that."

"My dear Chris!" he said. "And you take things like that to heart!"

"You see, they are true!" murmured Chris.

"They are not true. But all the same"—he began to smile again—"I can't for the life of me imagine why you won't marry me and get it over."

"No?" Chris suddenly looked up again; she was clinging to his arm very tightly with both hands. "It does seem rather silly, doesn't it?" she said, with resolute eyes raised to his. "Trevor, I—I'll think about it."

"Do!" he said. "Think about it quietly and sanely. And don't let yourself get frightened at nothing. As you say, it's silly."

"But you won't—press me?" she faltered. "You—you promised!"

"I keep my promises, Chris," he said.

But he was frowning slightly as he said it, and she was quick to note the fact. "Ah! don't be vexed with me," she pleaded very earnestly. "I know I'm foolish. I can't help it. It's the way I'm made."

She was on the verge of tears, and at once his hand closed with a warm and comforting pressure upon hers. "Chris! Chris! When will you learn not to be afraid of me?" he said. "I am not vexed with you, child. I am only wondering."

"Wondering?" she said.

"Wondering if I had better go away for a spell," he answered.

"Go away!" she echoed blankly.

"And give you time to know your own mind," he said.

"Trevor!" She turned suddenly white, so white that he thought for an instant that she was in physical pain; and then, feeling her clinging to him, he understood. "Oh, no!" she said vehemently. "No, no! Trevor, you won't? Say you won't! I—I couldn't bear that. Please, Trevor!"

"My dear," he said, "I shall never go away while you want me. But the question is, do you want me?"

"I do!" she declared, almost passionately. "I do!"

"You are quite sure?" He looked suddenly deep into her eyes, so suddenly that she could not avoid the look.

She quivered under it, but he did not release her. He searched her upturned face closely, persistently, relentlessly, till, with a movement of entreaty, she stretched up one hand and tremblingly covered his eyes.

"I am—quite sure," she said in a whisper. "And I—I don't like you to look at me like that."

He stood still, suffering himself to be so blinded, till, gaining confidence, she took her hand away.

"You won't ask me again, please, Trevor?" she said.

He smiled at her very kindly, but his voice, as he made answer, was grave. "No, dear, I shall never ask you that again."

She took his arm once more with evident relief. "Let us go up to the house," she said. "I expect Max is there already, waiting for us."

So they went up the weed-grown drive, and presently came into full sight of the house. It was a large, rambling building of stone, some of it very ancient, most of it covered with immense stacks of ivy. Another pair of iron gates divided park from garden, and as they approached these a lounging figure sauntered into view and came through to meet them.

Chris uttered a squeak of delight, and sprang forward. "Max!"

"Hullo!" said the new-comer.

He was a thick-set youth, with heavy red brows and a somewhat offhand demeanour. His eyes were green and very shrewd. They surveyed Mordaunt with open criticism. He was smoking a very foul-smelling cigarette.

Chris was very rosy. "Max," she said, "this is Trevor!"

"Hullo!" said Max again.

He extended a careless hand and gave his future brother-in-law a hard grip. There was no particular friendliness in the action, it was evidently his custom to grip hard.

"Come to investigate your new abode?" he said. "Are you going to pull it down?"

"It is not my present intention," Mordaunt said.

"Of course he isn't!" said Chris. "Don't be absurd, Max. It is going to be made lovely inside and out, and we are all going to live here."

"Are we?" said Max, with a sudden grin. "Who says so?"

He glanced at Mordaunt with the words, and it was Mordaunt who answered him—

"I hope you and your brothers will continue to look upon it as your home until you have homes of your own."

"Very rash of you!" commented Max, swinging round again to the gate. "Well, come inside and see it."

They went within, went from room to room of the old place, Max with the air of a sardonic showman, Mordaunt gravely attentive to details, Chris light-footed, eager with many ideas for its reformation. The mildewed walls and partially dismantled rooms, with their moth-eaten furniture and threadbare carpets, had no damping effect upon her spirits. She had a boundless faith in her *fiancé's* power to transform her ancient home into a palace of delight.

"If you really mean to buy it as it stands, I should recommend you to make a bonfire of the contents," said Max presently, as they stood all together in the deep bay window of a room on the first floor that looked out upon the park, with a glimpse beyond of distant hills. "But the place itself is an absolute ruin. I can't imagine how you are going to patch it up."

"I think it can be done," Mordaunt said. He was staring out somewhat absently, and spoke as if his thoughts were wandering.

Both brother and sister glanced at him. Then, "When are you going to get married?" asked Max.

Mordaunt came out of his reverie. "That," he said deliberately, "has still to be decided."

"Who is going to decide? You or Chris?" Max lighted another cigarette and pitched the match, still burning, from the window.

"Oh, Max!" exclaimed Chris. "How dangerous! Look! There is Cinders sniffing along the terrace! He is sure to burn his nose!"

She was gone with the words, and Max, with a brief laugh, returned to the charge.

"I conclude the decision rests with her."

"Well?" said Mordaunt. He spoke curtly; perhaps he resented the boy's interference, or perhaps he had had enough of the subject for that day.

"Look here," said Max. "I know Chris. She will keep you dangling for the next ten years if you will put up with it. If you want to be married soon, you will have to assert yourself."

Mordaunt was silent.

Max waited. Below them Chris flashed suddenly into view, darting with a butterfly grace of movement to the rescue of her pet.

Abruptly Mordaunt spoke. "I sometimes wonder if she is too young to be married."

"What?" Max removed his cigarette and stared at him. "She is as old as I am!"

Mordaunt looked back, faintly smiling. "Yes, I know. But—well, that's no argument, is it?"

"I suppose not. All the same"—Max leaned back nonchalantly against the window-frame—"if you mean to wait till she grows up, you'll wait a precious long time, and she will probably run away with another fellow while you are thinking about it."

Mordaunt clapped a restraining hand on his shoulder. "My friend," he said, "I don't permit that sort of thing to be said of Chris."

Maxwell's green eyes twinkled. "You don't, eh? That's rather decent of you. But, you know, there is such a thing as being too trusting. And the family of Wyndham are not conspicuously famous for their honourable scruples. Now, Chris is as much a Wyndham as the rest of us, and—I'm going to say it whether you like it or not, it's the truth also—she is a deal more likely to keep out of mischief if she marries young. You are no fool by the look of you. You know there is reason in what I say."

"You have said enough," Mordaunt said, with a touch of sternness.

"All right. The subject is closed. But—just tell me this. Do you—or do you not—want to marry her before the summer is over?"

"Why do you ask?"

"Because I want to know."

"Well"—Mordaunt's eyes studied him for a few seconds—"it is an unnecessary question."

"Because I know the answer?" questioned Max.

"Exactly."

"Very well." He straightened himself with a smile. "I think I can manage that for you."

"Wait!" Mordaunt said. "You mean well, but—I would rather you didn't attempt it. I would rather that Chris were left to settle this matter for herself."

"So she will. I know what I'm about, bless your heart! Chris always asks my advice and generally takes it. She will marry you all right before the end of the season. You leave it to me."

He turned from the window with the words, still smiling. "Give me five minutes alone with her," he said.

And Mordaunt, though more than half against his will, yielded the point, and let him go.

They lunched in the old oak-beamed dining-room—a meal presided over by Max, who played the host with a half-mocking air, while Chris, still eager upon the renovations, poured out plans, practicable and otherwise, for her *fiancé's* consideration.

"What a pity we have to get back!" she said regretfully when the time for departure drew near. "I want to begin right away, Trevor. Why can't we spend the night here? Wire to Aunt Philippa, Max. Say we are busy."

Max grinned. "What says Trevor?"

"Quite impossible," said Mordaunt, with a smile at her ardent face. "There isn't a bed for you to sleep on."

"I could sleep on the sofa with Cinders," she said. "We can sleep anywhere."

"They've slept on a heap of stones before now," remarked Max.

"I'm sure we haven't!" She whisked round upon him with a suddenness that was almost a challenge. "We haven't, Max!" she repeated.

He stuck a cigarette into his mouth. "All right, my dear girl. My mistake, no doubt. I thought you had."

"Don't be absurd!" ordered Chris, colouring vividly "We never did anything so—so disreputable." She twined her arm impulsively in Mordaunt's. "Don't believe him, Trevor!"

"I don't," he said, with his quiet eyes upon her upturned face.

Max laughed aloud. "Why don't you tell him the joke, Chris?"

"Because there isn't any joke, and you're very horrid," she returned with spirit. "Trevor, let's go!"

"I am ready," he said.

"Very well, then." Chris turned round with relief in her face and hastily tied her veil. "Please find Cinders, Max," she said. "And bring Trevor's coat. It's in the billiard-room. I suppose we really must go back this time, but you will bring me again, won't you, Trevor?"

"As often as you care to come," he said.

"Ah, yes! Only I'm so full of engagements just now. It's such a nuisance. One can never get away."

"What! Tired of London?" he said.

"Oh no, not really. But I want to be here, too. I love this place. You won't do anything in it without me, will you?"

"Not without your approval, certainly," he promised.

She turned back to him with her quick smile. "Trevor, thank you! I—I've decided to marry you as soon as ever I can—as soon as Hilda comes back from her honeymoon."

He was smoking a cigarette. He took it from between his lips and dropped it into an ash-tray. For a moment his face was turned from her. He seemed to be watching the smouldering ash. Then, "Really, Chris?" he said, looking down at her again.

She was tugging at her gloves. She thrust her hand out to him. "Button it, please!" she said, rather breathlessly, as if the exertion had exhausted her somewhat.

He took it, bent over it, suddenly pressed his lips to the soft wrist.

"Oh, don't!" said Chris, and snatched it from him.

When Max came back she was standing by the window, still fumbling at her glove, with her back turned, while her *fiancé* leaned against the mantelpiece, finishing his cigarette.

CHAPTER VIII
THE COMPACT

Wearily Bertrand de Montville turned his head upon the sofa-cushion, and opened his heavy eyes. He seemed to be listening for something, but evidently he considered that he had listened in vain, for his eyelids began to droop again almost immediately. He seemed to drift into a state of semi-consciousness.

The evening sunlight was screened from his face by blinds, but even so its deep shadows were painfully distinct. He looked unutterably tired.

There came a slight sound at the door, and again his eyes were open. In a moment, with incredible briskness, he was off the couch and half-way across the room before, seized with sudden dizziness, he began to falter.

Trevor Mordaunt, entering, made a dive forward, and held him up.

"Now, my friend, lie down again," he said, "and stay down till further orders."

"Ah, pardon me!" the Frenchman murmured, clutching vaguely for support. "I am strong, more strong than you think. I—I—"

"Lie down," Trevor reiterated. "You don't give yourself a chance, man. You forget you have been a helpless invalid for the past ten days. There! How's that? Comfortable?"

"You are always so good—so good!" panted de Montville very earnestly. "I know not how to thank you—how to repay."

"Just obey orders, that's all," said the Englishman, faintly smiling. "I want to get you well. No, you are not well yet—say what you like, you're not. I've let you get up for an experiment, but if you don't behave yourself back you go. Now lie still, quite still, while I open my letters. When you have quite recovered your breath we will have a talk."

He had assumed this tone of authority from the outset, and de Montville had submitted, in the first place because he was too ill to do otherwise, and later because, somewhat to his surprise, he found himself impelled thereto by his own inclination. It did not in any fashion wound his pride, this kindly mastery. He wondered at himself for tolerating it, and yet he offered no resistance. It was too great a thing to resist.

So, still panting a little, he subsided obediently upon Mordaunt's sofa while the latter busied himself with his correspondence.

There was a considerable pile of letters. Mordaunt opened one after another with the deliberation that marked most of his actions, but the pile dwindled very quickly notwithstanding. Some letters he dropped at once into a waste-paper basket, upon others he scribbled a few notes; two or three he laid aside for further consideration.

The last of all he held in his hand for several seconds unopened. The envelope was a large one and stiff, as if it contained cardboard. It was directed in an irregular, childish scrawl. Mordaunt, sitting at his writing-table, with his back to his guest, studied it gravely, thoughtfully. Finally very quietly he broke the seal.

There was a crackle of tissue-paper, and he drew out a photograph—the photograph of a laughing girl with a diminutive terrier of doubtful extraction clasped in her arms. Without any change of countenance he studied this also.

He laid it at last upon his table, and turned in his chair. "Have you had anything to drink?"

De Montville looked slightly disconcerted by the question. "But no!" he said. "I have not—that is to say, I would not—"

Mordaunt stretched a hand to the bell. "Holmes should have seen to it. What do you drink? Afraid I can't offer you absinthe."

"But I never drink it, monsieur."

"No? Whisky and soda, then?"

"What you will, monsieur."

"Very well. Whisky and soda, Holmes, and be quick about it." Mordaunt glanced at the clock, looked again at the photograph at his elbow, finally rose. "I want a talk with you, M. de Montville," he said, "if you feel up to it. Don't get up, please. There is no necessity."

But de Montville apparently thought otherwise, for he drew himself to a sitting position and faced his benefactor.

"I also," he said, "have desired to talk with you since long."

Mordaunt pulled up a chair. "Do you mind if I talk first?" he said.

"But certainly, monsieur." With quick courtesy the Frenchman made reply. His dark eyes were very intent. He fixed them upon the Englishman's face and composed himself to listen.

"It's just this," Mordaunt said. "I think we know each other well enough to dispense with preliminaries, so I will come to the point at once. Now you have probably realized by this time that I am a very busy man—have been for several years past. In my profession there is not much time for sitting still, nor, till lately, have I wanted it. But there comes a time in most men's lives when they feel that they would like to get out of the rash and enjoy a little leisure, take it easy—in short, settle down and grow old in comfort."

De Montville nodded several times with swift intelligence. "*Alors*, monsieur contemplates marriage," he said.

Mordaunt laughed a little. "Exactly, *mon ami*, and that speedily."

He broke off at the entrance of his servant, and for the next few seconds busied himself with the mixing of drinks. De Montville continued to watch him with keen interest. As Mordaunt handed him his glass he clutched the sofa-head and stood up.

"I drink to your future happiness," he said, with a sudden smile and bow, "and to the lady who will be so fortunate as to share it!"

Mordaunt held out his hand. "Thank you. Much obliged. But sit down, my dear fellow. I haven't quite finished what I want to say. And you are too shaky to be bobbing up and down. I was just going to point out where you come in."

De Montville gripped his hand with all his strength. "I can serve you, then? You have only to speak."

But Mordaunt would not speak till he was recumbent again. Then very quietly he came to the point.

"The upshot of it is that I want a secretary to take things off my hands a bit, and since I would rather have a pal than a stranger in that capacity I am wondering if you will take on the job."

"I!" Utter amazement sounded in de Montville's voice. He sat bolt upright for a space of seconds, staring into the impassive British face before him. "But you—you—joke!" he said at last, his voice very low.

"No, I am quite in earnest." Gravely Mordaunt returned his look. "I believe we might pull together very well. Think it over, M. de Montville, and if you feel inclined to give it a trial—"

"I wish that you would call me Bertrand," de Montville broke in unexpectedly. "It would be more convenient. My name is known in England, and—I do not like publicity. As for your—so generous—suggestion, monsieur, I have no words. I am your debtor in all things. I know well that it is of my welfare that you think. For myself I do not need to consider for a moment. I would accept with joy and gratitude the most profound. But, I ask you, are you altogether wise in thus reposing your confidence in a man of whom you know nothing, except that he was tried and condemned for an offence of which you had the goodness to believe him innocent? I repeat, monsieur, are you altogether wise?"

"From my own point of view—absolutely." Mordaunt spoke with a smile. He held up his glass. "You accept, then?"

"How could I do other than accept?" protested the Frenchman, with outspread hands.

"Then drink with me to the success of our alliance," said Mordaunt. "I believe it will work very well."

He prepared to drink, but de Montville made a swift movement to arrest him. "But one moment! First, monsieur, you will give me your promise that if in any manner I fail to satisfy you, you will at once inform me of it?"

Mordaunt paused, regarding him steadily. "Yes, I will promise you that," he said.

"Ah! Good! Then I drink with you, monsieur, to the success of our compact. It will be my pleasure and privilege to serve you to the utmost of my ability."

He drank almost with reverence, and set down his glass with a hand that trembled.

Mordaunt got up. "That is settled, then. By the way, the question of salary does not seem to have occurred to you. I don't know if you have any ideas upon the subject. Four hundred pounds per annum is what I thought of offering."

"Four hundred pounds!" De Montville stared at him in amazement. "Four hundred pounds!" he repeated, in rising agitation. "But no, monsieur! It is too much! I will not—I cannot—take—even from you—a gift so great. I—I—"

He waxed unintelligible in his distress, and would have risen, but Mordaunt's hand upon his shoulder kept him down. Mordaunt bent over him, very quiet and friendly, very sure of himself and of the man he addressed.

"That's all right, *mon ami*. It is not too much. It's a perfectly fair bargain, and—to please me if you like—I want you to accept it. You will find there is plenty to do, possibly more than you anticipate. So—suppose we consider it settled, eh?"

De Montville was silent.

"We'll call it done," Mordaunt said. "Have a cigarette!"

He held his case in front of the Frenchman, and after a moment de Montville took one. But he only balanced it in his fingers, still saying nothing.

"A light?" suggested Mordaunt.

He made a jerky movement, and glanced up for an instant. "Mr. Mordaunt," he said, speaking with evident difficulty, "what is—a pal?"

"A pal," Mordaunt said, smiling slightly, "is a special kind of friend, Bertrand—the best kind, the sort you open your heart to in trouble, the sort that is always ready to stand by."

"Such a friend as you have been to me?" questioned de Montville slowly.

"Well, if you like to say so," Mordaunt said. "I almost think we might call ourselves pals by this time. What say you?"

"I, monsieur?" He reached up and grasped the hand that rested on his shoulder. "For myself I ask no better," he said, in a voice that quivered beyond control, "than to be to you what you have been to me. And I will sooner die by my own hand than give you cause to regret your kindness."

"Which you never will," Mordaunt said. "Come, light up, man! Here's a match!"

He held it up, and de Montville had perforce to place the cigarette between his lips. His throat was working spasmodically, but with a valiant effort he managed to inhale a mouthful of smoke. He choked over it badly the next moment, however, and Mordaunt patted his back with much goodwill till he was better.

"There, my dear fellow, lie down now and take it easy. I'm dining out; but Holmes has special orders to look after you; and if you are wanting anything, in the name of common-sense ask for it."

With that he turned from the sofa, took up the photograph that lay upon his writing-table, hesitated an instant, then thrust it into his breast-pocket, and strolled out of the room.

CHAPTER IX
A CONFESSION

"So you don't like my photograph!" said Chris.

"Why do you say that?"

"I could see you didn't. What's the matter with it? Isn't it pretty enough? It's just like me."

"Yes, it's just like you," Mordaunt admitted.

"Then you don't like me?" suggested Chris.

He smiled at that. "Yes, I like you very much. But—"

"Well?" said Chris, her deep-sea eyes full of eager curiosity. "Go on, please!"

"Well," he said, "that photograph is not one that I could show to my friends."

"But why not—if it's just like me?"

He took her chin and turned her face gently to the light. "Try again," he said, "without Cinders."

"Without Cinders!" She stared at him mystified, then began to laugh. "Trevor, I believe you are jealous of Cinders!"

"Perhaps," he said. "Anyhow, I should prefer your portrait without him. You look like a baby of six cuddling a toy."

"I wonder what makes you so anxious to marry me," said Chris unexpectedly.

Mordaunt still smiled at her. "Strange, isn't it?" he said.

"Yes, I can't understand it in the least." She shook her head with a puzzled expression. "It's a pity you don't like that photograph. I'm sure Cinders has come out beautifully. And he isn't a bit like a toy."

"Yes, but I don't want Cinders."

Chris looked at him with sudden misgiving. "But, Trevor, when—when we are married—"

"Oh, of course," he said at once. "I didn't mean that. I haven't the smallest wish to part you from him. It's only his photograph I have no use for."

Her face cleared magically. "Dear Trevor, I quite understand. And I would go and be done again to-morrow if I had the money, but I haven't."

"Are you very hard up?" he asked.

She nodded. "Horribly. I'm very extravagant, too—at least, Aunt Philippa says so. I can't bear asking her for money. In fact, I—I—"

She hesitated, avoiding his eyes. "Shall I tell you something, Trevor?" she said in a whisper. "It's something I haven't told anyone else!"

"Of course tell me!" He took her two hands into his, holding them up against his heart.

"Well—it's a secret, you know—I—I—" She raised her face in sudden pleading. "Promise you won't be cross, Trevor."

"I promise, dear," he answered gravely.

"Well, I'm afraid it's rather bad of me. I haven't been paying for things lately. I simply couldn't. London is a dreadful place for spending money, isn't it? It's all quite little things, but they mount up shockingly. And—and—Aunt Philippa is bound to give me some money presently for my—my trousseau. So I thought—I thought—" She came nearer to him; she laid her cheek coaxingly against his breast. "Trevor, you said you wouldn't be cross."

He put his hand on her bright hair. "I am not cross, dear. I am only sorry."

Chris was inclined to be a little tearful. She did not quite know what had led her to tell him—it had been the impulse of a moment—but it was a vast relief to feel he knew.

"I'm not a very good manager, I'm afraid," she said. "But there are certain things one must have, and they do add up so. I believe it's the odd halfpennies and farthings that do it. Don't you ever find that?"

"I can quite imagine it," he said.

"Yes, they're so deceptive. I wonder why two-and-elevenpence three-farthings sound so much less than three shillings. It's a snare and a delusion. I don't think it ought to be allowed." She raised her head with her April smile. "I'm very glad I told you, Trevor. You're very nice about things. I was afraid you would be like Aunt Philippa, but you are not in the least."

"Thank you, Chris. Now I want to say something very serious to you. Will you listen—and take it seriously?"

She gave a little sigh. "I know exactly what it is."

"No, you don't know." Mordaunt looked at her with eyes that were gravely kind. "You are not to jump to conclusions where I am concerned," he said. "You don't know me well enough. What I have to say is this. I can't have you in difficulties for want of a little money. Those debts of yours must be settled at once."

"But, Trevor, Aunt Philippa—"

"Never mind Aunt Philippa. It has nothing to do with her. It is a matter between you and me. We will settle it without her assistance."

"Oh, Trevor, but—"

"There is no 'but,' Chris," he said, interrupting her almost sternly. "I am nearer to you than your aunt. Tell me—as nearly as you can—what those debts amount to."

Chris was looking a little startled. "But I—I don't know," she said.

"Well, find out and tell me." He smiled at her again. "It's all right, dear. Don't be afraid of me. I know it's hard to keep within bounds when there is a shortage of means. But I don't like debts. You won't run up any more?"

Chris still looked at him somewhat doubtfully. "I won't if I can help it," she said.

"You will be able to help it," he rejoined.

"Yes, but, Trevor, please let me say it. I don't think you ought to—to give me money before—before—Oh, do understand!" she broke off helplessly. "You generally do."

"I quite understand," he said, his hand on her shoulder. "But, my child, I think, considering all things, that you need not let that scruple trouble you. Since we are to be married in six weeks—"

"In six weeks, Trevor!" Again that startled look that was almost one of consternation.

"In six weeks," he repeated, with quiet emphasis. "Your cousin will probably be back from her honeymoon, and it will be the end of the season. Since, then, our marriage is to take place in six weeks, and that I shall then be responsible for you, I do not think you need be troubled about letting me help you out of this difficulty now. No one will know of it. It will set your mind at rest—and mine also."

"Ah, but, Trevor—" Chris spoke somewhat breathlessly—she was rubbing her hand nervously up and down his sleeve—"I'm not quite sure that—that it will set my mind at rest. I'm not sure that—that I want you to do it, or that I ought to let you even if I did, because, you see, because—"

"Because—?" he said.

She turned her head aside, avoiding his direct look. "Don't be angry, will you? But just—just supposing something happened, and—and—and we didn't get married after all?"

She ended rather desperately, in an undertone. But for the quiet hand on her shoulder she would have moved away from him; she might even have been tempted to flee altogether. As it was, she stood still, trembling a little, wondering if she had outrun his patience at last or if he had it in him still to bear with her.

He did not speak at once. She waited with a beating heart.

"Well?" he said, and at the sound of his voice she thrilled with relief. "It's as well to look all round a thing, I admit. We will consider that supposition if you like. Say something happens to prevent our marriage. What then? Is it to put an end to our friendship also?"

She turned slightly towards him. "I might never be able to repay you," she murmured.

"I see. And that would trouble you—even though we remained friends?"

She was silent.

"It has always been a puzzle to me," he said, "why money—which is the most ordinary thing in life—is the one thing that friends scruple to accept from each other. Gifts of any other description, all sorts of sacrifices, down to life itself, are offered and taken with no scruple of pride. But when it comes to money, which is of very small value in comparison, people begin to worry. Why, Chris, what are pounds, shillings, and pence between you and me? Surely we have climbed above that sort of thing, haven't we?"

The tenderness of his tone moved her, in a fashion compelled her. She went into his arms impulsively, she clung about his neck. Yet even then her scruples were not quite laid to rest.

"But—Trevor dear—just supposing we quarrelled? We might, you know, about Cinders or anything. And then—and then—"

"My dear," he said, "we certainly shall not quarrel about Cinders. I can't for the life of me picture myself quarrelling with you under any circumstances whatsoever. And even if we did, I don't think you would hate me so badly as to grudge me the satisfaction of knowing that I had been of use to you at an awkward moment. Don't you think we are getting rather morbid, Chris?"

"I don't know," she said, clinging closer. "I only know that you are miles and miles too good for me. And whatever makes you want me I can't think."

He put his hand under her chin, and turned her face up to his own. "I'll tell you another time. At the present moment I want to talk about—getting married."

He spoke the last two words very softly, holding her close lest she should shrink away.

But Chris, with her eyes on his, kept still and silent in his arms. Only she turned rather white.

He continued with the utmost gentleness. "Your cousin is going to be married on the fifteenth of this month. Can't we arrange our wedding for the fifteenth of next?"

"The fifteenth!" said Chris. "Isn't that St. Swithin's Day?"

She spoke so briskly that even Mordaunt was for the moment taken by surprise.

"St. Swithin's Day!" he echoed. "Well, what of it?"

She broke into her gay laugh. "Oh, please not St. Swithin's Day! Just imagine if it rained!"

"Chris!" he said. "You're incorrigible!"

His arms had slackened, and she drew away from him, breathing rather quickly.

"No, but really, wouldn't it be tragic? I shouldn't like a wet honeymoon, should you? Hadn't we better wait till August? Or shall you be wanting to go to Scotland?"

"No," he said. "I am not going to Scotland this year."

His eyes were still upon her, gravely watchful, but they expressed nothing of impatience or exasperation. Very quietly he waited.

"Shall we say August, then?" said Chris, in a small, shy voice, not looking at him.

"Will your aunt remain in town for August?" he asked.

"But we are not obliged to be married in town," she pointed out.

"Nor are we obliged to have a honeymoon, Chris," he said. "Shall we say St. Swithin's Day, and forego the honeymoon—if it rains?"

"Go straight home, you mean?" She turned back to him eagerly. "Oh, Trevor, I should like that! I do want to superintend everything there. Yes, let's do that, shall we? I always did think honeymoons were rather silly, didn't you?"

He smiled in spite of himself. "I daresay they are—from some points of view. It is settled, then—St. Swithin's Day?"

She nodded. "Yes. And we will go straight to Kellerton afterwards, and work—like niggers. It won't matter a bit then whether it rains or not. And Noel can spend his holidays with us and help. How busy we shall be!"

She laughed up at him, all shining eyes and dimples.

Again—in spite of himself—he laughed back, pinching her cheek. "Will that please you, my little Chris?"

"Oh, ever so!" said Chris.

He stooped and lightly kissed her hair. "Then—so let it be!"

CHAPTER X
A SURPRISE VISIT

It was raining—one of those sudden, pelting showers that descend from June thunder-clouds, brief but drenching. It was also very dark, and Bertrand had switched on the light. He was seated at Mordaunt's writing-table, his black head bent over a pile of letters. The pen he held moved busily, but not very quickly. He was writing with extreme care. It was evident that he meant his first day's work to be a success. He scarcely noticed the heavy downpour, being profoundly intent upon the work he had in hand. Only at a sharp clap of thunder did he glance up momentarily and shrug his shoulders. But he was at once immersed again in his occupation, so deeply immersed that at the opening of the door he did not turn his head.

Holmes paused just inside the room. "If you please, sir—"

"Ah, put it down, put it down!" said the Frenchman impatiently. "I am busy."

But Holmes, being empty-handed, did not comply with the request. He remained hesitating, obviously doubtful, till with a sharp jerk de Montville turned in his chair.

"What is it, then? I have told you—I am busy."

Holmes looked apologetic. He found the abrupt ways of the new secretary somewhat disconcerting. "It's a young lady, sir," he explained rather diffidently. "It's Miss Wyndham. She run in here for shelter, and, seeing as Mr. Mordaunt be out, I didn't know whether you would wish me to show her up or not, sir."

Bertrand was on his feet in a moment. "A young lady! Miss Wyndham! Who is—Miss Wyndham?"

"It's the young lady as Mr. Mordaunt is a-going to marry," said Holmes, dropping his voice confidentially. "I told her as Mr. Mordaunt weren't in, and she said as she'd like to wait. Didn't know quite what to do, sir. Would you like me to show her up?"

"But certainly!" De Montville's eyebrows had gone up an inch, but he lowered them hastily and smiled. Doubtless it was an English custom, this; he must not display surprise. "Beg her to ascend," he said. "Mr. Mordaunt may return at any moment. He would not wish his *fiancée* to remain below."

"Very good, sir." Holmes withdrew, leaving the door ajar.

Bertrand remained upon his feet, watching it expectantly.

At the sound of voices on the stairs he smiled involuntarily. But how they were droll—these English ladies! Would he ever accustom himself—

"Miss Wyndham, sir!" It was Holmes again, opening the door wide to usher in the unexpected visitor.

Bertrand bowed low.

The visitor paused an instant on the threshold, then came briskly forward. "Oh," she said, "are you the organ-grinder?"

He straightened himself with a jerk; he looked at her. And suddenly a cry rang through the room—a cry that came straight from a woman's heart, inarticulate, thrilled through and through with a rapture beyond words. And in a moment Bertrand de Montville, outcast and wanderer on the face of the earth, had shed the bitter burden that weighed him down, had leaped the dark dividing gulf that separated him from the dear land of his dreams, and stood once more upon the sands of Valpré, with a girl's hands fast clasped in his.

"*Mignonne!*" he gasped hoarsely. "*Mignonne!*" And again "*Mignonne!*"

Her answering voice had a break in it—a sound of unshed tears. "Bertie—dear! Bertie—dear!"

The door closed discreetly, and Holmes departed to his own premises. It was no affair of his, he informed himself stolidly; but it was a rum go, and he couldn't help wondering what the master would make of it.

"But why wasn't I told?" said Chris, yet hovering between tears and laughter. "They—Bertie—they said you were an organ-grinder!"

He let her hands go, but his dark eyes still shone with the wonder and the joy of the encounter.

"Ah!" he said. "And they told me—they told me—that you were—" He stopped abruptly with the dazed expression of a man suddenly hit in a vital place. All the light went out of his face. He became silent.

"Why—what is it?" said Chris.

He did not answer at once, and in the pause that ensued he resumed his burden, he re-crossed the gulf, and the sands of Valpré were left very, very far away.

In the pause also she saw him as he was—a man broken before his prime, haggard and tired and old, with the fire of his genius quenched for ever in the bitter waters of adversity.

With an effort he spoke. "It is nothing, *chérie*. You are the same. But with me—all is changed."

"Changed, Bertie? But how?"

He looked at her. His eyes dwelt upon the vivid, happy face, but all the spontaneous gladness had died out of his own; it held only an infinite melancholy.

"He—Mr. Mordaunt—has not told you?"

"No one has told me anything," she said. "What is it, Bertie? Have things gone wrong with you? Tell me! Was it—was it the gun?"

He bent his head.

"Oh, but I'm so sorry," she said. "Was it a failure, after all?"

She drew near to him. She laid a sympathetic hand upon his arm.

A sharp tremor went through him. He stooped very low and kissed it. "It was—worse than that," he said, his voice choked, barely audible. "It was—it was—dishonour."

"Dishonour!" She echoed the word, uncomprehending, unbelieving.

He remained bent over her hand. She could not see his face. "Have you never heard," he said, "of ex-Lieutenant de Montville—the man whom all France execrated three years ago as a traitor?"

"Yes," said Chris. "I've heard of him, of course. But"—doubtfully—"I don't read the papers much. I didn't know what he was supposed to have done. I only knew that everyone in England said he hadn't."

The Frenchman sighed heavily. "The people in England did not know," he said.

"No? Then you think he was guilty?"

He stood up sharply and faced her. "I know that he was innocent," he said. "But it could not be proved. That is what the English could never realize. And—*chérie*—I was that man. I was Lieutenant de Montville."

Chris was gazing at him in amazement. "You!" she said incredulously.

"I," he said. "They accused me of treason. They thought that I would sell my own gun—my own gun. They sent me to prison—*mon Dieu!* I know not how I survived. I suffered until it seemed that I could suffer no more. And then they gave me my liberty—they banished me from France. I came to England—and I starved."

"You starved, Bertie!" Her blue eyes widened with horrified pity. "You!" she said. "You!"

He smiled with wistful humour. "Men more worthy than I have done the same," he said.

"Oh, but you, my own *preux chevalier!*" Chris's voice trembled upon the words.

He made a quick, restraining gesture. "But no—not that!" he said. "Your friend always, *petite*, but your *preux chevalier*—never again!"

Chris smiled, with quivering lips. "You will never be anything but my *preux chevalier* so long as you live," she said. "Oh, Bertie, I'm so distressed—so grieved—to think of all you have had to bear. I never dreamt of its being you. You know, I never heard your name. We went away so suddenly from Valpré. I had no time to think of anything. I—I was very miserable—afterwards." Her voice sank; her eyes were full of tears. "I knew you would think I had forgotten, but indeed, indeed it wasn't that!"

"Ah, *pauvre petite!*" he said gently.

"And you didn't know my name either, did you?" she said. "I kept telling myself you would find out somehow and write—but you never did."

He spread out his hands. "But what could I do? Your name was not known. And I—I could not leave Valpré to seek you. My duties kept me at the fortress. And so—and so—I said that I would wait until my fortune was well assured, and then—then—" He stopped. "But that is past," he said, with an odd little smile that somehow cut her to the heart. "*Et maintenant* tell me of yourself, *petite*, of all your affairs. Much may arrive in four years. But first—you are happy, yes?"

Eagerly the dark eyes sought hers as he asked the question.

Chris looked back at him with a little frown. "Yes, I am happy, Bertie. At least—I should be happy—if it weren't for thinking of you. Oh, Bertie, that horrid gun! I always hated it!"

Again her voice quivered on the verge of tears, and again with a quick gesture he stayed her.

"We will speak of it no more," he said. "See! We turn another page in the book of life, and we commence again. Let us remember only, Christine, that we are good comrades, you and I. But it is a good thing, this *camaraderie*. It gives us pleasure, yes?"

She gave him her hands impulsively. "Bertie!" she cried. "We shall always be pals—always—all our lives; but don't—dear, don't smile at me like that! I can't bear it!"

He held her hands very tightly; he had wholly ceased to smile. But still gallantly he shielded her from the danger she had not begun to see. He did it instinctively, because of the love he bore her, and because of the innocence in her eyes.

"But what is it?" he said. "It is necessary that we smile sometimes, *chérie*, since to weep is futile, and laughter is always more precious than tears. Ah! that is better. You smile yourself. It is always thus that I remember my little friend of Valpré. She was ever too brave for tears."

He pressed her hands encouragingly, and again he let them go. But the strain was telling upon him. There was one subject which he could not trust himself to broach.

And for some reason Chris could not broach it either. She took refuge in every-day affairs; she told him of the giddy doings that kept her occupied from morning till night, of Cinders (the mention of whose name kindled a reminiscent gleam in the Frenchman's eyes), of the coming birthday dance, which he must promise to attend.

He shook his head over that; such gaieties were not for him. But Chris pressed the point with much persistence. Of course he must come. It would be no fun without him. Did he remember that birthday picnic at Valpré, and—and the night they had passed in the Magic Cave? She spoke of it with heightened colour and a hint of defiance which was plainly not directed against him.

"And I was afraid of the dragon," she said. "And you held my hand. I remember it so well. And afterwards I went to sleep, and slept all night long with my head on your shoulder."

"You were but a child," he said softly.

"But it seems like yesterday," she answered.

And then it was that the door opened very quietly, and Trevor Mordaunt came in upon them, sitting together in the gloom.

CHAPTER XI
THE EXPLANATION

There was nothing hurried in his entrance, nothing startling; but yet a sudden silence fell.

Out of it almost immediately came Bertrand's voice. "Ah, Mr. Mordaunt, you return to find a visitor. Miss—Wyndham is here. She came to seek you, but she found only—" he spread out his hands characteristically—"the organ-grinder."

He had risen with the words; so also had Chris. She went forward, but without her usual impetuosity.

"I have found an old friend, Trevor," she said, speaking quickly, as if embarrassed. "I have known Mr.—Mr.—what did you say your name was?" turning towards him again.

He shrugged his shoulders. "I am called Bertrand, mademoiselle."

She smiled in her quick way. "I have known—Bertrand—for years. At least, we used to know each other years ago, and—and we knew each other again the moment we met. It was a great surprise to me—to us both."

"And a great pleasure," said Bertrand, with a bow.

"An immense pleasure," said Chris, with enthusiasm.

"But, my dear girl," Mordaunt said, his quiet voice falling almost coldly upon their explanations, "what on earth made you come here of all places?"

"Oh," said Chris, leaping to this new point almost with relief, "it was raining, and thundering too. I hadn't an umbrella and I knew I should be drenched, and this was the nearest shelter I could think of, so I just came. It seemed the most sensible thing to do. I thought perhaps you would be pleased to see me. I even fancied you might give me tea."

There was a faint note of wistfulness in her voice though she was smiling. She stood before him with something of the air of a culprit.

"Of course Aunt Philippa wouldn't approve," she said.
"I know that. But—you always say you are not like Aunt Philippa, Trevor."

He took her hand very gently but with evident purpose into his own.

"I will give you tea with pleasure," he said, "but not here. Holmes shall call a taxi. I am afraid you must say good-bye to your friend now, unless —" he paused momentarily —"unless, Bertrand, you care to accompany us."

"Oh do, Bertie!" she said eagerly. "I want you. Please come!"

But Bertrand's refusal was instant and final.

"It is impossible," he declared. "I thank you a thousand times, but I have yet many letters to write, and the post will not wait."

"Letters?" said Chris curiously.

"M. Bertrand is my secretary," said Mordaunt quietly.

"Oh, is he? And you never told me! But what a splendid idea!" Chris stood between the two men, flushed, eager, charming. "I'm so glad, Bertie," she said impulsively. "You may think yourself very lucky. Mr. Mordaunt is quite the nicest man in the world."

Bertrand bowed low. "I believe it," he said simply.

"Then we shall see quite a lot of each other," went on Chris. "That will be great fun — just like old times. Oh, must I really go? I don't want to at all, and nothing will make me sorry that I came." She threw a gay smile at her *fiancé*, and withdrew her hand to give it to the friend of her childhood. "*Au revoir, preux chevalier!* You will come to my birthday party? Promise!" Then, as he still shook his head: "Trevor, if you don't bring him, I shall come all by myself and fetch him."

"No, you mustn't do that," Mordaunt answered with decision.

"Then will you bring him?"

"I will do my best," he promised gravely.

"Will you really? Oh, thank you, Trevor. I shall expect you then, Bertie. Good-bye!"

Her hand lay for a couple of seconds in his, and he bent low over it, but he did not speak in answer.

She went out of the room with the silent Englishman. He heard her laughing as they went downstairs. He heard her gay young voice a while longer in the hall below. Then came the throb of a motor and the closing of the street door. She was gone.

He stood quite motionless, listening to the taxi as it whirred away. And even after he ceased to hear it he did not move. He was gazing straight before him, and his eyes were the eyes of a man in a dream. They saw naught.

Stiffly at last he moved, and something like a shudder went through him. He crossed the room heavily, with the gait of one stricken suddenly old. He sat down again at the writing-table, and took up the pen that he had dropped how long ago!

He even wrote a few words slowly, laboriously, still with that fixed look in his eyes. Then quite suddenly he was assailed by a violent tremor. He pushed back his chair with a sharp exclamation, half-rose, then as swiftly flung himself forward and lay across the table, face downwards, gasping horribly, almost choking. His hands were clenched, and hammered upon the papers littered there. The pen rolled unheeded over the polished wood and fell upon the floor.

Seconds passed into minutes. Gradually the bony fists ceased their convulsive tattoo. The laboured breathing grew less agonized. The man's rigid pose relaxed. But still he lay with his arms outspread and his head bowed between them, a silent image of despair.

Slowly the minutes crawled by. Down in the street below a newsboy was yelling unintelligibly, and in the distance a barrel-organ jangled the latest music-hall craze; but he was deep, deep in an abyss of suffering, very far below the surface of things. There was something almost boyishly forlorn in his attitude. With his face hidden, he looked pathetically young.

The sound of the opening door recalled him at last, and he started upright. It was Holmes with the evening paper.

The man spied the pen upon the floor and stooped for it. Bertrand stretched out a quivering hand, took it from him, and made as if he would resume his writing. But the pen only wandered aimlessly over the paper, and in a moment fell again from his nerveless fingers.

Holmes paused. Bertrand sat with his head on his hand as if unaware of him.

"Can I get you anything, sir?" he ventured.

Bertrand made a slight movement. "If I might have—a little brandy," he said, speaking with obvious effort.

"Brandy? I'll get it at once, sir," said Holmes, and was gone with the words.

Returning, he found Bertrand so far master of himself as to force a smile, but his face was ghastly. There was a blue, pinched look about his mouth that Holmes, reminiscent of his hospital days, did not like. He had seen that look before.

But the first taste of spirit dispelled it. Very courteously Bertrand thanked him.

"You are a good man, Holmes. And I think that you are my friend, yes?"

"Very pleased to do anything I can for you, sir," said Holmes.

"Ah! Then I will ask of you one little thing. It is that you remember that this weakness—this malady of a moment—remain a secret between us two—between—us—two. *Vous comprenez; non?*"

His eyes, very bright and searching, looked with a certain peremptoriness into the man's face, and Holmes, accustomed to obey, made instinctive response.

"You mean as I am not to mention it to Mr. Mordaunt, sir?"

"That is what I mean, Holmes."

"Very good, sir," said Holmes. "You're feeling better, I hope, sir?"

Very slowly de Montville rose to his feet, and stood, holding to the back of his chair.

"I am—quite well," he said impressively.

"Very good, sir," said Holmes again, and withdrew, shaking his head dubiously as soon as he was out of the Frenchman's sight.

As for de Montville, he went slowly across to the window and, leaning against the sash, gazed down upon the empty street.

Not until he heard Mordaunt's step outside more than half an hour later did he move, and then very abruptly he returned to the writing-table and seized the pen anew. He was writing with feverish rapidity when Mordaunt entered.

Very quietly Mordaunt came up and looked over his shoulder. "My boy," he said, "I am very sorry, but that is not legible."

His tone was unreservedly kind, and Bertrand jerked up his head as if surprised.

He surveyed the page before him with pursed lips, then flashed a quick look into Mordaunt's face.

"It is true," he admitted, with a rueful smile. "I also am sorry."

"Leave it," Mordaunt said. "You are looking fagged, Yes, I mean it. It will keep."

"But I have done nothing!" Bertrand protested, with outspread hands.

"No? Well, I don't believe you ought to be doing anything at present. Come and sit down." Then, peremptorily, as Bertrand hesitated: "I won't have you overworking yourself. Understand that! I have had trouble enough to get you off the sick list as it is."

He spoke with that faint smile of his that placed most men at their ease with him. Bertrand turned impulsively and grasped his hand.

"You have been—you are—more than a brother to me, monsieur," he said, with feeling. "And I—I—ah! Permit me to tell you—I—am glad that Mademoiselle has placed herself in your keeping. It was a great surprise, yes. But I am glad—from my heart. She will be safe—and happy—with you."

He spoke with great earnestness; his sincerity was shining in his eyes. Mordaunt, looking straight down into them, saw no other emotion than sheer friendliness, a friendliness that touched him, coming from one who was so nearly friendless.

"I shall do my best to make her so," he made grave reply. "She has been telling me about you, Bertrand."

"Ah!" The Frenchman's eyes interrogated him for a moment and instantly fell away. "I am surprised," he said, "to be remembered after so long. No, I had not forgotten her; but that is different, *n'est-ce pas?* I think that no one would easily forget her." He smiled as though involuntarily at some reminiscence. "*Christine et le bon Cinders!*" he said in his soft voice. "We were all friends together. We were—" again his eyes darted up to meet the Englishman's level scrutiny—"what you call 'pals,' monsieur."

Mordaunt smiled. "So I gathered. It happened at Valpré, I understand."

Bertrand nodded. His eyes grew dreamy, grew remote. "Yes," he said slowly, "it happened at Valpré. The little one was lonely. We made games in the sand. We chased the crabs; we explored the caves; we played together— as children." He stifled a sudden sigh, and rose. "*Eh bien,*" he said, "we cannot be children for ever. We grow up—some quick—some slow—but all grow up at last."

He broke off, and took up the evening paper to cut the leaves.

Mordaunt watched him in silence—a silence through which in some fashion he conveyed his sympathy; for after a moment Bertrand spoke again, still dexterously occupied with his task.

"Ah! you understand," he said. "I have no need to explain to you that this meeting with my little friend who belonged to the happy days that are past has given me almost as much of pain as of pleasure. I do not try to explain—because you understand."

"You will get over it, my dear fellow," Mordaunt said, with quiet conviction.

"You think it?" Bertrand glanced up momentarily.

"I do," Mordaunt answered, with a very kindly smile. "In fact, I think, with all due respect to you, that you are younger than you feel."

"Ah!" There was not much conviction in Bertrand's response. He stood up and handed the paper to Mordaunt with a quick bow. "But—all the same—you understand?" he questioned, with a touch of anxiety.

"Of course I understand," Mordaunt answered gently.

CHAPTER XII
THE BIRTHDAY PARTY

"At last!" said Chris.

It was her birthday party, and she stood at the head of the stairs by her aunt's side, receiving her guests.

Very young she looked, a child still, despite her twenty-one years, and supremely happy. Her aunt, one of those ladies whose very smile is in itself an act of condescension, was treating her with unusual graciousness that night, and there was not a star awry in Chris's firmament.

She had just caught a glimpse of her *fiancé* in the crowd below her, and a hasty second glance had shown her that he was not unaccompanied. A slight man, olive-skinned, with a very small, black moustache and quick eyes that searched upwards restlessly, was ascending the stairs with him. In the instant that she looked those eyes found her, and flashed their quick recognition.

Chris waved her fan in eager greeting. "Ah, there he is!" she cried aloud.

"My dear child!" said Aunt Philippa.

Impetuously Chris turned to her. "He is a friend of mine, and Trevor's secretary. I told Trevor to bring him. He is French, and his name is Bertrand."

Her cheeks were flushed with excitement as she made this hasty explanation. She had purposely left it till a crowded moment, for Aunt Philippa was apt to be very searching in her inquiries, and Chris shrank at all times from being catechized by this somewhat formidable relative of hers.

"Trevor knows all about him; they are friends," she added, in response to a slight drawing of the brows, with which she was tragically well acquainted.

"All?" murmured Max in her ear from her other side, with a mischievous twinkle in his green eyes.

Chris ignored him, but she turned a vivid crimson, and the hand she stretched to Mordaunt was quivering with agitation. But in his quiet grasp it became still. She looked up into his eyes and smiled a welcome with recovered self-possession.

"Oh, Trevor, here you are! And you've brought Bertie as you promised." She gave her other hand to Bertrand with the words, but she did not speak to him—she went on talking to her *fiancé*. "I've had a tremendous day, and thank you a million times for—you know what. It's a good thing you booked your dances beforehand, for I haven't any left."

"Not one for me?" murmured Bertrand, as he bent over her hand.

She turned to him with a radiant smile. "Yes, yes, of course! Should I be likely to forget all old pal like you? Trevor, will you introduce him to Aunt Philippa?"

"My friend Mr. Bertrand," said Mordaunt promptly.

Mrs. Forest acknowledged the introduction with extreme chilliness. She strongly disapproved of Chris's faculty for developing unexpected friendships. The child was so regrettably free-and-easy in all her ways. Of course, if Trevor Mordaunt approved of their intimacy, and apparently he did, there was nothing to be said, but she herself could not regard it with favour. Once more she congratulated herself that her responsibilities where Chris was concerned were nearly at an end.

But if her greeting were cold, Bertrand scarcely had time to remark it, for his attention was instantly diverted by the red-haired youth who lounged behind her. Max, whose presence had been annoying his aunt all day, thrust out a welcoming hand to the new-comer.

"Hullo!" he said. "You, is it?"

Bertrand raised his brows. He gave his hand, after an instant's hesitation, with a non-committing, "Myself—yes."

Max drew him aside out of the crowd. "It's all right. I'm Chris's brother, and I shan't give you away. But how long do you expect to remain incog., I wonder? I knew your face the moment I saw you on the stairs."

"You know me?" said Bertrand, drawing back a little.

"Of course I know you. Who could help it? Your face is one of the best known in Europe. So you are the hero that Chris used to worship at Valpré! She mentioned the one fact to me, but not the other. She knows, I suppose?"

"Ah, yes, but it is a secret." Bertrand spoke wearily, as if reluctant to discuss the matter. "It is not my desire to be recognized. She knows that also."

"I never knew Chris could keep a secret before," commented Max.

A quick gleam shot up in the Frenchman's eyes. "Then you do not know her very well," he said.

Max smiled shrewdly, but did not contest the point. He seldom argued, and Chris herself at this moment intervened.

"Bertie, I've saved the supper extras for you. Don't forget. Max, you know most of the people here. Do introduce him, or find Jack—he will. I'm dancing the first with Trevor. Good-bye!"

She flashed her smile upon him, and was gone. Bertrand stood and watched her as she went away through the throng with Trevor Mordaunt. Everyone watched her, and nearly everyone smiled. She was so naïvely, so sublimely happy.

Her gay young laugh rang out as they began to dance. "Isn't it fun?" she said; and then, with her eyes turned to his, "Trevor, I've such a crowd of things to thank you for that I don't know where to begin."

"Then, my dear child, don't begin!" he said, with his indulgent smile.

She frowned at him. "You are not to call me 'child' any longer. I'm grown-up."

His smile remained. "Since when?" he said.

"That's a rude question which I am not going to answer. But, Trevor, you—you shouldn't have sent me all that money. It's much more than I want."

"I'm glad to hear it," he said; and, after a moment, "I hope you will spend it profitably."

"Oh, yes." Eagerly she made reply. "I've bought a new collar for Cinders—such a beauty, with bells! I thought it would be so useful if he went rabbiting."

"What! To warn the rabbits?"

"Oh, no! I never thought of that! Poor Cinders! It would spoil his sport, wouldn't it? And he's such a sportsman. I suppose I shall have to keep it for

Sundays after all. What a pity! I thought it would help us to find him if he got lost."

"But he always turns up again," said Mordaunt consolingly.

Her blue eyes flashed their sunshine. "Yes, yes, of course. And another thing I did which ought to please you very much."

The indulgence turned to approval on Mordaunt's face. "I can guess what that was," he said.

"Can you?" Chris looked delighted. "Well, you mustn't tell Aunt Philippa, because she would call it shocking extravagance, and I really only did it to please you."

"Oh! Then I am afraid I haven't guessed right." Mordaunt's expression became one of grave doubt.

Chris laughed aloud. "You will have to guess again. No, please go on dancing. One only gets hotter standing still."

"But, Chris," he said, "I want to know."

His tone was perfectly kind, as gentle as it always was when he addressed her, and yet the quick glance that she threw him was not without a hint of misgiving. The slender young body stiffened ever so slightly against his arm.

"I wonder if Bertie has found a partner," she said. "Do you think we ought to go and see?"

He guided her towards the entrance. A good many people were standing about, and one after another accosted Chris. She answered blithely enough, her hand still upon her *fiancé's* arm, but yet there was that about her that made him aware that she was not wholly at her ease. When he drew her towards a room beyond that led to a conservatory, she hung back.

"I want to find Bertie. Where is he?"

Jack Forest appeared at that moment, and she turned to him with evident relief. "Oh, Jack, where is Mr. Bertrand? I told Max to hand him over to you. He knows no one, and I do want him to have a good time."

"Be easy, my child," said Jack, with a cheery grin. "He is having the time of his life. The mater has taken him under her wing."

"Jack!" Chris stood aghast.

"Don't agitate yourself," said Jack. "It's all serene. He is thoroughly enjoying himself. Where are you two off to? Going to sit out in the dark? Shall I come and mount guard?"

"Oh, don't be ridiculous!" protested Chris. "Jack, remember our dance is the next."

Jack bowed with his hand on his heart. "I don't forget such things. Make the most of your time, Trevor. It's nearly up."

He departed with a careless swagger, and Chris turned to her quiet companion and gave a little shiver. "Why did we leave off dancing? I'm cold."

He led her across the hall to a settee. Someone had thrown a scarf upon it. He put it round her shoulders.

"It isn't mine," she said, "and it isn't that sort of cold either. I hope Aunt Philippa isn't teasing Bertie. Do you think she is?"

"I think he can take care of himself," Mordaunt said.

"Do you? I don't. Aunt Philippa is sure to say horrid things to him. I think we ought to go and find them—really."

There was a note of pleading in her voice, but Mordaunt did not respond to it. He sat and contemplated her, as if his thoughts were elsewhere.

He leaned forward at last and spoke very quietly. "Chris," he said, "forgive me for asking, but—you have paid your debts?"

The colour surged up all over her fair face. She began to pluck restlessly at her fan. But she said no word. Only as he took it gravely from her, she glanced up as though compelled, and for a single instant sheer panic looked at him out of her eyes.

"My dear," he said, "will you attend to the matter to-morrow?"

But still she was silent, quiveringly, piteously silent. The colour had gone out of her face now; she was as white as the dress she wore.

"You will?" he said gently.

She made a little sound that was like a repressed sob, and put her hand sharply to her throat.

"You will?" he said again.

"Yes," she whispered.

He dismissed the matter instantly, opened the fan he had taken from her, and began to admire it.

"Jack gave it to me," she said. "It's a birthday present. He always gives me nice things. So do you, Trevor. Your pendant is the loveliest thing I have ever seen."

He had sent her a pendant of turquoise and pearl, and it hung upon her neck at the moment. She fingered it lovingly.

"I shall go to bed in it," she said, "so as to have it all night long. It feels so delicious. I wish I could see it. It was the very thing I saw in Bond Street a few weeks ago, and wanted to wear at Hilda's wedding." She broke off with a sudden sigh. "It will be horrid when Hilda's married."

"Will it?" he said.

"Yes, horrid," she repeated with vehemence. "Aunt Philippa is going to turn all her attention to me then. Of course, I know she is very kind, but—well, I feel as if this is my last week of freedom. I shall be almost glad when—" She broke off abruptly. "Do let us go and rescue Bertie," she said, "before we get swallowed up in the crowd."

He got up at once and silently offered his arm. She slipped her hand within it, and gave it a little squeeze.

"We'll dance to the *finale* next time," she said lightly. "It's much more fun than talking."

She added carelessly, as they moved away together: "By the way, I had my photograph taken this morning. I don't know if you will like it. Shall I send you one?"

"Do," he said. And after a moment, smiling faintly: "Was that the thing that was to please me?"

She nodded, not looking at him.

He laid his hand for an instant upon hers. "Thank you, Chris," he said.

She turned instantly and smiled upon him. "You can give it to Bertie if you don't like it," she made blithe response.

CHAPTER XIII
PALS

"Ah! now, for a good talk," said Chris. "We have got at least half an hour. Are you tired, Bertie, or only bored?"

But he was neither, he assured her. He had enjoyed his evening greatly. No, he had not danced. He had found it enough diverting to look on tranquilly in a corner. *Mais oui*, everybody had been most kind, including his hostess, to whom he paid a special tribute of appreciation. He had found her as gracious as she was beautiful.

"Did she try to pump you?" asked Chris.

He raised his brows in humorous bewilderment. But to pump—what was it? To ask questions? Ah yes, she had asked him several questions. He had not answered all of them. He feared she had found him a little stupid. But she had been very patient with him, ah! so patient—he spread out his hands, with the old, quick smile, and Chris's peal of laughter echoed far and wide.

"Bertie, you're too heavenly for words! Then she didn't find out about Valpré? She thinks—I suppose she thinks—that Trevor introduced us to each other."

"I do not know what she thinks," the Frenchman made answer. "But no, we did not speak of Valpré! That is a secret, *hein*?"

"Not exactly a secret. I told Max. But Aunt Philippa—oh, she is so different. She never understands things," said Chris. "I daresay she will find out from Trevor as it is; but I hope she won't—I do hope she won't!"

He smiled comprehendingly. "But Mr. Mordaunt—he understands, yes?" he said.

She hesitated. "I never told even him about that night in the Magic Cave, Bertie."

"No?" he said, his quick eyes upon her. "But why not?"

She shook her head with vehemence. "I couldn't. Everyone—even Jack—made such a fuss at the time—as if—as if"—she turned crimson—"I had done something really wicked. I'm sure I don't know why. I always said so."

There was defiance as well as distress in her voice. Bertrand leaned a little towards her.

"Mr. Mordaunt would not think like that," he said, with conviction.

She looked at him dubiously. "I'm not so sure. He has extraordinary views on some things. I never quite know how he will take anything. Other people are the same. You are the only person I am quite sure of."

He smiled, but not as if greatly elated. "That is because we are pals," he said.

"Yes, I know. It's good to have a pal who understands." Chris spoke a little wistfully, but almost instantly dismissed the matter. "Why, I am forgetting! You haven't seen Cinders yet, and I told him you were coming. He is upstairs. Shall we go and find him?"

They went up together. Half-way up she slipped her hand into his, with a soft little laugh. "It's like old times, Bertie. Don't break the spell, *preux chevalier*. Let us pretend—just for to-night!"

They found Cinders imprisoned in a little sitting-room at the top of the house which Chris shared with her cousin. His greeting of Bertrand was effusive, even rapturous. Like his mistress, he never forgot a friend.

Afterwards they sat and talked of many things, chiefly connected with Valpré. There was so much to remember—Mademoiselle Gautier and her queer, conventual prejudices, Manon, the maid-of-all-work, and her funny stories of the shore.

"She quite believed in the spell," Chris said. "She almost frightened me with it."

"Without doubt there was a spell," said Bertrand gravely.

"You really think so? I never believed in it after that night."

"No?" he said. "And yet it was there."

Chris peered at him. "You talk as if it were something quite substantial," she said.

"It was substantial," he made answer, and then with a sudden smile into her wondering eyes: "As substantial, *chérie*, as my rope of sand that was to make my work endure like—like the Sphinx and Cleopatra's Needle and—and—" He broke off with his eloquent shrug, paused a moment, then—"and—our friendship, if you will," he ended.

"Ah, fancy your remembering that!" she said. "But I believe you remember everything."

"That is the spell," he said.

"Is it, Bertie? And do you remember the duel, and how you wouldn't tell me what it was all about? Tell me now!" she begged, as a child pleading for a story. "I always wanted to know."

But his face darkened instantly. "Not that, *petite*. He was bad. He was *scélérat*. We will not speak of him."

"But, Bertie, I'm grown-up now. I'm quite old enough to know," she urged, with a coaxing hand upon his arm.

He took the hand, turned it upwards, stroked the soft palm very reverently. "I pray that you will never be old enough, Chris," he said, and in the shaded lamplight she saw that his face had grown suddenly melancholy, almost haggard. "The knowledge of evil is a poisonous thing. Those who find it can never be young again."

His manner awed her a little. She did not pursue the point with her customary persistence. "Well, tell me what happened afterwards," she said. "He got well again?"

"Yes, *petite*."

"And—you forgave each other?"

"Never!" Bertrand raised his head and shot out the word with emphasis.

"Never, Bertie?" Chris looked at him, slightly startled.

He looked back at her, faintly smiling, but with the melancholy still in his eyes. "Never," he repeated. "That shocks you, no?"

"Not really," she said loyally. "I'm sure he was horrid. He looked it. Then—you are enemies still?"

"Enemies?" He shrugged his shoulders. "No, I think he would not consider me as an enemy now."

"And yet you never forgave him?"

"No, never." Again his denial was emphatic. After a moment, seeing her bewilderment, he proceeded to explain. "If he had apologized, if he had retracted the insult, then it is possible that a reconciliation might have been effected between us."

"But he didn't?" said Chris. "Then what happened? Did he do nothing at all?"

"For a long time—nothing," said Bertrand.

"And then?"

"Then," very simply he made reply, "he ruined me."

"Bertie!" She gazed at him with tragedy dawning in her eyes. "He ruined you! He!"

"He supplied the evidence against me," Bertrand said. "But it was clever. He spread a net—so"—he flung out his hands with an explanatory gesture—"a net that I see not nor suspect, and then when I am entrapped he draw it close—close, and—I am a prisoner." He shut his teeth with a click, and for an instant smiled—the smile of the man who fights with his back against the wall.

But the tragedy had grown from shadow to reality in the turquoise blue eyes of the girl beside him. "Oh, Bertie," she said, with a break in her voice, "then it was all my fault—mine!"

He turned towards her swiftly. "No, no, no! Who has said that? It is not true!" he declared, with vehemence.

"You said it yourself—almost," she told him. "And it is true, for if you hadn't fought him it would never have happened. Oh, Bertie! I'm beginning to think it was a dreadful pity I ever went to Valpré!"

He caught her hands and held them. "You shall not say it!" he declared passionately. "You shall not think it! *Mignonne*, listen! Those days at Valpré are to me the most precious, the most sacred, the most dear of my life. They can never return, it is true. But the memory of them is mine for ever. Of that can no one deprive me. While I live I shall cherish them in my heart."

He cheeked himself abruptly; she was gazing at him with a sort of speculative wonder that had arrested the tragedy in her eyes. At his sudden pause she began to smile.

"Bertie, dear, forgive me, but I can't help thinking what a funny Englishman you would have made! So you really don't think it was my fault? I'm so glad. I should break my heart if it were."

He stooped, catching her hands up to his lips, whispering inarticulately.

She suffered him, half-laughing. "Silly Frenchman!" she said softly.

And at that he looked up and let her go. "You are right," he said, speaking rather thickly. "I am foolish. I am mad. And you—you have the patience of an angel to support me thus."

"Oh no," said Chris. "I'm not a bit like an angel. In fact, I'm rather wicked sometimes—not very, you know, Bertie, only rather. Now let me show you my presents. I brought them up here on purpose."

So gaily she diverted the conversation, mainly because she had caught a gleam of tears in her friend's eyes and was aware that they had not been far from her own. It would never do for them to sit crying together on her birthday night. Besides, it was too ridiculous, for what was there to cry about? Bertrand was in a better position now than he had been for years. And she—and she—well, it was her birthday, and surely that was reason enough for being glad.

It was Bertrand who at length gently drew her attention to the time. They had been talking for the best part of an hour.

"Will not the supper dances be nearly finished?" he suggested.

"Oh, goodness!" exclaimed Chris. "Yes, long ago. We must fly. Say good-bye to Cinders. You will come and see him again soon, won't you? Come just as often as you can."

At the door she paused a moment, slipped a warm hand into his, and for the first time shyly broke her silence upon the subject of her approaching marriage.

"I'm so glad you are coming to live with us when we are married," she said. "I shall never feel lonely with you there."

"You would not be lonely without me," he made quick response. "You will have always your husband."

She caught her breath, and then laughed. "To be sure. I hadn't thought of that. But Trevor is always busy, and he is going to write a book too." She looked at him with sudden mischief in her eyes. "Yes, I am very glad you are coming," she said again. "When he doesn't want you with him you can come and play with me. And when it's summer"—her eyes fairly danced—"we'll go for picnics, Bertie, lots of picnics. You'll like that, *preux chevalier*?"

He smiled back upon her; who could have helped it? But he stifled a sigh as he smiled. Would life be always a picnic to her, he asked himself? He could not imagine it otherwise, and yet he knew that even upon this child of mirth and innocence the reality of life must dawn some day. Would it be a gracious dawning of pearly tints and roselit radiance, gradually filling that eager young soul to the brim with the greater joys of life? Or would it be fiery and terrible, a blinding, relentless burst of light, from which she would shrink appalled, discerning the wrath of the gods before ever she had realized their bounty?

Could it be thus with her, his little comrade, his bird of Paradise, his darling? He thought not. He believed not. And yet deep in the heart of him he feared.

And because of that lurking fear he vowed silently over the little friendly hand that lay so confidingly in his that never while breath remained in his body would he leave her until he knew her happiness—the ultimate happiness of her womanhood—to be assured.

It seemed to him that it was for this alone that he had been introduced once more into her book of life. All his hopes and dreams had passed; he was an old man before his time; but this one thing, it seemed, was left to him. For a while longer his name would figure with hers across the page. Only when the page turned his part would be done. She would not need him then. She would be a woman; and—*eh bien*, it was only the child Chris who could ever be expected to need him now. When she ceased to be a child the need—if such, indeed, existed—would be for ever past; and he would be no more to her than a memory—the memory of one who had played with her a while in the happy land of her childhood and had shared with her the picnics of those summer days.

This was the sole remaining aspiration of Bertrand de Montville—the man who in the arrogance of his youth had diced with the gods, and had lost the cast.

CHAPTER XIV
A REVELATION

"My dear, it is quite useless for you to attempt to justify your conduct, for it was simply inexcusable. No argument can possibly alter that fact. Everyone was waiting about for a considerable time in the supper-room, desirous of drinking your health, while you, it transpires, were hiding in a corner with this very questionable foreigner whom Trevor has been eccentric enough to befriend, but of whom I can discover practically nothing."

"But Trevor knows all about him, Aunt Philippa," pleaded Chris.

"That," said Aunt Philippa, "may or may not be the case. But so long as you are in my charge, I, and not Trevor, am the one to direct your choice of acquaintances, and I very strongly object to the inclusion of this Frenchman in the number. It is my desire, Chris, that you do not see him again during the rest of the time that you are under my roof. I intend to speak to Trevor upon the matter at the earliest opportunity. I consider that, in the face of what has occurred, he would be extremely ill-advised to retain this unknown foreigner in his employment, though I should imagine he has already arrived at that conclusion for himself. I could see that he was seriously displeased by your behaviour last night."

"Oh, was he?" said Chris blankly. "He didn't say so."

"He probably realized that it would be useless to express his displeasure at such a time. But let me warn you, Chris. He is not a man to stand any trifling. I have heard it from several quarters. Jack, as you are aware, knows him well, and he will tell you the same. You may try his patience too far, and that, I presume, is not your intention. Should it happen, I think that you would regret it all your life."

"But I haven't trifled! I don't trifle!" protested Chris, divided between distress and indignation.

Aunt Philippa smiled unpleasantly—she seldom displayed any other variety of smile. "That, my dear, is very much a matter of opinion. You had better go now to Hilda. She is waiting to see your bridesmaid's dress tried on."

Chris went, with a worried pucker between her brows. How curious it was that some people failed so completely to take a reasonable view of things! They made mountains out of molehills, and expected her to climb them—she, whose unwary feet were accustomed to trip so lightly along easy ways. And Trevor too—she caught her breath with a sharp shiver—was he really seriously displeased with her? He had given no hint of it when they had danced together, save that he had been somewhat grave and silent. But then, he was naturally so. She had not thought much of it; in fact, she had been thinking mainly of Bertie.

And here a sudden throb of dismay sent the blood to her heart. Aunt Philippa was going to speak to him upon this subject, was going to suggest unspeakable things, was going to talk over her conduct with him and make him furious in earnest. And then it would all come out about her having met Bertrand all those years ago. Trevor would mention that in the natural course of things, and then Aunt Philippa would tell him—would tell him—

"Chris, dear, what is the matter? You are as white as a ghost."

It was Hilda's voice gently recalling her. She came to herself with a start, and the hot blood rose to her cheeks with a rush.

"Are you very tired after yesterday?" her cousin asked. "I am afraid you got up too early."

"Oh, no!" said Chris. "I wasn't early at all. I didn't ride this morning. Jack has promised to come for me this evening instead."

She diverted Hilda's attention desperately. She could not make confidences in the presence of the dressmaker. Moreover, she was not sure that she wanted to talk even to Hilda about her pal from Valpré. It was true Hilda understood most things, but Aunt Philippa had somehow managed to inspire her with a sense of guilt. She knew she could not speak of Bertrand with ease to anyone now.

Besides, there was no time. The moment she was free she must manage somehow to communicate with Trevor. She must warn him of Aunt Philippa's intentions. She must explain to him.

She did not want him to know about that night in the Magic Cave. Everyone who heard of it was shocked, everyone except Max, and he made a speciality of never being shocked at anything. Why, it was even possible—here a new thought leaped up and struck her an unexpected blow—was it not more than possible that it was this self-same event that had given rise to the insult that had led to the duel? Of course that must be it! That was why Bertrand so persistently refused to enlighten her. How was it she had never before thought of it? It was the truth of course! How had she failed to see anything so glaringly apparent?

Yes, it was the truth. She had blundered upon it unawares, and now she surveyed it horror-stricken, remembering Bertrand's warning that the knowledge of evil was a poisonous thing. So must Eve have felt when first her eyes were opened to the wisdom of the gods.

She was free at last, and sped up to her room. The scribbled message that reached her *fiancé* an hour later was only just legible, but it spoke more eloquently of the state of mind of the writer than she knew.

"DEAR TREVOR,—

"Aunt Philippa says you are angry with me. Please don't be. Really there is nothing to be angry about, though she thinks there is, and she is going to try and persuade you to send Bertie away. Trevor, don't listen to her, will you? And, whatever you do, don't tell her about Valpré. I'm very bothered about it. Do be as kind as you always are to

> "Your loving
> CHRIS."

Mordaunt's answering note reached her late in the afternoon just before she set forth for her ride in the Park with Jack.

"MY DEAR LITTLE CHRIS,—

"My love to your Aunt Philippa, and I am just off to Paris for the inside of a week. I shall be back for your cousin's wedding. Ask her to reserve her lecture till then. Our friend Bertrand sends his *amitiés*. I send nothing, for you have it all.

> "Yours,
> TREVOR."

Chris kissed the note with a rush of tenderness—greater than she had ever managed to bestow upon the writer. That brief response to her appeal stirred her as she had never been stirred before. It was sweet of him to trust her so. She would never forget it, never, as long as she lived.

When Jack appeared to escort her, he noted her radiant face and shining eyes with approval.

"Why, you're looking almost pretty for once," he said. "What has happened to bring it about? It must be a recipe worth having."

"Don't be absurd!" she retorted, beaming upon him. "Who wants to be pretty?"

"It's better to be good certainly," he said. "I know you couldn't be both. But what's the joke? I think you might let me help laugh."

"There isn't a joke," she said. "And I'm not laughing. I've had a letter from Trevor, that's all. And he's going to Paris."

"Oh-ho!" said Jack.

"Now you're horrid!" she protested. "I don't want him to go in the least."

"Of course not," said Jack. "I've observed how remarkably depressed you were by the news."

"I shall be cross with you in a minute," said Chris.

"Heaven forbid!" said Jack. "When is he coming back?"

"In time for Hilda's wedding."

"And does he take the French secretary with him?"

"Oh, no, he can't go to France. I mean—I mean—"

Chris stopped in sudden confusion.

"I know what you mean," said Jack. "They would take too keen an interest in him over there. Isn't that it?"

"How did you know?" said Chris.

He laughed. "The proverbial little bird! I might add that a good many people know by this time."

"Oh, Jack, do they?" Chris looked at him in consternation. "He didn't want anyone to know."

"My dear child, in that case he should not have courted publicity as the guest of the evening last night."

"Jack! He wasn't the guest of the evening! How dare you say such things!"

Chris's rare displeasure actually was aroused now. Her slight figure stiffened, and she tapped her knee with her riding-switch. She never touched her animal with this weapon, whatever his idiosyncrasies, and certainly the horses she rode generally behaved with docility.

Jack surveyed her with amused eyes as they turned up under the trees. "All right," he said imperturbably. "He wasn't. My mistake, no doubt. But where on earth were you hiding during the supper extras? He was missing too. Curious, wasn't it?"

Chris came out of her temper with a winning gesture of appeal. "Jack dear, don't! I've heard such a lot about it from Aunt Philippa already. And why shouldn't I talk to my pals? You wouldn't like it if I didn't talk to you sometimes."

"Is he that sort of pal?" asked Jack.

She nodded. "Just that sort. And Trevor knows all about it and understands. I've just had a line from him to tell me so."

"Have you, though?" said Jack. "Then all I can say is Trevor is a brick—a very special kind of brick—and I hope you realize it."

"He's just the sweetest man in the world," said Chris with enthusiasm. "He is never horrid about things, and he never thinks what isn't."

"Lucky for you!" said Jack.

"Why?" She turned towards him sharply.

He began to smile. "Because, my dear, you have rather an unfortunate knack of making things appear—as they are not."

"I don't know what you mean," she protested. "It's very horrid of people to imagine things, and it certainly isn't my fault. Trevor understands that. He always understands."

"Let us hope he always will," said Jack.

"He would trust me even if he didn't," said Chris.

"At the same time," said Jack, "I shouldn't try his faith too far if I were you. If you ever overstepped it, I have a notion that it might be—well, somewhat unpleasant for you."

He spoke the words with a smile, but the silence with which they were received had in it something that was tragic. Chris was gazing straight before her as they rode. Her expression was curiously stony, as if, by some means, her customary animation had been suspended. Jack wondered a little. After a moment she spoke, without looking round. "Jack!"

"Your humble servant!" said Jack.

"I'm not laughing," she said. "I want you to tell me something. You know Trevor. You knew him years before I did. Have you ever seen him—really angry?"

"Great Jove! yes," said Jack.

"Many times?" There was a little quiver in her voice, but it did not sound exactly agitated.

"No, not many times. He isn't the sort of fellow to let himself go, you know," said Jack.

"No," she said. "But what is he like—when he is angry?"

Jack considered. "He's rather like a devil that's been packed in ice for a very long time. He doesn't expand, he contracts. He emits a species of condensed fury that has a disastrous effect upon the object thereof. He is about the last man in the world that I should choose to quarrel with."

"But why?" she said. "Would you be afraid of him?"

Jack considered this point too quite gravely and impartially. "I really don't know, Chris," he said at last. "I believe I should be."

"He can be terrible, then," she said, as if stating a conclusion rather than asking a question.

"More or less," Jack admitted. "But he is never unreasonable. I have never seen him angry without good cause."

"And then—I suppose he is merciless?"

"Quite," said Jack. "I saw him shoot a Kaffir once for knocking a wounded man on the head. It was no more than the brute deserved. I was lying wounded myself, and he took my revolver to do it with. But it was a nasty jolt for the Kaffir. He knew exactly what was going to happen to him and why, before it happened. Afterwards, when Trevor came back to me, he was smiling, so I suppose it did him good. He's a very deliberate chap. Some people call him cold-blooded. He never acts on impulse. And I've never known him make a mistake."

"I see." Chris swallowed once or twice as if she felt an obstruction in her throat. "I expect he would be like that with anyone," she said. "I mean if he had reason to be angry with anyone, he wouldn't spare them—whatever they were. I always felt he was like that."

"He's one of the best chaps in the world," said Jack warmly.

She assented, but not with the enthusiasm that had marked her earlier eulogy. She seemed, in fact, to have become a little *distrait*, and Jack, remarking the fact, suggested a canter.

They met several people whom they knew before they turned homewards, and it was not until they were leaving the Park that any further conversation was possible.

Then very suddenly Chris reined in and spoke. "Jack, before we go back, I want to ask you something."

"Well?" said Jack.

She made a pathetic little gesture towards him, and touched his knee with her riding-switch. Her blue eyes besought him very earnestly. "Jack, we—we are pals, aren't we? Or I couldn't possibly ask it of you. Jack, I—I've been foolish—and extravagant. And—" she became suddenly breathless—"I want twenty pounds—to pay some debts. Jack, could you—would you—"

"You monkey!" said Jack.

"I couldn't help it," she declared piteously. "I've spent a frightful lot of money lately. I don't know how it goes. It runs away like water. But I—want to get out of debt, Jack. If you will help me just this once, I'll pay you back when— when—when I'm married."

"Good heavens, child!" he said. "You shall have it twice over if you like. But why on earth didn't you tell me before? Don't you know it's very naughty to run up debts?"

She nodded. "Yes, I know. But I couldn't help it. There were things I wanted. And London is such an expensive place. You do understand, dear Jack, don't you?"

Jack thought he did. He was, moreover, too fond of his young cousin to treat her with severity. But he considered it his duty to deliver a brief lecture on the dangers of insolvency, to which Chris listened with becoming docility, thanking him with a quick, sweet smile when he had done.

Jack did not flatter himself that he had succeeded in making a very deep impression. He wondered a little what Trevor Mordaunt would have said under similar circumstances.

"I hope she will be straightforward with him," was his reflection. "But she is a Wyndham of the Wyndhams, and everyone knows that her father didn't suffer over-much from that complaint."

Which was true. Chris's father had been one of those baffling persons who are always in want of money and yet seem quite incapable of giving a clear account of their wants. His affairs had been in a perpetual muddle from the beginning of his career, and had probably ended so.

"Most unsatisfactory!" as Aunt Philippa invariably remarked, as a suitable conclusion to any discussion on the subject of her brother or any of his family. How she personally had managed to escape the general blight that rested upon them was a mystery that no one—not Aunt Philippa herself—had ever been able to solve.

CHAPTER XV
MISGIVINGS

Hilda Forest's wedding was one of the events of the season. All London went to it. Lord Percy Davenant, the bridegroom, was a man of many friends, and the bride's mother prided herself upon the width of her own social circle.

In the midst of the fuss and tumult the bride, very grave and serene, with shining eyes, went her appointed way. Everyone was loud in her praise. Her bearing was admirable. She was as one on whom a veil of happiness had fallen, and external things scarcely touched her.

She went through her part steadfastly and well, forgetful utterly of the watching crowds, conscious only of one being in all that critical multitude, holding only one thought in the silent sanctuary of her soul.

And Chris, the chief bridesmaid, walking alone behind her, watched and marvelled. She liked Lord Percy Davenant. He was big, good-natured, rollicking, and many a joke had they had together. But no faintest tinge of romance hung about him in her opinion. She could not with the utmost effort of the imagination see what there was in him to bring that light into Hilda's eyes.

It was odd, thought Chris, very odd. If it had been Trevor, now—She could quite easily have understood it if Hilda had fallen in love with him. And they would have been eminently well suited to one another, too. Yes, it was very strange, quite unaccountable! Here she remembered that Trevor was probably somewhere in the crowd behind her, and peeped over her shoulder surreptitiously to get a glimpse of him.

She was not successful, but she caught the eye of one of the bridesmaids immediately behind her, who leaned forward with a merry smile to whisper, "Your turn next!"

Chris turned back sharply. The words had a curious effect upon her; they gave her almost a sensation of shock. Her turn next to face this ordeal through which Hilda was passing with such supreme confidence! Would she feel as Hilda felt when she came to stand with Trevor before the altar?

Would that thrill of deep sincerity be in her voice also as she repeated the vows irrevocable which were even now leaving Hilda's lips? Would her eyes meet his with the same pure gladness of love made perfect?

A sudden tremor went through her. She shivered from head to foot. The scent of the flowers she held—Hilda's flowers and her own—seemed to turn her sick. She felt overpowered—lost!

Desperately she clutched her wavering self-control. This ghastly, unspeakable doubt must not conquer her. No one must know it—no one must see!

But she was as one slipping down a steep incline, faster and faster every second. The beating of her heart rose up and deafened her. It was like someone beating a tattoo in the church. She could not hear another word of the service. And she was suffocating with the nauseous sweetness of the bridal flowers. Wildly she looked around her. Where was Trevor? He would help her. He would understand—he always understood. But she sought him in vain. There was only the long line of bridesmaids behind her and a sea of indistinct faces on each side.

She lifted her head and gasped. She felt as if she were being smothered in flowers. Their heavy perfume stifled her. She understood now why some people wouldn't have flowers at their funerals. She had always thought it odd before.

She was slipping more and more rapidly down that fatal slope. The sunlight that lay in a great bar of vivid colours across the church danced before her eyes. She no longer saw the bridal couple in front of her. They had faded quite away, and in their stead was a terrible abyss of flowers—bridal flowers that made her sick and faint.

She swayed as she stood. Who was that speaking? Certain solemn words had pierced her reeling brain. She heard them as if they came from another world—

"Those whom God hath joined together let no man put asunder."

Those words would be uttered over her next. Perhaps they were meant for her even now. Surely it was her own wedding and not Hilda's, after all! She was being married, and she wasn't ready! Oh, it was horrible—horrible! And where was Trevor, or Bertie, or someone—anyone to hold her back from that dreadful, scented darkness?

Ah! An arm supporting her! A steady hand that took the flowers away! Trevor at last! She turned and clung to him weakly, crying like a frightened child. Her knees would not support her any longer, they doubled under her weight. But he lifted her without effort, almost as if she had been a child indeed, and carried her away.

He bore her to an open door that led out from the vestry, and there in the fresh air Chris revived. He set her on her feet, and made her lean against him. Jack hovered in the background, but he dismissed him.

"She is all right again. Go and tell your mother. It was an atmosphere to asphyxiate an ox."

Chris laughed very shakily. "I'm so sorry, Trevor. Did I make a scene?"

She would have withdrawn from his support, but he kept his arm about her. "No, dear. I chanced to be looking at you, and I saw you were going to faint. I am glad I was able to get you away in time."

"I couldn't help it," she said, not looking at him. "It was—it was—the flowers."

"I know," he said gently.

She leaned her head against him. It was throbbing painfully. "Oh, Trevor—it wasn't—only—the flowers," she whispered.

He put his hand over her aching temples. "Tell me presently, dear," he said.

She reached up and found the hand, drew it down over her face, and held it so for seconds, speaking no word. She touched it softly with her lips at last, and let it go.

"I'm well now," she said. "Take me back."

He looked at her searchingly. "You are sure?"

She smiled at him, though her eyes were still heavy. "Yes, I'll be quite good. I mustn't spoil Hilda's wedding by being silly, must I? You haven't brought Bertie, I suppose?"

He smiled a little. "He didn't get an invitation."

"Of course not. Trevor, you didn't think I was—flirting with him that night?"

"My dear child—no!"

"Because I never flirt," said Chris very earnestly. "It's a horrid thing to do. You'll never think that of me, will you? Or that I have ever trifled with you—or anyone?"

Trevor's eyes rested upon her with grave kindness. "My dear, why should I think these things of you?" he said.

She shook her head. "I don't know. Lots of people do. But you are different. I think you understand. You'll stay after it's over and have a talk, won't you?"

"Yes," he said.

She slipped her hand into his. "Now let's go back."

They went back. The ceremony was very nearly over. Chris took her place again, and followed the bride into the vestry afterwards.

Later, at the crowded reception, she was among the merriest, and very few noticed that she was paler than usual or that her eyes were deeply shadowed.

The wedded pair left early, and immediately afterwards the guests began to disperse. Mordaunt, who had been making himself generally useful, looked round for Chris as soon as a leisure moment arrived. But he looked in vain; she was not to be found.

He went through every room in search of her, but all to no purpose. For a while he lingered, waiting for her, talking to the few people who remained. But at length, as there was still no sign of her, he prepared to take his departure also, with the intention of presenting himself again later.

He was actually on the doorstep when Jack came striding after him. "I say, Chris wants you. I forgot to mention it. Make my apologies, for Heaven's sake! She must have been waiting an hour or more."

"What?" Mordaunt turned back sharply, frowning.

"Don't scowl, there's a dear chap," said Jack. "I'm awfully sorry. I had such a shoal of things to see to. She's upstairs, right at the top of the house, first door you come to. She said you were to go up and have tea with her and Cinders. Really, I'm horribly sorry."

"All right. So you ought to be," Mordaunt said, and left him to his regrets.

He was somewhat breathless when he arrived outside the door of Chris's little sanctum, but he did not pause on that account. He knocked with his hand already upon the handle, and almost immediately turned it.

"I can come in?" he asked.

A muffled bark from Cinders was the only answer—a warning bark, as though he would have the intruder tread softly.

Mordaunt trod softly in consequence, softly entered, softly closed the door.

He found his little *fiancée* crouched on the floor beside an ancient sofa, her arms resting upon it and her head sunk upon them. Cinders, very alert, bristling with importance, mounted guard on the sofa itself.

For Chris was asleep, curled up in her bridesmaid finery, a study in white and blue, with a single splash of vivid red-gold where the sunlight touched her hair.

Cinders growled below his breath as Mordaunt approached. He also wagged his tail, though without effusion. The visitor was welcome so far as he was concerned, but he must make no disturbance. A canny little beast was Cinders.

And so, noiselessly, Mordaunt drew near, and bent above the child upon the floor. He saw that she had been crying. Even in repose her face looked wan, and there was a soaked morsel of lace that had evidently been quite inadequate for the occasion crumpled up in one hand.

What was the trouble? he wondered, and wished with all his heart that Cinders could impart it. He had no doubt that Cinders knew.

It seemed almost cruel to awake her, but neither could he bring himself to leave her as she was. He looked to Cinders for inspiration. And Cinders, with a flash of intelligence that proved him more than beast, if less than human, lowered his queer little muzzle and licked his mistress's face.

That roused her. She stretched out her arms with a vague, sleepy murmur, smiled, opened her eyes.

"Oh, Trevor!" she said. "You!"

He stooped over her. "Chris, is anything the matter?"

She looked at him. "I don't know," she said slowly. "I forget."

"Poor child!" he said. "It's a shame to make you remember. But I'm afraid it is inevitable. Won't you lie on the sofa? You will find it more comfortable."

"No," said Chris. "I like the floor the best. You can sit on the sofa, if Cinders doesn't mind. Has everyone gone, downstairs? Hasn't it been a dreadful day?" She leaned her head against his knee with a sigh of weariness. "I do think getting married is a dreadful business," she said.

His hand was on her hair, the beautiful, burnished hair that Mademoiselle Gautier had deemed one of her most dangerous possessions. He did not try to see her face, and perhaps for that very reason Chris leaned against him with complete confidence.

"So you don't want to be married?" he said, after a moment.

"No, I don't!" she said, with vehemence. "I think marriage is dreadful—dreadful, when you come to look at it close." She moved her head under his hand; for an instant her face was raised. "Trevor, you don't mind my saying it, do you?"

"I want you to say exactly what is in your mind," he made grave reply.

"I knew you would." She nestled down again, and pulled his hand over her shoulder, holding it against her cheek. "I know I'm very unorthodox," she said. "Perhaps I'm wicked as well. I can't help it. I think marriage—except for good people like Hilda—is a mistake. It's so terribly cold-blooded and—and irrevocable."

She spoke the last words almost in a whisper. She was holding his hand very tightly.

He sat very still, and she wondered if he were shocked by her views, but she could not bring herself to ascertain. She went on quickly, with a touch of recklessness—

"It's only the good people like Hilda who can be quite sure they will never change their minds. In fact, I'm beginning to think that it's only the good people who never do. Trevor, what should you do if—if you were married to me, and then you—changed your mind?"

"I can't imagine the impossible, Chris," he said.

She moved restlessly. "Would it be quite impossible?"

"Quite."

"Even if you found out that I was—quite worthless?"

"That also is impossible," he said gravely.

She was silent for a space, then, "And what if I—changed mine?" she said, her voice very low.

"Have you changed your mind?" he asked.

She shrank at the question, quietly though it was uttered.

His hand closed very steadily upon hers. "Don't be afraid to tell me," he said. "I want the truth, you know, whatever it is."

"I know," she said, and suddenly she began to sob drearily, hopelessly, with her head against his knee.

He bent lower over her; he lifted her till he held her in his arms, pressed close against his heart.

"Yes, hold me!" she whispered, through her tears. "Hold me tight, Trevor! Don't let me go! I don't feel so—so frightened when you are holding me."

"Tell me what has frightened you," he said.

"I can't," she whispered back. "I'm just—foolish, that's all. And, Trevor, I can't—I can't—be married as Hilda was to-day. I can't face it—all the people and the grandeur and the flowers. You won't make me, Trevor?"

"My darling, no!" he said.

"It frightened me so," she said forlornly. "It seemed like being caught in a trap. One felt as if the guests and the flowers were meant to hide it all, but they didn't—they made it worse. I don't think Hilda felt like that, but then Hilda is so good, she wouldn't. Oh, Trevor dear, I wish—I wish we could go to Kellerton and live there without being married at all."

The words came muffled from his shoulder; she was clinging to him almost convulsively.

"But we can't, Chris," he said, his quiet voice coming through her agitation with a patience so immense that it seemed to dwarf even her distress. "At least, dear, you can go and live there if you wish, but I can't. Perhaps I am not indispensable."

"No, no!" she said quickly, as though the suggestion hurt her. "I want you."

"Then I am afraid you will have to marry me," he said. "We won't have a big wedding. It shall be as private as you like. I suppose you will want your brothers to be there."

"Why can't we run away together and get married all by ourselves?" suggested Chris. She raised her head and regarded him with sudden animation. "Wouldn't it be fun?" she said. "You could come for me in the motor, and we could fly off to some out-of-the-way village and be married before anyone knew anything about it. There would be no one to gloat over us and make silly jokes, no horrid show at all. Trevor," her face flashed into gaiety once more, "I'll go with you to-morrow!"

He smiled at her eagerness. "If I were to agree to that, you would run away in the night."

"Run away from you!" said Chris. She wound her arm swiftly about his neck. "As if I should!" she said reproachfully.

He looked at her, baffled in spite of his determination to understand. "You wouldn't want to do that, then?" he said.

She nestled to him with a gesture most winning. "Never, never, unless—"

"Unless—?" he repeated.

"Unless—for any reason—you were angry with me," she murmured, with her face hidden again.

He folded his arms more closely about her. "My little Chris, never be afraid of that," he said.

"Oh, but you might be," she protested.

"Never, Chris." He spoke gravely, with absolute conviction.

She turned her lips quickly to his. "Then let's run away together, shall we?"

He kissed her with great tenderness before he answered. "No, dear, no. It can't be done. What would your aunt say to it?"

"Surely if I don't mind that, you needn't!" she said.

But he shook his head. "I won't let you be pestered with preparations. We will keep it a secret from everyone outside. But I think we must let your Aunt Philippa into it. I think you owe her that."

"P'raps," admitted Chris, without enthusiasm. "But she is sure to want a big show, Trevor."

"Leave that to me," he said. "I promise you shall not have that. We will get it done early, and we will be at Kellerton for luncheon."

Her eyes shone. "How lovely! And the boys, too—and Bertie?"

He surveyed the eager face for a few seconds in silence. Then, "Chris," he said, "would it mean a very great sacrifice to you if I asked for the first fortnight with you alone?"

He was watching her closely, watching for the faintest suggestion of disappointment or hesitancy in the clear eyes, but he detected neither. Chris beamed upon him tranquilly.

"Why, I should love it! There's no end of things I want to show you. And we can make it all snug before Bertie and the boys come. But, of course" — she became suddenly serious — "I must have Cinders with me."

"Oh, we won't exclude Cinders," he said.

She laughed — the gay, sweet laugh he loved to hear. "That's settled, then. And you'll make Aunt Philippa promise not to tell, for of course that would spoil everything. Oh, and Trevor, you won't discuss Bertrand with her? Promise!"

He looked at her keenly for a moment, met only the coaxing confidence of her eyes, and decided to ask no question.

"My dear," he said, "as far as Bertrand is concerned, your Aunt Philippa and I have nothing to discuss."

"That's all right," said Chris, with relief. "Trevor, you've done me a lot of good. You are quite the most comforting man I know. I'm not frightened any more, and I'll never be such a little idiot again as long as I live."

She rose with the words, stood a moment with her hand on his shoulder, then stooped and shyly kissed his forehead.

"You always understand," she said. "And I love you for it. There!"

"I am glad, dear," he said gently.

But he did not look particularly elated notwithstanding. There had been moments in their recent conversation when, so far from understanding her, he had felt utterly and completely at a loss. He had not the heart to tell her so, for he knew that she was quite incapable of explaining herself; but the fact remained. And he wondered with a vague misgiving if he had yet succeeded — if, indeed, he ever would wholly succeed — in finding his way along the many intricate windings that led to her inmost heart.

CHAPTER XVI
MARRIED

It was certainly the quietest wedding of the season. People said that this was due to the bridegroom's well-known dislike of publicity; but, whatever the reason, the secret was well kept, and when Chris came out of the church on her husband's arm there was only Bertrand, standing uncovered by the carriage-door, to give her greeting.

She was smiling as she came, but it was rather a piteous smile. She had faced the ordeal with a desperate courage, but she had not found it easy. Only Trevor's steadfast strength had held her up. She had been conscious of his will acting upon hers throughout. With the utmost calmness he had quelled her agitation, had stilled the wild flutter of her nerves, had compelled her to a measure of composure. And now that it was over she felt that he was still in a fashion holding her back, controlling her, till she should have recovered her normal state of mind and be in a condition to control herself.

But the sight of Bertrand diverted her thoughts. Owing to her aunt's strenuous prohibition, she had not met him since the night of her birthday dance. She broke from Mordaunt to give him both her hands.

"Oh, Bertie," she cried, between tears and laughter, "it is good to see you again!"

He bent very low, so low that she only saw the top of his black head. "Permit me to offer my felicitations," he said, in a voice that was scarcely audible.

Her hands closed tightly for a second upon his. "You are pleased, Bertie?" she said, with a quickening of the breath.

He straightened himself instantly; he looked into her eyes. "But you are happy, yes?" he questioned.

"Of course," she told him hurriedly.

He smiled—the ready smile with which he had learned to mask his soul. "*Alors*, I am pleased," he said.

He helped her into the carriage, and turned, still smiling, to the man behind her. Yet he flinched ever so slightly from the grip of Mordaunt's hand. It was the merest gesture, scarcely perceptible; in a moment he had covered it with the quick courtesy of his race. But Mordaunt was aware of it, and for a single instant he wondered.

He took his place beside his bride, who tucked her hand inside his arm, with a little sob of sheer relief.

"Did I sound very squeaky, Trevor? I tried not to squeak."

He forgot Bertrand and everyone else but the trembling girl by his side. He laid a soothing hand on hers.

"My dear, you did splendidly. It wasn't so very terrifying, was it?"

"It was appalling," said Chris. "I kept saying to myself, 'Just a little longer and then that lovely new motor—my motor—and home.' You are going to give me my first lesson in driving to-day, aren't you? Say yes!"

He said "Yes," feeling that he was bestowing a reward for good behaviour.

She squeezed his arm. "And isn't it nice," she whispered, with shining eyes, "to feel that we are really going to stay there when we get there?"

He pressed the small, confiding hand. "You are glad, then, Chris?" he said.

"Oh, my dear, I should think I am!" she made answer. "I've been counting the days to the one when I shan't have to peck Aunt Philippa good-night. She never kisses properly and she won't let me. She says it's childish and unrestrained." She laid her cheek suddenly against his shoulder. "I've had no one to hug for ever so long—except Cinders," she said.

"Hasn't Cinders been enough?" he asked, with a hint of surprise.

She turned her face upwards quickly. "Trevor, you're not to laugh at me! It isn't fair."

He smiled a little. "I am not laughing, Chris, I assure you. I have always thought until this moment that Cinders was more precious to you than anyone else in the world."

"Oh, that's because you're a man," said Chris inconsequently. "Men always have absurd theories about women and the things they care for. As if we can't love heaps of people at the same time!"

"You can only love one person best," he pointed out.

"At a time," supplemented Chris, with a merry smile. "And you choose your person according to your mood. At least, I do. Oh, Trevor," with a sudden change of tone, "don't look! There's a hearse!"

She hid her face against him, and he felt a violent tremor go through her. He put his arm about her and held her close.

"My darling, what makes you so superstitious?"

"I'm not," she murmured shakily. "It isn't superstitious to believe in death, is it? It's a fact one can't get away from. And it frightens me—it frightens me! Think of it, Trevor! We only belong to each other till death us do part. Afterwards—who knows?—we may be in different worlds."

He pressed her closer, feeling her cling to him. "There is a greater thing than death, Chris," he said.

"I know! I know!" she whispered back. "But—I sometimes think—I'm not big enough for it. I sometimes wonder—if God gave me a heart at all."

"My little Chris!" he said. "My darling!"

She lifted a troubled face. The tears were in her eyes. "Don't you often think me silly and fickle?" she said. "And you'll find it more and more the more you see of me. You'll be disappointed in me—you'll be horribly disappointed—some day."

He looked down at her with great tenderness. "That day will never come, dear," he said. "If it did, I should blame myself much more than I blamed you. Come! You mustn't cry on our wedding-day. You're not really unhappy?"

"But I'm afraid," she said.

He dried her eyes and kissed her. "There is nothing to make you afraid," he said. "Haven't I sworn to love and cherish you?"

She nestled to him with a sigh. "It was very nice of you, Trevor," she said.

Her spirits revived during her motor-ride to Kellerton. The renovations there were in full swing. One portion of the house had been already made habitable for them. Mordaunt had had the entire management of this, but, as Chris gaily remarked, she would probably change everything round when she came upon the scene.

"I feel as if the holidays have just begun," she said to him as they sped over the dusty road. "And I'm going to work harder than I have ever worked in my life."

"If I let you," he said.

At which remark she made a face, and then, repenting patted his knee. "You will let me do what I like, I know. You always do."

"In moderation," said Trevor, with a smile.

She dismissed the matter as too trivial for discussion. "When are you going to let me drive?"

He gave her her first lesson then and there, an experience which delighted Chris so much that she refused to relinquish the wheel until they stopped at a country town for luncheon.

Here her whole attention was occupied in keeping Cinders from chasing the hotel cat, till Trevor caught and cuffed the miscreant, when her anxiety turned to indignation on her darling's behalf, and she snatched him away and kept him sheltered in her arms for the rest of their sojourn.

"I never punish Cinders," she said. "He's hardly ever naughty, and if he is he's always sorry afterwards."

Cinders, whose temper was ruffled, glared at Mordaunt and cursed him in an undertone throughout the meal, notwithstanding the choice morsels with which his young mistress sought to propitiate him.

"I do hope you haven't made him dislike you," she said, when at length they returned to the car. "He is rather tiresome with people he doesn't like."

"If he doesn't behave himself, we will send him to Bertrand to take care of," Mordaunt rejoined.

"Indeed we won't!" Chris declared, with warmth. "He has never been away from me day or night since I first had him."

At which declaration Mordaunt raised his eyebrows, and said no more.

He had always known Cinders for a dog of character, but not till that day had he credited him with the remarkable intuition by which he seemed to know—and resent—the fact that his mistress was no longer his exclusive property. It may have been that Chris herself imparted something of the new state of affairs to him by the very zeal of her guardianship. But undoubtedly, whatever its source, the knowledge had dawned in Cinders' brain and with it a fierce jealousy which he had never displayed in Mordaunt's presence before.

It was an afternoon of unclouded sunshine. Chris lay back in her seat, somewhat wearied but quite content, watching the cornfields with their red wealth of poppies, watching the long, white road before them, and now and then the unerring hands that held the wheel.

When at length they neared Kellerton she roused herself and became more animated. "It's been a lovely ride, Trevor. Let's go for one every day. Sometimes we might go down to the sea—it's only ten miles. But we will wait till Bertie comes for that. Ah, there is the lodge! How smart it looks! And they have actually taken the thistles out of the drive! I shouldn't have known it."

She sat up with eager delight in her eyes. The lodge-gates were open; they ran smoothly in without a pause and on up the long avenue to the old grey house.

Chris was enchanted. It was such a home-coming as she had never pictured.

"It's like a dream," she said. "I can't believe it's true. Everything looks so different. The garden was an absolute wilderness the last time we were here."

It had been turned into a paradise since then, and every second brought fresh discoveries to her ecstatic gaze.

"I didn't know it could be so lovely," she declared. "And you've done it all in a few weeks. Trevor, you're a magician!"

He smiled at her enthusiasm. "Oh, it isn't all my doing. I have only been down twice since the day you were here. I put it into capable hands, that's all. Nothing has been altered, only set to rights."

"It's lovely!" cried Chris.

Tired and thirsty though she was, she could hardly wait to have tea on the terrace before the house before she was off along the dear, familiar paths to her favourite nook under a great yew-tree whose branches swept the ground. A rustic seat surrounded the ancient trunk.

"This is my castle," said Chris. "This is where I hide when I don't want anyone to find me."

She stretched back a hand to her husband, and led him into her shadowy domain.

"The boys used to call it Hades," she said, in a hushed voice. "And I used to pretend I was Persephone. I did so wish Pluto would appear some day with his chariot and his black horses and take me underground. But," with a sigh, "he never did."

"Let us hope you have been reserved for a happier fate," Mordaunt said, with his arm about her.

She flashed him her quick smile. "You instead of Pluto! But I always thought he was rather fascinating, and I longed to see the underworld."

"I think the sunshine suits you best," he said.

"Oh yes, but just to see—just to know what it's like! I do so love exploring," insisted Chris.

He smiled and drew her out of her gloomy retreat. "Sometimes it's better not to know too much," he said.

"But one couldn't," she protested. "All knowledge is gain."

"Of a sort," he said. "But it is not always to be desired on that account."

A sudden memory went through Chris. She gave a sharp shudder. "Oh no!" she said. "One doesn't want to know horrid things! I forgot that."

He looked at her interrogatively, but she turned her face away. "Let's go back to the house. I wonder where Cinders is."

They returned to the house, and again Chris was lost in delight. A great deal yet remained to be done, but the completed portion was all that could be desired. They had chosen much of the furniture together, and she spent most of the evening in arranging it, with her husband's assistance, to her satisfaction.

But when at length the hour for dinner arrived he would not suffer her to do anything further.

"I believe you have done too much as it is," he said, "and after dinner I shall have something to show you."

She yielded readily enough. She certainly was tired. "I feel as if to-day had lasted for about six weeks," she said.

But her animation did not wane in spite of this, and she would even have returned to her labours after they had dined had Mordaunt permitted it. He was firm upon this point, however, and again without protest she yielded.

"You were going to show me something. What was it?"

"To be sure," he said. "I was going to show you how to write a cheque. Come over to the writing-table and see how it is done."

Chris went, looking mystified. "But I shall never write cheques, Trevor," she said.

"No? Why not?"

He drew up a chair for her and knelt down beside her.

"You are a woman of property now, Chris," he said, and laid a new cheque-book on the pad in front of her.

Chris gazed at it, wide-eyed. "But, Trevor, I haven't got any money at the bank, have I?"

"Plenty," he said, with a smile—"in fact, a very large sum indeed which will have to be invested in your name. That we will go into another day, but for present needs, if you are wanting money—"

"Yes?" said Chris eagerly.

He put a pen into her hand and opened the cheque-book.

She slipped her arm round his neck. "Trevor, I—I don't feel as if you ought. I—of course I—knew you would make me an allowance, but—but—you ought not to give me a lot of money all my own."

"My darling," he said gently, "don't forget that you are my wife, will you?"

She smiled a little shyly. "Do you know—I had forgotten—quite!"

He put his arm about her as she sat. "You must try to remember it, dear, because it's rather important. I know I might have made you an allowance, but I prefer that you should be independent. Only, Chris, I am going to ask a promise of you; and I want you to make it at the very beginning of our life together. That is why I have spoken on our wedding-night."

"Yes?" whispered Chris.

She had begun to tremble a little, and he pressed her to him reassuringly. "I want you to promise me that you will never run into debt, that if for any cause you find that you have not enough of your own you will come to me at once and tell me."

He spoke with grave kindness, watching her face the while. But Chris's eyes did not meet his own. She was rolling the pen he had given her up and down the blotting-pad with much absorption.

"Is it a promise, Chris?" he asked at length.

She threw him a nervous glance and nodded.

He laid his hand upon hers and held it still. "Chris, have you any debts now?"

She was silent.

"My dear," he said, "don't be afraid of me!"

There was that in his voice that moved her to the depths; she could not have said why. Impulsively, almost passionately, she went into his arms.

"I won't!" she said. "I won't! Trevor, I—I've been a little beast! That money you gave me on my birthday I didn't do—what you meant me to do with it. I just—spent it. I don't know how. And then—when you asked about it that night—I didn't dare to tell you, and I haven't dared since. I just let you think it was all right—when it wasn't. Oh, Trevor, don't be angry—don't be angry!"

"I am not angry," he said.

"Not really? But how you must despise me! It's just the way of the Wyndhams. We all do it. Trevor, why did you make me tell you?"

"My dear child," he said, "you must tell me these things. It is your only possibility of happiness, and mine also. Chris, never keep anything from me, for Heaven's sake! Don't you know that I trust you?"

"I don't deserve it!" sobbed Chris, clinging faster. "You don't know how bad I am!"

"Hush!" he said, with a restraining hand upon her head. "You have told me everything now?"

"Oh no, I haven't!" she whispered. "There are crowds of things I couldn't even begin to tell you. I have always warned you how it would be. I always said—"

Her agitation was increasing, and her words became inaudible. He saw that her nerves had given way under the long day's strain, and firmly, with infinite gentleness, he put a stop to further discussion of a subject that threatened to upset her seriously.

"Never mind," he said. "You will tell me by and bye, or if you don't I shall know it is all right. Chris, Chris, you mustn't get hysterical. You are worn out, dear, and it has upset your sense of proportion. Come, I am going to send you to bed. We will go into these money matters in the morning."

But Chris vehemently negatived this. "I don't want to—to spoil to-morrow. I—I shouldn't sleep for thinking of it. Oh, Trevor, let's settle it now. I'm going to be sensible—really. And—and—if you'll forgive me for all the bad things I've done up to to-day I—I will really try to tell you everything as it happens from now on. Will you, Trevor?"

She raised pleading, pathetic eyes, still wet with tears. He could feel her still quivering with the emotion she was striving to subdue. She was too near in that moment to resist—perhaps he would not have resisted her in any case; for he had it not in his heart to think ill of her.

"My darling," he said, "we will leave it at that. Only—in the future—trust me as I am trusting you."

He turned to the table and closed the cheque-book. "These debts are my affair. I will settle them. Just tell me what they are."

"Oh, but they are settled!" she told him. "I promised I would, you know."

"Then"—he looked at her—"someone lent you the money?"

Something in his tone made her shrink again. She hesitated.

"Chris!" he said.

Nervously she answered him. "Jack lent me forty pounds."

"Jack!" he said. "You weren't afraid to ask him, then?"

"Oh no!" she said quickly. "I'm not a bit afraid of Jack."

"Only of me, Chris!"

She gave herself back to him with a swift, shy movement. "It's the fear of vexing you," she said. "I don't mind vexing—other people. It's only you—only you. Trevor, say you understand!"

He did not answer her instantly, but the close holding of his arms drove all misgiving from her soul. He rose to his feet, raising her with him, pressing her to him faster and ever faster till her arms crept round his neck again, and she lay, a willing prisoner, against his heart.

And so holding her, at last he answered her tremulous appeal. "My darling, never be afraid of vexing me! Never be afraid that I shall not understand!"

She could not speak in answer. The wonder of his love for her had stricken her dumb; it had swept upon her like a wave, towering, immense, resistless, bearing her far beyond her depth.

She could only mutely lift her quivering lips; and he, moved to gentleness by her action, took her face between his hands with infinite tenderness, gazing down into her eyes with that in his own which cast out the last of her fear.

"My little Chris!" he said. "My wife!"

PART II

CHAPTER I
SUMMER WEATHER

"I think quite the worst part of being married is having to pay calls," said Chris.

"You do not like it, no?" said Bertrand, with quick sympathy.

"No," she rejoined emphatically. "And I don't see any sense in it either. No one ever wants afternoon callers."

"But that depends upon the caller, does it not?" he said.

"Not in the least," said Chris. "There's a stodginess about afternoon calling that affects even the nicest people. It's the most tiresome institution there is."

"Then why do it?" he suggested, with a smile.

She shook her head severely.

"Don't be immoral, Bertie! You're trying to tempt me from my duty."

"Never!" he declared earnestly.

"Oh, but you are; and I am not sure that you are not neglecting your own as well. What brought you out at this hour?"

He spread out his hands. "Mr. Mordaunt has ordered me to take a rest to-day."

Chris looked up at him sharply. "Aren't you well, Bertie?"

"But it is nothing," he said. "I have told him. It happens to me often—often—that I do not sleep. I have explained all that. But what would you? He is obstinate—he will not listen."

Chris patted a hammock-chair beside her. "Sit down at once. I knew there was something the matter directly I saw you this morning. But you always look horribly tired. Do you never sleep properly?"

He dropped into the chair and stretched up his arms with a sigh. "It is only in the morning that I am tired," he said. "It is nothing—a weakness that passes. Or if it passes not—I go."

"Go!" repeated Chris, startled.

He turned his head towards her. "That surprises you, yes? But how can I remain if I cannot work?"

"Oh, but you haven't been here a fortnight," she said quickly. "I expect the change of air has upset you. And it has been so hot too."

He acquiesced languidly, as if not greatly interested. His dark eyes watched her gravely. Evidently his thoughts had wandered from himself.

Chris was not slow to perceive this. "What are you thinking of?" she demanded.

"I am thinking of you," he answered promptly.

"What of me?" The blue eyes met his quite openly. Chris was always frank to her pals.

"I was thinking," he said, in his soft, friendly voice, "how you were happy, and how I was glad."

She threw him a quick smile. "How nice of you, Bertie! And how beautifully French! But, you know, I shan't be happy if you talk of leaving us. It will spoil everything, and I shall be absolutely miserable."

"You were not miserable before I joined you, no?" he said, smiling back at her.

"Of course I wasn't. But that was quite different. I knew all the while that you were coming. I should have been if anything had happened to prevent you."

"Really?" he said thoughtfully.

"Yes, really!" Chris was emphatic. "And I am sure there is nothing much the matter with you, Bertie; now, is there?"

He scarcely responded. "It will pass," he said. "And so you have arranged to make visits this afternoon?"

"Yes. Isn't it a bother?" Chris's brow wrinkled. "Noel wanted me to go and fish with him, but Trevor says I must go and see Mrs. Pouncefort, so I suppose I must. I hoped he would come too, but he has got to stay and interview the architect about that subsidence in the north wing. I wish you would come instead."

He shook his head. "No—no! That is not possible. Where does this lady live?"

"Sandacre way, towards the sea. Oh, do you know Rupert is coming over on Sunday with some brother officers? I had a card from him this morning. He is very fond of Mrs. Pouncefort—they all are. I don't know quite why. I believe they spend half their time there. Mr. Pouncefort is a dear little man—no one could help liking him. He has a yacht, and they always have a crowd of people staying there at this time of the year."

"*Alors*," he said, "it will amuse you to go there, no?"

Chris smiled. "Oh, not particularly. I would much rather stay with you and Trevor. Besides, I've such a lot to do."

She did not look overwhelmed with work as she leaned back in her hammock-chair, but she evidently intended to be busy, for a basket and scissors stood beside her.

Bertrand was much too courteous to suggest that she was not making the most of her time. Or perhaps he did not want to be left in solitary contemplation of that fleeting August morning. He lay silent for a little, and presently requested permission to smoke a cigarette.

"Of course," she said at once. "Why don't you go and lie in the hammock? I will come and rock you to sleep."

He thanked her, smiling, but declined.

She watched him light his cigarette with eyes grown thoughtful. Suddenly: "Bertie," she said, "are you very unhappy nowadays?"

He made a jerky movement, and dropped the match, still burning. Hastily he bent to extinguish it, but Chris was before him, her hand upon his arm, restraining him.

"No, sit still! It's all right. Tell me, please, Bertie! I want to know."

He shrugged his shoulders up to his ears, still smiling, but in a fashion that she was at a loss to interpret.

"But what a question, *petite*! How can I answer it?"

"I should have thought—-between friends—-" she began.

"*Ah, oui!* We are friends, are we not?" A curious expression of relief took the place of his smile, and she felt as if for some reason he had been afraid. "And you ask me if I am unhappy," he said. "*Mais vraiment*—I know not what to say!"

"Then you are!" she said, quick pain in her voice.

He looked down at the little friendly hand that lay upon his arm, but he did not offer to touch it. His eyes remained downcast as he spoke. "I am more happy than I ever expected to be, Christine."

"You like your work?" she questioned. "Trevor is kind to you?"

"He is—much too kind," the Frenchman answered, with feeling.

"But still you are unhappy?" she said.

"It is—my own fault," he told her, still not looking at her.

She rubbed his sleeve sympathetically. "Bertie, don't you think—if you tried very hard—you might manage to forget all that old trouble?"

There was a note of pleading in her voice, and he made a quick gesture as he heard it, as if in some way it pierced him.

She went on speaking, as he made no attempt to do so. "You know, Bertie, you really are quite young still, and there are such a lot of nice things left. It's such a pity to keep on grieving. Don't you think so? It seems rather a waste of time. And I do—so—want you to be happy."

At the quiver in her voice he glanced up sharply, but he instantly lowered his eyes again. And still he said no word. He only drew his brows together and bit his cigarette to a pulp.

Her hand came softly down his arm and lay upon his.

"Bertie," she said, in a whisper, "you're not—vexed?"

His hand clenched at her touch, but on the instant he looked up at her with a smile. "Vexed!" he said. "With you! A thousand times—no!"

She smiled back, reassured. "Then will you—please—try to forget what you have lost? I know it won't be easy, but will you try? It's the only possible way to be happy. And if you are not happy—I shan't be either."

He took her hand at last with perfect steadiness into his own. "You know not what I have lost," he said. "But—if I try to forget—that will content you?"

She nodded. "Yes, Bertie."

He looked at her intently for a moment, then, "*Eh Bien!*" he said briskly. "I will try."

"*Bon garçon!*" she said, with a merry smile. "That is settled, then. Why, there is Trevor! Has he finished that article of his already? He looked quite absorbed when I passed his window half an hour ago." She waved to him as he approached. "Why don't you wear a hat, you mad Englishman? Don't you know the sun is broiling?"

He smiled and ignored the warning. Bertrand sprang from his chair as he reached them, but Mordaunt instantly pressed him down again.

"No, no, man! Sit still! I have only come out for a moment."

"But I am going," Bertrand protested. "I cannot sit and do nothing. There are those accounts that you have given me to do. They are not yet finished. Also—"

"Also, they are not going to be done to-day," Mordaunt said, shaking him gently by the shoulder. "Chris, I am going to hand this fellow over to you for the next few days. You can do what you like with him so long as you don't let him do any work. That I absolutely forbid. You understand me, Bertrand?"

"But I cannot—I cannot," Bertrand said restlessly. "You are already much too good to me. You overwhelm me with kindness, and I—I make no return at all. No, listen to me—"

"I'm not going to listen to you," Mordaunt said. "You are talking nonsense, my friend, arrant drivel—nothing less. Chris will tell you the same."

"Of course," said Chris. "Besides, there are crowds of things you can do for me. No, he shan't be overworked, I promise you, Trevor. But I'm going to try a new cure. Just for this afternoon he is going to lie in the hammock and smoke cigarettes. But after to-day"—she nodded gaily at the perturbed Frenchman—"after to-day, Bertie, *nous verrons!*"

He smiled in spite of himself, but he continued to look dissatisfied till Mordaunt carelessly turned the conversation.

"Where's that young beggar Noel?"

"Fishing in the Home Meadow," said Chris.

"Quite sure?"

"I think so," she said. "Why?"

"Because he has taken one of my guns, and I believe he is potting rabbits."

Chris sat up with consternation in her eyes. "Trevor! I believe he is too! I heard someone shooting half an hour ago. And he has got Cinders with him! I know he will go and shoot him by mistake!"

"Or himself," said Mordaunt grimly.

"Oh, he won't do that," said Chris with confidence. "Nothing ever happens to Noel."

"Something will happen to him before long if he doesn't behave himself," observed Mordaunt. "My patience began to wear thin last night when I caught him asleep with a smouldering pipe on his pillow."

"Oh, but he always does what he likes in the holidays," pleaded Chris.

"Does he?" Mordaunt's voice was uncompromising.

She slipped a quick hand into his. "Trevor, you wouldn't spoil his fun?"

He looked down at her, faintly smiling. "My dear Chris, it depends upon the fun. I'm not going to have the place burnt down for his amusement."

"Oh no," she said. "But you won't be strict with him, will you? He will only do things on the sly if you are."

Mordaunt frowned abruptly. "If I catch him doing anything underhand—"

She broke in sharply in evident distress. "But we all do, Trevor! I—I've done it myself before now—often with Mademoiselle Gautier, and then with Aunt Philippa. One has to, you know. At least—at least—" His grey eyes suddenly made her feel cold, and she stopped as impulsively as she had begun.

There was a moment's silence, then quite gently he drew his hand away. "I think I will go and see what mischief the boy is up to."

She jumped up. "I'll come too."

He paused, and for a single instant his eyes met Bertrand's.
At once the Frenchman spoke.

"But, Christine, have you not forgotten your roses? It is growing late, is it not? And you will be out this afternoon. Permit me to assist you with them."

He picked up the basket as he spoke. Chris stopped irresolute. Her husband was already moving away over the grass.

"Come!" said Bertrand persuasively.

Chris turned with a smile and took the basket. "All right, Bertie, let's go. It is getting late, as you say, and I must get the vases filled."

They went away together to the rose-garden, and here, after brief hesitation, Chris voiced her fears.

"I'm so afraid lest Trevor should ever get really angry with any of the boys. They won't stand it, you know. And he—I sometimes think he is just a little hard, don't you?"

Mordaunt's secretary pondered this proposition with drawn brows. "No," he said finally, "he is not hard, but he is very honourable."

Chris laughed aloud. "That sounds just like a French exercise, Bertie. I don't see what being honourable has to do with it, except that the people who preen themselves on being honourable are just the ones who can't make allowances for those who are not. You would think, wouldn't you, that being good would make people extra kind and forgiving? But it doesn't, you know. Look at Aunt Philippa!"

Bertrand's grimace was expressive. "And Aunt Philippa is good, yes?"

"Frightfully good," said Chris. "I don't suppose she ever told a story in her life."

His quick eyes sought hers. "And that—that is to be good?"

Chris paused an instant, her attention caught by the question. "Why, I suppose so," she said slowly. "Don't you call that goodness?"

He spread out his hands. "Me, I think it is the smallest kind of goodness. One does not lie, one does not steal; but what of that? One does not roll oneself in the mud. And that is a virtue, that?"

Chris became keenly interested. "Do go on, Bertie! I had no idea you thought such a lot. I don't myself—often."

He laughed, his sudden pleasant laugh that he uttered now so rarely. "But I am no philosopher," he said. "Simply I think—a little—sometimes. And to me—to be honourable is no more a virtue than to wash the hands. One cannot do otherwise and respect oneself."

"No?" said Chris, a little dubiously. "Then, Bertie, if honour is not goodness, what is?"

He shrugged his shoulders. "Goodness? Bah! There is no goodness without love."

"Oh!" Chris's eyes opened wide. "You think—that?"

He nodded with vehemence. "*Si, chérie*! I think—that; more, I know it. I know that 'Love is the fulfilling of the law.' One does not need to go further than that. It is enough, no?" His eyes looked straight into hers; they were shining with the light that only friendship can kindle.

She smiled back at him. "I should almost think it is, Bertie. It is enough for you anyhow, since you believe it."

"Ah, yes," he said very earnestly. "I believe it, Christine. I should not be here now—if I did not believe it."

She puckered her brows a little. "I don't quite know what you mean," she said.

He turned from her questioning eyes, pulling his hat down over his own. "No," he said. "But—you know enough, *ma petite*, you know enough."

"I sometimes think I don't know anything," she said restlessly.

He stretched out a hand to her, as one who guides a child. "Ah, Christine," he said sadly, "but it is better to know the little than the much."

"You all say that," said Chris. "I think it is rather a horrid world for some things, don't you?"

"But the world is that which we make it," said Bertrand.

CHAPTER II
ONE OF THE FAMILY

"But, my dear chap, what bally rot! Anyone would think I'd never smoked a pipe or handled a gun before, when I've done both for years."

Noel Wyndham's smile was the most engaging part of him; it had the knack of disarming the most wrathful. It had served him many a time in the hour of retribution, and he never scrupled to make use of it. It was quite his most valuable asset.

"Don't be waxy, old chap," he pleaded, slipping an affectionate hand inside his brother-in-law's unresponsive arm. "I've been having such a high old time. And I'm not a bloomin' kid. I know what I'm about."

"All very well," Mordaunt said. "I don't object to anything in reason. But you are too fond of taking French leave with other people's property. That gun, for instance—"

"Oh, that's all right," the boy assured him eagerly. "It kicks most infernally, but I soon got the trick of it after a bruise or two. I say, you haven't seen anything of that little devil Cinders? He's gone down a rabbit-hole. Won't Chris be in a stew?"

Mordaunt possessed himself of the gun without further argument. "Then you'd better set to work and find him. Chris is going out this afternoon."

"In the motor?" Noel's eyes shone. "I'll go, too. You needn't bother about Cinders. He always turns up sooner or later. Don't tell Chris, or she'll spend the rest of the day hunting for him."

"She will probably want to know," observed Mordaunt.

"I shall say I never had him," said Noel unconcernedly. "He won't come to any harm, but you can turn that secretary fellow of yours on to the job if you're feeling anxious. I say, Trevor, we shan't want the chauffeur. Tell them, will you?"

"You certainly won't go without him," Mordaunt rejoined.

"And look here, Noel, you're not to tell lies. Understand?"

Noel looked up with a flicker of temper in his Irish eyes, "Oh, rats!" he said.

"Understand?" Mordaunt repeated. "It's the one thing I won't put up with, so make up your mind to that."

He spoke quite temperately, but with unswerving decision. His eyes looked hard into Noel's, and the boy's spark of resentment went out like an extinguished match.

"I say, I like you!" he said with enthusiasm. "You're a regular sport!"

"Thank you," Mordaunt returned gravely.

"And what about Chris?" Noel proceeded mischievously. "Isn't she allowed to tell lies, either?"

Mordaunt stiffened. "Chris knows better."

"Oh, does she?" Noel yelled derision. "My dear chap, you'll kill me! Why, she—she's about the worst of us. I never knew anyone lie quite like Chris when occasion arises."

He broke off. Mordaunt had shaken his arm free with an abruptness not far removed from violence.

"That's enough," he said sternly. "I don't advise you to say any more upon that subject."

"But I assure you it's the truth," Noel protested. "She can look you straight in the face and swear that black is white till you actually believe it. I assure you she can."

He spoke with such naïve admiration of the achievement that Trevor Mordaunt, on the verge of anger, found himself checked suddenly by an irrepressible desire to laugh.

Noel saw and seized upon his advantage. "But I daresay she wouldn't to you. She gets everything she wants without. I must say you're jolly decent to all of us. I'm sorry I took your gun—didn't know it was one you particularly valued. I'd get one of my own only I'm so beastly hard up. I suppose you couldn't lend me a fiver now, could you?"

He tucked his hand back into Mordaunt's arm persuasively, and smiled his winning smile. "I'll pay you back—with interest—when I come of age. That'll be in five years. I wouldn't ask you if I couldn't. But I daresay Chris can let me have it if you would rather not.

"No!" Mordaunt said very decidedly. "There must be no borrowing from Chris. I will give you five pounds if you are wanting it, but not to buy a gun with, and only on the understanding that for the future you come to me—and never to Chris—if you chance to be in difficulties."

"Oh yes, I'll promise that," said Noel readily. "But I don't want you to make me a present, old chap. I shall pay up some day. You shall have an I O U."

"Many thanks! I don't want one." Mordaunt began to smile. "Just keep straight and tell the truth," he said. "That's all the return I want."

"Really?" Noel's smile became a grin. "That's awfully decent of you. As a matter of fact, I don't believe even Chris could manage to deceive you. You're so beastly shrewd. But we'll call it a bargain if you like. You won't catch me trying to jockey you after this."

"Very well," Mordaunt said. "Then, on the strength of that, I want to know if you have ever had any money from Chris before."

"Why, of course I have!" Noel seemed surprised by the question. He spoke with the utmost frankness.

"How much?"

Mordaunt's smile had departed. He did not look altogether pleased, but Noel was quite unimpressed.

"Oh, goodness knows!" he said lightly. "She has my I O U's."

"Which she must find very satisfying," remarked Mordaunt. "Now look here, boy! There must be no more of this. You will have to keep within your allowance in future."

"My dear chap, it's all jolly fine—I can't!" protested Noel. "Why, I only get about twopence-halfpenny a term. It isn't enough to pay a cat's expenses, besides being always up to the eyes in debt."

Mordaunt heaved a sigh of resignation. "I suppose I had better look into your affairs. Write down as clear a statement of your debts as you can, and let me have it."

"I say—really?" Noel looked up eagerly. "You're not in earnest?"

"Yes, I am. And afterwards—you are to keep within your means, or if you don't I must know the reason why."

Noel grinned with cheery impudence. "You'll swish me, I suppose, to improve my morals? Wish I had as many sovereigns as I've had swishings. They would keep me in clover for a year."

Mordaunt laughed rather grimly. "I don't waste my time licking hardened sinners like you. I've something better to do."

Noel echoed his laugh with keen enjoyment. "You're rather a beast, but I like you. Have you paid Rupert's debts, too? He is always on the verge of bankruptcy. Shouldn't wonder if Max is as well, but he keeps his affairs so dark. I expect he is in the hands of the money-lenders—I know Rupert was years ago."

"I don't think he is now," Mordaunt said.

"Don't you? What's the betting on that? He could no more keep out of their clutches than he could fly over the moon. I say"—he suddenly burst into a peal of boyish laughter—"it's the funniest thing on earth to see you shouldering the family burdens. How you will wish you hadn't! And that French beggar you've adopted, too, who is safe to rob you sooner or later! Why don't you start a home for waifs and strays at once? I'll help you run it. I'll do the accounts."

Mordaunt laughed, in spite of himself. "Very kind of you! But I think there are enough of you for the present."

"All highly satisfactory," grinned Noel. "What a pity you didn't marry Aunt Philippa, I say! She would have been much more useful to you than Chris. Never thought of that, I suppose?"

"Never!" said Mordaunt.

"Poor old Aunt Phil!" Noel chuckled afresh. "She would have been in her element if you had only given her the chance. She hates us all like poison. I suppose you know why?"

"Haven't an idea," Mordaunt spoke repressively, "unless your general behaviour has something to do with it."

"Oh, very likely it has," Noel conceded. "But the chief reason was that our father diddled her out of a lot of money. He was hard up, and she was rolling. So he—borrowed a little." He glanced at Mordaunt with a queer grimace. "Most unfortunately he didn't live to pay it back. I shouldn't tell anyone this, but I don't mind telling you, as you are one of the family."

"And who told you?" Mordaunt inquired.

"Me? I overheard it."

"How?"

The question came sternly, but Noel was sublimely unabashed.

"The usual way. How does one generally overhear things? I hid behind a shutter once when Aunt Phil and Murdoch, our man of business, were having a talk. She pitched it pretty strong, I can tell you. I should have felt quite sorry for the old girl if I hadn't known that her husband had left her more than she could possibly know what to do with. As it was, I was rather glad than otherwise, for she's disgustingly mean over trifles. And people who can shell out and won't should be made to."

Mordaunt received this axiom in silence. As a matter of fact he was somewhat staggered by the information thus airily imparted. But he did not question the truth of it. He only wondered that he had never considered such a possibility before.

Another shout of merriment from the boy at his side made him look round. "Well? What's the joke?"

"You!" yelled the youngster, between his paroxysms. "I'm awfully sorry. You're such a good sort. But I can't help it. I say, Trevor—aren't you glad just—that you're one of the family?"

Mordaunt aimed a blow at him that he evaded with ease. "If you don't behave yourself I shall use the privilege in a fashion you won't care for," he said, "even if it is a waste of time."

At which threat Noel confidingly hooked his arm once more through that of his brother-in-law and begged him in a voice hoarse with laughter to stop rotting.

CHAPTER III
DISASTER

Chris and Noel set off in the motor that afternoon in excellent spirits to pay the projected call upon Mrs. Pouncefort.

They found the lady of the house at home, and spent an animated hour with her; for although she never appeared to welcome her visitors or to exert herself in any degree to entertain them, most of them seemed to find it difficult to get away.

When they departed at length they carried with them an invitation to a garden *fête* which had been arranged for the following week. It included the whole party, to Chris's great satisfaction.

"It will be the very thing for Bertie," she said. "It is just what he needs."

Noel, who entertained a sweeping prejudice against all foreigners, was inclined to dispute this, and a lively argument ensued in consequence, which lasted during the greater part of the run home.

Chris was at the wheel, being a fairly experienced driver by that time, though Mordaunt was very insistent that she should always have someone responsible by her side. On this occasion, however, Holmes, who was acting as chauffeur, had been imperiously relegated to the back seat by Noel, who intended to have his turn before the end of the ride. He had driven twice before under his brother-in-law's supervision, and he considered himself an expert.

As soon as they were through the lodge-gates, therefore, he began to clamour to change places with Chris. The worried Holmes protested in vain. Chris, though firmly refusing to sit behind, was quite willing to give her place at the wheel to her brother; and the change was speedily effected, remonstrance notwithstanding.

"We can't come to any harm on our own drive," was the careless consolation she threw to the perturbed man behind her, who then and there solemnly swore to his inner soul that whatever the outcome of the venture he would never again trust himself or the car to the tender mercies of the Wyndham family.

Finding himself thus ignored, he stood up and leaned over the boy's shoulder to give directions in the face of any sudden emergency that might arise, though Noel was obviously in no mood to pay any attention to them. As he remarked later, when recounting the adventure, he knew in his bones that there was going to be an accident; but the nature of it he could hardly be expected to foresee.

In fact, for a brief space all went well. The motor buzzed merrily along the drive, and it almost seemed as if the escapade would end without mishap, when, as they rounded the bend that led to the house, Noel unexpectedly put on speed. They shot forward at a great pace under the arching trees, and forthwith suddenly came disaster. Swift as a lightning flash it came—too swift for realization, almost too swift for sight. It was only a tiny, racing figure that darted for the fraction of a second in front of the car, and then— with a squeal half-choked—was lost in the rush of the wheels. It was only Cinders chasing a rabbit which he was destined never to catch.

Chris's shriek of agony rang as far as the house. In another moment she would have thrown herself headlong from the car, but Holmes was too quick for her. Not in vain had Holmes been through a three-years' war; not in vain did he hold himself responsible for the young wife of the master whom that war had taught him to love. Almost before she had sprung from her seat he had caught her, forcing her down again, holding her by grim strength from her mad purpose. She struggled with him fiercely, hysterically; but Holmes's grip never relaxed. She bore the marks of it upon her arms for weeks after.

And while he held her, baffling her utmost efforts to free herself, he was giving directions to Noel, whose nerve had departed completely with the shock of the catastrophe, giving them over and over again—steadily, insistently, and very distinctly, till they took effect at last, though only just in time.

They were dangerously near the house before, in response to the boy's frantic efforts, the car slackened and finally, under Holmes's reiterated directions, ran to a standstill.

Chris, in a perfect frenzy by that time, wrenched herself free and sprang down. Her husband, who had rushed from the house at her cry, was close to her as she reached the ground, but she sped away without so much as seeing him.

Back up the drive she tore, back to the shadowing trees, back to the piteous little blot in the shadow that was the only thing her world contained in that hour of anguish.

When they reached her she was sunk on the ground beside her favourite, crying his name, while he, whimpering, strove to drag his mangled body into her lap. She tried to lift him, but he yelped so terribly at her touch that she was forced to let him lie.

"Oh, Cinders, Cinders!" she cried, in an agony. "My little darling, what shall I do?"

Someone stooped over her; a quiet hand lay upon her shoulder. "Chris," it was her husband's voice, very grave and tender, "come away, dear. You can't do anything. The poor little chap is past our help."

She lifted a dazed face, staring uncomprehendingly.

"Come away," he repeated.

But when he tried to raise her she resisted him. "And leave him like this? No, never, never! Oh, Trevor, look—look! He is dying! Can't we do something—anything? Oh, he never cried like that before!"

"My dear, there is nothing that you can do." Very gently he made answer. "He can't possibly live. There is only one thing to be done, and that is to put him out of his pain as quickly as possible. But I can't do it with you here. So come away, dear! It's the kindest—in fact, it's the only—thing you can do."

"Are you going to—kill him?" gasped Chris in horror.

He nodded, with compressed lips. "There is no alternative. We can't let him suffer like this."

"Oh no, no, no!" Chris cried.

She would have thrown her arms about her darling, but he stopped her. He caught her wrists and held her back.

"Chris, you must not! When animals are hurt they will bite without knowing what they are doing. Chris, do you hear me? You must go."

But she would not. "Do you think I would leave him now—when he wants me most? And as if he would bite me—Cinders—Cinders—who never even growled at me!"

She bent over him again, beside herself with grief. Cinders, in the midst of his pain, tried gently to wag his tail. His brown eyes, faithful, appealing, full of love, gazed up at her. He had never seen his mistress in such trouble before, and the instinct to comfort her urged him even then, in the midst of his own. Again he made piteous efforts to crawl into her arms, but again he failed, and fell back, whimpering.

Chris covered her face. It was more than she could bear, and yet she could not—could not—leave him.

For a space that might have been minutes or only seconds she was left alone, tortured but impotent. A dreadful darkness had fallen upon her, a numbness in which Cinders, suffering and slowly dying, was the only reality.

Then again she became conscious of another presence. A quick hand touched her. A soft voice spoke.

"Ah, the poor Cinders! And he lives yet! *Chérie*, we will be kind to him, yes? We cannot make him live, but we will let him die quick—quick, so that he suffer no more. That is kind, that is merciful, *n'est-ce-pas?*"

She turned instinctively in answer to that voice. She held up her hands to the speaker like a child. "Oh, Bertie," she cried piteously, "is there nothing to be done? Nothing?"

"Only that, *chérie*," he made answer, very gently.

"Then"—she was sobbing terribly, but she suffered his hands to raise her—"don't let them—send me away, Bertie. I can't go—while he lives. It—it would hurt him more, if I went."

"No, no, *chérie*," he answered her reassuringly. "You will be brave, yes? See, I will hold your hand. We will go just across the road, but not beyond his sight. He will see you. He will know that you are near. There—there, *chérie*! Shut your eyes! It will be finished soon."

He put his arm around her, for she stumbled blindly. They went across the road as he had said, and halted under the trees on the farther side.

There followed a pause—an interval that was terrible—during which only the low crying of an animal in pain was audible.

Bertrand stood like a rock, still holding her. "But you will not look, *chérie*," he whispered to her softly. "It is deliverance—this death. Soon—soon he will not cry any more."

She pressed her face against his shoulder, wrapped in the close security of his arms, and waited, drawing each breath with difficulty, saying no word.

She did not know what was happening, and she dared not look. She could only wait in anguish for the whimpering that tore her heart to cease.

"Now, *chérie!*" whispered Bertrand at last, and she stiffened in his arms, preparing for she knew not what.

His hold tightened. For that instant he pressed her hard against his heart, so that she heard its quick beating.

The next there came a loud report—a sound that violently rent her stretched nerves, shattering them as glass is shattered by a stone. She drooped without sound like a broken flower, and the young Frenchman gathered her up, just as he had done on the occasion of their first meeting at Valpré, and bore her away.

CHAPTER IV
GOOD-BYE TO CHILDHOOD

Out of the dreadful darkness Chris groped her halting way, saw light, and, shuddering, closed her eyes again. But at once a voice spoke to her, soothingly, tenderly, calling her back.

Reluctantly she responded, reluctantly she returned to full consciousness, and knew that she was lying fully dressed upon a couch in the drawing-room. But at sight of her husband's face bending above her she shuddered again—a painful, convulsive shudder that shook her from head to foot.

He laid a quiet hand on her head, but she shrank away.
"Please, Trevor"—she faltered—"please, I want to be alone."

"Yes, dear," he made gentle reply. "Just drink this first, and I will leave you."

But she withdrew herself almost violently; she buried her face deep in the cushion. "I can't! I can't! Please don't ask me to. I am quite all right. I only want—to be alone."

She was shaking all over as one with an ague, and her words were hardly articulate. He waited a little for her trembling to pass, but it only increased till her whole body seemed to twitch uncontrollably. At last with the utmost quietness he stooped and deliberately raised her.

"Chris, my dear little girl, you mustn't let yourself go like this. I want you to take this stuff to steady you. Afterwards you will have a sleep and be better."

She did not absolutely resist him, but he felt her nervous contraction at his touch. The face she turned to his was ghastly in its pallor.

"I—I don't think I can, Trevor," she said, speaking very rapidly. "My throat won't swallow. It would only choke me. Please—please, if you don't mind—go away. I shall be all right if—if you will only go."

"I can't leave you like this," he said.

"Yes, yes, you can," she answered feverishly. "Oh, what does it matter? Trevor, I must be alone. I must! I must! Please go!"

Her agitation was growing with every second, and he saw that he must yield. He laid her back again without a word, smoothed the cushions, touched her hair, and softly departed.

She listened tensely for the closing of the door, relaxing instantly the moment she heard it. A great darkness descended upon her soul. She lay motionless, face downwards, too stunned for thought.

A long time passed. It was growing late. Over the quiet garden the summer dusk was falling. The swallows were swooping through it in their multitudes—the swallows that Cinders loved to chase. To-night no cheery, impudent bark pursued their flight. To-night all was still.

Did they miss him? she began to wonder dully. Did they ask each other where he had gone? And then, half-consciously, she began to listen for him, the scamper of the light feet, the gay jingle of his collar, till in a moment she almost fancied that she heard him scratching at the door.

She was half off the sofa before realization stabbed her, and she sank back numbly into her desolation.

Again a long time passed—an interval not to be measured by hours or minutes. The swallows ceased to circle and went to roost. It began to be dark. And still Chris lay alone, a huddled, motionless figure, prostrate, crushed, inanimate. Her hands and feet were like ice, but she did not know it. She was past caring for such trifles. All her abounding vitality seemed to be arrested, as if her very blood had ceased to circulate.

It was growing late when the door opened at last. A figure stood a moment upon the threshold, then entered, moving with a quick, light tread that might have been the tread of a woman. In the darkness it reached her, bent over her.

"*Ah, pauvre petite!*" said a soft voice, a voice so full of compassion that it thrilled straight to her silent heart and made it beat again. "All alone with your grief! You permit me to intrude myself, no?"

She turned and felt up towards him with an icy hand.
"Bertie!" she said. "You—might have come before!"

He knelt swiftly down beside her, pressing the little trembling fingers against his neck to give them warmth. "But you are so cold!" he said. "You must not lie here any more."

"Why not?" she said dully. "I don't think it matters, does it?"

"But of course!" he made quick rejoinder. "When you suffer we suffer also. Also"—he paused an instant—"Mr. Mordaunt awaits you, *petite*. Will you not go to him?"

She shivered. "Need I, Bertie? I don't want to."

It was the cry of a child—a child in distress—plunged for the first time in the bitter waters of grief, turning instinctively to the friend of childhood for comfort. "I don't want anyone but you," she said piteously. "You understand. You loved him—and Trevor didn't."

"Oh, but, Christine—" Bertrand began.

"No, he didn't!" she maintained, with sudden vehemence. "I always knew he didn't. He put up with him for my sake; but he never loved him. He never noticed his pretty little ways. Once—once"—she began to sob—"it was on our wedding-day—he slapped him—for chasing a cat! My sweet wee Cinders!"

She broke down utterly upon the words, and there followed such a storm of tears that Bertrand was forced to abandon all attempts to reason with her, and could only kneel and whisper soft endearments in his own language, soothing her, comforting her, as though she were indeed the child she seemed.

But it was long before she even heard him, not until the paroxysm had spent itself and she lay passive and utterly exhausted, with her hands fast clasped in his.

"You are good to me," she murmured then, and in a moment, "Why, Bertie, you're crying too!"

"Ah, pardon me!" he whispered, under his breath. "But to see you in pain, my little one, my bird of Paradise—"

"No," she said, a strange note of conviction in her voice, "I shall never be that any more now that Cinders is gone. I shan't be young like that any more. I—I shall grow up now, Bertie. I daresay Trevor will like me the better for it. But you won't, dear. You will be sorry, I know. We've been playfellows always, haven't we, even though you grew up and I didn't? Well"—there came a sharp catch in her voice—"we shall both be grown-up now."

And then, all in a moment, as if some panic urged her, she started up, drawing his hands close. "But we'll be friends still, won't we, Bertie? You won't talk of going away any more, will you? Promise me! Promise me, Bertie!"

He hesitated. "It might be better that I should go," he said slowly. "It is possible that—"

She interrupted him almost hysterically. "Oh no, no, no! I want you here. I want you, Bertie, Don't you understand?"

"But yes," he said. "Only, *petite*—"

"You will promise, then?" she broke in, as though she had not heard the last words. "Bertie, I'm so miserable. You—you—wouldn't add to it all!"

"No, *chérie*, by Heaven, no!" he said, with vehemence.

"Then you'll stay, Bertie? You will stay?" Very earnestly she besought him. Her tears were dropping on his hands. "Say you will!"

For a moment longer he hesitated; he tried to resist her, he tried to take a sane and temperate view. But those tears were too much for him. They were the one torture he could not endure. With a sharp gesture he flung his hesitation from him. Yet even then he left himself a way of escape lest the temptation should be more than he could bear.

"I will stay," he made grave reply, "as long as it would make you happy to have me with you—that is"—he checked himself—"if Mr. Mordaunt desire it also."

"But of course he does," said Chris. "He likes you. And I—I can't do without you, Bertie—not now."

He heard the desolate note in her voice, and he did not contradict her. Had he not sworn that while she needed him he would be at hand?

"*Eh bien*," he said soothingly. "I stay."

That comforted her somewhat, and presently, at his persuasion, she sat up and dried her eyes. It was too dark for them to see each other, but she held his hand very tightly; and there was comfort also in that.

"Now you will come away from here," he said. "Mr. Mordaunt is very troubled about you. He would not come to you himself because he thought that you did not desire him. But that was not true, no?"

Again that hard shudder went through Chris. She was silent for a little, them "Oh, Bertie," she whispered, "I wish—I wish—it hadn't been he who—who—" she broke off—"you know what I mean. You—saw!"

Yes, he knew. It was what Mordaunt himself had suspected, and loyally he entered the breach on his friend's behalf.

"*Chérie*—pardon me—that is not a good wish—not worthy of you. That which he did was most merciful, most brave, and he did it himself because he would not trust another. I wish it had been my hand—not his. Then you would have understood."

"I almost wish it had been!" whispered Chris; and then, her words scarcely audible, "But—but do you think—he—knew?"

"*Le pauvre Cinders?*" Very softly Bertrand spoke the dog's name. "No, Christine. He did not know. His head was turned the other way. His eyes regarded only you. And Mr. Mordaunt was so quiet, so steady. He aim his revolver quite straight, and his hand tremble—no, not once. Oh, believe me, *petite*, it was better to end it so."

"Yes, I know, only—only"—convulsively her hands closed upon his—"Bertie—Bertie—dogs do go to heaven, don't they?"

"I believe it, Christine."

"You do really—not just because I want you to?"

He drew her gently to her feet. "*Chérie*, I believe it, because I know that all love is eternal, and death is only an incident in eternity. Where there is love there is no death. Nothing that loves can die. It is the Divine Spark that nothing can ever quench."

He spoke with absolute conviction, almost with exultation; and the words went straight to Chris's heart and stayed there.

"You do comfort me," she said.

"I only tell you the truth," he made answer, "as I see it. We do not yet know the power of Love. We only know that it is the greatest of all. It is *le bon Dieu* in the world. And we meet Him everywhere—even in the heart of a dog."

"I shall remember that," she said.

Her hand still clung to his as they groped their way across the room. At the door for a moment she stayed him.

"I shall never forget your goodness to me, Bertie, never—never!" she said, very earnestly.

"Ah, bah!" he answered quickly. "But we are—pals!"

And with that he opened the door, almost as if impatient, and made her pass before him into the hall.

The lamplight dazzled Chris, and she stood for a moment uncertain. Then, as her eyes became accustomed to the change, she discovered her husband, standing a few yards away, looking at her.

He did not speak, merely held out his hand to her; and she went to him with a vagrant feeling of reluctance.

He put his arm about her, looking gravely into her wan face; but she turned from his scrutiny and leaned her head against his shoulder with a piteous little murmur of protest.

"Do you mind if I go to bed, Trevor?" she said, after a moment. "I—I'm very tired, and I don't want any dinner."

"You must have something, dear," he made answer, "but have it in bed by all means. I will bring it up to you in half an hour."

She made a slight movement which might have meant dissent, but which remained unexplained. For a little she stood passive, leaning against him as though she lacked the energy to go, but at length she made a move. Glancing round, she saw that Bertrand had departed.

"Where is Noel?" she asked.

"In his room."

She looked up sharply, detecting a hint of grimness in his voice. "Trevor"—she halted a little—"are you—vexed with anybody?"

His face softened at her tone. "Never mind now, dear," he said. "You are worn out. Get to bed."

She put her hand to her head with a weary gesture. "But why—why is Noel in his room?"

"Because I sent him there."

"You!" She stared at him, fully roused from her lethargy. "Trevor! Why?"

"I will tell you tomorrow," he said, frowning slightly. "I can't have you upset any more tonight."

"But, Trevor—"

"Chris, dear, go to bed," he said firmly. "If I don't find you there in half an hour, I shall put you there myself."

"Oh no!" she broke in. "Please don't come up. I shall get on better alone. And I have to say goodnight to Noel first."

"I am sorry, dear," he said, "but you can't. Noel is in disgrace, and I would rather you did not see him to-night."

"In disgrace! Trevor—why?"

He put his arm deliberately round her again, and led her to the stairs.

"Tell me why," she said.

"I will tell you tomorrow," he repeated.

But she would not be satisfied. She turned upon the first stair, confronting him. "Tell me now, please, Trevor."

He raised his brows at her insistence.

"Yes," she said in answer, "but I want to know. You don't—you can't—blame him for—for—" she faltered and bit her lip desperately—"you know what," she ended under her breath.

"I do blame him," he answered quietly. "I forbade him strictly to attempt to drive without someone of experience beside him."

"Oh!" A sharp note of misgiving sounded in Chris's voice. "You said that to me too!" she said.

He looked at her very gravely. "I did."

"Then—then"—she stretched a hand to the bannisters—"you are angry with me too?"

"No, I am not angry with you," he said, and she was conscious of a subtle softening in his tone. "I am never angry with you, Chris," he said emphatically.

"And yet you are angry with Noel," she said.

"That is different."

"How—different?"

He took her hand into his. "Do you know he nearly killed you?"

She started a little. "Me?"

He nodded grimly. "Yes. If it had been only himself, it wouldn't have mattered. But you—you!"

His arms went out to her suddenly; he caught her to him, held her passionately close for a moment, then lifted her and began to carry her upstairs.

She lay against his breast in quivering silence. It seemed that Cinders did not matter either so long as she was safe; and though she knew beyond all question that he was not angry with her, she was none the less afraid.

CHAPTER V
THE LOOKER-ON

"I think that it should be remembered that he is young," said Bertrand, "also that he has been punished enough severely already."

He leaned back in an easy-chair with a cigarette which he had suffered to go out between his fingers, and watched Mordaunt pacing up and down.

Mordaunt made no pretence of smoking. He walked to and fro with his hands behind him, his brows drawn in thought, his mouth very grim.

"My good fellow, he will have forgotten all that by to-morrow," he said, with a faint, hard smile. "I know these Wyndhams."

"I also," said Bertrand quietly.

Mordaunt glanced at him. "Well?"

The Frenchman hesitated momentarily. "I think," he said, "that you will find them more easy to lead than to drive."

Mordaunt's frown deepened. "They are all so hopelessly lawless, so utterly unprincipled. As for lying, this boy at least thinks nothing of it."

"Ah, that is detestable, that!" Bertrand said. "But he would not lie to you unless you made him afraid, *hein*?"

"He lies whenever it suits his purpose," Mordaunt said. "He would have lied about the speed of the motor if I would have listened to him. But it is his disobedience I am dealing with now. If I don't give that boy the sound thrashing he deserves for defying my orders, he will never obey me again."

Bertrand's eyes, very bright and vigilant, opened a little.
"But Christine!" he said.

"Yes, I know." Mordaunt came to a sudden halt. "Chris also must learn that when I say a thing I mean it," he said.

"Without doubt," the Frenchman conceded gravely. "But that is not all that you want. And surely it would be better to be a little lenient to her brother than to alienate her confidence from yourself."

He spoke impressively, so impressively that Mordaunt turned and looked at him with close attention. Several seconds passed before, very quietly, he spoke.

"What makes you say this to me, Bertrand?"

"Because you are my friend," Bertrand answered.

"And you think my wife is afraid of me?"

Bertrand's eyes met his with the utmost directness. "I think that she might very easily become afraid."

Mordaunt looked at him for several seconds longer, then deliberately pulled up a chair, and sat facing him.

"In Heaven's name, Bertrand, why?" he said.

Bertrand made a quick gesture, almost as if he would have checked the question, but when it was uttered he sat in silence.

"You can't tell me?" Mordaunt said at last.

He shrugged his shoulders. "If you desire it, I will tell you what I think."

"Tell me, then."

A faint flush rose in Bertrand's face. He contemplated the end of his cigarette as if he were studying something of interest. "I think, monsieur," he said at last, "that if you asked more of her, you would obtain more. She is afraid of you because she does not know you. You regard her as a child. You are never on a level with her. You are not enough her friend. Therefore you do not understand her. Therefore she does not know you. Therefore she is—afraid."

His eyes darted up to Mordaunt's grave face for an instant, and returned to the cigarette.

There followed a silence of some duration. At last very quietly Mordaunt rose, went to the mantelpiece, helped himself to a cigarette, and began to search for matches.

Bertrand sprang up to proffer one of his own. They stood close together while the flame kindled between them. After a moment their eyes met through a cloud of smoke. Bertrand's held a tinge of anxiety.

"I have displeased you, no?" he asked abruptly.

Mordaunt leaned a friendly hand upon his shoulder. "On the contrary, I am grateful to you. I believe there is something in what you say. I never gave you credit for so much perception."

Bertrand's face cleared. He began to smile—the smile of the rider who has just cleared a difficult obstacle.

"You have a proverb in England," he said, "concerning those who watch the game, that they see more than those who play. Shall we say that it is thus with me? You and Christine are my very good friends, and I know you both better than you know each other."

"I believe you do," Mordaunt said, smiling faintly himself. "Well, I suppose I must let the youngster off his thrashing for her sake. I wonder if he has gone to bed." He glanced at the clock. "It's time you went, anyhow. You are looking fagged to death. Go and sleep as long as you can."

He gripped the Frenchman's hand, looking at him with a kindly scrutiny which Bertrand refused to meet. He never encouraged any reference to his health.

"I am all right," he said with emphasis, but he returned the hand-grip with a warmth that left no doubt as to the cordiality of his feelings. He was ever too polished a gentleman to be discourteous.

Left alone, Mordaunt sat down at his writing-table to clear off some work which he had taken out of his secretary's hands earlier in the day. It was midnight before he finished, and even then he sat on for a long time deep in thought.

It was probably true, what Bertrand had said. Tenderly as he loved his young wife, he had not succeeded in winning her confidence. There was no friendship between them in the most intimate sense of the word, and so she feared him. His love was to her a consuming flame from which she shrank. Bitterly he admitted the fact, since there was no ignoring it. She was frightened at the very existence of his passion, restrain it how he would. She was his and yet not his. She eluded him, even when he held her in his arms.

His thoughts travelled backwards, recalling incident after incident, all pointing to the same thing. And yet he knew that he had been patient with her. He had held himself in check perpetually. And here again Bertrand's words recurred to him. If he had asked more, might he not have obtained more? Was it possible that he had failed to win her because he had not let her feel the compulsion of his love? Was it perchance his very restraint that frightened her? Had he indeed asked too little?

Again his thoughts went back and dwelt upon their wedding-night. He had kindled some answering flame within her then. She had not attempted to withhold herself. The memory of her shy surrender swept over him, setting the blood leaping in his veins anew. She had been his that night, and his throughout the brief fortnight that followed. They had been very intent upon the renovations, and no cloud had even shadowed their horizon. How was it she had slipped away from him since? Was it the advent of that tempestuous youngster that had caused the change? Undoubtedly Chris was less a Wyndham when alone with him. Or was there some other cause, arising possibly from some hidden fluctuation of mood, some restlessness of the spirit, of which he had had no warning? Her aunt's declaration that they were all lacking in stability recurred to him. Was it so with her? Was she fickle, was she changeable, his little Chris?

Her own words came back to him, uttered with tears upon her wedding-day: "Don't you often think me silly and fickle? You'll find it more and more, the more you see of me. You'll be horribly disappointed in me some day."

He rose abruptly. No, that day had not dawned yet. If she had slipped away from him, he, and he alone, was to blame. He had not won the friendship which alone brings trust, and he knew now that he could not hold her without it. As Bertrand had said, he had not been enough her friend. Even now she was probably crying herself ill in solitude over the loss of Cinders.

The thought quickened him to action. He turned out the light, and went swiftly from the room.

Upstairs, outside her door, he stopped to listen, but he heard no sound. She had cried herself to sleep, then, and he had not been there to comfort her. His heart smote him. Had she deemed him unsympathetic? She had seemed to wish to be alone, and for that reason he had left her as soon as he had satisfied himself that she had all she needed in a physical sense. She had not wanted him. She had shrunk from his touch. She had probably seen him go with relief. But—he asked himself the question with sudden misgiving— would it have been better if he had ignored her evident desire and stayed? He had feared exhaustion for her and had avoided any word or action that might have led to a renewal of her grief. Had he seemed to think too lightly of her sorrow? Had she been repelled by his very forbearance?

He passed on softly to his own room. The door that led from this into hers was ajar. He pushed it a little wider, and looked in.

It was lighted only by the moon, which threw a flood of radiance through the wide-flung windows. Every object in the room stood out in strong relief. Standing motionless in the doorway, Trevor Mordaunt sought and found his wife.

She was lying with her face to the moonlight, her hair streaming loose, the bedclothes pushed off her shoulders.

And there beside her, curled up in a big easy-chair, his black head lodged against her pillow, one hand clasped close in hers, lay Noel. Both had been crying, both were asleep.

For many seconds Mordaunt stood upon the threshold, gravely watching them, but he made no movement to draw nearer. At last noiselessly he withdrew, and closed the door.

The grimness had all gone from his face. He even smiled a little as he resigned himself to spending the night in his own room. The idea of disturbing the brother and sister never crossed his mind. It was enough for him that Chris had found comfort.

CHAPTER VI
A BARGAIN

"Luck!" said Rupert gloomily. "There never is any where I am concerned."

This in response to a question from his brother-in-law as to the general progress of his affairs. He sat in Mordaunt's writing-room, with one of Mordaunt's cigars between his lips, and a decidedly sullen expression on his good-looking face.

"I'm sick of everything," he declared. "I'm going to chuck the Army. It's never done anything for me. There's no chance of active service, and I loathe garrison work."

"The only question being, what else are you fit for?" said Mordaunt.

Rupert threw him a quick look. "I'll be your bailiff, if you like," he said. "I could do that."

Mordaunt raised his brows at the suggestion. "That is an idea that never occurred to me," he remarked.

"Why not? You want a bailiff, don't you?"

"A reliable one," said Mordaunt.

Rupert jumped in his chair as if he had been stung. "What the devil do you mean?"

"I mean"—Mordaunt regarded him steadily—"that I shouldn't care to trust my affairs to a man who can't look after his own."

Rupert's eyes flashed. "I am not to be trusted, then?"

Mordaunt continued to regard him, quite unmoved.

"You had better ask yourself that question, my dear fellow," he said "You are better qualified to answer it than I am."

Rupert relaxed again, dropping back listlessly. "I suppose you are right. I certainly don't make a great success of things. I believe I should get on better with you than with anyone else. But if you feel like that about it, there is no more to be said."

"You really want to be taken seriously, do you?" Mordaunt said.

"Of course I do!" Rupert turned towards him again with the lightning change of mood characteristic of him. "You must forgive me for being a bit touchy, old chap. It's this infernal thundery weather. May I have another drink?" He helped himself without waiting for permission. "Of course I want to be taken seriously. It's a billet that would suit me down to the ground. I know the place, every inch of it, and, as you know, I'm fond of it. I would look after your interests as though they were my own."

Mordaunt smiled. "But do you look after your own?"

Rupert clinked some ice into his tumbler, and thoughtfully watched it float.

"You've been so jolly decent to me," he said at length, "that I haven't the face to bother you with my affairs again."

"I suppose that means you are in difficulties," his brother-in-law remarked.

He nodded without looking up. "I'm never out of 'em. It's not my fault. It's my beastly bad luck."

"Of course," said Mordaunt dryly.

Rupert bobbed the ice against his glass and spilt some whisky-and-water in so doing. He looked decidedly uncomfortable.

"I can't help it," he said. "I was born in Queer Street, and I've lived there all my life. You fellows who are simply rolling in wealth haven't the smallest notion what it means."

"What is the good of saying that?" Mordaunt sounded impatient for the first time. "You know as well as I do that if you had twenty thousand a year you would spend twice the amount."

Rupert glanced at him sideways. "Hullo!" he said softly. "Beginning to size us up, are you?"

"I'm beginning to think"—Mordaunt spoke with force—"that your sense of honour is as much a minus quantity as your wealth."

"Honour!" Rupert looked up in genuine astonishment.

"Yes, honour," Mordaunt repeated grimly. "Do you call it honourable to run up debts that you have no possibility of paying?"

Rupert turned crimson. "Look here! I'm not going to stay here to be insulted," he said hotly. "I haven't asked for your help, and I'm damned if I'd take it if you offered it—after that."

He was on his feet with the words, but Mordaunt remained seated. "You can do as you like," he said quietly. "If you choose to take offence, that is your affair. I helped you before because I knew you were hard up and I was sorry for you. But there is no occasion for you to be hard up now. And I am not sorry for you this time. I think you deserve to be kicked."

"You be damned!" said Rupert fiercely.

Mordaunt's brows went up. He looked full into the boy's heated face, and though he said no word Rupert turned slowly white under the look. In the dead silence that followed he stood as tense as though he expected a blow. Yet Mordaunt made no movement, spoke no word.

It was Rupert who broke the silence finally, broke it hurriedly, stammeringly, as though it had become unbearable. "All right, old chap. I didn't mean quite that. But you—you shouldn't badger me. I'm not used to it."

"Sit down," Mordaunt said.

He obeyed awkwardly, and to cover his discomfiture took up his glass to drink. But before it reached his lips Mordaunt spoke again.

"Rupert!"

He started a little, and again the liquid splashed over.

"Put that down!" Mordaunt said.

Again dumbly he obeyed.

Mordaunt leaned forward and drew the glass out of his reach. "It has never been my intention to badger you," he said. "But I reserve to myself the privilege of telling you the truth. That is the fourth drink I have seen you mix this afternoon."

"I'm perfectly sober," Rupert asserted quickly.

"Yes, I know. But you are not as cool as you might be." Very keenly Mordaunt's eyes surveyed him, but they were not without a hint of kindness notwithstanding. "I mustn't call you a young fool, I suppose," he said, "but really you are not overwise. Now, what about these affairs of yours? Shall we go into them now or after tea?"

Rupert shrugged his shoulders sullenly. "I don't know that I care to go into them at all."

The kindliness went out of Mordaunt's eyes and a certain steeliness took its place. "As you like," he said. "Only let it be clearly understood that I will have no borrowing from Chris. I have forbidden her to lend money to any one of you. If you want it, you must come direct to me."

Rupert shifted his position, and looked out of the window. Down in the garden Chris was dispensing tea to three of his brother-subalterns, assisted by Noel. Bertrand was seated by her side, alert and watchful, ready at a moment's notice to come to her aid. It was his customary attitude, and it had been so more than ever since the death of Cinders. There was a protecting brotherliness about him that Chris found infinitely comforting: He understood her so perfectly.

She had not wanted to emerge from her seclusion to entertain her brother's friends on that sunny Sunday afternoon, but he had gently persuaded her. A change had come over Chris during the past four days. The violence of her grief had spent itself on the night that she and Noel had mingled their tears over the loss of their favourite, and she had not alluded to it since. She accepted her husband's sympathy with gratitude, but she shrank so visibly from the smallest allusion to her trouble that he found no opportunity for expressing it. He would not intrude it upon her. It was not his way, and she made him aware that for this also she was grateful.

But it was plainly from Bertrand that she drew her chief comfort. His very presence seemed to soothe her. He was just the friend she needed to help her through her dark hour.

That she fretted secretly Mordaunt could not doubt, but she was so zealous to hide all traces of it from him that he never detected them. He only missed her gay wilfulness and the sunshine of her smile. She responded to his tenderness even more readily than usual, but she did not open her heart to him. There seemed to be a barrier intervening that she could not bring herself to pass.

In his own mind he set this fact down to a certain feminine unreasonableness, imagining that she could not forget his share in the tragedy that had affected her so deeply. He trusted to time to soften the painful impression, and meanwhile, with his habitual patience, he set himself to wait till the physical strain had passed and the very sweetness of her nature should bring her back to him. He knew that all Bertrand's influence would be exercised in this direction, and his faith in his young secretary's discretion was considerable. Their brief conversation on the night of the disaster had rooted it more firmly than ever. Bertrand was so essentially a man of honour that he trusted him in all things as he trusted himself. Their code was the same, and their friendship of the kind that endures for life. If there were one thing on earth before all others upon which Trevor Mordaunt would have staked his all, it was this Frenchman's loyalty to himself. He was as staunch as Chris's brothers were unstable. He believed him to be utterly incapable of so much as an underhand impulse. And he was content that Chris should have for friend this man who was so close a friend of his own, upon whose nobility of character he had come to rely as a power for good that could not fail to raise her ideals and deepen in her that sense of honour which was still scarcely more than an undeveloped instinct in her soul.

His eyes followed Rupert's to the open window. The sound of chaffing voices rose clearly on the summer air, mingled with the chink of tea-cups.

"Shall we go?" Mordaunt said.

Rupert looked round with a laugh. "Did you see that ass Murphy stand on his head to drink his tea? It's his pet accomplishment. Yes, all right; let's go."

He got up, glanced at the whisky-and-soda on the table, then impulsively linked his arm in that of his brother-in-law, all his sullenness gone like a storm-cloud.

"You're quite right, old fellow. I have had as much of that stuff as is good for me. Forgive me for being such a bear. I didn't mean it."

Mordaunt paused. He had never dealt with anyone quite so bewilderingly changeable before. "I wish I knew how to treat you," he said, after a moment.

"Oh, pitch into me! It's the only way." Rupert's smile flashed suddenly upon him. "I've been an ungrateful brute, and I'm ashamed of myself. Seriously, Trevor, I'm sorry. I sometimes think to myself it's downright disgusting the way we all sponge on you. It's deuced good of you to put up with it."

Mordaunt still regarded him with close attention. But there was no doubt in his mind as to the boy's sincerity: he only wondered how long this contrite mood would last.

"I am always willing to help you to the best of my ability," he said. "But I think you might play the game. I can't keep pouring water into a sieve."

"It's not to be expected," Rupert agreed. "And I hate asking you for more money. I'm an absolute cur to do it. But—" he broke off, and pulled his hand free—"for goodness' sake, man, if you can—just this once—"

Mordaunt crossed the room to his writing-table, unlocked a drawer, took out a cheque-book.

"How much?"

"I say, you are a good chap!" Rupert protested. "Can you make it a hundred?"

"Will that settle everything?" Mordaunt asked.

"Oh, well—practically everything."

Mordaunt wrote the cheque in silence. He handed it over his shoulder finally to the boy behind him.

"It's for a hundred and fifty. I hope that will see you through. And look here, Rupert, do for Heaven's sake pull up and keep within bounds. I am quite willing to help you to a reasonable extent, but you must do your part, too. You are living at an insane rate. Do you keep an account of your expenditure?"

"Of course I don't!" Rupert seemed astonished at the question. "What on earth would be the good of that? It wouldn't reduce my expenses."

Mordaunt laid his cheque-book back in the drawer. "And you think you would make a good bailiff?" he said.

"Oh, that's different. Of course, you must have accounts for the management of an estate. You would have no cause to complain of me there. Are you going to think it over, I say?"

Mordaunt turned in his chair. "You really wish me to do so?"

"Rather!" Rupert spoke with enthusiasm. "If you knew how deadly sick I am of the life I live now!" he added, with strong disgust. "It's beastly hard work, too, in a sense, and nothing to show for it."

"I should work you hard myself," Mordaunt observed.

"I shouldn't mind that. I'd work like a horse here. It's what I've always wanted to do."

"And kick like a horse, too, if I ventured to find fault," said Mordaunt, smiling a little.

"No, I shouldn't. I'd take it like a lamb. Come, man, I've apologized."

There was a note of reproach in Rupert's voice. Mordaunt left his writing-table and faced him squarely.

"I'll make a bargain with you," he said. "If you can manage to keep straight between now and Christmas, and you are of the same mind then, I will take you on. Is it done?"

Rupert thrust out a hand with a beaming countenance. "Done, old fellow! And a thousand thanks! I'll do my part somehow if it kills me. Hullo, I say! There's Chris calling! Hadn't we better go?"

He was plainly desirous to end the interview, and Mordaunt did not seek to prolong it. "Come along, then!" he said. And they went out together arm-in-arm to join the group upon the lawn.

Two hours later, just before Rupert and his friends started upon their return journey, Bertrand happened to enter Mordaunt's writing-room, and was surprised to find the eldest Wyndham standing by the table with a glass of whisky-and-soda to his lips.

The surprise was mutual, and on Rupert's side so violent that he dropped the glass, which shivered upon the floor. He uttered a fierce exclamation as he recognized the intruder.

Bertrand was profuse in his apologies. "But I had no idea that there was anyone here! A thousand pardons, Mr. Wyndham! It was unfortunate—but very unfortunate. I am come only for Mr. Mordaunt's keys, which he left here by accident. I will ring for Holmes. He will remove this *débris*. And you will have another drink, yes?"

"I can't wait," Rupert said, almost inarticulately.

He remained standing at the table trying to compose himself, but he was white to the lips.

Bertrand regarded him with quick concern. "Ah, but how I have alarmed you!" he said. "My shoes are of canvas, and they make no sound. Will you, then, sit down for a moment, while I pour out another glass of whisky?"

He drew forward a chair with much solicitude, and took up a fresh glass. But Rupert swung away, turning his back upon him.

Prom the front of the house came the hoot of the waiting motor. Plainly his comrades were waxing impatient.

"But you will drink before you go?" urged the courteous Frenchman. "I am desolated to have deprived you—"

Rupert turned his face for an instant over his shoulder. It was no longer white, but crimson and convulsed with anger. His hands were clenched.

"Oh, go to the devil!" he cried violently, and with the words stamped furiously from the room.

Bertrand was left staring after him, petrified with amazement—too astounded to be angry.

At the end of a lengthy pause he turned and pocketed Mordaunt's keys, and rang the bell for Holmes to clear up the mess on the floor.

"*Mais ces anglais!*" he murmured to himself, with a whimsical shrug of the shoulders. "*Comme ils sont drôles!*"

CHAPTER VII
THE ENEMY

Mrs. Pouncefort's garden-party was an annual affair of some importance to which everyone, from the County downwards, was bidden, and from which very few absented themselves.

The Pouncefort entertainments were generally upon a lavish scale, were also largely attended by the military element of Sandacre society, and were invariably described in the local journals as "very smart affairs."

Had Chris been in her normal spirits she would have hailed the occasion with delight. She knew a good many people in the neighbourhood, and she was sure to meet all her friends there. It was, moreover, for this that she had successfully angled for an invitation for Bertrand. But when the day came she would have given a good deal for a legitimate excuse for remaining at home. The weather was hot, and she felt weary and disinclined for gaiety.

She said no word of her reluctance, however, for Bertrand had accepted his inclusion in the invitation with docility, and since she had decided that a little social change would be good for him, she would not draw back herself lest he should be tempted to do likewise.

Bertrand was her chief thought just then. She knew that her husband was dissatisfied with regard to his health, and undoubtedly he looked far from well, though he himself invariably declared that it was only the heat, and persistently refused to see a doctor. Not even Chris could shake this resolution of his, and he was so distressed when Mordaunt would not let him work that to keep him quiet Mordaunt was obliged to let him do a little. He made it as little as he could, however, and Bertrand spent a good deal of his time in the garden with Chris in consequence.

It certainly cheered her to have him, and for that reason he was the less inclined to rebel against the edict that sent him there. They had begun to read French together, Chris having developed a sudden keenness for the language which he was delighted to encourage. That the original idea had been devised for his pleasure he shrewdly suspected, but the carrying out of it contributed undoubtedly to her own. It occupied her thoughts and energies, and that was what she needed just then.

He knew perfectly well that she was as disinclined for social amusements as he was himself, but the same motive that prompted her urged him also. Each went with reluctance, but without protest.

Noel, who had achieved the most saintlike behaviour during the past week, went also. He made an ingratiating attempt at the last moment to persuade Mordaunt to let him drive. But Mordaunt was as adamant upon that point. He had issued a decree that Noel should drive no more during the summer holidays, and he meant to keep to it.

The prohibition did not extend to Chris, but she had shuddered at the bare mention of the motor ever since the accident, and he knew that she had not the faintest desire left to enlarge her experience in driving.

She was the last to leave the house on that sultry August afternoon, and Mordaunt saw at once that the ordeal of entering the car was a severe one. She even turned so white at the sight of it that he feared a breakdown.

"Come and sit with me," he said kindly.

She looked at him with a quick shake of the head. "No, I'll sit behind with Bertie if I may. Noel can sit with you."

Noel, who was already in the back seat, climbed over like a monkey, and Bertrand handed her in.

She sat very rigid until they were out of the avenue, and Bertrand was silent also. But as they turned into the road he began to talk, gently and persuasively, upon indifferent things, resolutely passing by her silence until with a wan little smile she managed to respond.

Long before they reached Sandacre she had quite recovered her self-command, and the flash of the sea upon the horizon brought from her a quick exclamation of pleasure.

"Ah, yes, it is beautiful, that!" he agreed with enthusiasm. "And there is the sand there, yes?"

She nodded. "I used to think we'd go and picnic there. But I don't think I want to now."

"Next year," suggested Mordaunt, without turning his head.

"Perhaps," she said, a little dubiously.

Bertrand said nothing. He was looking out to the wide horizon with a far look in his eyes, almost as though he saw beyond that sparkling sky-line, even beyond the sea itself.

The strains of the military band from Sandacre reached them as they turned in at the wide-flung gates. Chris's eyes kindled almost in spite of her. She loved all things military.

As for Bertrand, he sat bolt upright, with his head back, like a horse scenting battle. Glancing at him, Chris wondered at his attitude, till suddenly she recognized the strains of the Marseillaise.

She squeezed his hand in sympathy as he helped her to alight, and he looked at her with his quick smile of understanding. He was ever swift to catch her meaning.

They crossed a lawn that was crowded with people to a great cedar-tree, beneath which their hostess was receiving her guests. A large woman with a lazy smile was Mrs. Pouncefort, and wonderful dark eyes that were seldom wholly revealed—a woman who took no pains to please and yet whose charm was undeniable. Her monarchy was absolute and her courtiers many, but other women looked at her askance, half-conscious of a veiled antagonism. They were a little afraid of her also, though not one could have said why, since no bitter word was ever heard to pass her lips.

She greeted Chris with a cold, limp hand. "So nice of you to come. I hope you won't be bored. Ah, Mr. Mordaunt, how is Kellerton Old Park by this time? I hardly recognized it the day I called. Rupert tells me you have worked wonders inside as well as out."

"May I introduce our friend Monsieur Bertrand?" said Chris.

Bertrand brought his heels together and bowed low over the limp hand transferred to his. Mrs. Pouncefort smiled.

"There is a fellow-countryman of yours here. Where has he gone? Ah, there you are! Captain Rodolphe, let me introduce you to Mrs. Mordaunt and her French friend Monsieur Bertrand."

She extended one finger to Noel while making the introduction, and at once turned her attention elsewhere.

Chris found herself face to face with a heavy-browed man with an overbearing demeanour and a mouth and chin that sneered perpetually behind a waxed moustache and imperial. She stared at him for an instant with a bewildered feeling of having seen him somewhere before. Then, as she returned his bow, a stab of recognition pierced her, and she remembered where.

It flashed into her mind like a picture thrown upon a screen—that scene upon the sands of Valpré long, long ago, two men fighting with swords that gleamed in the sunlight, a child drawing near with wondering eyes to behold the conflict, and an unruly black terrier scampering to end it!

"I am delighted to make your acquaintance," declared Captain Rodolphe, "and that of your friend—M. Bertrand?"

He uttered the name interrogatively. Bertrand bowed very slightly, very stiffly, and was instantly erect again. "That is my name," he said, as he looked the other straight in the eyes.

Captain Rodolphe was smiling. "I think we have not met before? It is always a pleasure to meet a fellow-countryman in a strange land. That is well understood, is it not, Mrs. Mordaunt?"

His smooth speech brought her back to a situation that was not without serious difficulties, difficulties which he for one was apparently determined to ignore. Had he recognized her, she wondered? It seemed probable that he had not. But then there was nothing in his manner to indicate that he had recognized Bertrand either; yet of that there could be no doubt.

She heard her husband speaking to an acquaintance behind her, and instinctively she began to move away from him. She did not feel equal to effecting an introduction. She murmured something conventional about the gardens, and Captain Rodolphe at once accompanied her.

Bertrand walked in silence on her other side till, with an obvious effort, Chris included him in the conversation, when he responded instantly, with that ready ease of manner which had first drawn her to rely upon him. But though he showed himself quite willing, as ever, to help her, he did not once on his own initiative address the man who had been introduced for his benefit; and Chris, aware of an atmosphere that was highly charged with electricity, notwithstanding its apparent calm, began to cast about for a means of escape therefrom.

To rid herself of Captain Rodolphe was her first idea, but this was easier of thought than accomplishment. He was chatting serenely, in perfect English, and seemed to have taken upon himself the congenial task of entertaining her for some time to come. He also did not directly address her companion, unless she brought them into contact, and her efforts in this direction very speedily flagged. She could not expect two men, however courteous, to forget all in a moment the bitter enmity of years merely to oblige her. They were quite ready to ignore it in her presence, but the consciousness of it was more than Chris could endure with equanimity. It disconcerted her at every turn. She felt as if she trod the edge of a volcano, and her nerves, which had been so severely strained for the past week, could not face this fresh ordeal.

She turned at last in desperation, almost appealingly, to Bertrand. She knew he would understand. Had he ever failed her in this respect or in any other?

"Do you mind going to see if I have dropped my handkerchief in the car?" she asked him, with a nervous smile.

His smile answered hers. Yes, he understood. "I shall go with pleasure," he said, and with a quick bow was gone.

Chris breathed a little sigh of relief, and moved on with her escort into the rose-garden.

He seemed scarcely aware of Bertrand's departure. He was plainly engrossed in the pleasant pastime of conversing with her. Chris began to give him more of her attention. No, she certainly did not like the man. His sneer and his self-assurance disturbed her. He made her uncomfortably conscious of her own youth and inexperience. She almost felt as if he were playing with her.

He talked at some length upon roses, a subject upon which he seemed to be well informed, listened tolerantly to any remarks she made, and finally conducted her to a long shrubbery that led back to the lawn.

As they entered this, he lightly wound up the thread of his discourse and broke it off. "I have been wondering for long," he said, "where it was that I had seen you before. Now I remember."

She turned a startled face towards him. He was smiling with extreme complacence, but there was to her something sinister, something even threatening, about the bushy brows that shadowed his gleaming eyes. He put her in mind of a carrion-crow searching for treasures on a heap of refuse.

The impulse to deny all knowledge of him seized her—a blind impulse, blindly followed. "I think you must be mistaken," she said.

"How?" he ejaculated. "You do not remember Valpré—and what happened there?"

She saw her mistake on the instant, and hastened to cover it. "Valpré!" she said, frowning a little. "Yes, I remember Valpré, though it is years since I was there. But you—did I meet you at Valpré, Captain Rodolphe?"

He bowed with a gallantry that seemed to her exaggerated. "Only once, madame, but that once was enough to stamp you ineffaceably upon my memory. It was, in fact, a memorable occasion. And I forget—never!" Again with *empressement* he bowed. "And still you do not remember me?" he said.

There was a mocking glint in his eyes. It was as though with a smile he weighed her resistance, displaying it to herself as a quantity wholly negligible.

"I think you begin to remember now," he suggested.

And quite suddenly Chris saw what he had with subtlety set about teaching her, that to attempt to fence with him was useless.

"Yes, I remember," she said, and there was a hint of most unwonted malice in her capitulation. "Didn't I see you wounded in a duel?"

He smiled, and she saw his teeth. "If my memory be correct it was to madame herself that I owed that wound."

She felt the quick blood rush to her face. He had spoken with *double entendre*, but she did not perceive it until too late. She only remembered suddenly and overwhelmingly that the duel had been fought on her account, because of some evil word which this man had spoken of her in Bertrand's hearing. She could well believe it of him—the sneering laugh, the light allusion, the hateful insinuation underlying it. She was beginning to look upon the evil of the world with comprehending eyes—she, Chris, the gay of heart, the happy bird of Bertrand's paradise whom no evil had ever touched. And though she shrank from it as one dreading pollution, she dared not turn her back.

He went on with more daring mockery, still with lips that smiled. "Ah! I see you remember. That duel was an affair of interest to you, *hein*? You were—the woman in the case."

He leered at her intolerably, twisting his moustache.

But that was more than Chris could endure. He had taken her by surprise indeed, but he should not see her routed thus easily. She lifted her dainty head and confronted him with pride.

"Whatever the cause of the duel," she said very distinctly, "it was no concern of mine, and it was by the merest accident that I witnessed it. But in any case it is not a matter of sufficient importance to discuss now. Shall we go on?"

She put the question abruptly, with a little inward tremor, for the path was narrow and he had come to a stand immediately in front of her. He made a slight movement as if deprecating the obligation to detain her. His eyes were suddenly very evil and so intent that she could not avoid them. Yet still he smiled as though the situation amused him.

"But you joke!" he protested, with a snap of the fingers. "I did not suggest that it could be a matter of importance. It was all a *bagatelle*, a fairy-tale, that should not have had so serious an end. And your husband—he has heard the fairy-tale also? Or was it not of sufficient importance to recount to him?"

She would have turned from him at that, even though it had meant ignominious flight, but his eyes held her, and she dared not. She could only stand motionless, feeling her very heart grow cold.

Softly, jeeringly, he went on, still toying with the moustache that did not hide his smiling lips. "You have not told him yet? Ah! but it would amuse him. That night you passed with the fairies, a siren among the sirens, has he never heard of that? But you should tell him that! Or was it perhaps only a joke *à deux*, and not *à trois*? I have heard that the English husband can be strict, and you have found it so to your cost, *hein*?"

Her eyes blazed at the insult. For the first time in her life Chris was so possessed by fury as to be actually sublime. She drew herself to her full height. She met his mockery fearlessly, and, with a royal disregard of consequences, she trod it underfoot.

"Captain Rodolphe, be good enough to let me pass!"

He stood aside instantly. He was even momentarily abashed. He had not expected his game to end thus. She had seemed such an easy prey, this English girl. Her discomfiture had been almost too obvious. He certainly had not deemed her capable of this display of spirit.

Yet in a moment, even as, erect and disdainful, she passed him by, he was smiling again, a secret, subtle smile which she felt rather than saw. Emerging into the hot sunshine that beat upon the crowded lawn, she knew herself to be cold from head to foot.

CHAPTER VIII
THE THIN END

"Good-bye!" said Mrs. Pouncefort. "So glad you came. I hope you haven't been bored."

"Bored to extinction," murmured Noel. "Hi, Trevor! Let me drive, like a good chap. Do!"

"Certainly not," said Mordaunt, with decision. "You are going to sit behind. We shall meet the wind now, and Chris must come in front; it is more sheltered."

Chris submitted to this arrangement in silence. She was looking very tired. Her husband regarded her keenly as he tucked her in, but he said nothing.

"What do you think of Mrs. Pouncefort's latest?" grinned Noel, as they spun along the high-road. "I never met such a facetious brute in my life. How did you like him, Bertrand?"

"Who?" said Bertrand somewhat curtly.

"What did they call him—Rodolphe, wasn't it? That French chap with the beastly little beard."

"I did not like him," said Bertrand, with precision.

"That's all right," said Noel approvingly. "But he's reigning favourite with Mrs. Pouncefort, anyone can see with half an eye. Rum, isn't it? And little Pouncefort puts up with it like a lamb. But they say he's just as bad. Daresay he is, though he's quite a decent little beggar to talk to. I can't stand Mrs. Pouncefort at any price, while as for that Frenchman"—he made a hideous grimace—"I'm glad you are not all alike, Bertrand!"

Bertrand responded to the compliment without elation. He seemed preoccupied, and Noel, finding him uninteresting, turned his cheerful attention elsewhere.

Letters awaited them upon their return. Chris took up hers with scarcely a glance, and went up to her room.

Her husband, following a little later, found her sitting on a couch by the window, perusing them. She glanced up at his entrance.

"I have a letter from Aunt Philippa. She thinks we must be quite settled by this time, and she wants to spend a day or two here next week, before she goes to Scotland."

"I suppose we can put up with her for a day or two," said Mordaunt.

Her smile was slightly strained as she returned to the letter. "I suppose we shall have to."

He came and stood beside her, looking down at her bent head. The burnished hair shone warmly golden in the evening sunlight. He laid a quiet hand upon it. She started at his touch, and then sat very still.

"I have heard from Hilda too," she said, after a moment. "They are staying at Graysdale. Percy fishes all day and she sketches, when they are not motoring. It was very sweet of her to write by return."

A tear fell suddenly upon the open page. She covered it hastily with her hand. Her husband's pressed her head very tenderly.

"Chris," he said gently, "I wonder if you would like to go away for a little?"

She glanced up quickly, eagerly, with wet lashes. "Oh, Trevor!" she breathed.

He sat down beside her on the couch. "We will go to-morrow if you like," he said.

She slipped her hand into his. "I should love it!"

"Would you?" he said. "I have been thinking of it for some days, but I wasn't sure you would care for the idea."

"But your work?" she said. "Those articles you wanted to finish? And that political book of yours? And the alterations in the north wing, will they be able to get on with those with you away?"

"The literary work must stand over for a week or two," he said. "I shall leave Bertrand in charge of the rest."

"Bertrand!" She opened her blue eyes wide. "But—but he would be away, wouldn't he?" Then quickly: "He would go with us, of course? You didn't mean to leave him behind?"

He raised his brows ever so slightly. "I meant just us two, dear," he said. "Wouldn't you care for that?"

"Oh!" said Chris blankly. "But, Trevor, we couldn't possibly leave him. He isn't well. I—I shouldn't be happy about him. Besides—besides—" Her words faltered under his straight look; she made a little appealing gesture towards him. "Please understand," she said.

He took both her hands into his. "My dear, I do understand," he said, with the utmost kindness. "But I think he can be trusted to take care of himself for a little while. If you have any doubts upon the subject, ask him."

She shook her head. "No, it wouldn't do. I—I'd really rather not go away if it means—that. Besides, there is Noel. And next week there will be Aunt Philippa. I think we had better give up the idea, Trevor; I do really, anyhow for the present." She leaned nearer to him; her eyes looked pleadingly into his. "Say you don't mind," she begged him, a little tremulously.

"I am only thinking of you, dear," he answered.

She smiled with lips that quivered. "Well, don't think of me—at least, not too much. I only want you just to be kind to me, that's all. I—I shall be myself presently. You're very good to be so patient."

Her lips were lifted to his. He bent and kissed her. But as he went gravely away she had a feeling that she had disappointed him, and her heart grew a little heavier in consequence.

The sound of the piano in the drawing-room brought her down earlier than usual for dinner, and she found Bertrand playing softly to himself in the twilight. He had a delicate touch, and she always loved to hear him.

She had with difficulty trained him not to spring up at her entrance, but to-day he turned sharply round.

"Christine, what did that *scélérat* say to you?"

The abruptness of his speech did not disconcert her. She was never ill at ease with Bertrand, however sudden his mood. She came to the piano, and stood facing him in the dusk.

"He recognized me," she said.

"Ah!" Bertrand's exclamation was deep in his throat, like the growl of an angry dog. "And he said—?"

Chris hesitated.

Instantly his manner changed. He stretched out a quick hand. "Pardon my impatience! You will tell me what he said?"

Yet still she hesitated. His impetuosity had warned her to go warily if she would not have him embroiling himself in another quarrel for her sake.

"It doesn't matter much, does it?" she said, rather wearily. "I wasn't with him very long—no longer than I could help. He was objectionable, of course, but that sort of man couldn't be anything else, could he?"

"Tell me what he said," insisted Bertrand inexorably.

But still she hedged, trying to temper his wrath. "He didn't tell me anything new. I have known—for some time now—why you fought that duel."

"Ah! You know that? But how?"

She smiled wanly. "You forget I'm growing up, Bertie."

He winced at that suddenly and sharply, but he made no verbal protest. Only in the silence that followed there was something passionate, something which she never remembered to have encountered before in her dealings with him.

At the end of a long pause he spoke, with obvious constraint. "And you will not tell me what he said?"

"Is it worth while?" said Chris. "I daresay we shall never see him again."

"He insulted you, no?" said Bertrand.

She yielded, half-involuntarily, to his persistence. "He made some—rather horrid—insinuations. He spoke of the duel and of what happened at Valpré. And he asked—he asked if—Trevor knew."

A fierce oath burst headlong from Bertrand, the first she had ever heard him utter. He apologized for it instantly, almost in the same breath, but she was startled by the violence of it none the less, so startled that she decided then and there that, if she would keep the peace between him and his enemy, she must confide in him no further.

"But that was really all," she hastened to assure him. "I left him then, and—and I think we had better forget it, Bertie. Promise me you will."

He took the persuasive hand she laid upon his arm, but for several seconds he did not speak. It seemed as if he could not trust himself to do so.

At last, "Christine," he said, "I think that your husband ought to know."

She started at the words, almost snatching her hand from him. "Bertie! What do you mean? Know of what?"

He answered her with great steadiness; his eyes met hers unwaveringly. "Of that which happened at Valpré," he said.

She gazed at him in growing consternation. "Bertie, how—are you mad?—how could I tell him that?"

"With your permission, I will tell him," he said resolutely.

But she cried out at that, almost as if he had hurt her: "Oh no, no, never! Why should he know now? Don't you see how impossible it is? If I had ever meant to tell him, it ought to have been long ago."

"Yes," said Bertrand.

The quietness of his tone only agitated her still further. His evident determination terrified her. In that moment all her fear of her husband rose to towering proportions, a monster she dared not even contemplate. She clasped Bertrand's arm between her hands in wild, unreasoning supplication.

"Oh, you must not—you shall not! Bertie, you won't, will you? Promise me you won't—promise me! He wouldn't understand. He would want to know why I had never told him before. He would—he would—"

"Ah! but I would explain," Bertrand protested gently.

"But you couldn't! He would ask questions—questions I couldn't possibly answer. If he didn't say them he would look them. And his eyes are so terribly keen. They frighten me. They see—everything."

"But, *chérie*," he reasoned, "they could not see what is not there. You have nothing to hide from him. You have no shame. Why, then, have you fear?"

"I don't know," gasped Chris. "Only I know that he would never understand. He would think—he would think—"

"He would think that we have been—pals—for as long as we have known each other," said Bertrand soothingly. "He knows it already. It is true, is it not?"

But Chris's eyes had been opened too suddenly and tragically. Her sense of proportion was still undeveloped. "Yes, but he would never see it. You could never explain to him so that he would understand. He would think I had been deceiving him. He would think—Bertie, he would think"—her eyes dilated, and she drew in her breath sharply—"that—that you and I ought not to be friends any longer. Oh, don't tell him—please don't tell him. Indeed I am right. He trusts you, and—and he trusts me. But he wouldn't trust either of us any longer if he knew."

"Christine! Christine!"

"It is true," she asserted feverishly. "You don't know him as I do. Oh no, he has never been hard to me. But he could be hard. And he wouldn't forgive me—if he thought I had been hiding anything. Bertie, Bertie, you won't do it? Say you won't do it!"

"I do nothing without your consent," Bertrand answered quietly. "But I think that it is a mistake. I think—"

"Oh, thank you!" she broke in earnestly. "I know I can rely upon you to keep your word. I can, can't I?"

He smiled at a question which he would have borne from no other. "Until death, Christine," he said.

Her hands fell away from his arm. She was shaking all over. "I know I'm foolish," she said. "I can't help it. I was made so. And when Trevor begins to ask questions—" She broke off nervously. "What is that?"

A leisurely footfall sounded in the hall, a quiet hand pressed the electric switch by the door, and the room was flooded with light.

"Oh, don't!" Chris cried out sharply. "Don't!"

She put her hands over her face as if dazzled, and so stood quivering.

"What is it?" Mordaunt asked. "Did I startle you?"

He came to her. He drew her hands gently down. But she almost cowered before him, and he let her go.

"I think that she is tired," Bertrand said, his voice very low.

"Is that all?" Mordaunt asked, looking at him.

The Frenchman shrugged his shoulders, and made no reply. But Chris turned at the question, turned and confronted her husband with wide, scared eyes.

"Yes, I am tired," she said, speaking jerkily, breathlessly. "But—but I was startled too. I—I thought I heard Cinders—barking."

It was the first time she had ever deliberately lied to him, and her eyes met his full as she did it in desperate self-defence.

He looked at her very steadily for the space of several seconds after she had spoken, and in the silence Bertrand's hands clenched hard.

Quietly at length Mordaunt turned round to him. "Don't let me interrupt you," he said. "You were playing, weren't you? Chris and I are good listeners."

He took his wife's cold hand, and drew her to the sofa; and Bertrand, seeing there was nothing else to be done, turned back to the piano and resumed his playing.

Not another word was spoken by any of them until Noel came upon the scene, and airily dispelled the silence before he was aware of it.

CHAPTER IX
THE ENEMY MOVES

"And you mean to say that this French secretary of Trevor's actually lives in the house?" said Aunt Philippa.

"But of course he does," said Chris, opening her eyes wide.

"And is Trevor never away?" demanded Aunt Philippa.

"He hasn't been, but he talks of spending a night in town next week."

"And you will go with him?"

"No, I don't think so. It's too hot."

"Then I presume M. Bertrand will?"

Chris flushed a little. "I don't suppose so. He is feeling the heat too." She stretched up her hands above her head. "How I wish it would rain!"

Aunt Philippa continued her knitting severely in silence. They were sitting on the terrace awaiting the luncheon-hour. Across the garden came Noel's shrill whistle, and instinctively, before she remembered her aunt's presence, Chris answered it. The boy appeared at the farther end of the long lawn, and came racing towards them.

"Just seen the postman, Chris. Here's a letter for you—such a horrible fist, Sandacre post-mark, and sealed. Wonder who it's from?"

He leaned against her chair to recover his breath and regarded the envelope he held with frank interest.

Chris stretched up her hand for it. "I expect it's from Mrs. Pouncefort."

"Mrs. Pouncefort doesn't write like that!" protested Noel. "No woman could."

"May I have it?" said Chris.

He put it into her hand, but he still leaned against her chair. "Be quick and open it, I say! It looks important."

"I don't suppose it is," said Chris; but she opened it notwithstanding with some curiosity.

Aunt Philippa had arrived only the night before, but she was already very tired of her society, and any diversion was welcome.

"You don't mind?" she murmured to her aunt.

Her eyes were already upon the first page as she spoke. She frowned over the unfamiliar handwriting.

Noel studied it also over her shoulder. "What on earth—" he began.

She looked up suddenly, and crumpled the paper in her hand. "Noel, go away! How dare you!"

He stared at her in amazement. A sharp word from Chris was most unusual. Aunt Philippa looked up also.

"My dear girl, it isn't private, is it?" said Noel.

Chris was scarlet. She seemed to breathe with difficulty. "Of course it's private! All my letters are private!"

"But it comes from the Pounceforts," objected Noel. "I saw 'Sandacre Court' at the top of the page."

Chris sprang to her feet impetuously with blazing eyes. "And what if it does? You had no right to look over me. It was a hateful thing to do. What if it does come from Mrs. Pouncefort? Is it mine any the less for that?"

"Oh, don't get huffy!" remonstrated Noel. "Look at you! Anyone would think you had got the palsy. But you needn't pretend it's from Mrs. Pouncefort, because I know better."

"It—it is from Mrs. Pouncefort!" declared Chris.

"Which is a lie," rejoined Noel, with the utmost calmness. "I know you, my dear girl, I know you. You've told 'em before."

"Noel!" Aunt Philippa interposed her voice with extreme dignity. "You forget yourself. If you cannot speak with ordinary courtesy, be good enough to leave us."

Noel heeded the remonstrance no more than if it had been the buzzing of a fly. Chris's spark of temper had kindled his.

"Oh, you can swear it's the truth till all's blue," he declared, raising his voice recklessly. "But that doesn't make it so. In fact, it only makes the contrary all the more likely. Besides, you know you do lie, Chris, so you needn't deny it."

"Noel!"

It was not Aunt Philippa's voice this time, and it had in it so firm a note of authority that instinctively Noel turned.

Mordaunt, just returned from a ride, was standing in his shirt-sleeves at an open window above them. All the colour went out of Chris's face at sight of him, but he did not look at her.

"Come up here," he said to Noel. "I want to speak to you."

"Not coming," said Noel promptly.

"Come up here," Mordaunt repeated.

"What for?" Noel looked up at him, hands in pockets. "You'll be late for lunch if you don't buck up," he remarked, with a smile of cheery impudence.

His brother-in-law's face did not reflect his smile. It was grimly determined. "Come up here," he said again.

"Do go, Noel," Chris murmured uneasily.

"I won't," said Noel doggedly. "I'm not going to be pitched into for nothing. It was you who told the lie, not me."

"Oh, don't be absurd!" exclaimed Chris, in a fever of impatience. "Surely you're not afraid of him!"

"Anyone can see you are," retorted Noel. "I'll bet you daren't go yourself!"

She turned from him sharply without another word, and entered the house.

She met her husband on the threshold of his room, and pushed him impulsively back, her hands against his breast.

"Trevor, please don't be angry with him. He—we often go on like that. There is nothing to be angry about—indeed."

He took her hands and held them. She was panting a little; he waited while she recovered herself. Then, "Chris," he said very gently, "don't you think it is time you left off being afraid of me?"

"But when you are angry—" murmured Chris.

The Rocks Of Valpré | 235

"You have never seen me angry yet."

"You are not angry with Noel?" she asked quickly.

He smiled a little. "My dear child, Noel is no more capable of making me angry than that fly on the ceiling. But I am not going to have him behaving badly for all that."

"But he didn't," she urged, in distress. "It was all my fault. Trevor— Trevor, please don't say any more! He was quite right. I—I didn't tell the truth."

She made the confession in a broken whisper, with her face hidden against him. But a moment later she had sprung away in haste, for there came the clatter of careless feet upon the stairs, and Noel dashed suddenly upon the scene.

"Oh, I say, do stop jawing and come down," he said as he presented himself. "Poor Aunt Phil is ravenous for her lunch. What do you want me for, Trevor?"

But Mordaunt turned his back abruptly. "I don't want you now," he said. "You can go."

"Dash it!" Noel said. "What a rotter you are!" He flung himself full length upon the window-seat with elaborate nonchalance. "Run along, Chris," he said. "We're going to talk politics. Shut the door after you. That's right. Now, my good brother-in-law, what can I do for you?"

He sat up to slay a wasp on the window-pane, flicked the corpse in Mordaunt's direction with airy adroitness, and lay down again.

"Are you in a wax over anything?" he inquired, with a yawn.

Mordaunt turned quietly round. "Get up!" he said.

Noel laughed up at him engagingly. "You can't kick me so easily lying down, can you? But what do you want to kick me for? I'm quite harmless."

"I am not going to kick you," Mordaunt said. "It is not my way."

"All right, then. Why didn't you say so before?" Noel sat up and regarded him with interest. "Well?" he said at the end of an expectant pause. "Let's have it, man, and have done!"

"I have nothing to give you," Mordaunt returned. "I told you you could go."

Something in the tone rather than the words caught Noel's attention. He bounced suddenly from his lounging attitude to Mordaunt's side, and thrust an affectionate arm about his shoulders.

"What's the matter, old chap? You look as if you had found sixpence and lost half a crown."

"Perhaps I have," Mordaunt returned grimly.

He did not repulse the friendly overture; that also was not his way. But neither did he respond to it. He stood passive, looking out over the park with unobservant eyes.

"Cheer up, I say," urged Noel. "You're such a rattling good chap, you know. I'm getting awfully fond of you."

"Much obliged," said Mordaunt; but he did not seem highly gratified. In fact, his thoughts were plainly elsewhere.

Noel, however, would not be satisfied with this. "What are you grizzling about?" he said. "Tell a fellow!"

Mordaunt's eyes came down to him. "I wish you Wyndhams had a little sense of honour," he said.

"Oh, is that it?" said Noel. "Well, we are not top-heavy in that respect, I own. But, after all, it's not worth worrying about. We get on very nicely without it. And we wouldn't any of us sell a friend."

"I'm glad to know you draw the line somewhere," Mordaunt observed.

"Oh, rather! I wouldn't chouse you for the world. Chris wouldn't either. But we're both shy of you, you know, because you're so beastly moral." He gave his brother-in-law a warm hug to soften the effect of his words. "You may as well tell me what you wanted to say to me just now," he remarked.

"I was going to request you to behave like a gentleman," Mordaunt returned. "But as you don't seem to know what that means—" He paused, looking straight into the Irish eyes that met his with such sublime assurance. "Do you know what it means, Noel?" he asked.

Noel grinned. "You can take me in hand and teach me if it isn't too much trouble. I suppose you didn't like me to tell Chris she was lying about that letter. But she was, you know. There's no getting away from that fact, even if she is your wife."

"I'm not trying to get away from facts," Mordaunt said. "But I do object—strongly—to discourtesy. You may be her brother, but that doesn't entitle you to insult her. Plainly, I won't have it from you or anyone."

"I didn't insult her," declared Noel. "I only said I knew she was telling a cram. She knew it too."

"I know what you said," Mordaunt returned with brevity. "And you are not to say it again. Also, I must ask you to bear in mind that when I say a thing I mean it—invariably. I've had more than enough disobedience from you lately."

"Oh, I say," said Noel, winking gaily, "you don't want much, do you?"

Mordaunt relaxed a little. He put his hand on the boy's shoulder for a moment. "You can be quite a good chap if you try," he said.

Noel responded like a dog to a caress. "The mischief is to keep it up," he said. "But we won't quarrel anyhow. I'll make every allowance for you, old boy, for you're in a beastly unhealthy position; and you'll have to do the same—savvy? But for all that, that letter was no more written by Mrs. Pouncefort than by the man in the moon."

"That letter," Mordaunt said very deliberately, "is neither your affair nor mine."

Could he have seen Chris at that moment he might have changed his mind upon that point, but her young brother's careless chatter kept him from seeking her; nor would he very readily have found her had he done so.

For Chris was securely locked in a little room at the top of the house that had been her childhood's bedroom, and here with blanched face and hands that shook she was reading and reading again the letter that had given rise to so much discussion.

The handwriting was cramped and erratic, wholly unfamiliar, barely decipherable; but she had mastered the contents with tragic dexterity. Her understanding had leaped to the words.

"MY DEAR MRS. MORDAUNT," so went the letter, "You have probably forgotten my existence by this time, and it is with the utmost humility that I venture to recall it to your memory. For myself, it will always be a lasting pleasure to have met you again, and the fact that I share with you a secret of other days cannot but prove a bond between us. That secret I am prepared to guard faithfully, since—apparently—it is of value, if you on your part are ready to purchase my discretion with that of which all have need, but of which I temporarily am unhappily deficient. Briefly, madame, for the sum of five hundred pounds I will undertake that the episode of Valpré shall be consigned to oblivion so far as I am concerned. Otherwise, the strict husband may hear more than you have considered it convenient to tell him.

"Yours, with many compliments,
GUILLAUME RODOLPHE."

CHAPTER X
A WARNING VOICE

Five hundred pounds! Five hundred pounds! It represented her year's income to Chris.

All night long she lay wide-eyed and still, facing her problem with a quaking heart. It was like a suffocating weight upon her, crushing her down. Five hundred pounds! And the need thereof so urgent that it must be dealt with at once! But how to obtain it? How? How?

All through the dark hours she lay revolving the matter, questioning this way and that, bound hand and foot, yet not daring to contemplate the only sane means at her disposal of obtaining freedom. To tell her husband the simple truth, to throw herself unreservedly upon his generosity, to beg his forgiveness and his help—these were the things she could not do. As a matter of fact the truth had been so magnified by her fevered fancy that it had begun to appear monstrous even in her own eyes. Those far-off happenings at Valpré had become a dream with a nightmare ending. Not even Aunt Philippa could have distorted them to a more exaggerated semblance of evil. And to go to her husband now with such a story was utterly beyond Chris's powers of accomplishment. She lacked the courage to speak with simplicity and candour, and she was painfully aware that to give a halting account of the matter would be infinitely more dangerous than to keep silence. Already her husband's faith in her veracity had been shaken. Was it likely that he would accept unquestioning her assurance that this matter, which she had rigorously suppressed for so long and which she only imparted to him now under compulsion, was in reality one of trivial importance? Would he believe her? Had she ever fostered his belief in her? Could he in reason do so even if he desired?

Moreover, there was another obstacle. There was Bertrand. Though he had offered to speak for her, though he had desired to explain all, and though she knew that Trevor's faith in him was absolute, yet the presence of Bertrand in itself made candour impossible. Why this should be she did not know. It was a problem which she had not attempted to solve. But the fact remained. She dreaded unspeakably the possibility of having to describe the intimacy that had existed between herself and Bertrand in the old, free, Valpré days. She dreaded the keen searching of the grey eyes that, if they sought long enough, were bound to find her soul, and not only to find, but to enter it, to penetrate to its most hidden corner, and to draw out into the full light of day one of her most sacred possessions. She felt that she could not bear this probing. The very thought of it was horrible to her, and in connection with it the steady scrutiny of her husband's eyes became almost a thing abhorrent. Vaguely she knew, without realizing, that she cherished deep in that inmost shrine something which he must never see, something that it would be agony to show him, something that even now gnawed secretly at her quivering heart. She always shrank from his direct look, though she would not have him know it. The calm, level gaze frightened her, she knew not why. Perhaps the secret of all her fear of him lay hidden in this problem that she dared not face.

No, she could not endure a full revelation of the truth. Bertrand had declared that Mordaunt could not discover what was non-existent, but it was not this that Chris feared. It was something infinitely more terrible, a floating suspicion that might harden into actual fact at any moment.

And so her whole being was concentrated upon avoiding the catastrophe that instinct warned her to be impending. Everything hung upon the keeping of that secret which once had seemed to her so small a thing. It had grown to mighty proportions of late. She did not ask herself wherefore; but once in the night she smiled a piteous little smile at the recollection of Manon, the maid-of-all-work, and her story of the spell that bound all who entered the Magic Cave. She remembered how she had laughed over it; but Bertrand had not laughed. He had been quite grave; she remembered that also. He had even spoken as if he believed in it. For a little her thoughts dwelt upon that night, on the quick confidences he had poured out, on her own consternation over the nature of his enterprise, on the words he had uttered then to comfort her. She had never given them much thought before. To-night, lying by her husband's side, they returned to her, and for the first time she pondered them seriously. He had dismissed ambition and success, even the strife of nations, at a breath. He had been able to do so even then, when he was nearing the summit of his aspirations. "What are they?" he had said. "Only a procession that marches under the windows, only a dream in the midst of a great Reality."

What had he meant by that? she asked herself, and searched her memory for more. It came with a curious vividness, a winged message, straight and sure as an arrow. "We look out above them," he had said, "you and I" —

suddenly she heard the very thrill of his voice, and it pierced her through and through—"to the great heaven and the sun; and we know that that is life—the Spark Eternal that nothing can ever quench." Chris did not ask herself the meaning of that. She hid it away in her heart, quickly, quickly, lest seeing she should also understand.

It was very early in the morning when she slipped out of bed, and crept to the open window to watch the stars fade into the dawning. She would have liked to pray, but no prayer occurred to her. And so she knelt quite passive, gazing forth over the dim garden, too tired to think any longer, yet too miserable to sleep. She did not know that her husband's eyes gravely watched her throughout her vigil, and when presently she lay down again she still believed him to be sleeping.

In the morning inspiration came to Chris. She believed Rupert to be out of debt, thanks to Trevor's generosity. She would get him to raise the money for her. She knew he must have ways and means of so doing which were quite beyond her reach. At least, it seemed her only resource, and she would try it.

"Are you quite well, Chris?" her husband asked her when he rose at an early hour, as was his custom.

"Quite," said Chris. "Why?"

She looked at him nervously with heavy-lidded eyes.

He bent to kiss her before leaving the room. "Don't get up yet," he said kindly. "Stay in bed and have a sleep."

"But I—I have slept," she stammered.

He put the hair gently back from her forehead. "I know all about it," he said.

She started away from him in sheer panic. "About what?" she gasped, in a whisper; then, seeing his brows go up, "Oh, Trevor, I—I'm sorry. No, I haven't slept very well. But—"

"I thought not," he interposed quietly. "Well, sleep now, dear."

He turned to go, but impulsively she caught his hand, held it a moment, then suddenly put it to her lips. But she would not look at him, would not even raise her eyes again; and he, after the briefest pause, withdrew his hand, touched her cheek with it lightly, and so left her.

When they met again at the breakfast-table she was discussing with Aunt Philippa the best means of spending the day. Bertrand was not present.

He usually took chocolate at that hour in Mordaunt's room, where he could continue his secretarial work uninterrupted. Noel was not yet down.

Chris turned at once to address her husband. "I have had a line from Max. He is coming down for a few days I think he hasn't been well—overworking, he says."

"I can scarcely believe," said Aunt Philippa, with her acid smile, "that a Wyndham could ever suffer from that complaint."

"They don't over-rest, anyhow," said Mordaunt, with a glance at his wife's tired face. "I shall be very pleased to see him, Chris. Write and tell him so."

"I don't think I need write," she said. "He will be here this afternoon. Shall I ask Rupert to come over and dine, so that we can all be together— that is, if Aunt Philippa doesn't mind?"

"Pray do not consider me," said Aunt Philippa.

"Do exactly as you like," said Mordaunt quietly. "Rupert is always welcome so far as I am concerned."

Chris rose from the table as he sat down. "I will send him a note at once if I may, or I shall miss the post."

"Have you had any breakfast?" he asked, detaining her as she passed his chair.

"None at all," said Aunt Philippa.

"Oh, Aunt Philippa, I have, indeed!" protested Chris, colouring vividly. "Besides, I'm not hungry."

"Besides!" echoed Mordaunt, faintly smiling. "Drink a cup of hot milk before you go."

She made a wry face. "I can't. I hate it. Please don't keep me!"

"Then do as you are told," he said. "I thought I ordered you to stay in bed."

"Oh, don't be absurd!" said Chris; but she went back to her place and poured out the milk as he desired.

"Now drink it," he said, with his eyes upon her.

She obeyed him without further protest, finally setting the cup down with a sigh of relief.

Mordaunt rose to open the door. "You are not to do anything energetic to-day," he said.

She threw him a smile, half-shy, half-wistful, and departed without replying.

He turned back into the room and sat down. "I am not quite satisfied about Chris," he said.

"Neither am I," said Aunt Philippa, with unexpected severity.

He looked at her with awakened attention. "No?" he said courteously.

"No." Very decidedly came Aunt Philippa's reply. "I intended to speak to you upon the subject, my dear Trevor, and I am glad that an early opportunity for so doing has presented itself."

"You think she looks ill?" Mordaunt asked.

"Not at all," said Aunt Philippa. "The intense heat we have had lately is quite sufficient to account for her jaded looks. She has probably also been fretting unreasonably over the death of her dog. I believe that animal was the only thing in the world she ever really cared for."

Mordaunt rested his chin on his hand, and looked at her thoughtfully. "Indeed!" he said.

Neither his voice nor his face expressed anything whatever beyond a decorous gravity. Aunt Philippa began to feel slightly exasperated.

"She will get over that," she said, with a confidence that held more of contempt than tolerance. "None of the Wyndhams are fundamentally capable of taking anything seriously for long. You must have discovered their instability for yourself by this time."

"Not with respect to Chris." Was there a hint of sternness underlying the placidity of the rejoinder? There might have been, but Aunt Philippa was too intent upon the matter she had taken in hand to notice it.

"Oh, well," she said, "you haven't been married six weeks yet, have you? You will see what I mean sooner or later. But you may take it from me that all of them—Chris included—are without an atom of solidity in their composition. I warn you, Trevor, very seriously; they are not to be depended upon."

Mordaunt heard her without changing his position. His eyes looked straight at her from under lids that never stirred. "Is that what you have to say to me?" he asked, after a moment.

"It leads to what I have to say," returned Aunt Philippa with dignity.

She was quite in her element now, and enjoying herself far too thoroughly to be lightly disconcerted.

"Pray finish!" he said.

That gave her momentary pause. "I am speaking solely for your welfare," she told him.

"I do not question it," he returned.

Yet even she was aware that his stillness was not all the outcome of courteous attention. There was about it a restraint which made itself felt, as it were, in spite of him, a dominance which she set down to his forceful personality.

"The subject upon which I chiefly desire to speak a word of warning," she said, "is the presence in the house—the constant presence—of your young French secretary."

"Yes?" said Mordaunt.

He betrayed no surprise, but the word fell curtly, as if he found himself face to face with an unpleasant task and desired to be through with it as quickly as possible.

Aunt Philippa proceeded with just a hint of caution. "My dear Trevor, surely you are aware of the danger!"

"What danger?"

A difficult question, which Aunt Philippa answered with diplomacy. "Chris was always something of a flirt."

"Indeed!" said Mordaunt again.

His manner was so non-committal that Aunt Philippa began to lose her patience. "I should have thought that fact was patent to everyone."

"Never to me," said Chris's husband very deliberately.

Aunt Philippa smiled. "Then you are remarkably blind, my dear Trevor. Flightiness has been her chief characteristic all her life. If you have not yet found that out, I fear she must be deceitful as well."

"I am not discussing my wife's character," Mordaunt made answer very steadily.

"You prefer to shut your eyes to the obvious," said Aunt Philippa, beginning to be aware of something formidable in her path but not quite grasping its magnitude.

"I prefer my own estimate of her to that of anyone else," he made quiet reply.

Aunt Philippa made a slight gesture of uneasiness. The steady gaze was becoming a hard thing to meet. Had the man been less phlegmatic, she could almost have imagined him to be in a white heat of anger. He was so unnaturally quiet, his whole being concentrated, as it were, in a composure that she could not but feel to be ominous.

It was with an effort that the woman who sat facing him resumed her self-appointed task. "That I can well understand," she said. "But even so, I think you should bear in mind that Chris is young—and frail. You are not justified in exposing her to temptation."

"As how?"

Aunt Philippa hesitated for the first time in actual perturbation.

Mordaunt waited immovably.

"I think," she said at length, "that you would be very ill-advised if you went to town and left her here—thrown entirely upon her own resources."

"May I ask if you are still referring to my secretary?" he said.

She bent her head. "I have never approved of her being upon such intimate terms with him. She treats him as if—as if—"

"As if he were her brother," said Mordaunt quietly. "I do the same. I have many friends, but he is the one man in the world who possesses my entire confidence. For that reason I foster their friendship, for I know it to be a good thing. For that reason, if I were dying, I would confidently leave her in his care."

"My dear Trevor, the man has bewitched you!" protested Aunt Philippa.

His eyes fell away from her at last, and she was conscious of distinct relief, mingled with a most unwonted tinge of humiliation.

"I am obliged to you," he said formally, "for taking the trouble to warn me. But you need never do so again. Believe me, I am not blind; and Chris is safe in my care."

He rose with the words, and went to the sideboard for his breakfast. Here he remained for some time with his back turned, but when he finally came back to the table there was no trace of even suppressed agitation about him.

He sat down and began to eat with a perfectly normal demeanour. The silence, however, remained unbroken until Noel burst tempestuously into the room. No silence ever outlasted his appearance.

He flung his arms round his brother-in-law and embraced him warmly, with a friendly, "Hullo, you greedy beggar! Hope you haven't gobbled up everything! I'm confoundedly hungry. Morning, Aunt Philippa! I suppose you fed long ago? It's a disgusting habit, isn't it? But one we can't dispense with at present. Where's Chris?"

"Chris," said Aunt Philippa icily, "has already breakfasted, and so have I."

She moved towards the door as she spoke. Noel sprang with alacrity to open it, and bowed to the floor behind her retreating form.

"She looks like a dying duck in a thunderstorm," he observed, as he returned to the table. "What have you been doing to her? Has there been a thunderstorm?"

Mordaunt met his inquiring eyes without a smile. "Noel," he said, "if you can't be courteous to your aunt and your sister, I won't have you at the table at all—or in the house for that matter."

Noel uttered a long whistle. "I thought I smelt the reek of battle in the air! What's up? Anything exciting?"

"Do you understand me?" Mordaunt said, sticking to his point.

Noel broke into smiles. "Oh, perfectly, my dear chap! You're as simple as the Book of Common Prayer. But it would be a pity to kick me out of the house, you know. You'd miss me—horribly."

Mordaunt leaned back in his chair. "Then I'll give you a sound caning instead."

Noel nodded vigorous approval. "Much more suitable. I like you better every day. So does Chris. I believe she'll be in love with you before long."

"Really?" said Mordaunt.

"Yes, really." Noel was munching complacently between his words. "I never thought you'd do it. The odds were dead against you. She only married you to get away from Aunt Philippa. Of course you know that?"

"Really?" Mordaunt said again. He was not apparently paying much attention to the boy's chatter.

"Yes, really," Noel reiterated, with a grin. "It's solid, simple, sordid fact. The only chap she ever seriously cared about was a little beast of a Frenchman she chummed up with years ago at Valpré. I never met the beggar myself, but I'm sure he was a beast. But I'll bet she'd have married him if she'd had the chance. They were as thick as thieves."

At this point Mordaunt opened the morning paper with a bored expression, and straightway immersed himself in its contents.

Noel turned his attention to his breakfast, which he dispatched with astonishing rapidity, finally remarking, as he rose: "But you never can tell what a woman will do when it comes to the point—unless she's a suffragette, in which case she may be safely relied on to make a howling donkey of herself for all time."

CHAPTER XI
A BROKEN REED

"But, my good girl, five hundred pounds!" Rupert looked down at his sister with an expression half-humorous, half-dismayed. "What do you think I'm made of?" he inquired.

She stood before him, nervously clasping and unclasping her hands. "I must have it! I must have it!" she said piteously. "I thought you might be able to raise it on something."

"But not on nothing," said Rupert.

"I would pay it back," she urged. "I could begin to pay back almost at once."

"Why on earth don't you ask Trevor for it?" he said. "He's the proper person to go to."

"Oh, I know," she answered. "And so I would for anything else, but not for this—not for this! He would ask questions, questions I couldn't possibly answer. And—oh, I couldn't—I couldn't!"

"What have you been up to?" said Rupert curiously.

"Nothing—nothing whatever. I've done nothing wrong." Chris almost wrung her hands in her agitation. "But I can't tell you or anyone what I want it for. Oh, Rupert, you will help me! I know you will!"

"Steady!" said Rupert. "Don't get hysterical, my child. That won't serve anybody's turn. I suppose you've been extravagant, and daren't own up. Trevor is a bit of a Tartar, I own. But five hundred pounds! It's utterly beyond my reach."

"Couldn't you borrow it from someone?" pleaded Chris. "Rupert, it's only for a time. I'll pay back a little every month. And you have so many friends."

Rupert made a grimace. "All of whom know me far too well to lend me money. No, that cock won't fight. I've a hundred debts of my own waiting to be settled. Trevor wasn't disposed to be over-generous the last time I approached him. At least, he was generous, but he wasn't particularly encouraging. He's such a rum beggar, and I have my own reasons for not wanting to go to him again at present."

"Of course you couldn't go to him for this," said Chris. "But—Rupert, if you could only help me in this matter, I would do all I could for you. I would give you every farthing I could spare, indeed—indeed. I might even ask him for a little later on—not yet, of course, but by and bye, if I saw an opportunity. Oh, you don't know what it means to me—how much depends upon it."

"Why don't you tell me?" Rupert asked.

"Because I can't—I daren't!" Chris laid imploring hands upon his shoulders; her eyes besought him. "Dear Rupert, it isn't that I don't trust you. Don't think that! But it wouldn't do any good if you knew, and I simply can't talk about it. I've shown how much I trust you by asking you to help me out of my trouble. There is no one else in the world that I could ask—not even Max. He would make me tell him everything. But you won't, dear; I know you won't, will you?"

It was impossible not to be moved by her earnest pleading. Rupert slipped an arm around her. "You needn't be afraid of me," he said.

"I know I needn't," she answered, laying her cheek against him with a quick gesture of confidence. "And I am of everyone else—even of Bertie. It's absurd, isn't it? Fancy being afraid of Bertie!" She smiled through tears.

"He doesn't know, then?" said Rupert.

"Bertie? No, no, of course not! I wouldn't have him know for the world. He would go and do—something desperate." Chris's startled eyes testified to her dread of this contingency. "No, I haven't dared to tell anyone, except you. If you can't help me, there's no one left. I—I shall run away and drown myself."

"Oh, nonsense!" said Rupert. "There's a way out of every difficulty if one has the wit to find it. Keep cool, my dear girl! If you let yourself go, you will give your own show away."

"I know! I know!" gasped Chris. "But what can I do? It would kill me if Trevor knew!"

Rupert's arm tightened protectingly about her. At least they stood by each other, these Wyndhams. "Then Trevor mustn't know," he rejoined. "I'll manage it somehow if it's humanly possible. You must let me think it over. And in the meantime, for goodness' sake, keep cool. If Trevor were to see you now, he would know there was something up directly."

As a matter of fact, he himself had never seen his sister so agitated before. She was like a terrified bird in a trap. What on earth had she been doing? he wondered. What made her go in such abject fear of her husband that the very mention of his name was enough to send every vestige of colour from her face?

He grasped her trembling fingers reassuringly. "There! Leave it to me," he said. "I'll find a way out, never fear. I've been in a good many tight corners in my time, but I've always wriggled out somehow. I suppose you want the money soon?"

"At once," said Chris.

He made a grimace, as of one swallowing a nauseous draught. "All right, you shall have it. Now, don't worry any more. It's going to be all right." He patted her shoulder kindly. "Only, for Heaven's sake, don't do it again!"

She shivered, and turned away to hide her quivering lips. "If—if you can get me the money this once," she said, "I—I'll never ask you again, and I'll give you every farthing—every farthing—"

"My dear child, I don't want your farthings," responded Rupert cheerily. "If you can make it fifty pounds now, I shall be quite grateful. But I'll get you yours first, never mind how. Now, hadn't we better go back to the rest? Aunt Philippa will be wondering what we are conspiring about. By the way, when does she depart?"

"Soon, I hope," said Chris fervently.

He grinned. "Had enough of her, eh? So, I should imagine, has Trevor. He is keener on giving advice than taking it, if I know anything about him."

"She wouldn't dare to give Trevor advice," protested Chris.

"Ho! wouldn't she?" He laughed derisively, as they turned to leave the little room in the roof that was her refuge, but paused at the door to slip his arm through hers. "You're not to worry, young 'un," he said, with a patronage that did not veil concern. "Do you know you're looking downright ill?"

She smiled up at him wistfully. "Things have been pretty horrid lately. But I won't worry any more if—if you tell me I needn't."

"You needn't," he said, and impulsively he stooped and kissed her. He had always had a protecting tenderness for his little sister.

They descended to the drawing-room to find Aunt Philippa writing letters in solitary state. The rest of the company, with the exception of Mordaunt, who was at work in his own room, were in the billiard-room just beyond, and Chris and Rupert repaired thither, relieved to make their escape so easily.

They found Bertrand, who was an expert player, making a long break. He was playing against Max, whose opinion of him was obviously rising with this display of skill.

He was engaged upon a most difficult stroke when Chris entered, and she stopped behind him lest she should disturb his aim. But he turned round at once to her, leaving the balls untouched.

"*Mais non!*" he declared lightly. "I cannot play with my back to my hostess. It is an affair *très difficile,* and I must have everything in my favour."

"Oh, don't let me spoil your luck!" she said.

She came and stood at the end of the table to watch him.

"That would not be possible," he protested, as he applied himself again to the ball.

He achieved the stroke with that finish and dexterity that marked all he did.

"Oh, I say!" said Noel disgustedly. "You haven't a look-in, Max. He plays like a machine."

"You like not to be beaten by a Frenchman, no?" laughed Bertrand. "*Il faut que les anglais soient toujours, toujours les premiers, hein?*" He stopped suddenly, for Chris had made the faintest movement, as if his words had touched some chord of memory. He flashed her a swift look, and the smile died out of his face. He moved round the table, and again stooped to his stroke. "But what is success after all," he said, "and what is failure?"

"You ought to know," Max observed dryly, as again he made his point.

The Frenchman straightened himself. There was something of kinship between these two, a tacit sympathy that had taken root on the night of Chris's birthday, an understanding that called for no explanation.

"Yes," he said, with a quick nod, "I know them both. They are worth just—that." He snapped his fingers in the air. "They pass like"—he hesitated a moment, then ended with deliberation—"like pictures in the sand."

"The same remark applies to most things," said Rupert.

Bertrand glanced at him. "To all but one, monsieur," he said, in a queer tone that was almost tinged with irony.

Again he bent himself to a stroke with a quick, light grace, as though he regarded success as a foregone conclusion.

"Look at that!" said Noel in dejection, as the ball cannoned triumphantly down the table. "The gods are all on his side."

The stroke was a brilliant one, but Bertrand did not immediately straighten himself as before. He remained leaning across the table, as if he watched the effect of his skill.

There was a brief pause before very carefully he laid his cue upon the cloth and began to raise himself, slowly, with infinite caution, using both hands.

"No," he said, speaking jerkily, in a rapid undertone, as if to himself. "The gods—are no more—on my side."

A sharp gasp escaped him. He stood up, and they saw the sweat running down his forehead. "Will you—excuse me for a moment?" he said. "I have—forgotten *quelque chose.*"

He turned towards Chris with punctilious courtesy, clicked his heels together, bowed, and walked stiffly from the room.

CHAPTER XII
A MAN OF HONOUR

An amazed silence followed his exit; then, in a quick whisper, Chris spoke.

"He isn't well. I'm sure he isn't well. Did you see—his face—when he stood up?"

She turned with the words as if she would go after him, but Max checked her sharply. "No, you stay here. I'm going."

She paused irresolute. "Let me come too."

"Don't be silly," said Max. He frowned at her scared face for a moment, then smiled abruptly. "Don't be silly!" he said again. He passed down the room with what seemed to her maddening deliberation, opened the door, and went quietly out.

Aunt Philippa was still busy with her correspondence in the drawing-room. She glanced up as he went through. "Can you tell me what time the evening post goes out? I have just asked M. Bertrand, but he did not see fit to answer me."

"Then he couldn't have heard you," said Max. "The post goes out at nine-thirty."

"Ah! Then perhaps you would wait a moment while I direct this envelope, and you can then give it to a servant with orders to take it to the post-office at once."

Max drew his red brows together and waited.

The scratching of Aunt Philippa's pen filled in the pause. She directed her envelope, blotted it with care, stamped it with precision, finally handed it to her nephew with the request, "Please remember that it is important."

Max received it with reverence. "I shall treat it with the utmost veneration," he said. He knew that his aunt had a strong dislike for him, and he fostered it with much enjoyment upon every possible occasion.

He slipped the letter into his pocket as he left the room and promptly dismissed it from his mind.

He turned aside into the dining-room, rummaged for brandy and found it, and went with noiseless speed upstairs.

The door of Bertrand's room was unlatched, and he pushed it open without ceremony. Blank darkness met him on the threshold, but a sound within told him the room was tenanted. He switched on the light without delay, entered, and shut the door.

He found Bertrand seated huddled on the edge of his bed, gasping horribly for breath. He did not apparently hear Max enter. His close-cropped head was bowed upon his arms. His hands were opening and closing convulsively. He rocked to and fro almost with violence, but no sound beyond his spasmodic breathing escaped him.

Max set down the brandy and took him by the shoulders. "Look here," he said, "lie down. I'll help you."

Bertrand started a little at his touch, and Max had a glimpse of his tortured face as he glanced up. "*Fermez la porte!*" he said, in a choked whisper.

The door was already shut. Max wheeled and turned the key. "Now!" he said.

He stooped over the Frenchman, and with the utmost care lifted him back on to the pillows, unfastened his collar, then turned to fling the windows as wide as they would go. The night air, fragrant with rain, blew in, rustling the curtains. Bertrand turned his face towards it instinctively. His lips were blue; they worked painfully, as if, between his gasping, he were still trying to speak.

"Keep still!" Max said.

He mixed some brandy and water, and returning, slipped his arm under the pillow. "Don't exert yourself," he said. "I'll do it all."

Very steadily he held the glass for Bertrand to drink. He could take but very little at a time, so agonized was his struggle for breath. Max waited through each pause, closely watching the drawn face, never missing his opportunity. And gradually that little took effect. The anguish died out of Bertrand's eyes, and he lay still.

Max slipped his arm from beneath the pillow and stood up. "Don't move," he said. "You're getting better."

"You—will stay—with me?" whispered Bertrand.

"Yes."

He drew up a chair, and sat down, took the Frenchman's wrist between his fingers, and so remained for a long time.

Bertrand lay with closed eyes, his breathing still short and occasionally difficult, but no longer agonized.

There came the sound of flying feet along the corridor, and an impatient hand hammered on the door.

"Hullo, Bertrand! Are you all right? Chris wants to know," shouted a boyish voice.

Bertrand started violently, and a quiver of pain went through him. He fixed his eyes imploringly on Max, who instantly rose to the occasion.

"Of course he's all right. You clear out! We're busy."

"What are you doing?" Keen curiosity sounded in Noel's voice.

"Never mind! We don't want you," came the brotherly rejoinder.

"But I say—"

"Clear out!" ordered Max. "Go and tell Chris that Bertrand is writing a letter to catch the post; which reminds me," he added grimly, "you can also tell Holmes to come and fetch it in a quarter of an hour. Don't forget now. It's important."

He pulled the letter entrusted to his keeping from his pocket and tossed it on to the table.

Noel departed, and with an effort Bertrand spoke.

"But that was not the truth."

"Near enough," responded the second Wyndham complacently. "That is, if you don't want everyone to know."

Bertrand's brows contracted. "No—no! I would not that your sister should know, or Mr. Mordaunt."

"They will have to sooner or later," observed Max.

"Then—let it be later," murmured Bertrand.

Again there fell a silence, during which he seemed to be collecting his strength, for when he spoke again it was with more firmness.

"Mr. Wyndham!"

"All right, you can call me Max. I'm listening," said Max.

Bertrand faintly smiled. That touch of good-fellowship pleased him. Young as he was, this boy somehow made him feel that he understood many things.

"Then, Max," he said, "I think that you know already that which I am going to say to you. However, it is better to say it. It is not possible that I shall live very long."

He paused, but Max said nothing. He sat, still holding Bertrand's wrist, his gaze upon the opposite wall.

"You knew it, no?" Bertrand questioned.

"I suspected it," Max said. He turned slightly and looked at the man upon the bed. "This isn't your first attack," he said.

Bertrand shuddered irrepressibly. "Nor my second," he said.

"I can give you something to ease the pain," Max said. "But if you're wise you will consult a doctor."

Again a faint smile flickered over Bertrand's face. "I am not enough wise," he said, "to desire to prolong my life under these conditions."

"I should say the same myself," observed Max somewhat curtly.

He offered no further advice, but sat on, waiting apparently for further developments.

After a little Bertrand proceeded. "I have known now for some time that this malady was incurable. I think that I would not have it otherwise, for I am very tired. I am old too—much older than even you can comprehend. I have undergone the suffering of a lifetime, and I am too tired to suffer much more. But—look you, Max—I do not want to make suffer those my friends whom I shall leave behind. That is why I pray that the end may come quick—quick. And, till then—I will bear my pain alone."

"And if you can't?" said Max. "If it gets too much for you?"

"The good God will give me strength," the Frenchman said steadfastly.

Max shrugged his shoulders. "It's your affair, not mine. But I don't see why you shouldn't tell Trevor. He will be hurt by and bye if you don't."

But Bertrand instantly negatived the suggestion. "He is already much—much too good to me. I cannot—I will not—be further indebted to him. My services are almost nominal now. Also"—he paused—"if I tell him, I cannot remain here longer, and—I have made a promise that for the present I will remain."

Max's shrewd eyes took another quick look at him. "For Chris's benefit, I suppose?" he said, and though his tone was a question, it scarcely sounded as if he expected an answer.

Bertrand's eyes met his for an instant in a single lightning glance of interrogation. They fell again immediately, and there followed a considerable pause before he made reply: "I do not abandon my friends when they are troubled and they have need of me."

"Does Chris need you?" Max asked ruthlessly.

Again that swift glance shooting upwards; again a lengthy pause. Then, "*Vous avez la vue perçante,*" Bertrand remarked in a low tone.

"I can't help seeing things," Max returned. "I suppose it's my speciality. I knew you were in love with her from the first moment I saw you."

Bertrand made a slight movement, as if the crude statement hurt him; but he answered quite quietly, "You have divined a secret which is known to none other. I confide it to your honourable keeping."

The corners of Max's mouth went down. He looked as if he were on the verge of making some ironical rejoinder, but he restrained it, merely asking, "Are you sure that no one else knows it?"

"You mean—?" The words came sharply this time; Bertrand's eyes searched his face with keen anxiety.

"Chris herself," Max said.

"*La petite Christine! Ma foi, no!* She has never known!" Bertrand's reply was instant and held unshaken conviction.

"You seem very sure of that," Max observed.

"I am sure. Also"—a queer little smile of tenderness touched Bertrand's drawn face—"she never will know now."

"Meaning you will never tell her?" Max said.

"Me, I will die first!" Bertrand answered simply.

Max grunted. "Women have an awkward knack of finding things out without being told," he observed.

"She will never discover this while I live," Bertrand answered. "I am her friend—the friend of her childhood—nothing more than that."

"But if she did find out?" Max said.

"She will not."

"But—suppose it for a moment—if she did?" He stuck to his point doggedly, plainly determined to get an answer.

"In that case I should depart at once," Bertrand answered.

"Yes, and where would you go to?"

Bertrand was silent.

"You would go back to London and starve?" Max persisted.

"Perhaps." Bertrand spoke as though the matter were one of indifference to him. "It would not be for long," he said rather dreamily.

"Oh, rot!" Max's rejoinder was intentionally vehement. "Look here," he said, as Bertrand looked at him in surprise, "you can't go on like that. It's too damned foolish. If, for any reason, you do leave this place, you must have some plan of action. You can't let yourself drift."

"No?" Bertrand still looked surprised.

"No," Max returned vigorously. "Now listen to me, Bertrand. If I am to keep quiet about this illness of yours, you have got to make me a promise."

Bertrand raised his brows interrogatively.

"Just this," Max said, "that if you find yourself at a loose end, you will come to me."

Bertrand looked quizzical. "A loose end?" he questioned.

"You know what it means all right," Max returned sternly. "Is it a promise?"

"That I come to you if I need a friend?" amended Bertrand. "But—why should I do that?"

"Because I am a friend if you like," said Max bluntly.

Bertrand's hand closed hard upon his. "I have—no words," he said, in a voice from which all banter had departed.

Max gripped the hand. "Then it's a promise?"

Bertrand hesitated.

"You have no choice," Max reminded him. "And if you will come to me I can find a way to help you. It wouldn't even be difficult. And you would have skilled nursing and attention. Come, it's either that or Trevor will have to be told. He'll see that you don't go back to starve in the streets."

"I will not have Mr. Mordaunt told," Bertrand said quickly and firmly.

"Then you will give me this promise," Max returned immovably.

With a gesture of helplessness the Frenchman yielded. "*Eh bien*, I promise."

"Good!" said Max. He laid Bertrand's hand down and rose.

Yet a moment he stood above him, looking downwards. "You keep your promises, eh?" he asked abruptly.

Bertrand flushed. "I am a man of honour," he said proudly.

"Yes, I know you are." Max touched his shoulder with a boyish, propitiatory movement. "I beg your pardon, old chap. I'd be one myself if I could."

"But you—but you—" Bertrand protested in confusion.

"I am a Wyndham," said Max, with a bitter smile. "It doesn't run in our family, that. But I'll play the game with you, man, just because you're straight."

He patted Bertrand's shoulder lightly, and turned away. There were not many who knew Max Wyndham intimately, and of those not one who would have credited the fact that the innate honour of a French castaway had somehow made him feel ashamed.

CHAPTER XIII
WOMANHOOD

"A thousand thanks, *chère Madame*, for the generous favour which you have bestowed upon me! I shall make it my business to see that no rumour of your droll secret of Valpré ever reach the ear of the strict husband, lest he should imagine that among the rocks of that paradise there lies entombed something more precious to him than the gay romance of your youth.

"To this undertaking I subscribe my signature, with many compliments to the good secretary; and to you, *chère Madame*, my ever constant devotion.

"*Toujours à vous*, GUILLAUME RODOLPHE.

"P.S.—It is with profound regret that I find myself unable to visit you, but my duty recalls me to my regiment in Paris."

A faint sigh escaped Chris, the first breath she had drawn for many seconds. She stood by her dressing-table in the full glare of the electric light, dressed in white, her wonderful hair shining like burnished copper. She was to give her first dinner-party that night. It was not to be a very large affair, yet it was something of an ordeal in her estimation. She would probably have faced it more easily away from Aunt Philippa's critical eyes. But this was a condition not obtainable. Aunt Philippa had decided to remain some little time longer at Kellerton Old Park in consequence of an engagement having fallen through, a state of affairs that Noel regarded with a disgust too forcible to be expressed in words, and which had driven Max away within three days of his arrival.

Upon Chris had devolved the main burden of her aunt's society, and a heavy burden she had begun to find it. Aunt Philippa had apparently determined to spend her time in transforming her young niece into a practical housewife—a gigantic task which she tackled with praiseworthy zeal. She had already instituted several reforms in the household, and her thrifty mind contemplated several more. Chris's attitude, which had at first been one of indifference, had gradually developed into one of passive resistance. She was, as a matter of fact, too preoccupied just then to turn her attention to active opposition; but she did not pretend to enjoy the tutelage thus ruthlessly pressed upon her. She had been compelled to relinquish her readings with Bertrand, of whom she now saw very little; for, though rigidly courteous at all times, he consistently avoided Aunt Philippa whenever possible. She on her part treated him with disdainful sufferance, much as she had treated Cinders in the old days. She resented his presence, but endured it perforce.

Under these circumstances it was not surprising that there should occur moments of occasional friction between her niece and herself, especially since, under the most favourable conditions, they had never yet managed to discover a single point in common.

This constant jarring in the background of the ceaseless anxiety that consumed her night and day had worn Chris's nerves to a very thin edge, and now that relief had come at last in the form of the letter she held in her hand she was almost too spent to feel it. The tension had endured for so long that it seemed impossible that it could have relaxed all in a moment. She had received a roll of banknotes from her brother two days before, but that had in a fashion but added to her fever of unrest. Now that she knew them to be safe in the pocket of the blackguard for whom they were intended, now surely was the time for peace to return.

But had it? Standing there, still reading and re-reading those gibing words, she asked herself dully if ever peace could return to her—the thoughtless, happy peace of her childhood that she had valued so lightly— the careless security of a mind at rest. Had it gone from her for ever? Was that also buried among the rocks at Valpré? She wondered—she wondered!

There came a low knock at the door between her room and her husband's. She started violently. He had been in town for a few hours. She had not expected him back for another quarter of an hour at least.

"Oh no," she called out quickly, "you can't come in!"

Yet she stood as she was under the glaring light, the letter still clutched stiffly in her hand, her eyes still staring widely at the irregular, un-English writing. The letters seemed to writhe and squirm into life before her distorted vision, to wriggle like a procession of monstrous insects across the page. Were they insects or were they reptiles? She asked herself the question dazedly.

"Chris!" Her husband's voice came to her softly through the closed door. "Let me come in for a moment. I have something to show you."

"Wait!" she called back desperately. "Wait!"

Yet it was as if iron chains were loaded upon her. She could speak, but she could not move. Were they reptiles she was watching so intently? Or stay! Were they crabs? They were certainly rather like the funny little crabs that she and Cinders used to hunt for in the shallow pools of Valpré. She gave a little laugh. Surely it was the sort of thing that might have happened to Alice in Wonderland!

And then quite suddenly her brain flashed back to understanding, to vivid, appalling consciousness; and she knew that her husband was waiting to enter, while she held in her hand the one thing which she would have sacrificed her life sooner than let him see. The awfulness of the realization spurred her back to action. Her limbs were free again, though horribly—so horribly—unsteady. The letter seemed to burn her fingers. She dropped it into the small drawer in which she kept her trinkets, turned the key with feverish haste, and, withdrawing it, thrust it down inside her dress. The cold steel sent a shiver to her very heart, but it stilled the wild fever of her fear. When she turned from the dressing-table she had nerved herself; she was calm.

She crossed the room to the door at which Trevor stood waiting, and quietly opened it.

"How impatient you are!" she said, with a smile.

For a woman who held her fate at bay it was admirably done; but for Chris—little Chris of the sunny eyes and eager, impetuous actions—it was so overwhelming a failure that Mordaunt, standing on the threshold, made no movement to enter, but stood, and looked and looked, as though he had never seen her before.

She met the look as a duellist meets his opponent's blade, instantly but warily, summoning all the craft of her newly awakened womanhood to her aid. She was not conscious of agitation. Her heart felt as if it were turned to stone; it did not seem to be beating at all.

"Well," she said, as he did not speak, "have you got through your business in town?"

He did not answer her, but came straight forward into the room, took her by the shoulders, and drew her round so that she faced the light. "What have you been doing?" he said.

She faced him unshrinking, undismayed. The Chris of a few hours before would have drawn back in open fear from the piercing scrutiny of those grey eyes, but this Chris was different. This Chris was a woman with pale lips that smiled a baffling smile and eyes that barred the way to her soul, a woman who had found in her womanhood a weapon of defence that no man could thrust aside.

"I haven't been doing anything," she said indifferently, "except run round after Aunt Philippa—oh yes, and write up to town for some things I wanted. Aunt Philippa is really going to leave us to-day week. I can't think what we shall do without her, can you? Now tell me about your doings."

She lifted her face suddenly for his kiss, ignoring the fact that he was still holding her as if for inquisition.

He drew her sharply into his arms and held her fast. "You are very cold, sweetheart," he said.

She flushed a little at his action, though the lips he kissed were like ice. "I am tired," she said.

She expected him to set her free, but he did not. He held her closer still. Not till afterwards did she realize that it was the first time he had ever held her thus and she had not quivered like a frightened bird against his breast. She was scarcely thinking of him now. She was as one who stands before a scorching fire too rapt in reverie to feel the heat.

Yet after a little he did succeed in infusing a certain degree of warmth into her. Her arms went round his neck, though hardly of her own volition, and her lips returned his kiss. But there was no spirit in her. She leaned against him as if spent.

"Are you quite well, dear?" he asked her tenderly.

"Oh, quite! I am always well." She uttered a little tremulous laugh and raised her head from his shoulder. "Trevor," she said, "I am afraid you will think me very extravagant, but, do you know, I haven't any money to go on with. I had a notice from the bank to-day to say my account was overdrawn."

Again it was not the Chris he knew who uttered the words. It was a woman of the world to whom his passing displeasure had become a matter almost of indifference.

"Chris," he said abruptly, "what is the matter with you, child? Are you bewitched?"

That roused her. She suddenly realized that she was on dangerous ground, that to blind him she must recall the child who had vanished so inexplicably. And so for the first time she deliberately set herself to deceive this man who till now had ever impelled her to a certain measure of honesty. She did it with a sick heart—but she did it.

She laid her hands on the front of his coat, grasping it nervously, lifting pleading eyes to his.

"No, I'm not bewitched. I'm only pretending not to be frightened. Trevor, don't be vexed. I'm very sorry about it. Really I couldn't help it."

"It's all right, dear," he said at once, and his hands closed instantly and reassuringly upon hers. He smiled into her eyes. "It's very naughty, of course, but I'm glad you have told me. How much do you want?"

She hesitated momentarily. "I—I'm afraid rather a lot, Trevor."

"How much?" he repeated; and then, as she still hesitated, his hold tightened and his face grew grave. He looked straight down into her eyes. "Chris," he said, "you haven't forgotten, have you, that it is against my wish that you should let your brothers have money?"

She met the look unflinching. "No, Trevor."

He released her without further question. "Then you need not be afraid to tell me how much."

She made a little grimace. The part was getting easier to play. She was beginning to feel almost natural. But the other woman—the woman of the world who surely had never been Chris Wyndham—was still there in the background watching the farce and smiling cynically. Chris was beginning to be afraid of this new personality of hers. It was infinitely more formidable than her husband had ever been.

"How much, dear?" Mordaunt asked quietly.

She started slightly. "Thirty pounds," she said.

"Your account is overdrawn to that amount?"

"Yes." She glanced at him nervously. "I am very sorry," she said again.

He remained grave, but perfectly kind. "I will pay in fifty pounds to-morrow," he said. "That will take you to the end of the month."

"Oh, thank you, Trevor!" She threw him a quick smile of gratitude. "I will pay you back as soon as ever I can."

"No, it isn't a loan," he said.

"Oh, don't give it me!" Impulsively she broke in upon his words. It was growing strangely easy, this part she had to play. Or had she indeed been bewitched for those few dreadful seconds? Was she in reality herself again, the quick-hearted Chris he knew, and that other woman but a phantom born of the horrible strain she had undergone? She told herself that this was the true explanation, even while in her heart she knew otherwise.

"Don't give it me," she said again. "I would really rather you didn't."

"Why?" he asked.

She put out her hand to him with a little movement of entreaty. "I can't explain. But—I would like to pay it back if you don't mind."

He smiled at her persistence. "No, I don't mind, if you particularly wish it. Now come into my room for a moment. I want to show you something."

She went with him, her hand in his, not willingly but because she could not do otherwise.

He led her to the table, and pointed out a box upon it.
"That is for you, Chris."

"For me!" She looked at him as if startled. "What is it, Trevor?"

"Open it and see," he said.

She hesitated. She seemed almost afraid. "I hope it isn't anything very— very—"

"Open it and see," he repeated.

She obeyed him with hands that had begun to tremble, took out an object wrapped in tissue-paper, unfolded the coverings, and disclosed a jewel-case.

Then again she hesitated, standing as one in doubt. "Trevor, I—I—"

"Open it, dear," he said gently.

And mutely she obeyed.

Diamonds flashed before her dazzled eyes, a myriad sparkling colours shot spinning through her brain. She stood gazing, gazing, as one beneath a spell. For the passage of many seconds there was no sound in the room.

Then with a sudden movement she closed the case. It shut with a sharp snap, and she raised a haggard face.

"Trevor, it's lovely—lovely! But I can't take it—anyhow, not yet—not till I have paid you back."

"My dear little wife, what nonsense!" he said.

"No, no, it isn't! I am in earnest." Her voice quivered; she held out the case to him beseechingly. "I can't take it—yet," she said. "I thank you with all my heart. But I can't—I can't!"

Her words ended upon a sudden sob; she laid the case down again among its wrappings, and stood before him silent, with bent head. It was not easy to refuse this gift of his, but for some reason to accept it was a monstrous impossibility. He would not understand, of course, but yet—whatever he thought—she could not take it.

A long pause followed her last words. She shed no tears, but another sob was struggling for utterance. She put her hand to her throat to strangle it there.

And then at last Mordaunt spoke. "Chris, have you been doing something that you are afraid to tell me of?"

She was silent. Silence was her only refuge now.

He put his arm round her. "Because," he said very tenderly, "you needn't be afraid, dear, Heaven knows."

That pierced her unbearably. Woman though she was, she almost cried out under the pain of it.

She drew herself away from him. "Don't! please don't!" she said rather breathlessly. "You—you must take things for granted sometimes. I can't always be explaining my feelings. They won't stand it."

She tried to laugh, but could not. Again desperately she pressed her hand to her throat. How would he take it? She wondered. Would he regard it as a mere childish whim? Or would he see that he was dealing with a woman, and a desperate woman at that?

She scarcely knew what she expected of him, but most assuredly she did not anticipate his next move.

Quite quietly he picked up the jewel-case, and re-entered her room.

"It may as well go among your other treasures," he said. "You needn't wear it—unless you wish—until you have paid me back."

His tone was perfectly ordinary. She wondered what was in his mind, how he regarded her behaviour, why he treated her thus; not guessing that he had set himself resolutely, with infinite patience, to show her how small was her cause for fear.

He laid his hand upon the drawer that contained her trinkets, tried it, turned round to her, faintly smiling.

"May I have the key?"

She had followed him in silence, and now she stood still, The key! The key! It seemed to be searing her flesh, burning through to her very heart. She suddenly felt as if all the Fates were arrayed against her. Why—why—why had she chosen that drawer to guard her secret? Yet how could she have foreseen this? A mist swam before her eyes. Her new-found composure tottered.

"I—have lost it," she murmured.

"Lost it!" he echoed.

"I mean—I mean—" She was stammering now in open confusion—"I must have laid it down somewhere. I—I shall find it again, no doubt."

He turned fully round and looked at her. She clasped her hands to still her quivering nerves. This fresh ordeal was proving too much for her.

"I can't help it," she said, with white lips. "I often mislay things. I am careless, I know. But I always find them again sooner or later. I will have a look for it while you are dressing."

Her words ran on almost meaninglessly. She was speaking for the sake of speaking, because silence would have been too terrible to be borne, because if she had ceased to speak she must have screamed. Even as it was, the fact that her husband said nothing whatever was driving her almost to distraction.

Suddenly she realized that he was waiting for her to stop, that her words were making no impression, that he was not so much as listening to them, his attention being focussed upon her and her alone.

She broke off in desperation. She met his steady eyes. "Don't you—don't you believe me, Trevor?"

He did not instantly reply. For one dreadful moment she thought that he was going to answer in the negative. And then very deliberately he declined her direct challenge.

"I think," he said quietly, "that you don't know what you are saying."

And with that he went slowly back to his own room, taking the jewel-case with him. The door closed softly and she was left alone.

For many seconds thereafter Chris made no movement of any sort. It was as if she were afraid to stir. Her eyes were wide, gazing straight before her, as though fascinated by some scene of terror.

She moved at last stiffly, went to the window, drew a long, deep breath. She asked herself no questions of any sort. There was no need. For the first time in her life she was face to face with her own soul, beyond all possibility of self-deception.

The child Chris was gone for ever, the woman Chris remained, a woman with a tragic secret that must never be revealed. She knew now why she had fought so desperately to keep that episode of Valpré from her husband's knowledge. She only marvelled that the reason had never come home to her before. She knew now why she had always shrunk inwardly from the searching of his eyes. She had always dreaded that he might see too much, even that same secret of which she herself must have been vaguely conscious for years.

It was all clear to her now, so clear that she could never shut her eyes to it again. All her life long she must carry it in her heart, and no one must ever know. Sleeping and waking, she must keep it safely hidden. She must go on living a lie all her life, all her life.

She flung out her arms with a sudden gesture of fierce rebellion. Oh, why had she married? Why? Why? Why? Had she not always known in her heart that she was making a terrible, an irrevocable, mistake? How was it she had been so blind? Why had there been no one to warn her of the snare into which she was walking? Why had no hand held her back?

Trevor himself—but no, Trevor did not so much as know that she had left her childhood behind her yet. He was still wondering what childish peccadillo was troubling her, keeping her from accepting his gift. At least, he was very far from suspecting her actual reason; nor must he ever suspect.

Never, as long as they lived, must he know that she had refused the first thing of value that he had offered her since their wedding because in an instant of overwhelming revelation she had just recognized the fact that she loved—had loved for years—another man.

PART III

CHAPTER I
WAR

Two days before that on which Aunt Philippa had decided to take her departure Mordaunt went again to town. Noel, whose holidays were drawing to a close, accompanied him to the station in a state of high jubilation, albeit Holmes was in charge of the motor and there was not the faintest chance of his being allowed to take the wheel.

"I hope you're going to behave yourself," were Mordaunt's last words.

And the youngster's cheery grin and impudent "You bet, old chap!" ought to have warned him not to hope for behaviour too exemplary.

Noel, in fact, had been anticipating his brother-in-law's departure with considerable eagerness. Though he liked him thoroughly, he was an undoubted check upon his enjoyment. He kept him within bounds after a fashion which had at first amused but had of late begun somewhat to pall upon him; and Noel was only awaiting a suitable opportunity to kick over the traces and gallop free. On this occasion Mordaunt had decided to spend the night in town, so circumstances were propitious.

As for Mordaunt, he had dismissed Noel from his mind almost before the train was out of the station. But for her aunt's presence, he would have persuaded Chris to go with him, even though he knew that she had not the smallest wish to do so. He was growing very anxious with regard to her, and he was firmly determined that she should have a change of scene as soon as Noel's holidays and Aunt Philippa's protracted stay came to an end. It was not that she seemed ill, but she was very far from being herself, and there were times when he even fancied that she simulated gaiety for the deliberate purpose of deceiving him. He knew, too, that her sleep was often broken and troubled, but he never commented upon this; she was so plainly averse to any criticism from him or anyone. A shrewd suspicion had begun to take root in Mordaunt's mind to account for this unwonted reticence;

and because of it he treated her with the utmost patience and consideration, asking no question, giving no sign that he so much as noticed the change in her. He invariably turned from any subject she seemed to find distasteful. If she seemed unusually nervous or unreasonable, he passed it over, bearing with her with a tenderness that sometimes moved her in secret to passionate tears the while she asked herself what she had ever done that he should love her so.

For if she had ever doubted the quality of his love, she could not do so now. It surrounded her whichever way she turned, asking nothing of her, never intruding upon her, content simply to shelter her. And though the very fact of it hurt her, it comforted her subtly as well, lulling her fear of him, giving her a certain measure of confidence.

Of Bertrand, in those days, she saw less and less. In the first shock of realization she had instinctively avoided him, possessed by a haunting dread that he might guess her secret. But upon this point she was very soon reassured. The consistent and unwavering friendliness of his attitude quieted her misgivings, and nerved her to treat him, if with less intimacy, at least without visible awkwardness. Whether he noticed her avoidance or not she did not know, but he certainly seemed to be withdrawing himself more and more out of her life. His work with her husband apparently occupied all his thoughts, and then there was Aunt Philippa also to keep him at a distance. How it would be when her aunt departed Chris had no notion, but she was looking forward to that event with an eagerness almost feverish. All her natural sweetness notwithstanding, there were occasions upon which she actively disliked this domineering relative of hers. Aunt Philippa, on her part, who had never taken so much trouble with her niece before, openly marvelled at her intractability, which even the fact that Chris was one of those headstrong Wyndhams did not, in her opinion, wholly justify. No open rupture had occurred, but a very decided animosity had begun to smoulder between them, which a very little provocation might at any moment fan into open hostility.

Chris was leaning against a pillar of the porch when her brother returned. There was very decided dejection in her attitude.

"Cheer up!" Noel exhorted her, as he sprang from the car. "I've got a ripping plan."

He came and twined his arm in hers, and Chris smiled with a hint of wistfulness. She felt as if she had left Noel and his boyish pleasures very far behind of late.

"What do you want to do?" she said.

"Come into the gun-room and I'll tell you." Noel was all eagerness. "Coast clear?" he questioned. "Where's Aunt Phil?"

"Waiting for me to go and help her find fault with the gardeners." Chris was still smiling a little, but there was not much humour in her voice.

"Oh, rats! Don't go!" said Noel. "Come along into the gun-room, and help me make some fireworks. It will be much more fun."

A spark of the old ardour kindled in Chris's eyes. "Oh, are you going to make fireworks?" she said. "Have you got the ingredients?"

He nodded. "Nearly all. Come and see. What we haven't got we must manufacture. I know where there are plenty of cartridges."

Chris yielded to the eager pulling of his arm. "I suppose Trevor wouldn't mind for once," she said. She had grown unaccountably scrupulous in this respect.

But Noel jeered at the notion. "Who cares? It'll be all over long before he comes home to-morrow. We will have a regular jollification to-night. You and I will run the show, and Aunt Phil and Bertrand can look on and admire. I say, Chris, I've got a ripping receipt for Catherine wheels—not the big ones, those little things you hold and buzz round. You know!"

His enthusiasm was infectious. It drew her almost in spite of herself. Besides, it meant a temporary respite from the continual burden that weighed her down, and brief though it must be, she could not bring herself to refuse it. She went with him, therefore, with the feeling of one who has signed a truce with the enemy, and in a couple of minutes they were securely closeted in the gun-room, with the door locked against all intruders, and all thoughts of Aunt Philippa and any other troublous problems as resolutely excluded from their minds.

The hours of the morning literally flew. Luncheon-time found them absorbed in a most critical process.

"Bust lunch!" said Noel. "We can't possibly leave this now."

But Chris's sense of duty proved too strong for her inclination at this juncture, and she sallied forth from their retreat to rescue Bertrand from a *tête-à-tête* meal with her aunt.

There was a sparkle of merriment in her eyes when she entered the dining-room. The engrossing work of the morning had done her good. She was fully five minutes late, and Bertrand, who had presented himself sharp on the hour with military punctuality, was waiting by the window.

He came swiftly to meet her. She had not seen him before that day.

"You are looking well this morning," he said, in his quick, friendly way. "You have been busy, yes?"

His soft eyes interrogated her, as for an instant he held her hand. Never once had she found those eyes impossible to meet. They held the fidelity of unswerving friendship.

"Oh yes," she said, "busy in a fashion—a very childish fashion, Bertie. Noel and I are making fireworks!"

"Fireworks!" he echoed.

"Yes, we are going to have a grand display tonight. Will you come and look on?"

He smiled. "But yes," he said. "I think that I will come and take care of you."

She nodded. "Do! But they are not dangerous, not very. Where is Aunt Philippa?"

He spread out his hands whimsically. "She has not given me her confidence."

Chris laughed. Actually she was feeling almost lighthearted. Till that moment she had had a morbid dread of being alone with him, and now behold her dread vanishing in mirth! Surely she had been very foolish, like a child frightened at shadows!

"I wonder where she is," she said. "I am afraid I have been playing truant this morning. I shall have to apologize, though it was all Noel's fault. Do see if you can find Mrs. Forest," she added to a servant just entering. "Ask her if she is ready for luncheon."

"Mrs. Forest is out in the motor, and has not yet returned," was the information this elicited.

"How odd!" said Chris. "What had we better do?"

Bertrand shrugged his shoulders, still looking quizzical. "We must not lunch without her, *bien sûr*. Let us go into the garden."

They went into the garden, and walked for a space in the September sunshine.

They talked at first upon commonplace topics, and Chris was wholly at her ease. But presently Bertrand turned the conversation with an abrupt question.

"Christine, tell me, you have never seen that scoundrel Rodolphe again?"

She started a little, and was conscious that she changed colour, but she answered him instantly. "No, never. But—why do you ask?"

Very gravely he made reply. "I have feared lately that there was something that troubled you. I was wrong, yes?"

He looked at her anxiously.

She did not answer him, she could not.

"*Eh bien*," he said gently, after a moment. "It was not that. You have heard that he has been recalled to France—that there is a rumour that there have been revelations that may lead to a court-martial?"

"No!" said Chris in amazement. "Do you mean—"

He bent his head. "It is possible."

"That you may be vindicated?" she questioned eagerly. "Oh, Bertie!"

"It is possible," he repeated. "Yet I will not permit myself to hope. It is no more than a rumour. It is also possible that it may not even touch the old *affaire*, since he made no appearance at my trial."

"But if it did!" said Chris.

He gave her an odd look. "If it did, Christine?" he questioned.

"You would go back with flying colours," she said. "You would be reinstated surely!"

He shook his head. "I do not think it."

"You mean you wouldn't go?" she asked.

He turned his face up to the sun with a peculiar gesture. "Who can say?" he said, with closed eyes. "Me, I think that the good God has other plans for me. I may be justified—I do not know. But I shall wear the uniform of the French Army—never again."

He spoke perfectly calmly, with absolute conviction; but there was that in his face that startled her, something she had never seen before.

She put out a hesitating hand, and touched his sleeve. "Bertie!"

Instantly he looked at her, saw the scared expression in her eyes, and, smiling, pressed her hand.

"*Mais*, Christine, these things—what are they? Ambition, success, honour—loss, failure, shame; they seem so great in this little life of mortality. But, after all, they are no more than the tools with which the good God shapes us to His destiny. He uses them, and when His work is done He throws them aside. We leave them behind us; we pass on to that which is greater." He paused a moment, and his eyes kindled as though he were on the verge of something further; then suddenly they went beyond her, and he relinquished her hand. "Madame has returned," he said. "Let us go!"

Looking up, Chris saw Aunt Philippa upon the terrace above them.

The expression on her relative's face was one of severe and undisguised disapproval, as her gaze rested upon the two in the garden. Chris, as she moved to meet her, felt a sudden flame of indignation at her heart. How dared Aunt Philippa look at them so?

"We have been waiting for you," she said, speaking in some haste to conceal her resentment. "Has anything happened?"

Aunt Philippa replied in the measured accents habitual to her. "Nothing has happened. I have been to Sandacre Court, at Mrs. Pouncefort's invitation, to see the gardens. I waited for you, Chris, for nearly an hour this morning, but you did not see fit either to come to me or to send any word of explanation to account for your absence. Therefore I started late. Hence my late return."

Chris coloured. "I am sorry, Aunt Philippa. Noel wanted me. I am afraid I forgot you were waiting."

"It seems to me," said Aunt Philippa, with cutting emphasis, "that you are apt to forget every obligation when in Mr. Bertrand's society."

"Aunt Philippa!"

Furious indignation rang in Chris's voice. In a second—in less—it would have been open war, but swift as an arrow Bertrand intervened.

"Ah! but pardon me," he said, in his soft voice. "I am not responsible for Mrs. Mordaunt's negligence. She has been occupied with her affairs, and I with mine. Had she been in my society"—he smiled with a flash of the teeth—"she would not have forgotten her duties so easily. I am an excellent monitor, madame. Acquit me, I beg, of being accessory to the crime, and accept my sympathies the most sincere."

Aunt Philippa ignored them in icy silence, but he had accomplished his end. The evil moment was averted. Whatever Chris might have to endure later, at least she would be spared the added mortification of his presence during the infliction. Airily he turned the subject. He could overlook a snub more adroitly than Aunt Philippa could administer one.

They went into the house, and during the meal that followed Bertrand made himself gracefully agreeable to both ladies. So delicate were his attentions that Chris found herself more than once on the verge of hysterical laughter.

But when he left them at length, with many apologies, to resume his interrupted labours, her sense of humour ceased to vibrate. Never before had she desired her husband's presence as she desired it then.

Her hope that Aunt Philippa might retire to her room to rest was a very slender one, and destined almost from the outset to disappointment. Aunt Philippa was on the war trail, and she would not rest until she had tracked down her quarry.

She began at once to speak of her morning's visit to Mrs. Pouncefort, whom she knew as a London hostess. Personally, she disapproved of her, but she could not afford to pass her over, since her status in society was by no means inconsiderable, being, in fact, almost capable of rivalling her own.

"I should have remained to luncheon," she said, "but for the fact that you were here quite unchaperoned. Had you accompanied me, as I had hoped you would, I should not have had to hasten back in the heat."

"But I wasn't invited," said Chris, "and I know every inch of those gardens. I knew them long ago, before the Pounceforts came."

"The invitation," said Aunt Philippa, not to be diverted from her purpose, "was quite casual. You could quite well have accompanied me. In fact, I think Mrs. Pouncefort was surprised not to see you. However, we need not discuss that further. Doubtless you had your own reasons for desiring to remain at home, and I shall not ask you what those reasons were. What I do ask, and what I think I have a right to know, is whether you have had the proper feeling to tell your husband that the Captain Rodolphe you met at Pouncefort Court a little while ago is the man with whom you were so deplorably intimate at Valpré in your girlhood, or whether you have had the audacity to pretend that he was a total stranger to you."

Chris almost gasped at this unexpected attack, but its directness compelled an instant reply without pausing to consider the position.

"I was never intimate with Captain Rodolphe," she said quickly. "I never spoke to him before the other day."

And there she stopped suddenly short, arrested by the look of open incredulity with which her aunt received her hasty statement.

There was a moment's silence. Then, "Really!" said Aunt Philippa. "He gave Mrs. Pouncefort to understand otherwise."

Chris felt the blood rush to her face..This was intolerable. "What did he give Mrs. Pouncefort to understand?" she demanded.

"Merely that you were old friends," said Aunt Philippa, with the calm superiority of one not to be shaken in her belief.

"Then he lied!" said Chris fiercely.

Aunt Philippa said "Indeed!" with raised eyebrows.

Chris's hands clenched unconsciously. "He lied!" she repeated. "We are not friends! We never could be! I—I hate the man!"

"Then you know him well enough for that?" said Aunt Philippa.

Chris sprang to her feet with hot cheeks and blazing eyes. "Aunt Philippa, you have no right—you and Mrs. Pouncefort—to—to talk me over and discuss my acquaintances!"

"My dear child," said Aunt Philippa, "all that passed between us was a remark made by Mrs. Pouncefort to the effect that one of her guests, Captain Rodolphe—an old friend of yours whom she believed you had originally met at Valpré—had just returned to Paris. What led to the remark I do not remember. But naturally the name recalled certain regrettable circumstances to my mind, and I felt it my duty to ask if you had been quite candid with Trevor upon the subject. I am sincerely grieved to know that my suspicion in this respect was but too well founded."

"He was not the man I knew at Valpré" burst forth Chris, with passionate vehemence. "You may believe it or not; it is the truth!"

"Then, my dear," said Aunt Philippa, with the calmness of unalterable conviction, "there must have been two men who enjoyed that privilege."

Chris broke into a wild laugh—a laugh that had been struggling for utterance for the past hour.

"Two! Why, there were a dozen at least, some soldiers, some fishermen! Ask Trevor! He can tell you all about them—if he thinks it worth while!"

"And yet you have not mentioned Captain Rodolphe to him?" said Aunt Philippa. Her eyes were fixed unsparingly upon the girl's face, and she saw the colour dying away as swiftly as it had risen. "That is strange," she remarked, with emphasis.

"It is not strange!" flashed back Chris. The laugh had gone from her lips, leaving them white, but she faced her adversary unflinchingly. It was open war now—a fierce and bitter struggle for the mastery, for which she knew herself to be ill-equipped, but in which she must fight to the last. She knew that Aunt Philippa had always regarded her with cold dislike, and it dawned upon her in that moment that now—now that her position was assured, now that she was rich and popular and the wife of a man who was universally honoured in that great world of society in which her aunt had always striven for a leading place—the dislike had turned to a cruel jealousy that demanded her downfall. And she was horribly at her mercy; deep in her heart she knew that also, but she would not own it, even to herself. Aunt Philippa had not yet unmasked the truth. Until she succeeded in doing so, all was not lost.

"It is not strange," she repeated, and this time she spoke quietly, summoning all her strength to the unequal contest. "Captain Rodolphe was not of sufficient importance to mention to Trevor. Besides—"

"Although you hate him so bitterly!" Aunt Philippa reminded her.

Chris pressed on, ignoring the thrust. "Besides, Trevor does not need, does not so much as wish to be told of every little incident that ever happened in my life. He prefers to trust me."

"And have you never abused his confidence?" asked Aunt Philippa.

It was inevitable. She flinched ever so slightly, but she covered it with instant defiance. "What do you mean, Aunt Philippa?"

Aunt Philippa made no direct reply. She knew the value of insinuation in such a battle as this. "Ask yourself that question," she said impressively.

It might have provided a way of escape, at least temporarily, but Chris was too far goaded to see it. "Tell me what you mean," she said.

Aunt Philippa's thin lips smiled ironically. "My dear, are you really so blind, or is deceit the very air you breathe? Can you look me in the face and assure me that nothing has ever passed between you and your husband's secretary of which you would not wish him to know?"

That went home, straight to her quivering heart. For a moment the pain of it held her dumb. Then, with a gasp, she turned from the pitiless eyes that watched her.

"Oh, how dare you, Aunt Philippa! How dare you!" she cried in impotence.

"I trust that I am not afraid to do my duty," said Aunt Philippa, very gravely.

But Chris had already turned, completely routed, and fled from the scene of her defeat; nor did she pause until she had reached her haven at the top of the house, where, like a wounded bird, she crouched down in solitude and so remained for a long, long time.

Not till the afternoon was far advanced did any measure of comfort come to her stricken soul, and then at last she remembered that, after all, she was comparatively safe. Her husband's trust was still hers, implicit and unwavering, and she knew that he would not so much as notice a single hint from Aunt Philippa, however adroitly offered. That was her one and only safeguard, and as she realized it the bitterness of her heart gave place to a sudden burst of anguished shame. What had she ever done to deserve the generous, unquestioning trust he thus reposed in her? Nothing—less than nothing!

CHAPTER II
FIREWORKS

When Chris emerged from her seclusion, she found that her aunt had decided to suspend hostilities, and to treat her with the majestic condescension of the conqueror. It was something of a relief, for Chris was not fashioned upon fighting lines, and long-sustained animosity was beyond her. She was thankful for Noel's plans for the evening's entertainment as a topic of conversation, even though Aunt Philippa openly disapproved of the enterprise. She had begun feverishly to count the hours to her aunt's departure. She would not feel really safe, reassure herself how she might, until she was finally gone.

It was not until after dinner that Noel emerged from his lair in the gun-room and announced everything to be in readiness. He called Chris out on to the terrace to assist him, and Aunt Philippa and Bertrand were left—an ill-assorted couple—to watch and admire the result of his efforts. Aunt Philippa invariably maintained a demeanour of haughty reserve if she found herself alone with her host's French secretary, an attitude in which he as invariably acquiesced with an impenetrable silence which she resented without knowing why. He was always courteous, but he never tried to be agreeable to her, and this also Aunt Philippa resented, though she would have mercilessly snubbed any efforts in that direction had he exerted himself to make them.

The night was dark and still, an ideal night for fireworks. Noel began with the failures which he had not the heart to waste. He was keeping the choicest of his collection till the last. Consequently there were a good many crackling explosions on the ground with nothing but a few sparks to compensate for the noise, and Aunt Philippa very speedily tired of the din.

"This is childish as well as dangerous," she said. "I shall go to the library. There will at least be peace and quietness there."

"Without doubt," said Bertrand.

He accompanied her thither with a polite regard for her comfort for which he received no gratitude, and then returned to smoke his cigarette in comfort by the open French window that overlooked the terrace.

A ruddy glare lit up the scene as he took up his stand. The failures were apparently exhausted, and Noel had begun upon the masterpieces. Chris's quick laugh came to him, as he stood there watching. Yet he frowned a little to himself as he heard it, missing the gay, spontaneous, childish ring that he had been wont to hear. What had come to her of late? Was it true that she had told him on the night of Cinders' death? Was she indeed grown-up? If so—he changed his position slightly, trying to catch a glimpse of her in the fitful glare of one of Noel's Roman candles—had the time come for him to go? He had always faced the fact that she would not need him when her childhood was left behind. And certainly of late she had not seemed to need him. She had even—he fancied—avoided him at times. He wondered wherefore. Could it have been at her aunt's instigation? Surely not. She was too staunch for that.

There remained another possibility, and, after a little, reluctantly, with clenched teeth, he faced it. Had she by some means discovered that which he had so studiously hidden from her all this time? He cast his mind back. Had he ever inadvertently betrayed himself? He knew he had not. Never since her marriage had he given the faintest sign; no, not even on that fateful afternoon when she had clung to him in anguish of soul and he had held her fast pressed against his heart. He had been strictly honourable, resolutely loyal, all through. He had always held himself in check. He had never forgotten, never relaxed his vigilance, never once been other than faithful, even in thought, to the friend who trusted him. Yet—Max's words recurred to him, piercing him as with a stab of physical pain—without doubt women had a genius *incroyable* for discovering secrets. And if Chris were indeed a woman—was it not possible—

Again her laugh broke in upon his thoughts, and he turned swiftly in the direction whence it came. She was standing not more than a dozen yards from him, a red whirl of fire all about her, in her hand a whizzing, spitting-aureole of flame. The light flared upwards on her face and gleaming hair. She looked like some fire-goddess, exulting over the radiant element she had created. And, like a sword-thrust to his heart, there went through him the memory of her standing poised like a bird on the prow of a boat. Just so had she stood then; just so, goddess-like, had she exulted in the morning sunshine and the sparkling water; just so had her bare arms shone on the day that first he had consciously worshipped her, on the day that she had told him of her desire to find out all the secrets that there were. Ah! how much had she found out since then—his bird of Paradise with the restless, ever-fluttering wings? How much? How much?

A sudden cry banished his speculations—a cry uttered by her voice, sharp with dismay. "Oh, Noel! My sleeve!"

Before the words were past her lips Bertrand had leaped forth to the rescue. He traversed the distance between them as a meteor hurling through space. But even so, ere he reached her, the filmy lace that hung down from her elbow had blazed into flame. She had dropped the firework, and it lay hissing on the ground like a glittering snake. He sprang over it and caught her in his arms.

She cried out again as he crushed her to him, cried out, and tried to push him from her; but he held her fast, gripping the flaming material with his naked hands, rending it, and gripping afresh. Something white which neither noticed fluttered upon the ground between them. It must have actually passed through that frantic grip. It lay unheeded, while Bertrand beat out the last spark and ripped the last charred rag away from the soft arm.

"You are hurt, no?" he queried rather breathlessly.

"You, Bertie! What of you?" she cried hysterically, clinging to him. "Your hands—let me see them!"

"By Jove, that was a near thing!" ejaculated Noel, who had followed close upon Bertrand's heels. "I thought you were done for that time, Chris. How on earth did you manage it? You must have been jolly careless."

Chris did not attempt to answer. Now that the emergency had passed, she was hanging upon Bertrand almost in a state of collapse.

"Let us go in," the latter said gently.

"Yes, run along," said Noel, who had a wholesome dread of hysterics. "Don't be silly, Chris; there's no harm done. But if it hadn't been for this chap here you'd have been in flames in another second. I congratulate you, Bertrand, on your presence of mind. Not hurt yourself, I suppose?"

"I am not hurt," the Frenchman answered; but his words sounded as if speech were an effort to him, almost as if he spoke them through clenched teeth.

Chris straightened herself swiftly. "Yes, let us go in," she said.

She leaned upon Bertrand no longer, but she still held his arm. As they entered the drawing-room alone together, she turned and looked at him.

"Ah! I knew you were hurt," she said quickly. "Sit down, Bertie. Here is a chair."

He sank down blindly, his face like death; he had begun to gasp for breath. His hand groped desperately towards an inner pocket, but fell powerless before reaching it.

"Let me!" whispered Chris.

She bent over him, and slipped her own trembling hand inside his coat. Her fingers touched something hard, and she drew out a small bottle.

"Is it this?" she said.

His lips moved in the affirmative. She removed the stopper and shook out some capsules.

"*Deux!*" whispered Bertrand.

She put them into his mouth and waited. Great drops had started on his forehead, and now began to roll slowly down his drawn face. She took his handkerchief after a little to wipe them away, but almost immediately he reached up with a quivering smile and took it from her.

"I am better," he said, and though his voice was husky he had it under control. "You will pardon me for giving you this trouble. It was only—a passing weakness."

He mopped his forehead, and leaned slowly forward, moving with caution.

"But you are ill! You are in pain!" Chris exclaimed.

"No," he said. "No, I have no pain. I am better. I am quite well."

Again he looked up at her, smiling. "But how I have alarmed you!" he said regretfully. "And your arm, *petite*? It is not burnt—not at all?"

He took her hand gently, and put back the tattered sleeve to satisfy himself on this point.

Chris said nothing. Her lips had begun to tremble. But she winced a little when he touched a place inside her arm where the flame had scorched her.

He glanced up sharply. "Ah! that hurts you, that?"

"No," she said, "no. It is nothing." And then, with sudden passion: "Bertie, what does a little scorch like that matter when you—when you—" She broke off, fighting with herself, and pointed a shaking finger at his wrist.

It had been blistered by the flame, and his shirt-cuff was charred; but the injury was slight, remarkably so in consideration of the utter recklessness he had displayed.

He snapped his fingers with easy indifference. "Ah, bah! It is a *bagatelle*, that. In one week it will be gone. And now—why, *chérie*—"

He stopped abruptly. She had dropped upon her knees beside him, her hands upon his shoulders, her face, tragic in its pain, upturned to his.

"Bertie, why do you try to hide things from me? Do you think I am quite blind? You are ill. I know you are ill. What is it, dear? Won't you tell me?"

He made a quick gesture as if he would check either her words or her touch, and then suddenly he stiffened. For in that instant there ran between them once again, vital, electric, unquenchable, that Flame that had kindled long ago on a morning of perfect summer, that Flame which once kindled burns on for ever.

It happened all in a moment, so swiftly that they were caught unawares in the spell of it, so overwhelmingly that neither for the space of several throbbing seconds possessed the volition to draw back. And in the deep silence the man's eyes held the woman's irresistibly, yet by no conscious effort, while each entered the other's soul and gazed upon the one supreme secret which each had mutely sheltered there.

It was to the man that full realization first came—a realization more overwhelming than anything that had gone before, striking him with a stunning force that shattered every other emotion like a bursting shell spreading destruction.

He came out of that trance-like stillness with a gesture of horror, as if freeing himself from some evil thing that had wound itself about him unawares.

Her hands fell away from his shoulders instantly. She was white to the lips. She even for one incredible moment—the only moment in her life—shrank from him. But that impulse vanished as swiftly as it came, vanished in a rush of passionate understanding. For with a groan Bertrand sank forward and bowed his head in his hands.

"*Mon Dieu!*" he said. "What have I done?"

She responded as it were instinctively, not pausing to choose her words, speaking in a quick, vehement whisper, because his distress was more than she could bear.

"It is none of your doing, Bertie. You are not to say it—not to think it even. It happened long, long ago. You know it did. It happened—it happened—that day at Valpré—the day you—took me into your boat."

He groaned again, his head dropping lower. She knew that also! Then was she woman indeed!

There followed a silence during which Chris remained kneeling beside him, but she was no longer agitated. She was strangely calm. A new strength seemed to have been given her to cope with this pressing need. When at last she moved, it was to lay a hand that was quite steady upon his knee.

"Bertie," she said, "listen! You have done nothing wrong. You have nothing to reproach yourself with. It wasn't your fault that I took so long to grow up." A piteous little smile touched her lips, and was gone. "You have been very good to me," she said. "I won't have you blame yourself. No woman ever had a truer friend."

He laid his hand upon hers, but he kept his eyes covered. She could only see the painful twitching of his mouth under the slight moustache.

"Ah, Christine," he said at last, with an effort, "I have tried—I have tried—to be faithful."

"And you have never been anything else," she said very earnestly. "You were my *preux chevalier* from the very beginning, and you have done more for me than you will ever know. Bertie, Bertie"—her voice thrilled suddenly—"though it's all so hopeless, do you think it isn't easier for me now that I know? Do you think I would have it otherwise if I could?"

His hand closed tightly upon hers with a quick, restraining pressure. He could not answer her.

For some seconds he did not speak at all. At length, "Then—you trust me still, Christine?" he said, his voice very low.

Her reply was instant and unfaltering. "I shall trust you as long as I live."

He was silent again for a space. Then suddenly he uncovered his face and looked at her. Again their eyes met, with the perfect intimacy of a perfect understanding.

"*Eh bien*," Bertrand said, speaking slowly and heavily, as one labouring under an immense burden, "I will be worthy of your confidence. You are right, little comrade. We have travelled too far together—you and I—to fear to strike upon the rocks now."

He paused a moment, then quietly rose, drawing her to her feet. So for a while he stood, her hands clasped in his, seeming still upon the verge of speech, but finding no words. His eyes smiled sadly upon her, as the eyes of a friend saying good-bye. At last he stooped, and reverently as though he sealed an oath thereby, he pressed his lips upon the hands he held.

An instant later he straightened himself, and in unbroken silence turned and left her.

It was one of the simplest tragedies ever played on the world's stage. They had found each other—too late, and there was nothing more to be said.

CHAPTER III
THE TURN OF THE TIDE

It was evening when Mordaunt returned on the following day. He was met at the station by Noel. Holmes was in charge of the motor, and greeted his master with obvious relief. The care of the youngest Wyndham was plainly a responsibility he did not care to shoulder for long.

"All well?" Mordaunt asked, as he emerged from the station with his young brother-in-law hooked effusively on his arm.

"All well, sir," said Holmes, with the air of a sentry relaxing after long and arduous duty.

"Flourishing," said Noel, "though it's the greatest wonder you haven't come back to find Chris a heap of ashes. She would have been if Bertrand hadn't—at great personal risk—put her out."

"What has happened?" demanded Mordaunt sharply.

"All's well, sir," said Holmes reassuringly.

"Fireworks!" explained Noel. "My word, I made some beauties! I wish you could have seen 'em. I got singed a bit myself. But, then, that's only what one would expect playing with fire, eh, Trevor?" He rubbed his cheek ingratiatingly against Mordaunt's shoulder. "You needn't be anxious. Chris was really none the worse. But the Frenchman had a bad attack of blue funk when the danger was over, and nearly fainted. He's feeling ashamed of himself apparently, for I haven't seen him since. By the way, Aunt Phil and Chris had a mill yesterday, and the old lady is suffering from a very stiff neck in consequence. I asked Chris what she did to it, but she wouldn't tell me. Thank the gods, she goes to-morrow! You'll let me drive her to the station, won't you? I should like to go to heaven in Aunt Phil's company. She would be sure to get into the smartest set at once."

He rattled on in the same cheery strain without intermission throughout the return journey, having imparted enough to make Mordaunt thoroughly uneasy, notwithstanding Holmes's assurance.

The first person he met upon entering the house was Aunt Philippa. She accorded him a glacial reception, and explained that Chris had retired to bed with a severe headache.

"It's come on very suddenly," remarked Noel, with frank incredulity. "Where's Bertrand? Has he got a headache too?"

Aunt Philippa had no information to offer with regard to the French secretary! She merely observed that she had given orders for dinner to be served in a quarter of an hour, and therewith swept away to the drawing-room.

Mordaunt shook off his young brother-in-law without ceremony, and went straight up to his wife's room.

His low knock elicited no reply, and he opened the door softly and entered.

The room was in semi-darkness, but Chris's voice accosted him instantly.

"Is that you, Trevor? I'm here, lying down. I had rather a headache, or I would have come to meet you."

Her words were rapid and sounded feverish, as though she were braced for some ordeal. She was lying with her back to the curtained windows and her face in shadow.

Mordaunt went forward with light tread to the bed. "Poor child!" he said gently.

He stooped and kissed her, and found that she was trembling. Quietly he took her hand into his, and began to feel her pulse.

She made a nervous movement to frustrate him, but he gently insisted and she became passive.

"There is nothing serious the matter," she said uneasily. "I—I didn't sleep very well last night, that's all. I thought you wouldn't mind if I didn't come to meet you."

Mordaunt, with the tell-tale, fluttering pulse under his fingers, made gentle reply. "Of course not, dear. I think you are quite right to take care of yourself. Is your head very bad?"

"No, not now. I think I'm just tired. I shall be all right after a night's rest."

Again she tried to slip her hand out of his grasp, and after a moment he let it go.

"Please don't worry about me," she said. "You won't, will you?"

"Not if there is really no reason for it," he said.

She stirred restlessly. "There isn't—indeed. Aunt Philippa will tell you that. I was letting off fireworks with Noel only last night."

"And set fire to yourself," said Mordaunt.

She started a little. "Who told you that?"

"Noel."

"Oh! Well, nothing happened, thanks to—to Bertie. He put it out for me."

"I think there had better not be any more fireworks unless I am there," Mordaunt said. "I don't like to think of my wife running risks of that sort."

"Very well, Trevor," she said meekly.

"Where did the fireworks come from?" he pursued.

"We made them—Noel and I. We used some of your cartridges for gunpowder. He got saltpetre and one or two other things from the chemist. They were quite a success," said Chris, with a touch of her old light gaiety.

"And you are paying for it to-day," he said. "It will be a good thing when Noel goes back to school."

"Oh no," she answered quickly. "It wasn't the fireworks. I often have wakeful nights."

It was the first time she had ever alluded to the fact. He wondered if she would summon the courage to tell him something further. He earnestly hoped she would; but he hoped in vain. Chris said no more.

He paused for a full minute to give her time, but, save that she became tensely still, she made no sign. Very quietly he let the matter pass. He would not force her confidence, but he realized at that moment more clearly than ever before that she had only really belonged to him during the brief fortnight that they had been alone together. The two months of their married life had but served to teach him this somewhat bitter lesson, and he determined then and there to win her back as he had won her at the outset, to make her his once more and to keep her so for ever.

"I am going to take you away, Chris," he said. "You are wanting a change. Noel's holidays will be over next week. We will start then."

"Where shall we go?" said Chris, and he detected the relief with which she hailed the change of subject.

"We will go to Valpré," he said, with quiet decision.

"Valpré!" The word leaped out as if of its own volition. Chris suddenly sprang upright from her pillows, and gazed at him wide-eyed. In the dim light he could not see her face distinctly, but there was something almost suggestive of fear in her attitude. "Why Valpré?" she said, in a queer, breathless undertone as if she could not control her voice.

He looked down at her in surprise. "You would like to go to Valpré again, wouldn't you?"

She gasped. "I—I really don't know. But what made you choose it? You have never been there."

"No," he said. "You will be able to introduce me to all your old haunts."

She gasped again. "You chose it because of that?"

He put a steadying hand upon her shoulder. "Chris, what makes you so nervous, child? No, I didn't choose it because of that. As a matter of fact, I didn't choose it at all. I am due there on business in three weeks' time, but I thought we might put in a fortnight together there beforehand. Wouldn't you like that?"

She shivered under his hand, and made no reply. She only said, "What business?"

He hesitated a moment, then deliberately sat down upon the bed and drew her close to him. "You remember that blackguard Frenchman Rodolphe who was staying with the Pounceforts two or three weeks ago?"

"Yes," whispered Chris.

"He is to be court-martialled at Valpré, and I have accepted an offer to go as correspondent to the *Morning Despatch* and report upon his trial. As you know, I represented them at Bertrand's *affaire*, and this is a sequel to that. In fact, Bertrand himself is very nearly concerned in it. Certain transactions have recently come to light tending to show that the crime of which he was accused was not only committed by this same Rodolphe, but that he also deliberately manufactured evidence to shield himself at the expense of Bertrand, the author of the betrayed invention, against whom it seems he had a personal grudge. By the way, he managed skilfully to keep in the background at Bertrand's trial. I fancy he was away on some special mission at the time, and he did not appear. I never saw him before that day at Sandacre Court, and I did not so much as know then that he and Bertrand were acquainted. Did you know that?"

She started at the question, but answered it more naturally than she had before spoken. "Yes. I knew that Bertie had belonged to the same regiment. They did not speak to each other that afternoon. You see, I was there."

"Ah! And you never met him in the old Valpré days?"

Again she answered without apparent agitation; but her hands were fast gripped together in the gloom. "I may have seen him. I never spoke to him. Bertie was the only one I ever knew."

"Ah!" Mordaunt said again. He was plainly thinking of Bertrand's affairs. "Well, he is to stand his trial now, and I couldn't resist the chance of being present at it. He was recalled to Paris a week ago, and summarily arrested; but as popular feeling is running very high, the trial is to be held at Valpré, which is a fairly important military station. That means that the court-martial will take place probably in the fortress in which the crime was committed—a pleasing consummation of justice."

"And—Bertie will be vindicated?" breathed Chris.

"If Rodolphe is convicted," Mordaunt answered, "Bertrand will be in a position to return to France and demand a second trial, the outcome of which would be practically a foregone conclusion, and at which I hope I shall be present."

Chris drew a sharp breath. "Then—then he will go to Valpré too?"

"Not yet. He would be arrested and imprisoned if he did, and might possibly ruin his cause as well. No, he will have to play a waiting game for the present. I think myself it is the turn of the tide, but things may yet go against him. There is no knowing. He is better off where he is till we can see which way the matter will go. He doesn't want to spend the rest of his life in a fortress."

Chris shuddered uncontrollably at the bare thought. "Oh no—no! Trevor, you won't let him run any risk of that?"

"I shall certainly counsel prudence," Mordaunt answered. "If he runs any risks, it will be with his eyes open."

He paused a moment, then turned her face tenderly up to his own, and kissed it. "And you don't like the Valpré plan?" he said, with great gentleness.

She hesitated.

"We can go elsewhere if you prefer it," he said. "The court-martial will probably only take a few days. We can stay somewhere near while it is in progress. But I must have you with me wherever it is."

He spoke the last words with his arms closely enfolding her. She turned with sudden impulse and clasped him round the neck.

"Oh, Trevor," she murmured brokenly, "you are good to me—you are good!"

"My darling," he whispered back, "your happiness is mine—always."

She made a choked sound of dissent. "I'm horribly selfish," she said, with a sob.

"No, dear, no. I understand. I ought to have thought of it before."

She knew that he was thinking of Cinders, and that a return to the old haunts could but serve to reopen a wound that was scarcely closed. She was thankful that he interpreted her reluctance thus, even while she marvelled to herself as she realized how far she had travelled since the bitter day on which she had parted with her favourite. Looking back, she saw now clearly what that tragedy had meant to her. It had been indeed the commencement of a new stage in her life's journey. It was on that day that she had finally stepped forth from the summer fields of her childhood, and she knew that she would wander in them no more for ever.

The thought went through her with a dart of pain. They had been very green, those fields, and the great thoroughfare which now she trod seemed cruelly hard to her unaccustomed feet.

A sharp sigh escaped her as she gently withdrew herself from her husband's arms. "Shall we talk about it to-morrow?" she said.

CHAPTER IV
"MINE OWN FAMILIAR FRIEND"

Sitting in his writing-room with Bertrand that night Mordaunt imparted the news that concerned him so nearly.

The young Frenchman listened in almost unbroken silence, betraying neither surprise nor even a very great measure of interest. He sat and smoked, with eyes downcast, sometimes fidgeting a little with the fingers of one hand on the arm of his chair, but otherwise displaying no sign of agitation.

Only at the end of the narration did he glance up, and that was but momentarily, when Mordaunt said, "It transpires that this Rodolphe had an old score to pay off. You were enemies?"

Bertrand removed his cigarette to reply, "That is true."

"You once fought a duel with him?" Mordaunt proceeded.

Bertrand's eyelids quivered, but he did not raise them. He merely answered, "Yes."

"That fact will probably figure in the evidence," Mordaunt said. "The cause of the duel is at present unknown."

"It is—immaterial," Bertrand said, in a very low voice. He paused a moment, then said, "And you, you will be at the trial to report?"

"Yes. I am going. Chris will go with me."

"Ah!" The exclamation seemed involuntary. Bertrand's hand suddenly clenched hard upon the chair-arm. "You will take her—to Valpré?" he questioned.

"Probably not to the place itself," Mordaunt made answer. "I think she is not very anxious to go there. It has associations that she would rather not renew. We shall stay somewhere within easy reach of Valpré. Perhaps you can tell me of a suitable resting-place not too far away. You know that part of the world."

"I know it well," Bertrand said, and fell silent, as though pondering the matter. At the end of a lengthy pause he spoke, abruptly, with just a tinge of nervousness. "But why do you take her if she does not desire to go?"

Mordaunt raised his brows a little.

"You will pardon me," Bertrand added quickly, "but it occurs to me that possibly she may prefer to remain at home. And if that were the case you would not, I hope, consider my presence here as an obstacle, for"—again he flashed a swift look across—"it is not my intention to remain."

"What are your intentions?" Mordaunt asked.

Bertrand shrugged his shoulders. "I do not know yet. Circumstances will decide. But it is certain that I can trespass no more upon your kindness. I have already accepted too much from you—more than I can ever hope to repay. Moreover"—he paused—"I do not wish to inconvenience you, and since I cannot accompany you to France—" he paused again, and finally decided to say no more.

"Chris will go with me in any case," said Mordaunt quietly. "We have already arranged that. You would cause no inconvenience to anyone by staying here. In fact, it would be to my advantage."

"To your advantage!" Bertrand echoed the words sharply, as if in some fashion they hurt him; and then, "But no," he said with decision. "It has never been to your advantage to employ me. You have done it from the kindness of your heart, but it would have been better for you if you had entrusted your affairs to a man more capable. And for that reason I am going to ask you to find another secretary as soon as possible, one who will perform his duties faithfully and merit his pay."

"Is that the only reason?" Mordaunt asked unexpectedly.

There fell a sudden silence. Bertrand, with bent head, appeared to be closely examining the leather on which his fingers still drummed an uneasy tattoo. At last, "It is the only reason which I have to give you," he said, his voice very low.

"It is not a very sound one," Mordaunt remarked.

Again that quick shrug of the shoulders, and silence. Several moments passed. Then with an abrupt movement Bertrand rose, laid aside his cigarette, which had gone out, and seated himself at the writing-table.

A pile of letters lay upon it that had arrived by the evening post. He began to turn them over, and presently took up a paper-cutter and deftly slit them open one by one.

Mordaunt sat and smoked as one lost in thought. Finally, after a long silence, he looked up and spoke.

"Why this sudden hurry to dissolve partnership, Bertrand?" he asked, with his kindly smile. "Is it this Rodolphe affair that has unsettled you? Because surely it would be wiser to wait and see what is going to happen before you take any decided step of this sort."

"Ah! It is not that!" Bertrand spoke with a vehemence that sounded almost passionate. "It is nothing to me—this affair. It interests me—not that!" He snapped his fingers contemptuously. "No, no! The time for that is past. What is honour, or dishonour, to me now—me who have been down to the lowest abyss and who have learned the true value of what the world calls great? Once—I admit it—I was young; I suffered. Now I am old, and—I laugh!"

Yet there was a note that was more suggestive of heartbreak than of mirth in his voice. He applied himself feverishly to extracting a letter from an envelope, while Mordaunt sat and gravely watched him.

Suddenly, but very quietly, Mordaunt rose, strolled across, and took the fluttering paper out of his hands. "Bertrand!" he said.

The Frenchman looked up sharply, almost as if he would resent the action, but something in the steady eyes that met his own altered the course of his emotions. He leaned back in his chair with the gesture of a man confronting the inevitable.

Mordaunt sat down on the edge of the writing-table, face to face with him. "Tell me why you want to leave me," he said.

There was determination in his attitude, determination in the very coolness of his speech. It was quite obvious that he meant to have an answer.

Bertrand contemplated him with a faint, rueful smile. "But what shall I say?" he protested. "You English are so persistent. You will not be content with the simple truth. You demand always—something more."

"There you are mistaken," Mordaunt made grave reply. "It is the simple truth that I want—nothing more."

"*Ciel!*" Bertrand jumped in his chair as if he had been stabbed in the back. "You insult me!"

Mordaunt's hand came out to him instantly and reassuringly. "My dear fellow, I never insult anyone. It is not my way."

"But you do not believe me!" Bertrand protested. "And that is an insult—that."

"I believe you absolutely." Very quietly Mordaunt made answer. The hand he would not take was laid with great kindness on his shoulder. "I happen to know you too well to do otherwise. Why, man," he began to smile a little, "if all the world turned false, I should still believe in you."

"*Tiens!*" The word was almost a cry. Bertrand shook the friendly hand from his shoulder as if it had been some evil thing, and almost with the same movement pushed his chair back sharply out of reach. "You should not say these things to me!" he stammered forth incoherently. "I do not deserve them. I am not—I am not what you imagine. You do not know me. I do not know myself. I—I—" He broke off in agitation and sprang impetuously to his feet.

With a gesture half-hopeless, half-appealing, he turned and walked to the window, as if he could no longer bear to meet the level, grey eyes that watched him with so kindly a confidence.

There fell a silence in the room while Mordaunt, still sitting on the writing-table, deliberately finished his cigarette. That done, he spoke.

"Don't you think you had better tell me what is the matter?"

Bertrand jerked his shoulders convulsively; it was the only response he made.

Mordaunt waited a few moments more. Then, "Very well," he said, without change of tone or countenance. "We will dismiss the subject. If you really mean to leave me, I will accept your resignation in the morning, but not to-night. If—as I hope—you have thought better of it by then and decide to remain, nothing further need be said. Will that satisfy you?"

Bertrand wheeled abruptly, and stood facing him, the length of the room intervening. His mouth worked as if he were trying to speak, but he said nothing whatever.

Mordaunt turned without further words to the letter in his hand, and studied it in silence. After a pause Bertrand came slowly back to the writing-table. He had mastered his agitation, but he looked unutterably tired.

Mordaunt moved to one side at his approach. "Sit down!" he said, without raising his eyes.

Bertrand sat down, and began to turn his attention to sorting the letters he had opened. Mordaunt stood motionless, reading with bent brows.

Suddenly he spoke. "There is something here I can't understand."

Bertrand glanced up. "Can I assist?"

"I don't know. Read that!" Mordaunt laid the letter before him. "I can't account for it. I think it must be a mistake."

Bertrand took the letter and read it. It was an intimation from the bank that in consequence of the bearer cheque for five hundred pounds presented and cashed the week before, Mordaunt's account was overdrawn.

"What cheque can it be?" Mordaunt said. "Have you any idea?"

Bertrand shook his head. "But no! It is perhaps some charity—a gift that you have forgotten?"

"My good fellow, I may be careless, but I'm not so damned careless as that." Mordaunt pulled out a bunch of keys with the words. "Let me have a look at my cheque-book. You know where it is."

Yes, Bertrand knew. He was as cognizant of the whereabouts of Mordaunt's possessions as if they had been his own, and he had as free an access to them. Such was the confidence reposed in him.

He took the keys, selected the right one, stooped to fit it into the lock. And then suddenly something happened. A violent tremor went through him. He clutched at the table-edge, and the keys clattered to the ground.

"Hullo!" Mordaunt said.

Bertrand was staring downwards with eyes that saw not. At the sound of Mordaunt's voice he started, and began to grope on the floor for the keys as if stricken blind.

"There they are, man, by your feet." Mordaunt stooped and recovered them himself. "What's the matter? Aren't you well?"

Bertrand lifted a ghastly face. "I am quite well," he said. "But—but surely the bank would not cash a cheque so large without reference to you!"

Mordaunt looked at him a moment. "I have been in the habit of drawing large sums," he said. "But I usually write a note to the bank to accompany a cheque of this sort."

He turned to the drawer and unlocked it. His cheque-book lay in its accustomed place within. He took it out and commenced a careful examination of the counterfoils of cheques already drawn.

Bertrand sat quite motionless, with bowed head. He seemed to be numbly waiting for something.

Mordaunt was very deliberate in his search. He came to the end of the counterfoils only, but went quietly on through the sheaf of blank cheques that remained, gravely scrutinizing each.

Minutes passed. Bertrand was sunk in his chair as one bent beneath some overpowering weight, the pile of letters untouched before him.

Suddenly Mordaunt paused, became tense for an instant, then slowly relaxed. His eyes travelled from the open cheque-book to the man in the chair. He contemplated him silently.

After the lapse of several seconds, he laid the open book upon the table before him. "A cheque has been abstracted here," he said.

His voice was perfectly quiet. He made the statement as if there were nothing extraordinary in it, as if he felt assured that there must be some perfectly simple explanation to account for it, as if, in fact, he scarcely recognized the existence of any mystery.

But Bertrand uttered not a word. He was as one turned to stone. His eyes became fixed upon the cheque in front of him, but his stare was wide and vacant. He seemed to be thinking of something else.

There fell a dead silence in the room, a stillness in which the quiet ticking of the clock on the mantelpiece became maddeningly obtrusive. For seconds that dragged out interminably neither of the two men stirred. It was as if they were mutely listening to that eternal ticking, as one listens to the tramp of a watchman in the dead of night.

Then, at last, with a movement curiously impulsive, Trevor Mordaunt freed himself from the spell. He laid his hand once more upon his secretary's shoulder.

"Bertrand!" he said, and in his voice interrogation, incredulity, even entreaty, were oddly mingled. "You!"

The Frenchman shivered, and came out of his lethargy. He threw a single glance upwards, then suddenly bowed his head on his hands. But still he spoke no word.

Mordaunt's hand fell from him. He stood a moment, then turned and walked away. "So that was the reason!" he said.

He came to a stand a few feet away from the bent figure at the writing-table, took out his cigarette-case, and deliberately lighted a cigarette. His face as he did it was grimly composed, but there were lines in it that very few had ever seen there. His eyes were keen and cold as steel. They held neither anger nor contempt, only a tinge of humour inexpressibly bitter.

Finally, through a cloud of smoke, he spoke again. "Have you nothing to say?"

Bertrand stirred, but he did not lift his head. "Nothing," he muttered, almost inarticulately.

"Then"—very evenly came the words—"that ends the case. I have nothing to say, either. You can go as soon as you wish."

He spoke with the utmost distinctness. His head was tilted back, and his eyes, still with that icy glint of amusement in them, watched the smoke ascending from his cigarette.

There was a brief pause. Then Bertrand stumbled stiffly to his feet. He seemed to move with difficulty. He turned heavily towards the Englishman.

"Monsieur," he said with ceremony, "you have—I believe—the right to prosecute me."

Mordaunt did not even look at him. "I believe I have," he said.

"*Alors*—" the Frenchman paused.

"I shall not exercise it," Mordaunt said curtly.

"You are too generous," Bertrand answered.

He spoke without emotion, yet there was something in his tone—something remotely suggestive of irony—that brought Mordaunt's eyes down to him. He looked at him hard and straight.

But Bertrand did not meet the look. With a mournful gesture he turned away. "I shall never cease to regret," he said, "the unhappy fate that sent me into your life. I blame myself bitterly—bitterly. I should have drawn back at the commencement, but I had not the strength. Only monsieur, believe this"—his voice suddenly trembled—"it was never my intention to rob you. Moreover, that which I have taken—I will restore."

He spoke very earnestly, with a baffling touch of dignity that seemed in some fashion to place him out of reach of contempt.

Mordaunt heard him without impatience, and replied without scorn. "What you have taken can never be restored. The utmost you can do is to let me forget, as soon as possible, that I ever imagined you to be—what you are not."

The simplicity of the words effected in an instant that which neither taunt nor sneer could ever have accomplished. It pierced straight to Bertrand's heart. He turned back impulsively, with outstretched hands.

"But, my friend—my friend—" he cried brokenly.

Mordaunt checked him on the instant with a single imperious gesture of dismissal, so final that it could not be ignored.

The words died on Bertrand's lips. He wheeled sharply, as if at a word of command, and went to the door.

But as he opened it, Mordaunt spoke. "I will see you again in the morning."

"Is it necessary?" Bertrand said.

"I desire it." Mordaunt spoke with authority.

Bertrand turned and made him a brief, punctilious bow. "That is enough," he said, and left the room martially, his head in the air.

CHAPTER V
A DESPERATE REMEDY

The clock on the mantelpiece struck two, and Mordaunt rose from his chair to close the window. The night was very still and dark. He stood for a few moments breathing the moist air. From somewhere away in the distance there came the weird cry of an owl—the only sound in a waste of silence. He leaned his head against the window-sash with a sensation of physical sickness. His heart was heavy as lead.

"Trevor!"

It was no more than a whisper, but he heard it. He turned. "Chris!"

She stood before him, her white draperies caught together with one hand, her hair flowing in wide ripples all about her, her eyes anxiously raised to his.

"Trevor," she said, "what is the matter?"

There was a species of desperate courage in the low question. The fingers that grasped her wrapper were tightly clenched.

He closed the window. "Have you been lying awake for me?" he said. "I am sorry."

"Something is the matter," she said with conviction. "Won't you tell me what it is? I—I would rather know."

"I will tell you in the morning, dear," he said gently. "You must go back to bed. I am coming myself now."

But Chris stood still. "I want to know now, please, Trevor," she said. "I shall not sleep at all unless I know."

He put his arm about her, looking down at her with great tenderness. "Must I tell you now?" he said, a hint of weariness in his voice.

She did not resist his touch, but neither did she yield herself to him. She stood within the encircling arm, looking straight up at him with wide, resolute eyes.

"It is something to do with Bertie," she said, in the same tone of unquestioning conviction.

He raised his eyebrows. "What makes you think so?"

She frowned a little. "It doesn't matter, does it? Won't you tell me what has happened?"

He hesitated momentarily; then; "Yes, I will tell you," he said. "Bertrand is leaving to-morrow—for good."

He felt her stiffen against his arm, and for the first time he noticed her pallor and the unusual steadfastness of her eyes. He realized that she was putting strong restraint upon herself, and the fact made her strangely unfamiliar to him. He was accustomed to vivid speech and impetuous action. He scarcely knew her in this mood, although he recognized that he had seen it at least once before.

"Why?" Her lips scarcely moved as they asked the question. Her eyes never left his face.

He drew her to the writing-table on which his cheque-book still lay open at the place whence a cheque had been abstracted with its counterfoil.

"Sit down," he said, "and I will tell you."

She sat down in silence.

He knelt beside her as he had knelt on their wedding-night, and took her cold hands into his own.

"I think you know," he said quietly, "that I have always trusted Bertrand implicitly."

"You trust everyone," she said, with a small, aloof smile, as if she were trying to appear courteous while her thoughts were elsewhere.

"Yes, to my undoing," he told her grimly. "I trusted him to the utmost, and—and he has betrayed my trust."

She started at that, but instantly controlled herself. "In what way?" she asked him, her voice scarcely above a whisper.

He drew the cheque-book to him. "If you look at this cheque and the next," he said, "you will see that there is one missing. There has been a cheque taken out."

"Yes?" said Chris.

Her eyes rested for a moment upon the cheque-book, and returned to his face. They held a curious expression as of relief and doubt mingled.

"That is how he betrayed my trust," he told her quietly. "He used that cheque to forge my signature and withdraw a sum of money from my account which under ordinary circumstances I should probably never have missed. As he is aware, I keep a large account, and I am in the habit of drawing large cheques. As it chanced, the account was not quite so large as usual, and it did not quite cover the amount withdrawn. Consequently my attention was called to it, and I looked into the matter and discovered—this."

"Yes?" said Chris. "Yes?"

She was breathing very fast. It was evident that her agitation was getting beyond her control.

He clasped her hands closer, with a warm and comforting pressure. He knew—or he thought he knew—what this revelation would mean to her. Had not Bertrand been even more her friend, her trusted counsellor, than his own?

"That is all the story, dear," he said gently. "We have got to face it as bravely as we can. He will leave in the morning, so you need not see him again."

She made a quick, involuntary movement, and her hands slipped from his.

"Not see him again!" she repeated, staring at him with wide eyes. "Not see him again!"

"I think it would be wiser not," he said, very kindly. "It would only cause you unnecessary pain."

She uttered a sudden breathless little laugh. "Trevor—am I dreaming? Or—are you mad? You don't—actually—believe he did this thing?"

His face hardened a little. "He had the sense not to attempt to deny it. There was no question as to his guilt. He was the only person besides myself who had access to my cheque-book."

"But—" Chris said, and paused, as if to collect her thoughts. "How much was taken?" she asked after a moment.

"That," Mordaunt observed, "is the least important part of the whole miserable business."

"Still, tell me," she persisted.

"He took five hundred pounds."

"Trevor!" She gasped for breath, and turned so white that he thought for a moment she would faint.

He put his arm round her quickly. "Chris, we won't discuss it any further to-night. You must go back to bed. You will catch cold if you stay here any longer."

But for the first time in her life she resisted him. She drew away from him. She almost pushed him from her.

"Five hundred pounds!" she said, speaking through white lips. She was shivering violently from head to foot. "But—but—what should Bertie want with five hundred pounds?"

"I didn't inquire what he did with it." Mordaunt's answer came with implacable sternness. "I haven't the least curiosity on that point. It is enough for me that he took it."

"Oh, Trevor, how hard you are!" The words rushed out like the cry of a hurt creature, and suddenly Chris's hands were on his shoulders, and her face, pinched and desperate, looked closely into his. "You have so much— so much!" she wailed. "You don't know what temptation is!"

He rose to his feet instantly and lifted her to hers. She was sobbing terribly, but without tears. He held her to him, supporting her.

"Chris, Chris!" he said. "Don't, child, don't! I know what this means to you. It means a good deal to me too, more than you realize. But for Heaven's sake let us stand together over it. Let us be reasonable."

There was strong appeal in his voice; for in that moment, though he held her to his heart, he knew that the gulf between them had suddenly begun to widen. He saw the danger in a flash of intuition, but he was powerless to avert it. They viewed the matter from opposite standpoints. Did they not view all matters moral thus? She could condone what he could only condemn, and because of this she deemed him hard and feared him.

He bent his face to hers as he held her. His lips moved against her forehead. "Chris," he said softly, "don't cry, dear! Listen to me. I'm not going to punish him. He will have to go of course. As a matter of fact, he meant to do so in any case. But it will go no further than that. There will be no prosecution."

She turned her face up quickly, and he saw that her eyes were dry, though her breathing was spasmodic. "You couldn't prosecute an innocent man," she said. "And he is innocent. I know he is innocent. You say he didn't deny it. It was because he wouldn't stoop to deny it. He knew you would never believe him if he did."

The words came fast and passionate. She drew back from him to utter them, and for the first time he read a challenge in her desperate eyes.

He let her go out of his arms. He had tried to bridge the gulf, but the distance was too great. His tenderness only gave her courage to defy him.

With a stifled sigh he abandoned the conflict. "As I said before, there is no question of his guilt," he said, with quiet emphasis. "Far from denying it, he even announced his intention of restoring what he had taken. That, of course, is also out of the question. He will probably never be in a position to do so. But in any case it is beside the point. It is useless to discuss it further."

She broke in upon him almost fiercely. "Trevor, won't you believe me when I say that I know—I know—he is innocent?"

He looked at her. "How do you know it?"

She wrung her hands together. "Oh, I have no proof! Can't you believe me without proof?"

He was watching her intently. "I believe in your sincerity, of course," he said. "But I am afraid I don't share your conviction."

"But you must—you must!" she cried. "I know him better than you do. I know him to be incapable of the tiniest speck of dishonour. I swear that he is innocent! I swear it! I swear it!"

He put out a restraining hand. "Chris, don't say any more! You are only upsetting yourself to no purpose. Come, child, it is useless to go on—quite useless."

She flung out her arms with a gesture of utter despair. "You won't believe me?"

He turned to lock up his cheque-book. "I have answered that question already," he said, without impatience.

She drew near to him. Her blue eyes burned with a feverish light. Her face was haggard. "Trevor, what would you say if—if—I told you he were shielding someone—if I told you he were shielding—me?" Her voice sank upon the word.

He turned sharply round, so sharply that she shrank. But he made no movement towards her. He only looked full and piercingly into her face. At the end of ten seconds he spoke, so calmly that his voice sounded cold.

"I am afraid I shouldn't believe you."

His eyes fell away from her with the words. He dropped his keys into his pocket and switched off the light from his writing-table.

Chris was shivering again, shivering from head to foot. She could barely keep her teeth from chattering. He came to her and put his arm round her.

She glanced up at him nervously, but his quiet face told her nothing. Almost involuntarily she suffered him to lead her from the room.

CHAPTER VI
WHEN LOVE DEMANDS A SACRIFICE

When Chris awoke, the morning sunshine was streaming in through the open windows, and she was alone. She came back to full remembrance slowly, as one toiling along a difficult road. Her brain felt very tired. She lay vaguely listening to the gay trill of a robin on the terrace below, dreading the moment when the dull ache at her heart should turn to active pain.

A cheery whistle on the gravel under her windows roused her at last. She took up her burden again with a great sigh.

"O God!" she whispered, as she turned her heavy head upon the pillow, "do let me die soon—do let me die soon!"

But there was no voice nor any that answered.

Wearily at length she raised herself. It was curious how ill she felt. She looked longingly back at her pillow.

At the same instant the gay whistle in the garden gave place to a cracked shout. "Hullo, Chris! Aren't you going to get up to-day? Do you know what time it is?"

She started, and looked at her watch. Ten o'clock! In amazement and consternation she sprang from the bed. Bertrand was to leave in the morning; so Trevor had told her. She must—she must—see him before he left! Doubtless Trevor had hoped that she would sleep on till the afternoon, and so miss him. How little he knew! How little he understood!

With a bound she reached the window, there a sudden dizziness attacked her. She clutched at the curtain with both hands. What if he had gone already? What if she were never to see him again?

Desperately she steadied herself. She must not give way thus. She looked out and saw Noel, walking along the edge of the balustrade that bounded the terrace. His arms were outstretched, and he balanced himself with extreme difficulty. It looked perilous, but she knew him well enough to feel no anxiety, notwithstanding the fact that there was a fall of twelve feet on one side of him.

After a few moments she commanded herself sufficiently to call down to him, "Noel, where is everybody?"

He looked up, lost his balance, and sprang down upon the terrace. "By Jove! Aren't you dressed yet? What are we coming to? Trevor is gone to ride round the estate, wouldn't have me for some reason. Bertrand is in his room with the door locked, says he is busy—all bally rot, of course. And Aunt Phil, thank the gods! is packing her trunk to leave by the five o'clock train. By the way, Trevor said I was to see you had some breakfast. What would you like? I'll bring it up to you myself in two shakes."

Chris felt an unexpected lump rise in her throat. Somehow the tenderness of her husband's love hurt her more than it comforted just then. She knew that he had absented himself and deputed Noel to wait upon her because he had divined that she would prefer it. His intuition frightened her also. Was he beginning to divine other things as well? Recalling his intent look of the night before, the wonder struck chill to her heart. Yes, she was thankful that he had gone; but it would be horribly hard to meet him again after she and Bertrand had said good-bye. Aunt Philippa's departure, eagerly though she had anticipated it, would make it harder. Very soon Noel also would be gone, and they would be alone together. How would she keep her secret then? How hide her soul from those grave, keen eyes that probed so deeply?

Ah! but he trusted her; he trusted her! Back to the old sheet-anchor flew her whirling thoughts. His faith in her was invincible, unassailable. It kept her safe. It sheltered her from every danger. It was her single safeguard in temptation; without it she would be lost.

She swallowed the lump in her throat, and leaned from the window to give her brother the instructions he awaited.

Turning back into the room, she found a note in her husband's handwriting lying on her table. She took it up.

"I do not forbid you to see Bertrand," it ran, "though I think you would be wiser not to do so. I have already taken leave of him. He refuses to be open with me, so there is no more to be said. It is by his own wish that he is leaving to-day. As I said to you last night, I shall take no legal steps against him, but that does not alter the fact that he is a criminal, and for that reason your friendship with him must cease. I am sorry, but it is inevitable. I think you will see it for yourself by and bye, but till then my prohibition must be enough. I cannot be disobeyed in this matter. Bear it in mind, dear, and believe that, even though I may seem hard, I am acting for your welfare, which is more to me than anything else on earth.

"Yours,
TREVOR."

Her face was white and strained as she read the note through. She seemed to hear her husband's quiet voice in every sentence. Never till that moment had she fully realized the fact that he had the right thus to guide and restrain her actions. Never till that moment had she found her will in direct opposition to his. A sudden passion of rebellion swept upon her, possessed her. It was intolerable, impossible; she could not submit to the mandate.

To give up her friend—the dear knight of her girlhood's dreams—to see him never again, to close her heart to him, to shut out the very memory of him, to take up her life without him—no, never, never, never! Her throbbing heart cried out against it. It was not to be borne. A fury akin to hatred surged up within her. There was no man living who could make her do this thing.

Fiercely she tore the paper across and across, and flung the fragments from her. Never would she consent to this! She would defy him sooner!

Defy him! It was as if a voice spoke suddenly in her soul, asking a quiet question. Could she defy him and still hide her secret? Would not the steady eyes read her through and through the instant that her will resisted his? Would he not know in a moment? Was it not even possible that he had begun already to suspect?

Again she recalled his intent look of the night before, and her heart misgave her. Had she betrayed herself? Had he seen behind the veil? She shivered at the thought, and for a few moments she was overwhelmingly afraid. How would she ever meet those eyes again?

But when presently Noel presented himself she had recovered her self-command. She even compelled herself to eat some breakfast, while he balanced himself on the window-sill and made careless conversation. It was evident that he knew nothing of Bertrand's impending departure, and she was relieved that this was so. She could not have borne his curiosity or his comments.

"What are you going to do to-day?" she presently inquired.

"When you've had a decent meal, I'm going for a ride," he answered promptly. "Can't waste the whole day hanging about and Fiddle's spoiling for a gallop. You won't come, I suppose?"

She shook her head. "No. I couldn't, anyhow. I must stay with Aunt Philippa to-day. I've had quite a lot to eat. Don't wait."

He sprang to his feet at once. "You haven't done badly, have you, considering you've been lazing in bed instead of working up an appetite in the open air? I say, Chris, there's nothing the matter, is there?"

"Of course not," she returned briskly. "Why?"

"You're not looking exactly chirpy," he said, regarding her critically. "And Trevor was positively bearish this morning. He hasn't been bullying you, has he?"

"Of course not," she said again. "How absurd you are!"

He looked incredulous. "Don't you stick it!" he warned her. "If he tries it on, you come to me. I'll settle him."

She laughed and turned the subject. "Hadn't you better start? It's getting late."

"P'raps I had. Good-bye, then!" He bent unexpectedly and kissed her cheek. "We'll go for a picnic to-morrow," he said, "to celebrate Aunt Phil's departure. Keep your pecker up! She'll soon be gone."

He marched away, whistling, and Chris was alone.

She rose and finished her dressing with feverish haste. Now was her time.

Noel had said Bertrand was in his room. She must see him alone. But how should she let him know? If she went in search of him she might encounter Aunt Philippa and be detained. She went down to her husband's room, and rang the bell there.

Holmes answered it in some surprise, knowing his master to be out; but she gave him no time for speculation.

"Holmes," she said, "I believe Mr. Bertrand is somewhere in the house. I wish you would find him, and say I am waiting to speak to him on a matter of importance. I am going into the garden. He will find me under the yew-tree."

Holmes departed with his customary dispatch. There was something indefinable about his young mistress that made him wish his master were at hand. He made his way to Bertrand's room and knocked.

There was no immediate reply; then, "I am busy," said Bertrand from within.

"If you please, sir!" said Holmes.

There was a movement in the room at once, and the door opened. "Ah! It is the good Holmes!" said Bertrand. "I thought that it was Monsieur Noel. What is it, then? You bring me a message?"

He looked at the man with sleepless eyes that shone curiously bright. In the room behind him a portmanteau, half-filled, lay upon the floor.

For a single instant Holmes hesitated before delivering his message. Then he gave it punctiliously, word for word.

"I am obliged to you," said Bertrand courteously. "I shall go to Mrs. Mordaunt at once."

He crossed the threshold therewith, but paused a moment outside the room.

"Holmes," he said, "I go to London by the 11.50. Will you arrange for my luggage to be taken to the station?"

Holmes's well-ordered countenance expressed no surprise. "Very good, sir. And you yourself, sir?" he said.

"I shall walk," said Bertrand.

"You would like me to finish packing for you, sir?" suggested Holmes.

"Ah! That would be very good." Bertrand's voice expressed relief. He stepped back into the room to slip a sovereign into the man's hand.

But Holmes drew back. "Thank you, sir. I'd rather not, sir."

Bertrand's brows went up. "How? But we are friends, no?" he questioned.

"I don't know, sir," said Holmes, respectful but firm. "Anyhow, I'd rather not, sir."

"*Eh bien!*" The Frenchman shrugged his shoulders and turned. "*Adieu*, Holmes!" he said.

"Good-day, sir!" said Holmes.

He stood in the middle of the room till Bertrand had gone, then with an expressionless face he betook himself to the door of Aunt Philippa's room.

Here he knocked again, and, receiving Mrs. Forest's permission to enter, presented himself on the threshold.

"I have come to say, madam, that Mrs. Mordaunt is in the garden under the old yew," he announced deferentially. "Will you be good enough to join her there?"

Aunt Philippa, in the midst of her own preparations for departure, received the news with considerable surprise. It was not Chris's custom to send her messages of any description. The summons fired her curiosity; but her dignity would not allow her to hasten overmuch to answer it.

"I will be with Mrs. Mordaunt in a few minutes," she said.

And Holmes departed, impassive still but with a mind uneasy. He wished with all his soul that the master had not chosen to absent himself that morning. Perhaps he was unreasonably nervous, but there seemed to be tragedy in the very air.

Bertrand, traversing the lawn bareheaded, was keenly aware of tragedy; but it did not delay his steps. He went down the shady path that led to Chris's retreat at a speed that left him breathless. He paused with his hand to his heart as he reached the yew-tree before plunging into the gloom beneath its great, drooping branches. He was living too fast, and he knew it, could almost feel his life running out like the sand in an hour-glass. But a great recklessness possessed him. If his strength could only be made to last for a couple of hours more, he did not care what happened to him, how soon the sand ran out.

He had suffered more during the past night than he had ever thought to suffer again. He had fought a desperate fight, and it had cost him nearly all his strength. He knew instinctively that he must make the most of what was left. Afterwards—afterwards—when the ordeal was over, he would sink down and rest, it mattered not where. If he lived long enough, he would keep his promise to Max Wyndham. If not,—well, he would not be needing human help. The gods had nearly done with him, and he was too weary to care. If he could only be faithful a little longer—a little longer! Nothing would matter afterwards, and the pain would be over then.

"Bertie, I am here!"

He started, and for a moment that which he had been fighting down all night showed in his eyes. He thrust it away out of sight. He answered her with his usual courteous confidence.

"Ah! You are there, Christine! You will pardon me for keeping you waiting. I came as soon as your message reached me."

He lifted one of the great yew-branches and stepped beneath as if entering a tent. It fell behind him, and in the green gloom they were face to face.

"Were you going without saying good-bye?" said Chris.

She stood before him, very pale and quiet. Her eyes did not meet his quite fully.

He spread out his hands. "I knew not if you would wish to see me."

"Don't you know me better than that?" she said. He did not answer her. Evidently she did not expect an answer, for she went on almost at once. "Bertie, why did you let Trevor think you had robbed him?"

He made a sharp gesture of protest, but remained silent.

She laid her hand on his arm. "Come and sit down, Bertie! And please answer me, because I want to know."

He went with her to the rustic seat against the tree-trunk. He was gripping his self-control with all his strength.

"Mr. Mordaunt must think what he will," he said at length, with an effort. "He can never judge me too severely."

"Why do you say that?" Chris asked the question quickly, nervously, as if she had to ask it, yet dreaded the answer.

"I think you know, Christine," he answered, his voice very low.

She shrank a little. "But that money, Bertie? You knew nothing of that?"

He was silent for a moment; then, "We will not speak of that," he said firmly. "I could not stay here in any case, so—it makes no difference."

"No difference that he should think you a thief!" exclaimed Chris.

He turned his eyes downwards, staring heavily at the ground between his feet. "I ask myself," he said, "if I am any better than a thief."

"Bertie!" There was quick distress in her voice this time. "But you have done nothing wrong," she declared vehemently, "nothing whatever!"

He shook his head in silence, not looking at her.

"And you are ill," she went on, passing the matter by as if not trusting herself. "What will you do? Where will you go?"

He sat up slowly and faced her. "I go to London," he said, "and I must start now. Do not be anxious for me, Christine. I have money enough. Mr. Mordaunt offered me more this morning. But I had no need of it, and I refused."

He spoke quite steadily. He was braced for the ordeal. He would be strong until the need for strength was past.

But with Chris it was otherwise. For her there was no prospect of relaxation. She was but at the beginning of her trial, and her whole soul shrank from the contemplation of what lay before her. The dear dreams of her childhood had flickered out like pictures on a screen. And she had awakened to find herself in a prison-house from which all her life long she could never hope to escape. Did some memory of the arms that had enfolded her so often and so tenderly come to her as she realized it? If so, it was only to stab her afresh with the bitter irony of Fate that had lavished upon her the love of a man who had filled her life with all that woman's heart could desire, and yet had failed to give her happiness.

And so, when Bertrand spoke of going, the newly awakened heart of her rose up in sudden, hot revolt. His departure was inevitable, and she knew it, but her endurance was not equal to the strain. She had deemed herself stronger than she was.

She threw out her hands with a passionate gesture. "Bertie! What shall I do without you? I can't go on by myself. I can't—I can't!"

It was like the cry of a child, but in it there throbbed all the deep longing of her womanhood. Ah! why had her eyes been opened? Surely she had been happier blind!

He took the outflung hands and held them. He looked into her eyes. "But, *chérie,*" he said, "you have your husband."

"I know—I know!" Piteously the words came from her. "He is very good to me. But, Bertie, he—has never been—first. I know it now. I didn't know before, or I wouldn't have married him. I swear I would never have married him—if I had known!"

"*Chérie,* hush!" Almost sternly he checked her, though his eyes were unfailingly kind. "You must not say it, Christine. Words always make a bad thing worse. Think instead how great is his love for you. Remember—oh, remember that you are his wife! The sin was mine that you could ever forget it. But you have not forgotten it, *mignonne!* Tell me that you have not! Tell me that when you think of me it will be as a friend who gives you no regrets, the friend of your childhood, little Christine—the comrade with whom you played in the sunshine; no more than that—no more than that!"

Very earnestly he besought her, holding her hands lightly clasped between his own, ready at her slightest movement to let them go. But she made no effort to withdraw them. She only bent her head and wept as though her heart were breaking.

"*Chérie, chérie!*" he said, and that was all; for he had no words wherewith to comfort her. He had wrought the mischief, but the remedy did not lie with him.

His own lips quivered above her bowed head; he bit them desperately.

After a little she commanded herself sufficiently to speak through her tears. "Bertie, you once said—that there was no goodness without Love. Then why—why is Love—wrong?"

"Love is not wrong, *chérie.*" Instant and reassuring came his answer. "Let us be true to Love, and we are true to God. For Love is God, and in every heart He is to be found; sometimes in much, sometimes in very, very little, but He is always there."

"I don't understand," said Chris. "If that were so—why mustn't we love each other? Why is it wrong?"

"It is not wrong." Again with absolute assurance Bertrand spoke. "So long as it is pure, it is also holy. There is no sin in Love. We shall love each other always, dear, always. With me it will be more—and ever more. Though I shall not be with you, though I shall not see your face or touch your hand, you will know that I am loving you still. It will be as an Altar Flame that burns for ever. But I will be faithful. My love shall never hurt you again. That is where I sinned. I was selfish enough to show you the earthly part of my love—the part that dies, just as our bodies die, setting our spirits free. For see, *chérie*, it is not the material part that endures. All things material must pass, but the spiritual lives on for ever. That is why Love is immortal. That is why Love can never die."

She listened to him in silence, scarcely comprehending at the moment words that later were to become the only light to guide her stumbling feet.

"Would you say that you love the dead no more because you see them not?" he questioned gently. "The sight—the touch—what is it? Only the earthly medium of Love; Love Itself is a higher thing, capable of the last sacrifice, greater than evil, stronger than death. Oh, believe me, Christine, Death is a very small thing compared with Love. If our love were of the spirit only, Death would be less than nothing; for it is only the body that can ever die."

"But why can't we be happy before we die?" whispered Chris. "Other people are."

He shook his head. "I doubt it, *chérie*. With death in the world there can be no perfection. All passes—all passes—except only the Love that is our Life."

He paused a moment, seeming to hesitate upon the verge of telling her something more; but in that instant she raised her head and he refrained.

"Ah, Christine," he said sadly, "I never thought that I should make you weep like this."

"Oh, it's not your fault, Bertie." She smiled at him, with quivering lips. "It's just life. But—dearest—I want you to know all the same—that I'm glad—I'm glad I love you so. And—whether it's right or wrong, I can't help it—I shall always love you—best of all."

His eyes shone at the words. A passionate answer sprang to his lips, but he stopped it unuttered. "We are not responsible for that which we cannot help," he said instead. "Only—my darling"—for the first time the English word of endearment passed his lips, spoken almost under his breath—"never permit the thought of me to come between you and your husband. Be faithful, Christine—be faithful!"

She made no answer of any sort; but her eyes were hopeless.

He waited a while, still holding her hands while tenderly he watched her. At last, "I must go, *chérie*," he whispered.

Her face quivered. Suddenly and impetuously as of old she spoke. "Bertie, once—long ago—you meant to marry me, didn't you?"

His own face contracted. "Do not let us torture ourselves in vain," he urged her gently.

"But it is true!" she persisted.

He hesitated an instant. "Yes, it is true," he said.

She leaned her head back, looking him straight in the eyes. There was a light in hers that he had never seen before. They gleamed like stars, seeing him only. "Bertie," she said, and her voice thrilled upon the words, "I was yours then, and I am yours now. I have always belonged to you, and you to me. Bertie, I—am coming with you."

His violent start testified to the utter unexpectedness of her announcement. Such a possibility had not, it was obvious, suggested itself to him. He turned white to the lips.

"Christine!" he stammered incredulously.

Feverishly she broke in upon his astonishment. "Oh, don't be shocked! It is absolutely the only way. I cannot stay here without you. Trevor will keep us apart. He will not let me even write to you. He says that our friendship must cease. And it cannot—it cannot! Bertie, don't you see? Don't you understand? Don't you—want me?"

A note of despair rang in her voice. Her hands suddenly gripped each other in agonized misgiving. But on the instant his gripped closer, holding them crushed against his breast in fierce reassurance. His eyes shone full into hers, and for one moment of fiery rapture which both were to remember all their lives their souls mingled, became fused in one, forgetful of all beside.

Out of the silence the man's voice came, low and passionate. "*Le bon Dieu* knows how I want you, my bird of Paradise! But yet—but yet—" Something seemed to choke his utterance. He gave a sudden gasp, and bowed his head forward upon her shoulder.

Her arms were round him in an instant. "What is it, dearest? You are ill!"

"No," he said. "No." But still he gasped for breath, and she fancied that he repressed a shudder.

He raised his head after a moment. "Pardon me, *chérie*. I am only— weak. Christine, all my life—all my life—I shall remember—how you were ready—to give up all—all—for me. But, *mignonne*, I cannot take such a sacrifice. I dare not. Go back to your husband, *chérie*. It is your duty. You are his, not mine. We will not stain our love thus. Christine"—his voice broke—"*ma mignonne*, I love you too well—too well—to do this thing. You shall not be ruined—for my sake."

"Oh, but, Bertie!" she pleaded. She was clinging to him now; her eyes implored him. "Think of me here without you! Never to see you again— never to have a single word from you any more! Bertie, I can't bear it—I can't bear it! It will be no sacrifice to me to come with you. I don't mind hardship. I'm used to poverty, But here—but here—"

Her voice broke also, she could say no more. His arms went round her, straining her to him. His face was close to hers. But his eyes were the eyes of a man in torture.

"I know—I know all," he whispered. "Yet—my darling—you must stay—and I must go. When Love demands a sacrifice—"

"I will sacrifice anything—everything—all I have!" she cried out wildly.

"We must sacrifice each other," he said. "That is the test of our love, *chérie*. That is the sacrifice that Love demands."

He spoke quite quietly, with the calmness of one who knew and faced the worst. The torture in his eyes had turned to dumb endurance. "Only thus," he said—"only thus can we be true to our love. We sacrifice the little for the much. *Mignonne*, believe me, it is worth it. You are mine, and I am yours. So be it, then. Let us be—faithful."

He spoke with the utmost tenderness; yet was she awed. Her sudden rebellion died. It was as though a quiet hand had been laid upon her heart, stilling her pain. For one moment she looked with him across the long, dark furrows of mortal life into the great Beyond, and knew that he had spoken the truth. Their love was worth the sacrifice.

"Oh, Bertie," she said, in a whisper, "you are right, dear, you are right."

His eyes flashed swift understanding into hers; yet for a moment his arms tightened about her, as if her submission made it harder for him to let her go.

She waited till they relaxed, and then she laid her hands upon his shoulders. "Bertie," she said very earnestly, "forget I ever asked it of you!"

He shook his head instantly, with a sudden, transforming smile that revealed in him the young, quick spirit that had caught hers so long ago. "Oh no—no!" he said. "It will be to me the most precious memory of my life. By it I shall always remember—the so great generosity—of your love."

The smile went out of his face. He leaned nearer to her. She read irresolution in his eyes, and a quiver that was half of hope and half of apprehension went through her. Was he going to fail, after all, in the moment of victory? If so—if so—

But he restrained himself. She saw him fight down the impulse that urged him inch by inch until he had it in subjection. Under her watching eyes he conquered. He showed her the Omnipotence of Love.

Quietly, with no exaggeration of reverence, he knelt before her. He took her hands into his own, turned them upwards, pressed his lips to each palm, let them go.

The silence between them was like a sacrament. She never knew how long it lasted. It was a farewell more final than any words.

At last, "God keep you, my Christine!" he said. "God bless you!"

He rose to his feet, but he did not look at her again.

She could not speak in answer; there was no need of speech. He knew her heart as he knew his own.

And so in silence, with bent head, he left her. And the sun went out of her sky.

CHAPTER VII
THE WAY OF THE WYNDHAMS

When Mordaunt returned from his ride, it was close upon the luncheon-hour. He went straight upstairs to prepare for the meal.

Chris's room was empty. He wondered where she was, but Noel bounded in and enlightened him before he descended.

"She's doing the pretty to Aunt Philippa," he reported. "Only three more hours now! Hip, hip, hooray!"

His yell caused Mordaunt to fling the towel he was using at his head, a compliment which seemed to please him immensely. He draped it round his neck and proceeded to deliver himself of that which he had come to say.

"Look here, Trevor, you've been bullying Chris, haven't you? You needn't say you haven't, because I know you have."

"Did she tell you so?" Mordaunt sounded grim.

Noel turned to look at him. "No. She said you hadn't. But she always tells a cram when it suits her purpose. I knew you had all the same."

Mordaunt was silent.

"She's horribly down in the mouth," Noel proceeded. "She never used to be before she married you. It's a pretty beastly thing to have to say, but someone ought to say it, and if I don't no one else will."

"Go on," said Mordaunt. "Your sense of duty does you credit."

"Don't be a beast! It isn't duty at all. I'm simply pointing out the obvious. I should think you could see it for yourself, can't you?"

Mordaunt brushed his hair in silence.

"It's got to stop anyhow," Noel went on with determination. "She's not to be bullied. It's worse than shabby,—it—it's damned mean to—to treat her as if—as if—" He became suddenly agitated and lost the thread of his discourse.

Mordaunt had laid down his brushes to listen. His eyes were gravely attentive. They held no indignation. "Go on," he said again. "You are quite right to use strong language if you consider the occasion requires it."

But Noel's flow of language had failed him. He sprang suddenly at his brother-in-law, and caught him by the shoulders. "Oh, do stop it, old chap!" he urged, with husky vehemence. "We all of us rely on you. And if you fail us—can't you see we're done for?"

Mordaunt looked down at him with a faint smile. "Perhaps I had better tell you what has happened," he said. "The trouble at the present moment is that Bertrand has robbed me, and has left in consequence."

"Great Scotland!" ejaculated Noel. "How much did he take?"

"Five hundred pounds. That's a detail of small consequence." Mordaunt spoke with grim precision. "It has upset Chris—quite naturally. But even you can hardly hold me responsible for that."

"I should think not! I say, I'm sorry I spoke." Impetuously Noel hugged him to obliterate the effect of his words. "I'm a silly ass. You mustn't mind me. Do you know, I always thought he would somehow, though Chris was so keen on him."

"I was keen on him too," Mordaunt observed, without much humour.

"I'm awfully sorry, old chap. It's a bit of a facer for you. But, you know, you can't trust foreigners. It doesn't do. There was that chap at Valpré. He simply bewitched Chris. She never would hear a word against him, but I'm sure he was a bounder. I've often thought since that he probably manoeuvred that cave business. They're such a wily lot, these Frenchies."

"What cave business?" There was a hint of sharpness in Mordaunt's voice; his brows were drawn.

Noel looked surprised. "Why, the time they got hung up by the tide all night. Mean to say you never heard of it? Oh, my eye!" he broke off blankly. "Then I've let the cat out of the bag!"

"Don't distress yourself. It is of no importance." Mordaunt's tone was suddenly very deliberate. He turned away and began to put on his coat. "Are you ready for luncheon? I'm going down now."

Noel surveyed him doubtfully. "You won't let on I told you, will you?" he said uneasily. "Chris may have asked me to keep it dark."

"I don't suppose she did." Very quietly Mordaunt made reply. "She has more probably forgotten all about it. But I won't give you away in any case. You are ready? Then suppose we go!"

They descended together to find Aunt Philippa and Chris awaiting them in the hall. Chris scarcely looked at her husband. She was very pale.

He followed her to her end of the table to pour her out a glass of wine.

"Please don't!" she said nervously. "I don't like it. I can't drink it."

"I think you can," he answered. "Try!"

He went to his own place, and proceeded to engage Aunt Philippa in conversation. But Aunt Philippa was looking even more severe than usual, and responded so indifferently to his efforts that he presently suffered them to flag. There fell a dead silence. Then Noel struck in with furious zest, and Mordaunt turned to him with relief. But Chris scarcely opened her lips.

At the end of the meal he addressed her with quiet authority. "Chris, you must rest this afternoon. Your aunt will excuse you."

"Certainly," said Aunt Philippa stiffly.

Chris rose from the table in unbroken silence. She came slowly down the long room. Mordaunt got up to open the door, and followed her out.

"Don't worry about me, please!" Chris besought him as he closed the door behind them. "I shall be all right to-morrow."

He ignored the protest, and accompanied her upstairs. She glanced at him uneasily as they went. "I can't help being—unhappy just for to-day," she murmured. "You—you couldn't expect me—not to care?"

He did not speak till they reached her room. Then: "You saw Bertrand," he said, in a tone that was hardly a question.

"Yes." She began to tremble a little. "I am sorry," she said. "But—I had to." She stood before him, not meeting his eyes, waiting for him to speak. "I couldn't let him go—for good—without saying good-bye," she said, as he remained silent.

He took her gently by the shoulders. "Chris, look at me!"

She drew back, yet in a moment with a desperate effort she raised her eyes to his. He laid his hand upon her forehead, and looked at her long and searchingly.

She endured the look in quivering silence, but she turned so deathly pale under it that he thought she would faint. Quietly he let her go.

"You will lie down now?" he said.

"Yes," she answered, under her breath.

"Don't be in a hurry to get up," he said. "I will explain to your aunt that I do not wish you to be disturbed, and I shall see her off myself."

He went to the windows and drew the curtains. She watched him silently. As he turned back into the room, she spoke.

"Trevor, are you angry with me?"

He paused, as if the question were unexpected. "No," he said, after a moment.

Her eyes shone unnaturally bright in the twilight. "You understand that—that I couldn't obey your wishes about not seeing—Bertrand—before he left?"

"I did not forbid you to see him," he said.

"But—you are vexed because I did," she persisted.

He came quietly back to her. "I believe you did the only thing possible to you," he said, in a tone she could not fathom. "Therefore there is no more to be said. Won't you lie down?"

She complied without further words. He covered her with a rug, but she shivered under it as one with an ague. He brought a quilt, and laid that also over her.

She reached out then, and caught his hand. "Trevor, forgive me!"

He bent over her. "My dear, I am not angry with you."

"Ah, but—but—" She broke off helplessly; there was something about him that unnerved her. Suddenly and inexplicably the longing surged over her to be caught to his breast and held there safe from all the tumult, the misery, the vain regrets, that tortured her quivering soul. But she could not tell him so, could not bring herself to pour out all the truth. For the first time she saw how wide was the gulf that had opened between them—that gulf which he had tried in vain to span the night before—and her heart died within her. She knew that she was powerless, that now in the hour of her adversity, now when she felt her need of a protector and comforter as never before, she dared not confide in him, dared not throw herself upon his mercy, and trust to his generosity to understand and to forgive.

And so she could only hold his hand very tightly, too agitated to utter any plea, afraid to keep him, yet even more afraid to let him go, lest, apart from her, that dread gulf should widen into an abyss too terrible for contemplation.

He waited for a little beside her, to give her agitation time to subside. But it only increased till it became so painfully obvious that he could ignore it no longer.

"Is there something you want to tell me?" he asked her gently. "I am quite ready to listen to you. Only don't be so distressed. Really there is no need."

His tone was perfectly kind, but the caressing note she was wont to hear in it was absent. She shivered afresh, conscious of a chill. She could not answer him; her throat seemed incapable of producing sound.

A while longer, with absolute patience, he waited. Then; "I think you must let me go, dear," he said. "I am doing you more harm than good just now. By and bye, when you are calmer, we will have a talk."

And so by his very forbearance he committed the greatest mistake of his life. If he had stayed then, she might have been persuaded to tell him all that was in her heart. But—the bitter irony of it!—though she was possessed by a passionate longing to do so, in face of his quiet restraint she could not. In fear of the physical effect upon her, he held her back. And she was powerless to pass the barrier. Without his supporting tenderness, she could not lay bare to him the misery and the pain which in no other way could be relieved.

She loosened her hold upon his hand, and as he gently withdrew it she felt as if her last chance of peace were taken away. She turned her face into the pillow and lay still, and a moment later the soft closing of the door told her he had gone.

She listened to his quiet tread along the passage, and an overwhelming sense of desolation swept over her. He had left her alone to cope with her trouble, and the burden of it was greater than she could bear.

She did not know that he returned a little later and listened for many seconds at the door, fearing that she might be spending her solitude in tears. She never heard him there, or even then her tragedy might have been lifted from her. She was lying quite still, with clenched hands, staring dry-eyed into space; for she had no tears to shed.

And he, deeming her sleeping, went softly away again, to sit on the terrace and await Aunt Philippa, who had retired to make her final preparations.

A long time passed before she made her appearance, and he was beginning to wonder with some uneasiness if she had decided to postpone her departure after all, when at length she joined him, ready dressed for the journey. She sat down beside him, looking very handsome and dignified.

"I am glad of this opportunity of seeing you alone, my dear Trevor," she began, "as, after long deliberation, I have at last decided to take you into my confidence upon a matter that has been greatly troubling me."

Mordaunt laid aside the proof of an article with which he had been occupying himself, and replied with his customary courtesy, "I am always glad if I can be of use to you."

"Thank you," said Aunt Philippa.

She carried a bag upon her wrist, and she proceeded to open and search within it. Finally she extracted, a piece of folded notepaper, and handed it to him.

"Will you read that first?" she said. "It will make a difficult task easier."

Mordaunt took the paper, saw that it was a letter, and proceeded to read it under her watching eyes.

There followed a long, quiet pause before he said, "I presume that this is not addressed to you."

"There," said Aunt Philippa, "you are quite correct."

"Then—" He folded it sharply, and made as if he would hand it back to her, but altered his purpose and closed his fingers upon it instead. "Will you explain?" he said.

Aunt Philippa proceeded to do so in her most judicial manner. "That letter I found on the terrace yesterday morning and, believing it to be one of my own that had blown out of my window, I picked it up and later placed it in my letter-case. In the evening I took it out with the intention of answering my correspondent, but upon perusing it, I discovered it to be the communication which you hold in your hand. As you perceive, it was written from Sandacre Court about a week ago, and I now realize that it is not the first letter which the writer has sent to this house. You may remember a discussion arising one morning on the subject of a letter from Sandacre Court. That letter, I am now convinced, was written by the same hand, and these facts point to the very unpleasant conclusion that the man who wrote them—Guillaume Rodolphe—has been levying blackmail. He is apparently aware of a most unfortunate episode which occurred at Valpré in Chris's early girlhood—"

Mordaunt held up his hand abruptly; his face was set in iron lines. "I have already heard of the episode to which you refer," he said.

"Indeed!" said Aunt Philippa. "And may I ask how long you have been aware of it?"

He hesitated momentarily. "Is that material?"

"I think it is," she rejoined. "If Chris has brought herself even at the eleventh hour to be open with you, none will rejoice more sincerely than I. It has always been my principle that wives should have no secrets from their husbands. But, knowing her as I do, I question very much if this can be the case. I have remonstrated with her myself upon the subject, but she refused so stubbornly to listen to me that I cannot but feel that the time has come for me to take my own measures. I should not be doing my duty otherwise. Painful as it is to me, I feel it incumbent upon me to tell you the truth. Now, my dear Trevor, are you aware that there has to-day been a scene between your wife and your secretary which I can only describe as—a love passage? Has she confessed this to you? Because, if not, you must no longer remain in ignorance of the true state of affairs. Chris has deceived me throughout in the most flagrant manner. Had I known—as I now know—that the man who caused the Valpré scandal and your secretary, Bertrand de Montville, a criminal exile living upon your charity, were one and the same person, I would never have permitted you to marry my niece and expose her afresh to a temptation which she had already shown herself unable to resist."

Her last words were somewhat hurried, for Mordaunt had risen to his feet, and there was that in his eyes that warned her that if she paused for a single instant they would never be uttered at all. And Aunt Philippa never liked to leave a task unfinished. That which she undertook she invariably carried through undeviatingly, whatever the cost, and notwithstanding any adverse circumstances which might arise during its accomplishment.

She finished her sentence therefore, and then resigned herself to the martyrdom of being grossly misunderstood.

For that he utterly misread her motives was apparent from his very expression, even before he said with extreme deliberation: "Mrs. Forest, you will oblige me very greatly by not pursuing this subject any further. As I said to you before, Chris is in my keeping now, and it will be my first care to see that no harm comes to her. As to my secretary, he has left me for good, and I doubt if I ever see him again."

"I see," said Aunt Philippa. "You have quarrelled with him then?"

"I have." Sternly he made reply. He still held the note she had given him crumpled in his hand.

Aunt Philippa stiffened her neck severely. "And you left them alone to say good-bye! My dear Trevor, are you mad, or only criminally indifferent to your own interests?"

"I am neither," he said.

"And do you know what happened?"

"I do not wish to know."

She contemplated him for a moment in silence, then: "Your own servant has more common sense," she said.

"Do you mean Holmes?" He spoke with absolute composure, not as one vitally interested; but his eyes made her nervous, they were so still and intent.

"I do mean Holmes," she said. "He came to me in the course of the morning and informed me that his mistress was under the yew-tree and wanted me. I thought his message unusual at the time. When I went out to the yew-tree about ten minutes later, I understood the meaning of it. They were together there, in each other's arms. I did not interrupt them, for I felt it my duty to ascertain, if possible, how far the mischief had gone. But I was not successful. The interview came to an end almost at once. He knelt down upon the ground and kissed her hands, after which he got up and went away. I did not hear what he said to her, but it was certainly no word of farewell. Personally I am convinced that his leave-taking was not final. As for Chris herself, she seemed dazed, and I left her to recover."

Aunt Philippa paused. He had not interrupted her, but she did not feel his silence to be reassuring. She found it impossible to meet his look any longer, though she made a valiant effort to do so.

"I hope you will believe," she said, after a moment, "that nothing but a most urgent sense of duty has impelled me to tell you this."

He did not answer, and she began to flounder a little, finding his silence hard to fathom.

"I felt that you ought to be upon your guard. As I have told you before, not one of the Wyndhams is to be trusted. I think you have been too generous in this respect, and have laid yourself open to deception. However—now that I have warned you once more, you will perhaps be more careful in the future. I can only hope that my warning has come in time."

Again she paused, but still he remained silent, looking straight at her with a steely regard that never altered.

She mustered her forces at length to ask a direct question. "What do you propose to do with regard to that letter you hold in your hand?"

With a quiet movement he transferred it to his pocket. "I have not had time to consider the matter," he said.

She was momentarily surprised, and showed it. "I thought you would know what to do at once," she said. "It was, in fact, my reason for telling you of it. I felt that something ought to be done—and quickly."

"Something will be done," Mordaunt answered quietly. "You have placed the matter in my hands, and I shall deal with it. I think I need not ask you to refrain from mentioning it to anyone else?"

"You need not," said Aunt Philippa with dignity.

"Thank you. And that is all you wish to say to me?"

She met his steady eyes for an instant and at once looked away again. "All," she replied, "except that I think it was a great pity that you refused so persistently to profit by my former warning. It might have averted much trouble both for yourself and for Chris."

He made her a slight bow. "I fear I am not unique," he said, "in preferring to conduct my own affairs in my own way."

When Aunt Philippa took her departure that afternoon it was in a most unwonted state of doubt, not unmingled with apprehension. Despite his moderation, she had an uneasy feeling that her communication to Trevor Mordaunt had set in motion a devastating force which nothing could arrest or divert until it had spread destruction over all that lay in its path.

CHAPTER VIII
THE TRUTH

In answer to her husband's low knock, Chris turned from her dressing-table. She had switched on the electric light, and had taken down her hair, preparatory to dressing for dinner. It hung all about her in magnificent ripples of ruddy light and shade. Her face, in the midst of it, looked very small and tired. She was clad in a plain white wrapper, that fell away from her neck and arms, giving her a very childish appearance.

"Yes, I'm getting up," she said, with the flicker of a smile. "I couldn't sleep."

He entered and closed the door behind him in silence.

"Has Aunt Philippa gone?" she asked.

He responded briefly, "Three hours ago."

"Ah!" She stretched out her arms with the gesture of one freed from an irksome burden, but they fell again immediately, almost as if a fresh burden had taken its place.

She stood for a few seconds motionless, looking straight before her. Finally, with a hint of nervousness, she turned her eyes upon her husband; they shone intensely blue in the strong light.

"We shall soon be quite alone," she said.

His eyes did not answer hers. They looked remote and cold. "Come and sit down," he said.

He seated himself on the couch from which she had just risen. Chris caught up a slide from the dressing-table, and fastened back her hair with fingers that trembled inexplicably.

Then she went to him. "Trevor," she said, and there was pleading in her voice, "do you know, I don't want to talk about anything. I think one gets over some troubles best that way. Do you mind?"

He took her wrists very quietly, and drew her down beside him. "What were you trying to tell me this afternoon?" he said.

She shivered and turned her face away. "Nothing, really nothing. I was foolish and upset. Please let me forget it."

She would have withdrawn from his hold, but his hands tightened upon her. "Won't you reconsider the matter?" he asked. "It would be better for us both if you told me of your own accord."

"Trevor!" She turned to him swiftly, flashing into his face a look of such wild alarm that he was touched, in spite of himself.

"My dear," he said, "I have no wish to frighten you. But you must see for yourself that it is utterly impossible for us to go on like this. You are keeping something from me. I want you to tell me quite quietly and without prevarication what it is."

She turned white to the lips. "There is nothing, Trevor. Indeed, there is nothing," she said.

His face changed, grew stern, grew implacable. He bent towards her, still holding her firmly by the wrists. He looked closely into her eyes, and in his own was neither accusation nor condemnation, only a deep and awful questioning that seemed to probe her through and through.

"For Heaven's sake," he said, "don't lie to me!"

And Chris shrank, shrank from that dread scrutiny as she would have shrunk from naked steel. She did not attempt to speak another word.

For seconds that seemed to her agonized senses like hours, he held her so, waiting, waiting for she knew not what. Her heart thumped within her like the heart of a terrified creature fleeing for its life. She began to pant audibly through the silence. The strain was more than she could bear.

"Chris!" he said.

She started violently; every pulse leaped, every nerve jarred. But she did not lift her eyes to his; she could not.

"Don't tremble," he said, his voice very cold and even. "Just tell me the truth. Begin with what happened at Valpré."

Her white lips quivered. "What—how much—do you know?"

"I will tell you that," he said, "when you have answered me quite fully and unreservedly."

She cast an imploring look at him that did not reach his eyes. "But, Trevor, nothing happened," she told him piteously. "That is to say, nothing beyond—" She broke off short. "I was only a child. I didn't know," she ended, in a confused murmur.

"What didn't you know?" Stern and pitiless came the question. His hands were holding her wrists tightly locked. There was compulsion in their grasp.

She answered him because she could not help it, but her words were wild and incoherent. "I didn't know what it meant. I didn't see the harm of it. I was too young. It all happened before I realized. And even then—even then—I didn't understand—that it was serious—until—until— the duel. Trevor—Trevor, you are hurting me!"

His hold relaxed, but he did not set her free. "Was that duel fought on your account?" he asked.

"Yes," she whispered.

"In what way?"

She was silent.

"Answer me," he said.

She clenched her hands in sudden, strenuous rebellion. "I don't know. I never heard."

"Was it because you had compromised yourself with Bertrand de Montville?"

Very deliberately he asked the question, so deliberately that she could not evade it.

"It is not fair to—to put it like that," she said.

"I am waiting to hear your own version," he told her grimly.

"You have only heard Aunt Philippa's, so far?" she hazarded.

"I have heard nothing whatever about what happened at Valpré from your aunt," he answered. "But that is beside the point. Are you quite incapable of telling me the truth?"

She winced sharply. "Trevor! Why are you so cruel? I have done nothing wrong."

"Then look at me!" he said.

But she would not, for his eyes terrified her. Nor could she bring herself to speak of Valpré under their piercing scrutiny. Only close-locked in his arms could she have poured out the poor little secret that she had sacrificed so much to keep. Not the nature of the adventure itself, but the fact that she had given her love to the man who had shared it with her, held her silent. She could not spread her love before those pitiless eyes, and to disclose the one without the other had become impossible to her.

And so she remained silent, counting the seconds as she felt his forbearance ebb away.

When at last he moved and released her, she cowered almost as if she expected a blow. Yet when he spoke, though there was in his tone a subtle difference, his words came with absolute composure. She could almost have imagined that he was smiling.

"Since you refuse to be open with me," he said, "you compel me to draw my own conclusions. Now, with regard to this letter which you received a week ago from Captain Rodolphe—you have another letter from him somewhere in your possession?"

He took the missive from his pocket and opened it as if he would read it again. But the sight was too much for Chris. It tortured her beyond endurance, galvanizing her into sudden, unconsidered action. She snatched it from him and tore it passionately into fragments.

"You shall not!" she cried. "You shall not!"

With the words she sprang to her feet, and stood before him, goaded to frenzy, challenging his calm.

"Where did you find it?" she demanded.

"It was found on the terrace," he said.

She flung out a trembling hand. "Ah! Then I dropped it that night that my dress caught fire. I thought it was burnt. And you found it—you dared to read it!"

He did not attempt to explain his action. Perhaps he realized he was more likely to obtain the truth from her thus than by endless cross-questioning. "Yes, I have read it," he said.

She made a desperate gesture. "And because of this—because of this— you—you accuse me of—"

"I have accused you of nothing," he said sternly. "I have only asked you to tell me the truth. I hoped you would do so of your own free will, but since you will not—"

"Yes?" she cried back. "Since I will not—?"

"I shall find another means," he answered.

He rose abruptly. They stood face to face. There was no shrinking about Chris now. She was braced to defiance.

"Where is that other letter?" he said.

"I have destroyed it."

She uttered the words with quivering triumph, strung to a fever-pitch of excitement in which fear had no part.

His eyes went to her jewel-drawer.

"It is not there," she said. "The letter I hid there was the one you have just read."

She spoke rapidly, but she was no longer incoherent. Her words came without effort, and he knew that she was telling the truth as the victim in a torture-chamber might tell it, because she was goaded thereto and incapable at the moment of doing otherwise. He also knew that, notwithstanding this, she was scarcely aware of what she said. Out of the agony of her soul, because the pain was unbearable, she had yielded without knowing it.

"I only kept this letter," she said, "in case he ever asked for more. But it doesn't matter now—nothing will ever matter any more. You know the worst, and"—fiercely—"you are welcome to know it. I—I'm even glad! I've nothing left to be afraid of."

She drew in her breath hysterically. She was on the verge of dreadful laughter, but she caught it back, instinctively aware that she must keep her strength—this unwonted strength of desperation that had come to her—as long as possible.

He heard her without emotion. His face was grim and mask-like, frozen into hard, unyielding lines.

"It is certainly best that I should know it," he said. "But I have not yet heard all. How much did this Rodolphe charge for his silence?"

She had almost answered him before she remembered, and checked the words upon her lips. "No, I don't think I need tell you that," she said.

"That is better than telling me a lie," he rejoined. "As a matter of fact, there is no need, as you say, for you to tell me. I know what sum he asked for, and I know how he obtained it."

He spoke with steady conviction, his eyes unwaveringly upon her. For seconds now she had endured his look without flinching. As she had said, there was nothing left for her to fear. But at his words her face changed, and unmistakable apprehension took the place of despair.

"No, no!" she said quickly. "He did not obtain it in that way. At least—at least—Trevor, I swear to you that Bertrand knew nothing of that."

"You need not take that trouble," he said coldly.

She gripped her hands together. "You don't believe me—but it is the truth. Bertrand never knew that I had heard from Captain Rodolphe."

"You deceived him too, then?" Pitilessly he asked the question. He also had begun to feel that nothing could ever matter any more.

She wrung her hands in anguish. Her face was still raised to his, white and strained and desperate—the face of a woman who would never dissemble with him again. "Yes," she said, "I deceived him too."

"Then"—slowly he uttered the words—"it was you who forged my name upon that cheque? It actually was you whom he was shielding? And you tell me that he did not know what it was for?"

"He did not know," she said. She would not have given such an explanation of her own volition at that moment, but—since upon this point she could not tell him the truth—it was simpler to let it pass. What did it matter, after all? Let him think her a thief also if he would! She was past caring what he thought.

"And when do you expect to meet again?" Mordaunt asked, with great distinctness.

She flinched as if he had struck her. "Oh, haven't you tortured me enough?" she said.

His jaw hardened. He stepped suddenly to her and took her by the shoulders. His eyes appalled her. It was as if a devil looked out of them. She shrank away from him in sheer physical terror.

"Oh, you needn't be afraid," he said. "I shan't hurt you. Why should I? You are nothing to me. But—for the last time—let me hear you speak the truth. You love this man?"

The words, curt and cold, might have fallen from the lips of a stranger, so impersonal were they, so utterly devoid of any emotion.

Wide-eyed, she faced him, for she could not look away with his hands upon her, compelling her.

"You love this man?" he repeated, his speech still cold but incisive—a sharp weapon probing for the truth.

She caught her quivering nerves together, and valiantly answered him. "I do!" she said. "I do!" And as she spoke, the power within her surged upwards, defying constraint, dominating her with a mastery irresistible. She suddenly stripped her heart bare of all reserve and showed him the love that agonized there. "I have always loved him!" she said. "I shall love him till I die!"

It was a woman's confession, in which triumph and anguish were strangely mingled. In a calmer moment she would never have made it, but that moment was supreme, and she had no choice. Regardless of all consequences, she told the burning truth. She would have told it with his hands upon her throat.

In the silence that followed the avowal she even waited for violence. But she was unafraid. The greatness of the power that possessed her had lifted her above all fear. She trod the heights where fear is not. And all-unconsciously, in that moment she won a battle which she had deemed irrevocably lost.

Mordaunt's hands fell from her, setting her free. "In Heaven's name," he said, "why didn't you go with him?"

She did not understand his tone. It held neither anger nor contempt, and so quiet was it that she could still have fancied it almost indifferent. Yet, inexplicably, it cut her to the heart.

"I'll tell you the truth!" she said, a little wildly. "I—I would have gone with him. I offered—I begged—to go. But he—he sent me back."

"Why?" Again that deadly quietness of utterance, as though, indeed, a dead man spoke.

Her throat began to work spasmodically, though she had no desire to weep. She felt as if her heart were bleeding from a mortal wound.

With an effort that nearly choked her, she made reply.

"He said—it was—my duty."

"Your duty!" He repeated the word deliberately. Though the devil had gone out of his eyes, she could not meet them any longer. Not that she feared to do so; but the pain at her heart was intolerable, and it was his look, his voice, that made it so.

Almost as if he divined this, he turned quietly from her. He walked to the window and opened it wide, as if he felt suffocated. The wind was moaning desolately through the trees. There was the scent of coming rain in the air.

He spoke with his back to her, without apparent effort. "I release you from your duty," he said. "Go to him! Go to him—now!"

She gazed at him, dumbfounded, not breathing. But he remained motionless, his hands clenched, his face to the night.

"Go to him!" he repeated. "I shall set you free—at once. Go—and tell him so!"

Then, as still she neither moved nor spoke, he slowly turned and looked at her.

From head to foot she felt his eyes comprehend her, and from head to foot, under his look, she shuddered. She spoke no word; she was as one paralysed.

Very quietly he pulled the window to behind him, still with his eyes upon her. In that moment he was complete master of himself. He stood aloof, shrouded, as it were, in an icy calm. She had no clue to his thoughts. She only knew that by some means, inexplicable and irresistible, he bound her even as he set her free.

"You understand me?" he said, his voice cold, level, pitilessly distinct. "It is my last word upon the subject. You and I have done with each other. Go!"

It was literally his last word. As he uttered it, his eyes fell away from her. He crossed the room with even, unhurried tread, opened the intervening door that led into his own, passed through with no backward glance, and shut it steadily behind him.

As for Chris, she stood numbly gazing after him till only the panels of the door met her look. And then, her strength leaving her, without sound she sank downwards and lay crumpled, inanimate, broken, upon the floor.

PART IV

CHAPTER I
THE REFUGEE

Autumn on a Yorkshire moor.

Hilda Davenant leaned back and looked from her sketch to the moor with slight dissatisfaction in her calm eyes.

"What's the matter with it?" said Lord Percy.

He was lying in the faded heather beside her, sucking grass-stems with bovine enjoyment. He surveyed the faint pucker on his wife's forehead with lazy amusement.

She looked down at him. "It isn't nearly good enough."

He laughed comfortably. "Put it away! It'll do for my birthday. I shan't look at it from an artist's point of view."

She smiled a little. "Oh, any daub would do for you. You simply don't know what art is."

"Exactly," he rejoined tranquilly. "Any daub will do, provided your hand lays on the colours. But nothing less than that would satisfy me. Come! Isn't that a pretty speech? And you didn't angle for it either!" He caught her hand and rubbed it against his cheek. "You are civilizing me wonderfully," he declared. "I never knew how to make pretty speeches before I met you."

"Surely I never taught you that!" she protested. "I am never guilty of empty compliments myself."

"Nor I," smiled her husband. "I say what I think to you always. Now what do you say to coming for a stretch? There's an hour left before I need buzz down to the station and meet Jack. You will admit I have been very good and patient all this time. Pack up your painting things, and I'll trek back to the house with them."

"No. We will go together," Hilda said. "Why not?"

"I thought you would prefer to sit and admire the landscape," he said.

She smiled and made no response.

"A case in point!" laughed Lord Percy. "But here the compliment would not have been empty since you obviously prefer my company to the solitude of a Yorkshire moor."

She looked at him with the smile still in her eyes, but she did not put the compliment into words. Only, as she rose to leave the scene of her labours, she slipped her hand within his arm.

"I have been thinking a great deal of Chris lately," she said. "I wish she would write to me again."

"I thought your mother was there," said Lord Percy.

"She has been. I believe she left them yesterday. But then, she does not give me any detailed news of Chris. I have a feeling that I can't get rid of that the child is unhappy."

"She has no right to be," rejoined her husband. "She's married about the best fellow going."

"Who understands her about as thoroughly as you understand art."

"Oh, come!" he remonstrated. "Mordaunt is not quite such a fool as that! The little monkey ought to be happy enough—unless she tries to play fast and loose with him. Then, I grant you, there would be the devil to pay."

Hilda smiled. "I can't help feeling anxious about her. It has always been my fear that, when the glamour of first love is past, Trevor might misjudge her. She is so gay and bright that many people think her empty. I know my mother does for one."

"Your mother might," he conceded. "Trevor wouldn't—being a man of considerable insight. Tell you what, though, if you want to satisfy yourself on the score of Chris's happiness, we will get them to put us up for a night when we leave here for town three weeks hence. How will that suit you?"

"I should love it, of course," she said. "But wouldn't it be rather far out of our way?"

"I daresay the car won't mind," said Lord Percy.

They walked back to the house that a friend had lent for their three-months' honeymoon. It nestled in a hollow amongst trees, the long line of moors stretching above it. They were well out of the beaten track. Few tourists penetrated to their paradise. Near the house was a glade with a miniature waterfall that filled the place with music.

"That waterfall makes for laziness," Lord Percy was wont to declare, and many were the happy hours they had spent beside it.

They passed it by without lingering to-day, however, for both were feeling energetic. Briskly they crossed the little lawn before the house, and entered by a French window.

"Better secure some refreshments before we go on the tramp," suggested Lord Percy. "I've got a thirst already. Hullo! What on earth—"

He broke off in amazement. A slight figure had risen up suddenly from a settee in a dark corner; and a woman's face, wild-eyed and tragic, confronted them.

"Great Scott! Who is it?" said Lord Percy Davenant.

And "Chris!" exclaimed Hilda, at the same moment.

As for Chris, she stood a second, staring at them; then: "Trevor has turned me out, so I've come to you," she said her white lips moving stiffly. "I've nowhere else to go."

With the words she stumbled forward, feeling vaguely out before her as though she saw not. Hilda started towards her on the instant, caught her, folded warm arms about her, held her fast.

"My darling!" she said, and again, "My darling!"

But Chris heard not, nor saw, nor felt. She had reached the end of her strength, and black darkness had closed down upon her agony, blotting out all things. She sank senseless in her cousin's embrace....

It was long before they brought her back, so long that Hilda became frightened and dispatched her husband in the motor for a doctor, wholly forgetting her brother's expected visit in her anxiety.

Lord Percy ultimately returned with the local practitioner, whom he had dragged almost by force from the bedside of a patient ten miles away. He, too, had forgotten Jack, but remembered him as he set down the doctor, and whirled away again in a cloud of dust, leaving him to announce himself.

Chris had by that time recovered consciousness, in response to Hilda's strenuous efforts, but she had scarcely spoken a word. She lay on the sofa in the drawing-room, cold from head to foot, and shivering spasmodically at intervals. She drank the wine that Hilda brought her with shuddering docility; but it seemed to have no effect upon her. It was as if the blood had frozen at her very heart.

"Get her to bed," were the doctor's orders, and he himself carried Chris up to Hilda's room.

She was perfectly passive in their hands, but quite incapable of the smallest effort, and so painfully apathetic that Hilda grew more and more uneasy. She had never imagined that her gay, light-hearted Chris could be thus. It wrung her heart to see her. She was like a dainty flower crushed into the dust of the highway.

"Nervous prostration consequent upon severe mental strain," was the doctor's verdict later. "You will have to take great care of her, and keep her absolutely quiet, or I can't be answerable for the consequences. She is in a very critical state, and"—he paused a moment—"I think her husband ought to be with her."

"Ah!" Hilda said, and no more.

He passed the matter over. "Don't let her talk at all if you can prevent it, and reassure her in every way possible. I will send a composing draught, or she will be in a high fever before the morning."

"You fear for the brain?" Hilda hazarded.

"I fear—many things," he answered uncompromisingly.

He took his departure just as Lord Percy and his guest arrived, and Hilda paused upon the step to greet her brother.

He sprang from the car before it came to a standstill, and she saw on the instant that he was in a towering fury. Jack Forest, the kindly, the easy-going, the careless, was actually white with anger.

He scarcely stopped to greet her. "Where is Chris?" he demanded.

"She is in bed," Hilda answered, seeing he had heard the whole story. "No," as he turned inwards, "you can't see her. Indeed you mustn't, Jack. The doctor says—"

"Damn the doctor!" said Jack. "I'm going to see her, in bed or not. Where is she?"

He was half-way upstairs with the words, and Hilda's protest fell upon empty air. She could only follow and look on.

Jack opened the first door he came to, and found himself in Chris's presence. He strode straight across the room, as one who had a perfect right, stooped over her as she lay, and gathered her up into his arms.

"My little sweetheart!" he said, and kissed her fiercely over and over again.

That woke her from her lethargy, as no more tender ministrations could have done. She wound her arms about his neck, and clung to him like a lost child.

"Oh, Jack!" she said. "Oh, Jack!" and burst into an agony of tears.

Hilda closed the door softly, and went away. Jack's treatment seemed the best, after all.

When she saw him again he was quite calm, but there was about him a grimness of purpose with which she was not familiar. He drew her aside.

"Look here! I can't sleep on this. I'm going to see Trevor—at once. If I don't bring him to reason, I shall probably shoot him; but I haven't told her that. All she wants is to be left in peace, and peace she shall have, whatever the cost."

"But, my dear boy, quarrelling with Trevor on her behalf won't make for peace," Hilda ventured to point out.

He acknowledged the truth of this with a brief nod. "All the same, I'm damned if I'll stand by and see him wreck her life. Let me know how she goes on. Send a wire to the club to-morrow. No, don't! I'll wire to you first, and let you know where I am. I'm going straight back to the station now. With any luck I ought to catch the afternoon express. Where's Percy?"

"You must have something to eat," urged Hilda. "You've had nothing whatever."

He frowned impatiently. "Oh, rats! I can feed on board. I shan't starve."

But she knew, with sure intuition, that the moment he was out of her presence all thought of refreshment would leave his mind.

She saw him go, and then returned to Chris.

She found her sitting up in bed, rocking herself to and fro, and crying, crying, crying, the tears of utter despair. But this distress, despite its violence, was better—Hilda knew it instinctively—than her former cold inertia. She gathered her to her breast, and held her close pressed till her anguish had somewhat spent itself.

By degrees and haltingly the story of Chris's tragedy was unfolded.

"I've told Jack everything," she said at last. "And now I've told you, but we won't ever talk about it any more. Jack is going to see Trevor, and—and try to make him understand. I didn't want him to, but he would do it. But he has promised me that Trevor shan't follow me here. Do you think he will be able to prevent him? Do you? Do you?"

She shuddered afresh uncontrollably at the bare thought, and Hilda had some difficulty in calming her.

"Dearest, I am sure he will never come to you against your will," she said, with conviction. "I am sure you needn't be afraid. But oh, Chris, my darling, he is your husband. Always remember that!"

"I know! I know!" Feverishly Chris made answer, and Hilda knew that she must not pursue this subject. "But I can never see him again, never— never—never! I think it would kill me. Besides—besides—" She broke off inarticulately, and Hilda did not press her to finish.

She found that she must not speak much of Bertrand either, though she did venture to ask why the Valpré escapade had ever been kept from Trevor in the first place.

"I really can't quite explain," Chris answered wearily. "When it dawned on me that vile things had been said and actually a duel fought because of it I felt as if I would rather die than let him know. Besides, at the back of my mind, I think I somehow always knew—though I did not realize—that— Bertie—came first with me, and I—I was terrified lest Trevor should suspect it. Of course it doesn't matter now," she ended. "He knows it all, and—as he says—we have done with each other." She uttered a long, quivering sigh, and turned her face into the pillow.

"My darling, so long as you both live, that can never be," Hilda said very earnestly. "Whatever mistakes you have made, you are still his and he is yours. Nothing can alter that."

"He doesn't think so," said Chris. "In fact, he—he told me to go to Bertie, so that—so that"—she shivered again—"he could set me free."

"Oh, Chris, he did—that?"

"Yes, I think he meant it for my sake as much as for his own. But I couldn't do it. You see, I don't know where Bertie has gone for one thing.

And then—I know Bertie would have thought it wrong. You see"—the tears were running down her face again—"we love each other so much, and—and love like ours is holy. He said so."

"I wonder how he learned that," Hilda said. "It is not a creed that most men hold."

"But Bertie is not like most men." Very softly came Chris's answer, and through her tears her eyes shone with the light that is kindled by nothing earthly. "Bertie has come through a great deal of suffering," she said. "It has taught him to know the good from the bad. And—he said I shouldn't be ruined for his sake. As if I cared for that!" she ended, smiling wanly.

"Thank God he did for you!" Hilda said.

"Oh, do you think it matters?" said Chris.

CHAPTER II
A MIDNIGHT VISITOR

It was a dark, wet night. The rain streamed from the gutters and pattered desolately on the pavement below. It had rained for hours.

Trevor Mordaunt sat alone, with a pipe between his teeth, his windows flung wide to the empty street, and listened to the downpour. He had arrived in town that afternoon to make a few necessary arrangements before leaving England. These arrangements completed, there was nothing left to do but to await the next morning for departure.

It was not easy, that waiting. He faced it with grim fortitude, realizing the futility of going to bed. It was possible that he might presently doze in his chair, but ordinary sleep was out of the question, and he would not trouble himself to court it. Tossing all night sleepless on his pillow was a refinement of torture that he did not feel called upon to bear.

He had spent the previous night tramping the country-side, but he could not tramp in London, and though he was not aware of fatigue, he knew the necessity for bodily rest existed, and he compelled himself to take it.

So he sat motionless, listening to the rain, while the hours crawled by.

The roar of London traffic rose from afar, for the night was still. Now and then a taxi whirred through the sloppy street, but there were few wayfarers. Once a boy passed whistling, and the man at the window above stiffened a little, as if in some fashion the careless melody stirred him, but as the whistler turned the corner he relaxed again with his head back, and resumed his attitude of waiting.

It was nearly midnight when a taxi hummed up to the flaring lamp-post before the house, and stopped to discharge its occupant. Mordaunt heard the vehicle, but his eyes were closed and he did not trouble to open them. He had laid aside his pipe, and actually seemed to be on the verge of dozing at last. The window-curtain screened him from the view of any in the street, and it did not occur to him that the new arrival could be in any way connected with himself.

It was, therefore, with a hint of surprise that he turned his head at the opening of the door.

"Mr. Wyndham to see you, sir," said Holmes. "Says it's very particular, sir."

"Who? Oh, all right. Show him in." A bored note sounded in Mordaunt's voice. "And you needn't sit up, Holmes. I'll let him out," he added.

"Very good, sir," said Holmes, without enthusiasm. He never liked to retire before his master.

Mordaunt rose with a faint touch of impatience. He expected to see Max, and wondered that the news of his arrival in town had reached him so quickly. But it was Rupert who entered, and turned to satisfy himself that the door was shut before he advanced to greet his brother-in-law.

Mordaunt stood by the window and watched the precaution with a certain grim curiosity. He fancied he could guess the reason of this midnight visitation, but as the boy came towards him and halted in the full light he saw that he was mistaken. There was no indignant questioning visible on Rupert's face. It looked only grey and haggard and desperate.

"Look here," he said, speaking jerkily, as if it were only by a series of tense efforts that he spoke at all. "I've come to tell you something. I don't know how you'll take it. And I may as well admit—that I'm horribly afraid. Do you mind if I have a drink—just to help me through?"

Mordaunt closed the window, and came quietly forward. Just for a moment he fancied that Rupert had already fortified himself in the manner indicated for the ordeal of meeting him, and then again he realized that he was mistaken. The eyes that looked into his were perfectly sane, but they held an almost childlike appeal that made his heart contract suddenly. He bit his lip savagely. Why on earth couldn't the fellow have left him alone for this one night at least?

He forced himself to be temperate, but there was no warmth in his tone as he said, "I've no objection to your having a drink if you want it. I suppose you've got into a scrape again, and want me to help you out?"

"No, it's not that—at least, not in the sense you mean."

Hurriedly Rupert made answer. He looked for a moment at the glasses on the table, but he did not attempt to help himself. Suddenly he shivered.

"Ye gods! What an infernal night! I had to walk ever so far before I found a taxi. I came up by the evening train—couldn't get off duty sooner.

I thought you would be off to Dover before I got here. And I—and I—" He broke off blankly and became silent, as if he had forgotten what he had meant to say.

Mordaunt leaned over the table, and mixed a drink with the utmost steadiness. "Sit down," he said. "And now drink this, and pull yourself together. There's nothing to be in a funk about, so take your time."

He spoke with authority, but his manner had the aloofness of one not greatly interested in the matter in hand. He resented the boy's intrusion, that was all.

Rupert accepted his hospitality in silence. This obvious lack of interest increased his difficulties tenfold.

Mordaunt went back to his chair by the window, and relighted his pipe. He knew he was being cold-blooded, but he felt absolutely incapable of kindling any warmth. There seemed to be no warmth left in him.

Rupert gulped down his drink, and buried his face in his hands. He felt that the thing he had come to do was beyond his power to accomplish. He could not make his confession to a stone image. And yet he could not go, leaving it unmade.

In the long pause that followed it almost seemed as if Mordaunt had forgotten his presence in the room. The minutes ticked away, and he made no sign.

At last, desperately, Rupert lifted his head. "Trevor!"

Mordaunt looked at him. Then, struck possibly by the misery of the boy's attitude, he laid down his pipe and turned towards him.

"Well, what is it?"

Vehemently Rupert made answer. "For pity's sake, don't freeze me up like this, man! I—I—oh, can't you give me a lead?" he broke off desperately.

"You see, I don't know in the least what you have come to say," Mordaunt pointed out. "If it has anything to do with—recent events"—he spoke with great distinctness—"I can only advise you to leave it alone, since no remonstrance from you will make the smallest difference."

"But it hasn't," groaned Rupert. "At least, of course, it's in connection with that. But I've come to try and tell you the truth—something you don't know and never will know if I don't tell you. And—Heaven help me!—I'm such a cur—I don't know how to get through with it."

That reached Mordaunt, stirring him to activity almost against his will. He found himself unable to look on unmoved at his young brother-in-law's distress. He left his chair and moved back to the table.

"I don't know what you've got to be afraid of," he said, with a touch of kindliness in his tone that deprived it of its remoteness. "I'm not feeling particularly formidable. What have you been doing?"

Rupert groaned again and covered his face. "You'll be furious enough directly. But it's not that exactly that I mind. It's—it's the disgusting shabbiness of it. We Wyndhams are such a rotten lot, we don't see that part of the business till afterwards."

"Hadn't you better come to the point?" suggested Mordaunt. "We can talk about that later."

"No, we can't," said Rupert, with conviction. "You'll either throw me out of the window or kick me downstairs directly you know the truth."

"I'm not in the habit of doing these things," Mordaunt remarked, with the ghost of a smile.

"But this is an exceptional case." Rupert straightened himself abruptly, and turned in his chair, meeting the quiet eyes. "Damn it, I'll tell you!" he said, springing to his feet with sudden resolution. "Trevor, I—I'm an infernal blackguard! I forged that cheque!"

"You!" Sternly Mordaunt uttered the word. He moved a step forward and looked Rupert closely in the face. "Are you telling me the truth?" he said.

"I am." Rupert faced him squarely, though his eyelids quivered a little. "I'm not likely to lie to you in this matter. I've nothing to gain and all to lose. And I shouldn't have told you—anyway now—if Noel hadn't come over this morning with the news that you had kicked out your secretary for the offence I had committed. Even I couldn't stick that, so I've come to own up—and take the consequences."

He braced himself, almost as if he expected a blow. But Mordaunt remained motionless, studying him keenly, and for many seconds he did not utter a word.

At last, "Bertrand knew of this," he said, in a tone that held more of conviction than interrogation.

"No, he didn't. He knew nothing, or, if he did, it was sheer guess-work. I never suspected that he knew." Rupert's hands were clenched. He was face to face with the hardest task he had ever undertaken.

"He knew, for all that." Mordaunt's brows contracted; he seemed to be following out a difficult problem.

Finally, to Rupert's relief, he turned aside. "Go on," he said. "I'll hear the whole of it now. What did you do with the money?"

Rupert's teeth closed upon his lower lip. "That's the only question I can't answer."

"Why not?" The question was curt, and held no compromise.

"Private reasons," Rupert muttered.

"Family reasons would be more accurate," Mordaunt rejoined, in the same curt tone. "You gave it to—Chris."

The momentary hesitation before the name did not soften its utterance. It came with a precision almost brutal.

Rupert made a slight movement, and stood silent.

"You are not going to deny it?" Mordaunt observed, glancing at him.

He turned his face away. "What's the good?"

"Just so. You had better tell me the whole truth. It will save trouble."

"But I don't see that there is anything more to tell." Rupert spoke with an effort. "I stole the cheque in the first place—that Sunday afternoon—you remember? I was a bit top-heavy at the time. That's no excuse," he threw in. "I daresay I should have done it in any case. But—well, you know the state of mind I was in that day. You had just been beastly generous, too. And that reminds me; you left your keys behind, do you remember? I came in for another drink and saw them. The temptation came then, and I never stopped to think till the thing was done. Bertrand nearly caught me in the act. He didn't suspect anything at the time, but he may have remembered afterwards."

"Probably," said Mordaunt. "You weren't frank with me that day, then? There were debts you didn't mention."

Rupert nodded. "You were a bit high-handed with me. That choked me off. Still, though in an evil moment I took the cheque out of your book,

I loathed myself for it afterwards. I hadn't the strength of mind to destroy it, or the courage to send it back. But"—he turned back again and met Mordaunt's eyes—"I wasn't going to use it, though I was cur enough to keep it, and to like to feel it was there in case of emergency. I didn't mean to use it—on my oath, I didn't. I don't expect you to believe me, but it's true."

"I believe you," Mordaunt said quietly. "And—the emergency arose?"

Rupert nodded again. "Chris came to me—in great distress. Couldn't tell me what she wanted it for. You weren't to know, neither was Bertrand. She couldn't use her own without your finding out. And so—as it seemed urgent—in fact, desperate—and as it was for her—" He broke off. "No, I won't shelter myself in that way. I did it on my own. She didn't know. No one knew. If Bertrand suspected, he must have thought I took it for my own purposes. Heaven knows what she wanted it for, but she was most emphatic that it shouldn't get round to him."

"And you tell me she did not know how you obtained the money? Are you certain of that?" Mordaunt's tone was deliberate; he spoke as one who meant to have the truth.

"Why, man, of course I am! What do you take her for? Chris—my sister—your wife—"

"Stop!" The word was brief, and very final. "We need not go into that. She may not have known at the time, but she suspected afterwards. In fact, she knew."

"Is that what you quarrelled about?" Eagerly Rupert broke in. "Noel tried to get it out of her, but she wouldn't tell him. You'll find out where she's gone, and set it right? She can't be very far away."

"That," Mordaunt said, in a tone from which the faintest hint of feeling was excluded, "is beside the point. We will not discuss it."

"But—" Rupert began.

"We will not discuss it." Mordaunt repeated the words in the same utterly emotionless voice, and Rupert found it impossible to continue. "In fact, there seems to be nothing further to discuss of any sort. Can I put you up for the night?"

Rupert stared at him.

"Well?" Mordaunt's brows went up a little.

"Are you in earnest?" the boy burst out awkwardly. "I mean—I mean—don't you want to—to—give me a sound kicking?"

"Not in the least." A steely glint shone for a moment in the grey eyes. "I don't think that sort of treatment does much good, as a rule. And I have not the smallest desire to administer it. If you think you deserve it, I should imagine that is punishment enough."

Rupert swung round sharply on his heel. "All right. I'm going. If you want me, you know where to find me. I shan't run away. And I shan't try to back out. What I've said I shall stick to—if it means perdition."

"And what about the Regiment?" Quietly Mordaunt's voice arrested him before he reached the door. "Or doesn't the Regiment count?"

Rupert stopped dead, but he did not turn. "The Regiment"—he said—"the Regiment"—he choked suddenly—"they'll be damned well rid of me," he ended, somewhat incoherently.

"Come back!" Mordaunt said.

He made an irresolute movement, but did not comply.

"Rupert!" There was authority in the quiet voice.

Unwillingly Rupert turned. He came back unsteadily, with features that had begun to twitch.

Mordaunt moved to meet him. The coldness had gone out of his eyes. He took Rupert's arm, and brought him back to the table.

"I think you had better let me put you up," he said. "You can sleep in my room; I'm not wanting it for to-night. There, sit down. You mustn't be a fool, you know. You are played out, and want a rest."

"I—I'm all right," Rupert said.

He made as if he would withdraw his arm, but changed his intention, and stood tense, battling with himself.

"Oh, man!" he burst out at last, hoarsely, "you—you don't know what a—what a—cur I feel! I—I—I—" Words failed him abruptly; he flung round and sank down again at the table with his head on his arms, too humbled to remember his manhood any longer.

"My dear fellow, don't!" Mordaunt said. He put his hand on the boy's heaving shoulders and kept it there. "There's no sense in letting yourself go. The thing is done, and there is no more to be said, since neither you nor I can undo it. Come, boy! Pull yourself together. I am going to forget it, and you can do the same. I think you had better go to bed now. We shall have time for a talk in the morning. What?" He stooped to catch a half-audible sentence.

"You'll never forget it," gasped Rupert.

"Yes, I shall—if you will let me. It rests with you. I never wish to speak or think of it again. I have plenty of other things to think about, and so have you. That's settled, then. I am going to see if I can find you something to eat."

He stood up. His face had softened to kindness. He patted Rupert's shoulder before he turned away.

"Buck up, old chap!" he said gently, and went with quiet tread from the room.

CHAPTER III
A FRUITLESS ERRAND

"Hullo, Jack!" Noel sprang to meet his cousin with the bound of a young panther. "Where on earth have you come from? My good chap, you're positively drenched! You've never walked up from the station!"

"And missed the way twice," said Jack grimly. He shook Noel off without ceremony. "Where is Trevor? I have come to see him."

"Oh, he's cleared out; went to town this afternoon, says he's going to Paris to-morrow. There's been no end of a shine, you know. Chris bolted last night. Heaven only knows where she's gone. I think she might have told me first."

"I can tell you," said Jack. "She is with Hilda at Graysdale. I have just come from there. Trevor is in town, you say?"

Noel nodded. "Bertrand's gone too, you know. That was the beginning of it. Trevor kicked him out for robbing him. Beastly little thief! I told Trevor he would long ago. I say, you are not going again!"

Jack, still standing on the mat, was consulting his watch. "If there is another up train to-night I must catch it. There's a motor here, isn't there? Send round word that it is wanted."

"But there isn't a train!" Noel protested. "I know the last one goes at nine-fifty, and it's past ten now. Have you all gone raving mad? I always thought you, anyhow, had a little sense."

Jack uttered a grim laugh. "Well, find a time-table. I must go by the first train in the morning, whatever the hour. I've got to see Trevor before he leaves England."

"You won't get any sense out of him," Noel remarked. "I told him he was a beastly cad myself before he went, and he didn't even punch my head. Oh, I say, Jack, this place is pretty ghastly with no one in it. I can't stick it much longer."

"Just get me a drink," Jack said, "and we will discuss your affairs at length."

Noel departed with his customary expedition. He returned with drinks for two, which he proceeded to mix with a lavish hand.

"I'm not going to let you have that," Jack observed. "You have dined, and I haven't. Get me some food like a good chap, and then we will have a talk."

Noel submitted meekly. He was fond of Jack. Returning with sufficient to satisfy his cousin's immediate needs, he seated himself on the table while he ate, and embarked upon a more detailed account of the happenings of the past two days.

"I only saw Chris for a few minutes," he said in conclusion. "She looked pretty desperate, and seemed horribly scared. But she wouldn't tell me why. I knew there was something up, of course. Trevor had told me she was upset about Bertrand. But I had no idea she was going to cut and run. I don't know if Trevor had, but I couldn't get anything out of him. It's my belief the silly ass was jealous."

Jack grunted.

"I didn't know what to do," Noel ended. "So I thought I'd stick on here till someone turned up."

"You ought to be going back to school," Jack remarked.

Noel leaned carelessly down upon his elbow and looked him straight in the eyes. "I'm not going," he said.

"Why not?"

"I've other things to think about. I'm going to Graysdale. Can you lend me a couple of quid for the journey? I'll pay you back when I come of age."

Jack surveyed him with one brow uplifted. "Suppose I can't?"

"I shall tramp, that's all." Noel made unconcerned response. He was accustomed to fend for himself, and the prospect of such an adventure was rather alluring than otherwise.

Jack smiled a little. He liked the boy's independence. "What do you want to go to Graysdale for?" he asked.

"To look after Chris, of course."

"Hilda can do that."

"Not in the same way. You needn't try to put me off. I'm going." Noel got off the table with his hands in his pockets and broke into a whistle.

Jack went on with his meal in silence.

Finally Noel came round and stood beside him. "That's understood, is it?" he said. "One of us ought to be with her, and as you and Rupert are chasing after Trevor, and Max is in town, it looks like my job. Anyhow, I'm going to take it on."

"All right," Jack said. "Go and prosper. I'm not sure that you will be wanted. But that's a detail. I daresay Chris may like to have you."

Noel grinned boyishly. "You're a white man, Jack! I'm jolly glad you turned up. Between ourselves, I don't mind telling you that I've been in a fairly stiff paste all day. It's a beastly feeling, isn't it? I'd have looked after her better if I'd known."

"You're a white man too," said Jack kindly. "Mind you behave like one."

They parted for the night soon after, to meet again very early in the morning, and finally separate upon their various errands.

Noel departed upon his in obviously high spirits; but he maintained his air of responsibility notwithstanding, and Jack took leave of him with a smile of approval.

He himself telegraphed to Hilda as soon as he arrived in town, and acquainted her with the fact of the boy's advent. He directed her to send her answering message to him at Mordaunt's rooms, and then proceeded thither with the firm determination to see the owner thereof without further delay.

Holmes admitted him, and imparted the information that his master was at breakfast with the eldest Mr. Wyndham, who had arrived overnight.

Jack's jaw hardened at the news. He had not expected to find Rupert accepting his brother-in-law's hospitality. He shrugged his shoulders over the volatility of the Wyndhams, and announced curtly that he desired to see Mr. Mordaunt in private.

"Will you come into the smoking-room, sir?" asked Holmes.

"Certainly. But tell him I can't wait," said Jack.

He marched into the smoking-room therewith, and Holmes softly closed the door upon him. The window by which Mordaunt had sat all night long was open, and the sounds of the street below came cheerily in. Jack crossed over and quietly shut it.

Turning from this, his eyes fell upon a photograph on the mantelpiece. He went up to it and took it between his hands. Gaily the pictured face laughed up at him—Chris in her happiest, wildest mood, with Cinders clasped in her arms; Chris, the child of the sunny eyes that no shadow had ever darkened!

Something rose suddenly in Jack's throat. He gulped hard, and put the portrait back. Was it indeed Chris—the broken-hearted woman he had held in his arms but yesterday? Then was the Chris of the old days gone for ever.

Someone entered the room behind him and he wheeled round.

"Good morning," said Mordaunt.

He offered his hand, but Jack ignored it and his greeting alike.

He stood for a couple of seconds in silence, looking at him, while Mordaunt waited with absolute composure. Then, "I daresay you are wondering what I have come for," he said. "Or perhaps you can guess."

"Why should I?" Mordaunt said.

Jack frowned abruptly. He had met this impenetrable mood before. But he would not be baffled by it. It was no moment for subtleties. He went straight to the point.

"I have come to tell you that Chris is at Graysdale with Hilda," he said.

Mordaunt's brows went up. He said nothing.

But Jack was insistent. "Did you know that?"

"I did not." Very deliberately came Mordaunt's answer; it held no emotion of any sort. The subject might have been one of utter indifference to him.

"Then where did you think she was?"

There was an undernote of ferocity in Jack's question, almost a hint of menace; but Mordaunt seemed unaware of it.

"Forgive me for saying so, Jack," he said. "But that is more my affair than yours. I have nothing whatever to discuss with you, nor do I hold myself answerable to you in any way for my actions."

"But I do," Jack said curtly. "I have always held myself responsible for Chris's welfare. And I do so still."

Mordaunt listened unmoved. "You can hardly expect me to acknowledge your authority," he said, "since my responsibility in that respect is greater than yours."

"I have no desire to dictate to you," Jack answered quickly. "But I do claim the right to speak my mind on this matter. Remember, it was I who first brought you into her life."

Mordaunt shrugged his shoulders slightly. "As to that, I am fatalist enough to believe that we should have met in any case. But isn't that beside the point? I have declined to discuss the matter with anyone, and I am not going to make an exception of you."

"You must," Jack said. He threw back his shoulders as if bracing himself for a physical conflict. He was plainly in earnest.

Mordaunt turned to the table and sat down. "You are wasting your time," he said. "Argument is quite useless. I have already decided upon my plan of action, and quarrelling with you is no part of it."

"What is your plan of action?" Jack demanded.

Mordaunt took out his cigarette-case. "I shall start for Paris in a couple of hours. Meantime"—he glanced up—"I suppose you won't smoke? Have you had any breakfast?"

"Then you mean to desert her?" Jack said.

Mordaunt's face remained immovable. He began to smoke in dead silence.

Jack's teeth clenched. "I am going to have an answer," he said.

"Very well." Coldly the words fell; there was something merciless in their very utterance. "Then I will answer you; but it is my last word upon the subject. My wife followed her own choice in leaving me, and it is my intention to abide by her decision. If you call that desertion—"

"I do," Jack broke in passionately. "It is desertion, nothing less. She left you—oh, I know all about it—she left you because you literally scared her away. You terrified her into going; there was nothing else for her to do. She had done nothing wrong. But you—you dared to suspect her of Heaven knows what. You dared to think that Chris—my Chris—was capable of playing you false, you who were the only man on earth I thought good enough for her. And do you know what you have done? You have broken her heart!" He took the portrait from the mantelpiece and thrust it in front of the man at the table. "That," he said, and suddenly his voice was quivering, "that was the child you married. I gave her into your care willingly, though, God knows, I worshipped her. No, you didn't cut me out. I was never in the running. I never so much as made love to her. I always knew she was not for me. When she accepted you, I thought it was the best thing that could possibly happen. I felt she would be safe with you. You were the one fellow I would have chosen to guard her. And she needed guarding. She was as innocent and as inexperienced as a baby. She didn't know the world and its beastly ways. I thought you were to be trusted to keep her out of the mud; I could have sworn you were. But you withdrew your protection just when she needed it most. You practically turned her out, cut her adrift. She might have gone straight to the bad for all you cared. And now, like the damned blackguard that you are, you are going to clear out and leave her to break her heart!"

Fiercely the words rushed out. Jack, the placid, the kindly, the careless, was for the moment electrified by a tornado of feeling that swept him far beyond the bounds of his customary easy *bonhomie*. He towered over the man in the chair as if at the first movement he would fell him to the ground.

But Mordaunt remained quite motionless. He had removed his cigarette, and sat looking straight up at him with steely eyes that never changed. When Jack ceased to speak, there fell a silence that was in a sense more fraught with conflict than any war of words.

Through it at length came Mordaunt's voice, measured and distinct and cold. "It is not particularly wise of you to take that tone, but that is your affair. I have already warned you that you are wasting your time. Your championship is quite superfluous, and will do no good to anyone. I think you will see this for yourself when you have taken time to think it over. Wouldn't it be as well to do so before you go any further—for your own sake, not for mine?"

"I am not thinking of myself at the present moment," Jack responded sternly, "or of you. I'm thinking of Chris—and Chris only. Man, do you want to kill her? For you're going the right way to do it."

The cigarette between Mordaunt's fingers slowly doubled and crumpled into shapelessness, but the steely eyes never altered. They barred the way inflexibly to the man's inmost soul. He uttered neither question nor answer.

But Jack was not to be silenced. "I tell you, she is ill," he said. "I saw her myself yesterday. She was simply broken down. I never saw such a change in anyone. I couldn't have credited it. Hilda is horribly anxious about her. She is going to wire to me here as to her condition."

"Why here?" Very calmly came the question.

Jack explained. Almost in spite of himself his own heat had died down, cooled by that icy deliberation. "I went to Kellerton yesterday in search of you, found only Noel there, but had to spend the night as it was late. I came on by the first train, and wired to Hilda to send her message here in case you may be wanted. It ought to come through in about an hour."

"And you propose to wait for it?"

"Yes, I do." Jack paused an instant; then, "You must wait too," he said doggedly. "She isn't very likely to want you, and I've sworn you shan't frighten her any more; but you shan't abandon her either while there is the faintest chance that she may want you."

"There is not the faintest." Mordaunt glanced down at the thing that had once been a cigarette which he still held between his fingers, contemplated it for a moment, then rose and went to the mantelpiece for an ash-tray. "You have taken a good deal upon yourself, Jack," he said. "But I have borne with you because I know that your position is a difficult one. You say you know everything. That may be so, and again it may not. In either case, our points of view do not coincide. I will wait until that telegram comes; but it is not my intention to go to my wife—whatever it may contain."

Jack bit his lip savagely. "In short, you don't care what happens to her!" he said. "You want to be rid of her—one way or another. And you don't care how!"

He spoke recklessly, uttering the thought that had come uppermost in his mind without an instant's consideration. Perhaps instinctively he sought to rouse the devil that till then had been held in such rigid control. But the effect of his words was such as he had scarcely looked for.

Mordaunt turned with the movement of a goaded creature and gripped him by the shoulder. "You believe that?" he said.

They stood face to face. Mordaunt was as white as death. His eyes in that moment were terrible. But it seemed to Jack that they expressed more of anguish than of anger, and he felt as if he had seen a soul in torment. He averted his own instinctively. It was a sight upon which he could not look.

"Do you believe it?" Mordaunt said, his voice very low.

"No!" Impulsively Jack made answer. That instant's revelation had quenched his own fire very effectually. "Forgive me!" he said. "I—didn't understand."

The hand on his shoulder relaxed slowly. There fell a silence. Then, "All right, Jack," Mordaunt said very quietly.

And Jack knew that he had dropped the veil again that shrouded his soul's agony.

"You will wait here for that telegram?" Mordaunt asked, after a moment.

"Yes, please."

"Will you come into the other room? Rupert is with me."

"No. I'll wait here, thanks."

"Very well. I shall see you again." Mordaunt crossed to the door, then paused, and after a moment came slowly back to the table.

He stood before it in silence, looking down upon the portrait that Jack had laid there as one looks upon the face of the dead.

His face showed no sign of softening, yet Jack made a last effort to move him. "You're not going to let her fret her heart out for you? You'll go back to her if she is wanting you? Damn it, Trevor! You can't know what she is suffering! And after all—she is your wife!"

Mordaunt's mouth hardened. He made no response.

"Surely you don't—you can't—think evil of her?" Jack said.

Mordaunt raised his eyes slowly. "You have said enough," he said, with quiet emphasis. "As for this portrait, take it if you value it. I never cared for it myself."

"Never cared for it!" Jack ejaculated.

"No. It never conveyed very much to me. I did not regard her in that light."

"Then you never knew her," Jack said with conviction.

"Possibly not." Mordaunt turned away once more. "Most of us are blind," he said, "until our eyes are opened. I am going to send you in some breakfast if you are sure you prefer to stay here."

He went out quietly, leaving Jack marvelling at his own docility. The last thing he would have expected of himself was that at the end of the interview he also would be accepting the hospitality of the man he had come almost prepared to shoot. The turn of events forced him into a species of unwilling admiration. There was no denying the fact that, mismanage his own private affairs as he might, this was a born leader of men.

Mordaunt himself brought him his sister's telegram some time later.

He remained in the room while Jack opened it, but he betrayed no impatience to hear its contents. As for Jack, he stood for several seconds with the message in his hand before he looked up.

"I suppose you will have to see it," he said then reluctantly.

"That is as you like."

But though the words were emotionless, Mordaunt's eyes searched his face, and in answer to them Jack held out the paper.

"I am sorry," he said.

"In no danger. Keep Trevor away," was the message it contained.

"As I thought," Mordaunt observed, and handed it back without further comment.

"She will be wanting you presently," Jack said uneasily, "You know how women change."

And Mordaunt smiled, a grim, set smile. "Yes, I know," he answered.

CHAPTER IV
THE DESIRE OF HIS HEART

The night was very hot, even hotter than the day had been. Only the whirring electric fan kept the air moving. It might have been midsummer instead of the end of September.

Bertrand de Montville, seated in an easy-chair and propped by cushions, raised his head from time to time and gasped for breath. He held a newspaper in his hand, for sleep was out of the question. He had been suffering severely during the day, but the pain had passed and only weariness remained. His face was yet drawn with the memory of it, and his eyes were heavily shadowed. But the inherent pluck of the man was still apparent. His pride of bearing had not waned.

He was reading with close attention a report upon the chief event of the hour—the trial of Guillaume Rodolphe at Valpré. It had been in progress for four days, and was likely to last for several more. The report he read was from the pen of Trevor Mordaunt, an account clear and direct as the man himself. So far the evidence had seemed to turn in Bertrand's favour, and, his protestations notwithstanding, it was impossible not to feel a quickening of the pulses as he realized this fact. Would they ever send for him? He asked himself. Would they ever desire to do justice to the man they had degraded?

It was evident that the writer of the account before him thought so. However Mordaunt's opinion of the man himself had altered, his conviction on the subject of his innocence of that primary crime had plainly remained unshaken. He had not allowed himself to be biased by subsequent events.

"And that is strange—that!" the Frenchman murmured, with his eyes upon the article. "Perhaps *la petite Christine* has convinced him. But no—that is not probable."

He broke off as the door opened, and a quick smile of welcome flashed across his face. He stretched out both hands to the new-comer.

"All right. Sit still," said Max.

He sauntered across the room, his coat hanging open and displaying evening dress, and gave his hand into Bertrand's eager clasp. It was a very cool hand, and strong with a vitality that seemed capable of imparting itself.

He looked down at Bertrand with a queer glint of tenderness in his eyes. "I shouldn't have come up at this hour," he said, "but I guessed you would be awake. How goes it, old chap? Pretty bad, eh?"

"No, I am better," Bertrand said. "I am glad that you came up."

Max drew up a chair, and sat down beside his *protégé*. For nearly three weeks now Bertrand had been with him. A post-card written from a squalid back-street lodging had been his first intimation that the Frenchman was in London, and within two hours of receiving it Max had removed him to the private nursing-home in which he himself was at that time domiciled. For, notwithstanding his youth, Max Wyndham was a privileged person, and owned as his greatest friend one of the most distinguished physicians in London.

His natural brilliance had brought him in the first place to the great man's notice; and though he was but a medical student, his foot was already firmly planted upon the ladder of success. There was little doubt that one day — and that probably not many years distant — Max Wyndham would be a great man too. Even as it was, his grip upon all things that concerned the profession he had chosen was so prodigious that his patron would upon occasion consult with him as an equal, detecting in him that flare of genius which in itself is of more value than years of accumulated knowledge. He had the gift of magnetism to an extraordinary degree, and he coupled with it an unerring instinct upon which he was not afraid to rely. Equipped thus, he was bound to come to the front, though whether the Wyndham blood in him would suffer him to stay there was a proposition that time alone could solve.

His effect upon Bertrand was little short of magical. Sitting there beside him with the wasted wrist between his fingers, and his green eyes gazing at nothing in particular, there was little about him to indicate a remarkable personality. Yet the drawn look passed wholly away from the sick man's face, and he leaned back among his pillows with a restfulness that he had been very far from feeling a few seconds earlier.

"So you are reading all about the Rodolphe *affaire*," Max said presently.

"It is Mr. Mordaunt's own report," Bertrand explained. "It interests me—that. I feel as if I heard him speak."

Max grunted. He had asked no question as to the circumstances that had led to Bertrand's departure, and Bertrand had volunteered no information. It had been a closed subject between them by mutual consent. But to-night for some reason Max approached it, warily, as one not sure of his ground.

"When do you hope to see him again?"

A slight flush rose in Bertrand's face. "Never—it is probable," he said sadly.

"Ah! Then you had a disagreement?"

Bertrand looked at him questioningly.

Max smiled a little. "No, it isn't vulgar curiosity. Fact is, I came across my cousin Jack Forest to-day. You remember Jack Forest? I've been dining with him at his club. We hadn't met for ages, and naturally we had a good deal to say to one another."

He paused, gently relinquishing his hold upon Bertrand's wrist, and got up to pour something out of a bottle on the mantelpiece into a medicine-glass.

"Drink this, old chap," he said, "or I shall tire you out before I've done."

"You have something to say to me?" Bertrand said quickly.

Max nodded. "I have. Drink first, and then I will tell you. That's the way. You needn't be in a hurry. You were going to tell me about that disagreement, weren't you? At least, I think you were. You have been rash enough to trust me before."

"But naturally," Bertrand said. He handed the glass back with a courteous gesture of thanks. "And I have not had cause to regret it. I will tell you why I disagreed with Mr. Mordaunt if you desire to know. It was because he found that he had been robbed, and that I"—he spread out his hands—"was the robber."

Max stared. "Found that you had robbed him! You!"

Bertrand nodded several times, but said no more.

"I don't believe it," Max said with conviction.

Bertrand smiled rather ruefully. "No? But yet the evidence was against me. And me, I did not contradict the evidence."

"I see. You were shielding someone. Who was it? Rupert?"

At Bertrand's quick start Max also smiled with grim humour. "You see, I know my own people rather well. I'm glad it wasn't Chris, anyway. Then she had nothing at all to do with your quarrel with Trevor?"

"Nothing," Bertrand said—"nothing." He paused a moment, then added, with something of an effort, "But I had decided that I would go before that. Mr. Mordaunt did not know why."

"Because of Chris?" There was a touch of sharpness in Max's voice.

Bertrand bent his head. "You were right that night. A man cannot hope to hide his heart for ever from the woman whom he loves."

"You told her, then?"

"It arrived without telling," Bertrand answered with simplicity.

"That means she cares for you?" Max said shrewdly.

Bertrand looked up. "*Mais c'est passé,*" he said, his voice very low. "You have guessed the truth, but you only know it. Her husband—"

"My dear fellow, that's just the mischief. He knows it too," Max said.

"He!" Bertrand started upright.

Instantly Max's hand was upon him, checking him. "Keep still, Bertrand! You can't afford to waste your strength. Yes, Trevor knows. He knew on the very day you left. He found out that that blackguard Rodolphe had been blackmailing her. He had a scene with Chris, and she left him."

"Rodolphe! *Le canaille! Est-ce possible? Alors,* she is not—not with him— at Valpré—as I thought?" gasped Bertrand.

"No. She has not been near him since. I knew nothing of this till to-day. She hardly ever writes. I thought—as you did—that she had gone to France with Trevor. Instead of that, Jack tells me, she has been with his sister in Yorkshire all this time. She has been ill, is so still, I believe. They are coming to town to-morrow, to Percy Davenant's flat. Jack is very worried about it. He saw Trevor before he left England, but couldn't get him to listen to reason. He seems to have made up his mind to have no more to do with her, while she is fretting herself to a skeleton over it, but daren't make the first move towards a reconciliation. It probably wouldn't do any good if she did. He is as hard as iron. And if his mind is once made up—" Max left the sentence unfinished, and continued: "I think I shall go to Valpré and see what I can do. This has gone on long enough, and we can't have Chris making herself ill. I should think even he would see the force of that. This trial business will be over in a few days, and if I don't catch him he may go wandering, Heaven knows where. But it won't do. He must come back to her. I shall tell him so."

But at that Bertrand laid a nervous hand upon his arm. "My friend," he said, "you will not persuade him."

Max looked at him, and was confronted by eyes of gleaming resolution. "I believe I shall," he said. "I can persuade most people."

"You will not persuade him," Bertrand repeated. "That *scélérat* has poisoned his mind. Moreover, you do not even know what passed between us."

"I don't need to know," Max said curtly.

Bertrand began to smile. "And you think you can plead your sister's cause without knowing, *hein*? No, no! the affair is too much advanced. There is only one man who can help the little Christine now. He would not listen to you, *mon cher*, if you went. But—to me, he will listen, even though he believes me to be a thief; for he is very just. I know that I can make him understand. And for that I shall go to him to-morrow. As you say, we cannot let *la petite* fret."

He spoke quite quietly, but his eyes were shining with a fire that had not lit them for many a day.

"My dear chap, you can't go. You're not fit for it." Max spoke with quick decision. "I won't let you go, so there's an end of it."

But Bertrand laughed. "So? But I am more fit than you think, *mon ami*. Also it is my affair, this, and none but I can accomplish it. See, I start in the morning, and by this hour to-morrow I shall be with him."

"Folly! Madness!" Max said.

But indomitable resolution still shone in the Frenchman's eyes. "Listen to me, Max," he said. "If I spend my last breath thus, why not? I have not the least desire to cling to life. And is that madness? I love *la petite* more than all. And is that folly? Why should I not give the strength that is still in me to accomplish the desire of my heart? Is mortal life so precious to those who have nothing for which to live?"

"Rot!" Max said fiercely. "You have plenty to live for. When this scoundrel Rodolphe is disposed of they will be reinstating you. You've got to live to have your honour vindicated. Does that mean nothing to you?"

Bertrand shrugged his shoulders. "It would interest me exactly as the procession under the windows interests those who watch. The procession passes, and the street is empty again. What is that to me?" He snapped his fingers carelessly. But the animation of his face had transformed it completely, giving him a look of youth with which Max was wholly unfamiliar. "See!" he said. "*Le bon Dieu* has given me this thing to do, and He will give me the strength to do it. That is His way, *mon ami*. He does not command us to make bricks without straw."

Max grunted. "Whatever you do, you will have to pay for," he observed dryly. "And how are you going to get to Valpré without being arrested?"

"But I will disguise myself. That should be easy." Bertrand laughed again, and suddenly stretched out his arms and rose. "I am well," he declared. "I have been given the strength, and I will use it. Have no fear, Max. It will not fail me."

"I shall go too, then," Max said abruptly. "Sit down, man, and be rational. You don't suppose I shall let you tear all over France in your present condition by yourself, do you? If you excite yourself in this fashion, you will be having that infernal pain again. Sit down, I tell you!"

Bertrand sat down, but as if he moved on wires. "No," he said with confidence, "I shall not suffer any more to-night. You say that you will go with me? But indeed it is not necessary. And you have your work to do. I would not have you leave it on my account."

"I am coming," Max said, with finality, "And look here, Bertrand, I shall be in command of this expedition, and we are not going to travel at break-neck speed. You will not reach Valpré till the day after to-morrow. That is understood, is it?"

Bertrand hesitated and looked dubious.

"Come, man, it's for your own good. You don't want to die before you get there." Max's tone was severely practical.

"Ah no! Not that! I must not fail, Max. I must not fail." Bertrand spoke with great earnestness. He laid an impressive hand on his companion's arm. For a moment his face betrayed emotion. "I cannot—I will not—die before her happiness is assured. It is that for which I now live, for which I am ready to give my life. Max—*mon ami*—you will not let me die before—my work—is done!"

He spoke pantingly, as though speech had become an effort. The strain was beginning to tell upon him. But his eyes pleaded for him with a dumb intensity hard to meet.

Max took his wrist once more into his steady grasp. "If you will do as I tell you," he said, "I will see that you don't. Is that a bargain?"

A faint smile shone in the dark eyes at the peremptoriness of his speech. "But how you are despotic—you English!" protested the soft voice.

"Do you agree to that?" insisted Max.

"*Mais oui.* I submit myself—always—to you English. How can one—do other?"

"Then don't talk any more," said Max, with authority. "There's no time for drivel, so save your breath. You will want it when you get to Valpré."

"Ah, Valpré!" whispered Bertrand very softly as one utters a beloved name; and again more softly, "Valpré!"

CHAPTER V
THE STRANGER

A long wave broke with a splash and spread up the sand in a broad band of silver foam. The tide was at its lowest, and the black rocks of Valpré stood up stark and grotesque in the evening light. The Gothic archway of the Magic Cave yawned mysteriously in the face of the cliff, and over it, with shrill wailings, flew countless seagulls, flashing their wings in the sunset.

The man who walked alone along the shore was too deeply engrossed in thought to take much note of his surroundings, although more than once he turned his eyes towards the darkness of the cave. A belt of rocks stretched between, covered with slimy, green seaweed. It was evident that he had no intention of crossing this to explore the mysteries beyond. Just out of reach of the sea he moved, his hands behind him and his head bent.

All through the day he had been pent in a stuffy courtroom, closely following the evidence that, like a net of strong weaving, was gradually closing around the prisoner Guillaume Rodolphe. All France was seething over the trial. All Europe watched with vivid interest.

Another man's name had begun to be uttered on all sides, in court and out of it, coupled continuously with the name of the man who was standing his trial. Bertrand de Montville, where was he? All France would soon be waiting to do him justice, to pay him high honour, to compensate him for the indignities he had wrongfully suffered. He would have to face another court-martial, it was true; but the outcome of that would be a foregone conclusion, and his acquittal would raise him to a pinnacle of popularity to which he had surely never aspired, even in the days when ambition had been the ruling passion of his life.

Undoubtedly he would be the hero of the hour, if he could be found. But where was he? Everyone was asking the question. None knew the answer. Some said he was in England, awaiting the turn of events, abiding his opportunity; others that he was already in France, lying hidden in Paris, or even risking arrest at Valpré itself. The police were uniformly reticent upon the subject, but it was generally believed that there would be small difficulty in finding him when the moment arrived. Some went so far as to assert that he had actually been arrested, and was being kept a close prisoner by the authorities, who were plainly in fear of serious rioting. Whatever the truth of the matter, the fact remained that the tide of public opinion had set very strongly in his favour, and was likely to wax to a tumultuous enthusiasm exceedingly difficult to cope with when the object thereof should present himself.

With all of this Trevor Mordaunt was well acquainted; but he, on his part, was firmly convinced that Bertrand would keep away until he himself had left France. To come to Valpré now would be to court a meeting with him, and this, he was convinced, Bertrand would do his utmost to avoid. The break between them had been quite final. Moreover, he probably believed that Chris was at Valpré also, and he had apparently determined not to see her again. But here an evil thought forced its way. Might they not, quite possibly, be in communication with one another? It had presented itself many times before, that thought, and he had sought to put it from him. But to-night it would not be denied. It conquered and possessed him. Was it at all likely that the parting between them had been final?

Only that afternoon evidence had been given of the episode that had led to the duel on the Valpré sands more than four years before. He had listened with a set face to the account of the insult and the subsequent challenge, and though no name had been mentioned, he had known and faced the fact that the woman in the case had been his wife. Even then, Bertrand had regarded her as his peculiar charge, as under his exclusive protection. And she—had she not told him with burning unrestraint that she had always loved this man, would love him till she died?

With the gesture of one who relinquishes his hold upon something he has discovered to be valueless, Trevor Mordaunt turned in his tracks and began to walk back over the long stretch of sand. He looked no longer in the direction of the Magic Cave, but rather quickened his steps as though he desired to leave it far behind. But there was no escaping that all-mastering suspicion. It went with him, closely locked with his own spirit, and he could not shake it off.

Back to his hotel he walked, with no glance at sea or shining sunset, and went straight to his own room. There was a private sitting-room adjoining, which he was wont to share with some of his fellow-journalists. They used it as a club writing-room when the proceedings of the court-martial were over for the day. He had his notes in his pocket; his report was not yet written. He remembered that he must catch the midnight mail, and decided that he would not stop to dress. That day's sitting had been longer than usual, and his walk along the shore had made him late.

He passed straight through his bedroom, therefore, and into the sitting-room that overlooked the sea. A small, round-backed man, with a shag of black hair upon his face, was sitting by the window. There were three other men in the room, all writing busily. All, save the man by the window, glanced up at Mordaunt's entrance and nodded to him. They were all English, with the exception of the stranger, who was obviously French.

Mordaunt looked at him questioningly, but no one volunteered an explanation. He had evidently been sitting there for some time. His gaze was fixed upon the darkening sea. It was plain that he had no desire to court attention.

Quietly Mordaunt crossed the room to him. He was crouched like a monkey, his chin on his hand, and made no movement at his approach.

Mordaunt reached him, and bent a little. "*Est-ce que vous attendez quelqu'un, monsieur?*"

Dark eyes flashed up at him, and sharply Mordaunt straightened himself.

"I await Mr. Mordaunt," a soft voice said.

There was an instant's pause before, "That is my name," Mordaunt said very quietly.

"*Eh bien, monsieur*! May I speak with you—in private?"

The stranger rose shufflingly. He had the look of an old man.

"Come this way," Mordaunt said.

He re-crossed the room, his visitor hobbling in his wake. No one spoke, but all surveyed the latter curiously, and as the door of Mordaunt's bedroom closed upon him there was an interchange of glances and a raising of brows.

But nothing passed behind the closed door that would have enlightened any of them. For Mordaunt scarcely waited to be alone with the man before he said, "I must ask you to wait some time longer if you wish to speak to me. I am not at liberty at present."

"If I may wait here—" the stranger suggested meekly.

"Yes. You can do that. Have you dined?"

"But no, monsieur."

Mordaunt rang the bell. His face was quite immovable. He stood and waited in silence for an answer to his summons.

Holmes came at length. He betrayed no surprise at sight of the stranger in the room, but stood stiffly at attention, as though prepared to remove him at his master's bidding.

"Holmes," Mordaunt said very distinctly, "this—gentleman has private business with me, and he will wait in this room until I am able to attend to him. Will you get him some dinner, and see that no one but yourself comes into the room while he is here?"

"Very good, sir," said Holmes.

He looked his charge over with something of the air of a sentry taking stock of a prisoner, and turned about.

"See that he has all that he wants," Mordaunt added.

"Very good, sir," Holmes said again, and withdrew.

Mordaunt turned at once towards the other door. "I may be a couple of hours," he said, and passed through gravely into his sitting-room.

The trio assembled there glanced up again at his entrance with professional curiosity, but Mordaunt's face was quite inscrutable. Without speaking, he went to the table, took out his notebook, and began to write. The evidence had that evening been completed, and the trial adjourned for two days. It was his intention to write a short *résumé* of the whole, and this he proceeded to do with characteristic clearness of outline. His pen moved rapidly, with unwavering decision, and for upwards of an hour he was immersed in his task, to the exclusion of all other considerations.

The three other men in the room completed their own reports, and went out one by one. The hotel was full of journalists from all parts, and the dinner-hour was always a crowded time. It was considered advisable by the English *coterie* to secure the meal as early as possible, but to-night Mordaunt neglected this precaution. He did not look up when the others left, or stir from his place until the article upon which he was engaged was finished.

He threw down his pen at last, and leaned back to run his eye over what he had written. It was a very brief inspection, and he made no corrections.

Finally he shook the loose sheets together, added two or three sketches from his notebook, thrust them into a directed envelope, and went to the door.

Holmes came to him at once along the passage.

"Get this sealed and dispatched without delay," Mordaunt said. "The gentleman is still waiting, I suppose?"

"Still waiting, sir," said Holmes.

"He has dined?"

"If you can call it dining, sir."

"Very well. You can go, Holmes."

But Holmes lingered a moment. "Won't you dine yourself, sir?"

"Later on. I am engaged just now. All right. Don't wait."

Holmes shook his head disapprovingly without further words, and turned to obey.

Mordaunt closed the door and turned the key, then walked slowly across the room to the window by which the Frenchman had sat that afternoon, and opened it wide. The night was very dark, and through it the sea moaned desolately. The wind was rising with the tide and blew in salt and cold, infinitely refreshing after the stuffy heat of the day. He leaned his head for a while against the window-frame. There was intense weariness in his attitude.

He uttered a great sigh at last and stood up, paused a moment, as though to pull himself together, then, with his customary precision of movement, he turned from the open window and walked across to the door that led into the next room. His face was somewhat paler than usual, but perfectly composed.

Without hesitation he opened the door and spoke. "Now, Bertrand!"

CHAPTER VI
MAN TO MAN

There was a quick movement in answer to the summons, and in a moment the visitor presented himself. He had taken the false hair from his face, and his gait was no longer halting. He looked up at Mordaunt with sharp anxiety as he came through.

"No one else has recognized me?" he asked.

"I believe not."

He drew a quick breath of relief. "*Bien!* It has been an affair *très difficile.* I have feared detection *mille fois.* Yet I did not expect you to recognize me so soon."

"You see, I happen to know you rather well," Mordaunt said.

The Frenchman spread out his hands protestingly. The excitement of the adventure had flushed his face and kindled his eyes. He looked younger and more ardent than Mordaunt had ever seen him. The weariness that had so grown upon him during his exile had fallen from him like a cloak. "But you do not know me at all!" he said.

Mordaunt passed over the remark as if he had not heard it. "What have you come for?" he asked.

"To see you, monsieur." The reply was as direct as the question. A momentary challenge shone in Bertrand's eyes as he made it.

But Mordaunt remained coldly unimpressed. "It was not a very wise move on your part," he remarked. "You will be arrested if you are discovered. The authorities are not ready for you yet. They are quite capable of suppressing you for good and all if it suits their purpose."

"I know it. But that is of no importance after to-night." Bertrand stood and faced him squarely. "After to-night," he said, "they may do what they will. I shall have accomplished that which I came to do."

"And that?" said Mordaunt. He looked back into the eager eyes with the aloofness of a stranger. His manner was too impersonal to express either enmity or contempt.

The keenness began to die out of Bertrand's face, and a certain dignity took its place. "That," he made answer, "is to tell you the truth in such a fashion that, although you think that I am a thief, you will believe it."

"I do not think that you are in a position to tell me anything that I do not know already," Mordaunt answered quietly. "By the way, it may interest you to hear that the affair of the cheque has been cleared up. I wronged you there, but I do not think that I was responsible for the wrong."

"I was responsible," Bertrand said, his voice very low. "I deceived you. And for that you will not pardon me, no?"

But the level grey eyes looked through and beyond him. "That," Mordaunt said, "is a matter of small importance now. Deceptions of that kind are never excusable in my opinion; but as I do not expect you to share my point of view, it seems scarcely worth while to discuss it."

Bertrand bowed stiffly. "It is not of that that I desire to speak. Of myself you will think—what you will. I have merited—and I will endure—your displeasure. But of *la petite*"—he paused—"of Christine"—he faltered a little, and finally amended—"of *madame votre femme*, you will think only that which is good. For that is her nature, that. And for me," his voice throbbed with sudden passion, "I would rather bear any insult than that you should think otherwise of her. For she is pure and innocent as a child. Do you not see that I would sooner die than harm her? And it has always, always been so. You believe me, no?"

Mordaunt's face was as stone. "I shouldn't go on if I were you," he said. "You have nothing whatever to gain. As I have told you, I know already all that you can tell me upon this subject, and what I think of it is my affair alone. It is a pity that you took the trouble to come here. If you take my advice, you will leave me on the earliest opportunity."

"But you are mistaken. You do not know all." Impulsively Bertrand threw back the words. "You cannot refuse to listen to me," he said. "I appeal to your honour, to your sense of justice. If you knew all, as you say, you would not leave her thus. If you believed her to be blameless—as she is— you would not abandon her in her hour of trouble. I tell you, monsieur"— his breath quickened suddenly and he caught his hand to his side—"if you know the truth, you are committing a crime for which no penalty is enough severe."

He broke off, panting, and turned towards the open window.

Mordaunt said nothing whatever. His face was set like a mask. The only sign of feeling he gave was in the slow clenching of one hand.

After a few moments Bertrand wheeled round. "See!" he said. "I have followed you here to tell you the truth face to face, as I shall tell it—*bientôt*— to the good God. You shall bind me by any oath that you will, though it should be enough for you that I have nothing at all to gain, as you have said. I shall hide nothing from you. I shall extenuate nothing. I shall tell you only the truth, man to man, as my heart knows it. For her sake, you will listen, yes?"

His voice slipped into sudden pleading. He stretched out his hands persuasively to the impassive Englishman, who still seemed to be looking through him rather than at him. He waited for an answer, but none came.

"*Eh bien!*" he said, with a quick sigh of disappointment. "Then I shall speak in spite of you. I begin with our meeting four years ago among the rocks of Valpré. It was an accident by which we met. I was working to complete my invention, and for the greater privacy I had taken it to the old cave of the contrabandists upon the shore—a place haunted by the spirits of the dead—so that I was safe from interruption. Or so I thought, till one afternoon she came to me like a goddess from the sea. She had cut her foot among the stones, and I bound it for her and carried her back to Valpré. She was only a child then, with eyes clear as the sunshine. She trusted herself to me as if I had been her brother. That is easy to comprehend, is it not?"

Again he paused for an answer, but Mordaunt said no word; his lips were firmly closed.

With a characteristic lift of the shoulders Bertrand continued. "*Après cela* we met again and then again. *La petite* was lonely, and I, I played with her. I drew for her the pictures in the sand. We became—pals." He smiled with a touch of wistfulness over the word that his English friend had taught him. "We shared our secrets. Once—she was bathing"—his voice softened imperceptibly—"and I took her into my boat and rowed her back. It was then that I knew first that I loved her. Yet we remained comrades. I spoke to her no word of love. She was too young, and I had nothing to offer. I said to myself that I would win her when I had won my reputation, and in the meantime I would be patient. It was not very difficult, for she did not understand. And then one day we went to explore my cavern—she called it the Magic Cave, of which she was the princess and I her *preux chevalier*. We were as children in those days," he put in half-apologetically, "and it was her *fête*. *Bien*, we started. *Le petit* Cinders went with us, and almost before we had entered he ran away. We followed him, for Christine was very anxious. I had never been beyond the second cavern myself, and we had only one lantern. We came to a place where the passage divided, and here we agreed that she should wait while I went forward. I took the lantern. We could hear him yelp in the distance, and she feared that he was hurt. So I left her alone, and presently, hearing him, as I thought, in front of me, I ran, and stumbled and fell. The lantern was broken and I was stunned. It was long before I recovered, and then it was with great difficulty that I returned. I found her awaiting me still, and Cinders with her. It was dark and horrible, but she was too brave to run away. I heard her singing, and so I found her. But by that time the sea had reached the mouth of the cave, and there was no retreat. We had no choice. We were prisoners for the night. It might have happened to anyone, monsieur. It might have happened to you. You blame me—not yet?"

Again the note of pleading was in his voice, but Mordaunt maintained his silence. Only his eyes were no longer sphinx-like. They were fixed intently upon the Frenchman's face.

Bertrand went on as though he had been answered. "I kept watch all through the night, while she slept like an infant in my arms. You would have done the same. In the morning when the tide permitted, we laughed over the adventure and returned to Valpré. She went to her governess and I to the fortress. By then everybody in Valpré knew what had happened. They had believed that we were drowned, and when we reappeared all were astonished. Later they began to whisper, and that evening the villain Rodolphe, being intoxicated, proposed in my presence an infamous toast. I struck him in the mouth and knocked him down. He challenged me to a duel, and we fought early in the morning down on the sand. But that day the gods were not on my side. Christine and Cinders were gone to the sea to bathe, and, as they returned, they found us fighting. *Le bon* Cinders, he precipitate himself between us. *La petite* rush to stop him—too late. Rodolphe is startled; he plunge, and my sword pierce his arm. *C'était là un moment très difficile. La petite* try to explain, to apologize, and me—I lead her away. *Après cela* she go back to England, and I see her not again. But Rodolphe, he forgive me—never. That, monsieur—and only that—is the true story of that which happened at Valpré. The little Christine left—as she arrived—a pure and innocent child."

He stopped. Mordaunt's eyes were still studying him closely. He met them with absolute freedom.

"I will finish," he said, "and you shall then judge for yourself. As you know, I had scarcely attained my ambition when I was ruined. It was then that you first saw me. You believed me innocent, and later, when Destiny threw me in your path, you befriended me. I have no need to tell you what your friendship was to me. No words can express it or my desolation now that I have lost it. I fear that I was never worthy of your—so great— confidence." His voice shook a little, and he paused to steady it. "It was my intention—always—to be worthy. The fault lay in that I did not realize my weakness. I ought to have left you when I knew that *la petite* was become your fiancée."

For the first time Mordaunt broke his silence. "Why not have told me the truth?"

Bertrand raised his shoulders. "I did not feel myself at liberty to tell you. Afterwards, I found that her eyes had been opened, and she was afraid for you to know. It did not seem an affair of great importance, and I let it pass. We were pals again. She gave me her confidence, and I would sooner have died," he spoke passionately, "than have betrayed it. I thought that I could hide my heart from her, and that only myself would suffer. And this I can say with truth: by no word, no look, no action, of mine were her eyes opened. I was always *le bon frère* to her, neither less nor more, until the awakening came. I was always faithful to you, monsieur. I never forgot that she belonged to you—that she was—the wife of—my friend."

Something seemed to rise in his throat, and he stopped sharply. A moment later very slowly he sat down.

"You permit me?" he said. "I am—a little—tired. As you know, I began to see at last that I could not remain with you. I resolved to go. But the death of Cinders prevented me. She was in trouble, and she desired me to stay. I should have grieved her if I had refused. I was wrong, I admit it. I should have gone then. I should have left her to you. I do not defend myself. I only beg you to believe that I did not see the danger, that if I had seen it I would not have remained for a single moment more. Then came the day at Sandacre, the encounter with Rodolphe. I knew that evening that something had passed between them; what it was she would not tell me. I tried to persuade her then to let me tell you the whole truth. But she was terrified— *la pauvre petite*. She thought that you would be angry with her. She feared that you would ask questions that she could not answer. She had kept the secret so long that she dared not reveal it."

"In short," Mordaunt said, "she was afraid that I should suspect her of caring for you."

His words were too quiet to sound brutal, but they were wholly without mercy. Bertrand's hands gripped the arms of his chair, and he winced visibly.

Yet he answered with absolute candour. "Yes, monsieur. I believe she was. I believe that it was the beginning of all this trouble. But had I known that Rodolphe would use his knowledge to extort money from her, I would not have yielded—no, not one inch—to her importunity. I did not know it. Christine was afraid of me also. I had fought one duel for her; perhaps she dreaded another. And so the mischief was done."

"And who told you that she had been blackmailed?" Mordaunt demanded curtly.

Bertrand made answer without hesitation. "I heard that two days ago from Max."

"Max?"

"Her brother, Max Wyndham."

"And who told him?"

Bertrand's black brows went up. "I believe it was his cousin Captain Forest."

"Ah! So he sent you, did he? I might have known he would." For the first time Mordaunt spoke with bitterness.

"Monsieur, no one sent me." There was dignity in Bertrand's rejoinder, a dignity that compelled belief. "I came as soon as I knew what had happened. I came to redress a great wrong. I came to restore to you that which is your own property—of which, in truth, you have never been deprived. With your permission, I will finish. On the night of the fireworks, the night you were in London, I—betrayed myself. I cannot tell you how it happened. I know only that my love became suddenly a flame that I could not hide. She had been in danger, and me—I lost my self-control. The veil was withdrawn, I could hide my love no more. I showed her my heart just as it was, and—she showed me hers."

Bertrand rose with none of his customary impetuosity and stood in front of Mordaunt, meeting the steady eyes with equal steadiness.

"I tell you the truth," he said. "We understand each other, and we love each other. But you—you are even now more to her than I have ever been.

She has need of you as she has never had of me. You are the reality in her life. I"—he spread out his hands—"I am the romance."

He paused as if to gather his strength, then went rapidly on. But his face was grey. He looked like a man who had travelled fast and far. "Monsieur," he said very earnestly, "believe me, I do not stand between you. I love her—I love you both—too much for that. My one desire, my one prayer, is for her happiness—and yours. Do not, I beseech you, make me an obstacle. You are her protector. Do not leave her unprotected!"

Again for an instant he paused, seeming to strive after self-control. Then suddenly he relinquished the attempt. He flung his dignity from him; he threw himself on his knees at the impassive Englishman's feet. "Mr. Mordaunt," he cried out brokenly, "I have told you the truth. As a dying man, I swear to you—by God—that I have hidden nothing. Monsieur—monsieur—go back to her—make her happy—before I die!"

His voice dropped. He sank forward, murmuring incoherently.

Mordaunt stooped sharply over him. "Bertrand, for Heaven's sake—" he began, and broke off short; for the face that still tried to look into his was so convulsed with agony that he knew him to be for the moment beyond the reach of words.

He lifted the huddled Frenchman to a chair with great gentleness; but the paroxysm did not pass. It was terrible to witness. It seemed to rack him from head to foot, and through it he still strove to plead, though his speech was no more than broken sound, inexpressibly painful to hear, impossible to understand.

Mordaunt bent over him at last, all his hardness merged into pity. "My dear fellow, don't!" he said. "Give yourself time. Haven't you anything with you that will relieve this pain?"

Bertrand could not answer him. He made a feeble gesture with his right hand; his left was clenched and rigid.

Mordaunt began to feel in his pockets; his touch was as gentle as a woman's. But his search was unavailing. He only found an empty bottle. Bertrand had evidently taken the remedy it had contained earlier in the evening.

He turned to get some brandy, but Bertrand clutched at his sleeve and detained him. "Max is here," he gasped. "Find Max! He—knows!"

His hand fell away, and Mordaunt went to the door. Holmes had returned to his post in the passage. He came forward as the door opened.

"Mr. Max Wyndham is somewhere here," Mordaunt said. "Go and find him, and bring him back with you—at once."

Holmes nodded comprehension and went.

Mordaunt turned back into the room. Bertrand had slipped to the floor again, and was lying face downwards. His breathing was anguished, but he made no other sound.

Mordaunt poured out some brandy and went to him. He knelt down by his side and tried to administer it. But Bertrand could not drink. He could only gasp. Yet after a moment his hand came out gropingly and touched the man beside him.

Mordaunt took it and held it.

"You—believe me?" Bertrand jerked out.

"I believe you," Mordaunt answered very gravely.

"You—you forgive?"

Painfully the question came. It went into silence. But the hand that had taken Bertrand's closed slowly and very firmly.

"*Et la petite—la petite—*" faltered Bertrand.

The silence endured for seconds. It seemed as if no answer would come. And through it the man's anguished breathing came and went with a dreadful pumping sound as of some broken machinery.

At last, slowly, as though he weighed each word before he uttered it, Mordaunt spoke.

"You may trust her to me," he said.

And the hand in his stirred and gripped in gratitude, Bertrand de Montville had not spent himself in vain.

CHAPTER VII
THE MESSENGER

"Roses!" said Chris. "How nice!"

She held the white blossoms that Jack had sent her against her face, and smiled.

It was a very pathetic smile, a wan ghost of gaiety, possessing more of bravery than mirth. She lay on a couch by the window, looking out under the sun-blinds at the dusty green of the park. Though October had begun, the summer was not yet over, and the heat was considerable. It seemed oppressive after the fresh air of the moors, and Hilda watched her cousin's languor with some anxiety. For her face had scarcely more colour than the flowers she held.

"Is the paper here?" asked Chris.

She also was closely following the progress of the Valpré trial. Though she never discussed it, Hilda was aware that it was the only thing in life in which she took any interest just then.

She gave her the paper containing the last account that Mordaunt had written, and for nearly an hour Chris was absorbed in it. At last, with a sigh, she laid it down, and drew the roses to her again.

"It's very dear of Jack to send them. Hilda, don't you want to go out? You mustn't stay in always for me."

"I want you to come out too, dear," Hilda said.

"I? Oh, please, dear, I'd rather not." Chris spoke quickly, almost beseechingly. She laid a very thin hand upon Hilda's. "You don't mind?" she said persuasively.

Hilda took the little hand and stroked it. "Chris darling," she said, "do you know what is the matter with you?"

The quick blood rushed up over the pale face, spread to the temples, and then faded utterly away. "Yes," whispered Chris.

Hilda leaned down, and very tenderly kissed her. "I felt sure you did. And that's why you will make an effort to get strong, isn't it, dear? It isn't as if it were just for your own sake any more. You will try, my own Chris?"

But Chris turned her face away with quivering lips. "I think—and I hope—that I shall die," she said.

"Chris, my darling—"

"Yes," Chris insisted. "If it shocks you I can't help it. I don't want to live, and I don't want my child to live, either. Life is too hard. If—if I had had any choice in the matter, I would never have been born. And so if I die before the baby comes, it is the best thing that could possibly happen for either of us. And I think—I think"—she hesitated momentarily before a name she had not uttered for weeks—"Trevor would say the same."

"My dear child, I am quite sure he wouldn't!" Hilda spoke with most unaccustomed vigour. "I am quite sure that if he knew of this, he would be with you to-day."

"Oh no, indeed!" Chris said. She spoke quite quietly, with absolute conviction. "You don't know him, Hilda. You only judge him from outside. If he knew—well, yes, he might possibly think it his duty to be near me. But not because he cared. You see—he doesn't. His love is quite dead And"—she began to shiver—"I don't like dead things; they frighten me. So you won't let anyone tell him; promise me!"

"But, my dear, he would love the child—his child," urged Hilda softly.

"Oh, that would be worse!" Chris turned sharply from her. "If he loved the child—and—and—hated the mother!"

"Chris! Chris! You are torturing yourself with morbid ideas! Such a thing would be impossible."

"Not with him," said Chris, shuddering. "He is not like Percy, you know. You think him gentle and kind, but he is quite different, really. He is as hard—and as cold—as iron. Ah, here is Noel!" She broke off with obvious relief. "Come in, dear old boy. I've been wondering where you were."

Noel came in. He usually haunted Chris's room during the day. The Davenants had done their utmost to persuade him to go to school, but Noel had taken the conduct of his affairs into his own hands, and firmly refused.

"I shan't go while Chris is ill," he declared flatly. "We'll see what she's like at the mid-term."

Jack's authority was invoked in vain, for Jack was on the youngster's side.

"I've squared him," said Noel, with satisfaction. "Of course, I'm sorry to be a burden to you, Hilda, but I'll pay up when I come of age."

Which promise invariably silenced Hilda's protests, and made Lord Percy chuckle.

Aunt Philippa was still absent upon her autumn round of visits, a circumstance for which Noel was openly and devoutly thankful. Not that her influence was by any means paramount with him, but her presence might of itself have been sufficient to drive him away. The only person who could really manage him was his brother-in-law, but as he had apparently forgotten Noel's very existence, it seemed unlikely that his authority would be brought to bear upon him. Meanwhile, Noel swaggered in and out of his sister's presence, penniless but content, and Chris plainly liked to have him.

On the present occasion he interrupted their conversation without apology, pushed Chris's feet to one side, and seated himself on the end of the sofa.

"Do you mind if I smoke?" he said to Hilda.

"Yes, I do," said Hilda.

"All right, then. You'd better go." He pulled a clay pipe out of his pocket, and an envelope that contained tobacco. "I know Chris doesn't mind," he said, with a twinkling glance in her direction. "Also, my cousin, someone wants you in the next room."

"Who is it?" said Hilda.

"Don't ask me," said Noel.

She hesitated momentarily. "Well, I suppose I must go. But mind, Noel, you are not to smoke in here."

"Say please!" said Noel imperturbably.

"Please!" said Hilda obediently.

He rose and accompanied her to the door. "Madam, your wishes shall be respected."

He opened the door with a flourish, bowed her out, closed it, and softly turned the key.

Then he wheeled round to his sister with gleaming eyes. "That's done the trick, I bet. Trevor has just turned up with Jack. But you needn't be afraid. I shan't let him in."

"What!" said Chris.

She started up, uttering the word like a cry.

Noel left the door swiftly, and came to her. "It's all right, old girl. Don't you worry yourself. We'll hold the fort, never fear. He shan't come in here, unless you say the word."

Chris's hands clutched him with feverish strength. Her face was deathly. "Oh, Noel!" she breathed. "Oh, Noel!"

He hugged her reassuringly. "It's all right, I tell you. Don't get in a blue funk for nothing. He's not coming in here to bully you."

But Chris only clung faster to him, not breathing. The sudden shock had sent all the blood to her heart. She felt choked and powerless.

"There! Lie down again," said Noel. "I'm here. I'll take care of you. I knew he would turn up again; it's what I've been waiting for. But I swear he shan't come near you against your will. That's enough, isn't it? You know you are safe with me."

She could not answer him, but she crouched back upon the sofa in response to his persuasion. She was shaking from head to foot.

Noel sat solidly down beside her. "Don't be frightened," he said. "We're going to have some fun."

"What—what can he have come for?" whispered Chris.

"Goodness knows! But he isn't going to get it, anyway. Good old Hilda! She went like a bird, didn't she? I call this rather amusing."

Noel began to whistle under his breath, obviously enjoying the situation to the utmost.

But Chris restrained him. "I want to listen," she murmured piteously.

He became silent at once, and several seconds crawled away, accompanied by no sound save the interminable buzzing of a fly on the window-pane.

Noel arose at length and with a single swoop of the hand captured and killed it. Then he went back to Chris.

"I say, don't look so scared! No one is going to hurt you."

The words were hardly uttered before Hilda's light step sounded outside, and her hand tried the door.

Chris started violently, and cowered among her cushions. Noel chuckled softly.

"Chris dear, what is the matter? Let me in!" Anxiety and persuasion were mingled in Hilda's voice.

Noel's chuckle became audible. "She isn't going to. She doesn't want anyone but me. Do you, Chris?"

Chris made no reply. She was staring at the door with starting eyes.

Noel went leisurely across and set his back against it. His eyes still gleamed roguishly, but his mouth had ceased to smile.

"I say, Hilda," he said, over his shoulder, "if you want to do Chris a good turn, tell that beastly cad behind you to go. I shan't let him in, anyhow, not if he stays till doomsday. So he may as well clear out at once."

"My dear Noel, how can you be so absurd?" Hilda's placid tones held real annoyance for once.

But the cause of it was quite unimpressed.

"Your dear Noel is acting up to his lights," he returned, "and he has no intention of doing anything else, absurd or otherwise. Chris is nearly scared out of her wits, so you had better take my advice sharp."

This last information took instant effect upon Hilda. She turned her attention to Chris forthwith.

"My dear, do let me in! There is nothing whatever to frighten you. I promise you shall not be frightened. Chris, tell that absurd boy to open the door—please, dearest!"

"I—can't!" gasped Chris.

"She isn't going to," said Noel. "You run along, Hilda. And you can tell Trevor with my love that if he'll clear out now I'll meet him at any time and place he likes to mention and have a damned old row."

"Very good of you!" Another voice spoke on the other side of the door, and Noel jumped in spite of himself. "But at the present moment you don't count. Is Chris there? I want to speak to her."

The leisurely tones came, measured and distinct, through the closed door, and Chris covered her face and shivered. "Oh, you'll have to let him in!" she said. "Only—don't go away! Don't leave me alone with him!"

"Chris!" Mordaunt's voice, calm and unhurried, addressed her directly. "Jack is here with me. Will you let us in?"

Chris lifted a haggard face. "Open the door, Noel!" she said.

"Why?" demanded Noel, with sudden ferocity. "We are not going to knock under to him. Why should we?"

"It's no use," she said. "We can't help it. Besides—besides—" She broke off with something like a sob, and rose from the sofa.

Noel looked at her under drawn brows. "You really mean it?"

"Yes." She pushed the hair from her forehead, and made a great effort to still her agitation. "I do mean it, Noel. I—wish it."

"All right." The boy whizzed round and turned the key.

He met Mordaunt face to face on the threshold with clenched hands, his face dark with passion. "If you hurt her—I'll kill you!" he said.

Had Mordaunt laughed at him, he would probably have attempted to carry out his threat then and there, for his mood was tempestuous. But the quiet eyes that met his blazing ones held no derision. They went beyond him instantly, seeking the girlish figure that leaned against the sofa-head for support; but a hand grasped his shoulder at the same moment and turned him back into the room.

"I shan't quarrel with you on that account," Mordaunt said. "You can stay if you like, and satisfy yourself."

Jack entered behind him, and went straight to Chris. He took her quivering hands into his, and held them fast.

"That boy deserves to be horsewhipped for startling you like this," he said.

She smiled at him wanly, but not as if she heard his words. "You will stay with me, Jack?" she said beseechingly.

"If you wish it, dear. But Trevor wants to say something rather private. Really, you have nothing to be afraid of."

His kindly eyes looked down reassuringly into hers. They seemed to reason with her, to persuade and soothe at the same time.

But Chris's hands clung to his. "Don't—don't go!" she said. "I want you—I want you, Jack."

"Suppose we sit down," said Jack practically. "Trevor, I wish you'd kick that boy downstairs. It would do him good and me too. This isn't a family conclave."

"Noel can stay," Mordaunt answered quietly. He was still looking towards his wife, but he did not seem to be regarding her very intently. "You are mistaken in thinking that I have anything to say to Chris in private. I have only come to tell her what I have already told you, that Bertrand is at Valpré, ill and wanting her. I will take her to him—if she will come."

"Trevor!" She turned to him with eyes of sudden horror—horror so definite that it swamped all her personal shrinking. "How is he ill? You—you have hurt him!"

"I have done nothing to him," Mordaunt answered. "He is suffering from heart-disease, and cannot be moved. I must start from Charing Cross in an hour. Will you come with me?"

"To go to him?" Her eyes were still dilated, but they did not waver from his.

"To go to him." He repeated the words with precision, and waited for her answer.

But Chris sat in silence, her hands in Jack's.

"Look here," Noel broke in abruptly, "if Chris goes, I go."

"Very well," Mordaunt said. "If Chris desires it, you may."

Chris came out of her silence with a little shudder, and turned to the man beside her. "Jack, tell me what to do!"

"I think you had better go, dear," Jack said.

"But if—but if—oh, is he very ill?" She looked again at her husband.

"He is very ill indeed," Mordaunt said.

"You think I ought to go?" She asked the question with an obvious effort.

"I have come to fetch you," he said.

"Then—he is dying!" she said, with sudden conviction.

Mordaunt was silent.

Abruptly she left Jack and went up to him. "Trevor," she said, "would you want to take me to him if—if—"

"If—?" he repeated quietly.

"If you thought I was doing wrong to go?"

He made a slight movement, as if the question were unexpected. "I should have explained to you," he said, "that your brother Max is in charge of him, so that when I am not with you—and, as you know, I am attending the Rodolphe trial—you will not be alone."

"Oh, Max is there!" she said, with relief. "But what is he doing at Valpré?"

"He went there with Bertrand."

"But I thought Bertrand could not go to France," she hazarded.

"He went in disguise."

"Why?" Her lips trembled upon the word.

"Because he had something to say to me." With the utmost calmness his answer came.

"Ah!" She started and turned so white that he put out a hand to steady her.

She laid her own within it, as it were instinctively, because she needed support.

"What was it?" she whispered.

He looked at her gravely. "Are you afraid to be alone with me?" he said.

"No."

"Then—quick march!" said Jack, with his hand through Noel's arm.

They went out together, Noel glancing back for the smallest sign from his sister to remain.

But she made none. She stood quite still, with her hand in her husband's, waiting.

As the door closed Mordaunt spoke. "Have you been ill?"

"No," she said faintly. "Not—not really ill."

She was aware of his close scrutiny for a moment, but she made not the slightest attempt to meet it.

"You want to know what Bertrand said to me," he said. "And you have a right to know. He told me the whole history of your friendship from the beginning to the end."

"He told you about—about Valpré?" Her eyelids quivered, as if she wished to raise them but dared not.

"Yes."

"Then you know—" Her hand fluttered in his.

"I know everything," he said.

Her white face quivered piteously. "And you—you are still angry?"

"No, I am not angry." He led her back to the sofa. "Sit down a minute," he said. "I don't think you are quite fit for this, and if you are going back with me to Valpré, you will need to reserve your strength."

He sat down beside her, both her hands firmly clasped in his, as if thereby he would impart to her the strength she lacked.

"You mean me to go, then?" murmured Chris.

"Don't you want to go?" he asked.

"If he really wants me—" she faltered. "And if you—you wish it, too."

"My dear," he said, "do my wishes make any real difference?"

She caught her breath sharply, and bent her head that he might not see her face. "Yes," she whispered, under her breath.

"Very well," he said, "I wish it, too."

She was silent, but suddenly her tears began to fall upon the strong hands that held hers. She would have given anything to have repressed them at that moment. With her whole soul she shrank from showing him her weakness, but it overpowered her. She bowed her head lower still, and wept.

He sat quite motionless for seconds, so that even in the depth of her distress she marvelled at his patience. But at last, very gently, he moved, let her hands go, and rose.

He stood awhile turned from her, his face to the window, though the sun-blind was all that could have met his view; finally, with grave kindness, he spoke.

"I think I had better leave you to prepare for the journey. There is not much time at your disposal, and you will probably need it all. It is settled that Noel is to go with us?"

"You won't mind?" she whispered.

"I think it a very good plan," he answered.

He turned round and came back to her. She had commanded herself to a certain extent, but still she could not raise her face. She waited tensely as he approached, possessed by a sudden, almost delirious longing to feel the touch of his lips.

Her desire surged into leaping hope as he stopped beside her. Would he—could he? But he did not stoop. He only laid his hand for a moment upon her head.

"Chris," he said, "try to think of me as a friend—and don't be afraid."

She thrilled at the low-spoken words. In another moment she would have conquered all hesitation and sprung up to feel his arms about her, to hide her face against him, to open to him all her quivering heart. But for that moment he did not wait.

With the utterance of the words his hand fell, and he moved away.

The opening and the closing of the door told her he had gone.

CHAPTER VIII
ARREST

"Ah, but what a night for dreams!"

The cool salt air came in from the sea like a benediction, blowing softly about the sick man by the window, sending a gleam of life into eyes grown weary with long suffering. He leaned back upon his pillows for the first time in many hours.

"It is as if the door of heaven had opened," he said.

"You're not going yet, old chap!" Max answered, a curious blending of grimness and tenderness in his voice.

"But no—not yet—not yet." Softly Bertrand made answer, but resolution throbbed in his words also. "I must not fail her—my little pal—my bird of Paradise. But the night is very long, Max, *mon ami*. And the darkness—the darkness—"

Max's hand came quietly down and closed upon his wrist. "I'll see you through," he said.

"Yes—yes. You will help me. You are one of those created to help. That is why you will be great. The great men are always—those who help."

The words came slowly, sometimes with difficulty, but the young medical student made no attempt to check them. He only sat with shrewd eyes upon the sick man's face and alert finger on his wrist, marking the waning strength while he listened. For he knew that the night was long.

Years afterwards it came to be said of him that his patients never died until his back was turned. It was not strictly true, but it conveyed something of the magnetism with which he wrought upon them. He knew the crucial moment by instinct, when to grapple and when to slacken his hold, and he never went by rule.

And so on that his second night of vigil by the side of a dying man, though he recognized speech as a danger, he made no effort to silence him. He knew that weariness of the spirit that finds no vent was a greater danger still.

"So you think I have a future before me?" he said.

"I am sure of it." Bertrand spoke with conviction. "It will not be an easy future, *mon ami*. Perhaps it will not be happy. Those who climb have no time to gather the flowers by the way. But—it will be great. You desire that, yes?"

"In a fashion," Max said. "I don't know that I consider greatness in itself as specially valuable. Do you?"

"I?" said Bertrand. "But I have passed all that. There was a time when ambition was to me as the breath of life. I thought of nothing else. And then"—his voice dropped a little—"there came a greater thing—the greatest of all. And I knew that I had climbed above ambition. I knew success and fame as a procession that passes—that passes—the mirage in the desert— the dream in the midst of our great Reality. I knew all this before my ruin came. It was as if a light had suddenly been held up, and I saw the work of my life as pictures in the sand. Then the great tide rushed up, and all was washed away. But yet"—his voice vibrated, he looked at Max and smiled— "the light remained. For a time, indeed, I was blind, but the light came back to me. And I know now that it was always there."

He paused, and turned his head sharply.

"What is it?" said Max.

"I heard a sound."

"There are plenty of sounds in this place," Max pointed out.

"Ah! but this was different. It sounded like—" He stopped with a gasp that made Max frown.

Undoubtedly there was a sound outside, the tread of feet, the jingle of a sword. Max got up, still frowning, and went to the door.

He had barely reached it before there came a loud knock upon the panels, and a voice cried: "*Ouvrez!*"

Max's knowledge of French was exceedingly limited, but that fact by no means dismayed him. He turned round to Bertrand for a moment.

"I'm going to have a talk with this johnny. Don't agitate yourself. You are not to move till I come back."

"*Ouvrez!*" cried the voice again.

"All right?" questioned Max.

Bertrand was leaning forward. His eyes were very bright, his breathing very short. "They have come—to take me," he said.

"I'll see them damned first," said Max. "You keep still, and leave it to me."

His hand was on the door with the words. A moment more he stood, thick-set and British, looking back. Then with a curt nod, he opened the door, and passed instantly out, pulling it after him.

Half a dozen soldiers filled the passage. The one who had knocked—an officer—stood face to face with him.

"Now what do you want?" asked Max.

He stood, holding the door-handle, his red brows drawn, a glint of battle in the green eyes beneath them. And so, during a brief silence, they measured each other.

Then quite courteously the Frenchman spoke. "Monsieur, my duty brings me here. Will you have the goodness to open that door?"

"It's a good thing you can speak English," Max remarked, with his one-sided smile. "What do you want to go in there for? The room is mine."

"And you are entertaining a friend there, monsieur." The Frenchman still spoke suavely; he even smiled an answering smile.

"That is so," Max said. "Do you know his name?"

"It is Bertrand de Montville." There was no hesitation in the reply. He looked as if he expected the Englishman to move aside, as he made it. But Max stood his ground.

"And what is your business with him?" he asked.

The officer's brows went up. "Monsieur?"

"You have come to arrest him?" Max questioned.

The Frenchman hesitated for a moment, then: "I must do my duty," he said.

The green eyes contemplated him thoughtfully for a space. Then, "I suppose you know he is dying?" Max said slowly.

"Dying, monsieur!" The tone was sharp, the speaker plainly incredulous.

Max explained without emotion. "He is suffering from an incurable disease of the heart, caused by hardship and starvation. If you go in and agitate him now, I won't give that for his chances of lasting through the night."

He snapped his fingers without taking his eyes from the other's face.

"Is it true?" the Frenchman said.

"It is absolutely true." Max spoke quietly, but there was force behind his words. "You can do what you like to safeguard him, though he is quite incapable of getting away. You can surround the house and post sentries at the door. But unless you want to kill him outright, you won't take him away from here. You can send one of your own doctors to certify what I say. You don't want to kill him, I presume?"

The Frenchman was listening attentively. It was evident that Max Wyndham was making an impression.

"My orders are to arrest him and to take him to the fortress," he said.

"Dead or alive?" asked Max.

"But certainly not dead, monsieur. All France will be calling for him to-morrow."

"That's the funny part of it," said Max. "France should have thought of that before. Well, sir, if you want him to live, all you can do is to wait. I will keep him going through the night, and you can send a doctor round in the morning."

"You are a doctor?" asked the Frenchman keenly.

"No. I am a medical student."

"And you are friends, *hein?*"

"Yes, we are friends. It was I who brought him here."

"But what a pity, monsieur!" There was a touch of kindly feeling in the words.

"Yes," Max acknowledged grimly. "It was a pity. But his reason for coming was urgent. And, after all, it made little difference. It has only hastened by a few weeks the end that was bound to come."

"You think that he will die?"

"Yes." Max spoke briefly. His tone was one of indifference.

The Frenchman looked at him curiously. "And what was his reason for coming?"

"It was a strictly private one," Max said. "This trial had nothing to do with it. It will certainly never be made public, so I am not at liberty to speak of it."

"And has he done—that which he left England to do?"

"Not yet, sir, but he may do it—if he lives long enough." Again Max's tone was devoid of all feeling. He still stood planted squarely against the closed door.

"And you think he will not do that?"

"On the contrary," said Max, "I think he will—if I am with him to keep him going."

He spoke with true British doggedness, and a gleam of humour crossed the Frenchman's face. He made a brief bow.

"M. de Montville is fortunate to possess such a friend," he said.

The corner of Max's mouth went down. "As to that," he said dryly, "he might do a good deal better, and a very little worse. Now, sir, what are you going to do?"

The Frenchman looked quizzical. "It seems that I must take your advice, monsieur, or risk very serious consequences. I shall leave a guard here during the night, and I must ask you to give me the key of this door. *Après cela*"—he shrugged his shoulders—"*nous verrons.*"

Max turned without protest, opened the door, and withdrew the key. He stood a moment listening before he turned back and laid it in the officer's hand. His face was grave.

"I think I must go to him," he said. "You will see to it that he is not disturbed?"

"No one will enter without your permission," the Frenchman answered. "And you, monsieur, will remain with him until I return."

"I see," said Max. Again, for an instant, the fighting gleam was in his eyes, then carelessly he laughed. "Well, I shan't try to run away. He and I are down in the same lot. You would find it harder to turn me out than to keep me here."

"I believe it, monsieur." There was no irony in the words or in the bow that accompanied them. "And I repeat, he is a happy man who possesses your friendship."

"Oh, rats!" said Max, and suddenly turned scarlet. "You are talking through your hat, sir. If you've quite done, I'll go."

It was the most boyish utterance he had permitted himself, and as he gave vent to it he was so obviously ill at ease that the Frenchman smiled.

"But you are younger than I thought," he said. "Will you shake hands?"

Max gave his customary hard grip. They looked into each other's eyes for a moment, and separated with mutual respect.

Five seconds later Max had returned to his self-appointed task of helping a dying man to live through the night.

CHAPTER IX
VALPRÉ AGAIN

"How dark it is!" said Chris. "And how we are crawling!"

She turned her white face from the carriage-window with the words. They were the first she had uttered since leaving Paris.

Neither of her two companions responded at once. Noel was curled up in the farther corner asleep, and her husband sitting opposite was writing rapidly in a notebook. He stopped to finish his sentence before he looked up. She was conscious of a little sense of chill because he did so.

"Why don't you try to get a sleep?" he said then. "We shall not reach Valpré for another two hours."

"I can't sleep," she said.

Her eyes avoided his instinctively. They were more nearly alone together at this moment than they had been since their brief interview that morning at the Davenants' flat. It seemed weeks ago to Chris already.

"Have you tried?" he asked.

"No."

He did not make the obvious rejoinder, but glanced again at his writing, added something, and put it away. Then, with his usual deliberation of movement, he left his seat and came over to her side.

She had a moment of desperate shyness as he sat down. "Don't let me interrupt you," she said nervously.

He ignored the words, as if he considered them foolish "I should like you to get a little sleep," he said. "You have had a long day. Look at that fellow over there, setting the good example."

"He hasn't so much to think about," said Chris, with a smile that quivered in spite of her.

"Are you thinking very hard?" he asked.

"Yes." She brought out the word with an effort, for suddenly she wanted to cry again, and she was determined to keep back her tears this time.

He made no comment, but sat and looked at the blank darkness of the window.

After a time she mastered herself, and stole a glance at his grave face.

"You—I suppose you will be busy at the court again to-morrow?" she said.

"Yes." He turned to her in his quiet way. "It will be the last day in all probability."

"You think the verdict will be made known?"

"Yes."

She shivered a little. "And the sentence?"

"The sentence will probably not be disclosed till later."

She shivered again, and he reached forward and drew the window a little higher.

"I'm not cold," she said quickly. "Trevor, aren't you—just a little—sorry for him?"

"For whom?"

"For the prisoner—for—for Captain Rodolphe." She stammered the name with downcast eyes.

"No." Very calmly and very decidedly came his answer. "I have no pity for a man of that sort. I think he should be shot."

"Oh, do you?" she said with a gasp.

"Yes, I do. A treacherous scoundrel like that is worse than a murderer in my opinion. So is anyone who is fundamentally untrustworthy."

"Oh, but—but—Trevor—," she said, and suddenly there was a note of pleading in her halting words, "that includes the weak people with the wicked. Don't you think—that is rather hard?"

"Quite possibly." He made the admission in a tone she did not understand, and relapsed into silence.

She felt as if the subject were closed, and did not venture to pursue it.

But after a moment he surprised her by a quiet question: "Why don't you try to convince me that I am wrong?"

She looked up at him quickly, as if compelled. His eyes were waiting for hers, met them, held them.

"I am not suggesting that you should defend Rodolphe," he said. "You were not thinking of him. He is not one of the weak."

"I was thinking of myself," she said. "And—and—and—" She wavered and stopped.

"Rupert?" he suggested.

She caught her breath. "What made you think of him?"

"You were thinking of him, were you not?"

She made a gesture of helplessness. "Yes."

"I see," he said. "But you needn't be anxious about Rupert. He came to me long ago and told me the truth."

She opened her eyes wide. "What made him do that?"

"He heard that Bertrand was bearing the blame for his misdeeds, and he had the decency to be ashamed of himself."

"Oh!" said Chris. She was silent for a moment, still meeting his steady gaze. Suddenly her mouth quivered and she turned from them. "Trevor, I—I am ashamed too."

"Hush!" he said.

The word was brief, it sounded stern; but in the same instant his hand found hers and held it very tightly.

She mastered herself with a great effort in response to his insistence. "Were you very angry with him?" she whispered.

"No."

"You didn't—punish him in any way?"

"No. I told him to forget it and said I should do the same. As a matter of fact, I had forgotten it until this moment." Mordaunt's tone was unemotional; he released her hand as he was speaking, and again she was conscious of that small sense of chill.

"You forgave him, then?" she said.

"Yes, I did." He paused a moment; then: "By and bye," he said, "Rupert will take on the management of the Kellerton estate, and I think he will probably be a great help to me."

Chris's eyes shot upwards in amazement. "Trevor! Not really?"

He smiled a little. "Yes, really. It is the sort of life that suits him best; and he will be pretty busy, so it ought to keep him out of mischief."

"Oh, but, Trevor—" she said, and stopped short.

"Well?" he said gently.

"I didn't think you would do that," she murmured in confusion. "I didn't think you would ever trust any of us again."

"You think I may regret it?" he said.

She turned her face to the window and made no answer.

He sat beside her for a little longer in silence, then rose, bundled up a travelling-rug to form a cushion, and arranged it in her corner. "Lean against that," he said kindly. "I know you can sleep if you don't try not to."

She thanked him with trembling lips, and as he turned away she caught his hand for a moment and held it to her cheek.

He withdrew it at once though with absolute gentleness. He did not speak a word.

Thereafter she closed her eyes and tried to sleep, but the drumming of the train was in her ears perpetually, and she could not forget it. Present also was the consciousness of her husband's quiet watchfulness. Though he held aloof from her, his care surrounded her unceasingly. Not once had she felt it relax since she had placed herself in his charge. Did he guess? she asked herself, and trembled inwardly. He was being very kind to her in a distant, measured fashion. Was that the reason for it? Could it be?

Her thoughts went back to her talk with her cousin, to the bitter words she had uttered. Would he really care if she were to die? Would he? Would he? She longed to know.

But of course he would not, or he could not be so cold. For Bertrand's sake he had come to fetch her. He had evidently forgiven Bertrand just as he had forgiven Rupert. He forgave everybody but her, she thought to herself forlornly. For his wife alone he could not make allowances.

Again the hot tears welled up, and her closed lids could not keep them back. The dumb anxiety that had gnawed at her heart all through the day returned upon her overwhelmingly, became a burden too heavy to be borne. She covered her face and sobbed.

"Chris!" Her husband's voice came down to her in the depths of her distress. His hand pressed her head. "Leave off crying," he said. "You mustn't cry."

She turned her face upwards, all blinded with tears. "Trevor, I know—I know we shan't be in time!"

They were not the words she wanted to say to him, but they came uppermost and were uttered almost before she knew. She wondered if they would make him angry, but it was too late to recall them. She reached out her hands to him imploringly.

"Oh, forgive me for caring so much!"

"Hush!" he said again very gently. "I understand."

He put the hair back from her forehead, and dried her eyes. There was something almost maternal in his touch.

"You mustn't cry," he said again. "I think you will be in time, and if you are, you will need all your strength; so you mustn't waste it now. Come, you are going to be brave?"

"I'll try," she said faintly.

"See if you can get to sleep," he said.

"But I know I can't," whispered Chris.

"I think you can." He spoke with grave conviction.

"Will you—will you hold my hand?" faltered Chris.

He took it at once. She felt his fingers close steadily upon it, and a sense of comfort stole over her. She clasped them very tightly, and closed her eyes.

The train drummed on through the night, bearing her back to Valpré, back to the old enchantments, to the sands, the caves, and the rocks. She began to hear again the long, low wash of the sea. Or was it the sound of wheels that raced over the metals? Before her inner vision came the spreading line of foam that had rushed how often to catch her dancing feet. And the quiet pools crystal-clear among the rocks, with the sunshine that turned their pebbly floors to gold, so that they became palaces of delight, draped with exquisite curtains of rose and palest green, peopled with scuttling crabs that were not really crabs at all, but the spellbound retinue of the knight who dwelt in the Magic Cave.

She looked towards the Gothic archway, expectant, with quickening breath. Surely he would be coming soon! Ah, now she saw him—a radiant, white-clad figure, with the splendour of eternal youth upon him and the Deathless Magic in his eyes.

And suddenly her own eyes were opened, so that she knew beyond all doubting that the spell that bound him—that bound them both—was the spell of Immortality, the Divine Passport—Love the Indestructible.

Thereafter came a wondrous peace, solacing her, calming her, wrapping her round. Once she stirred, and was conscious of a quiet hand holding hers, lulling her to a more assured restfulness. And so at last she slipped into the quiet of a deep slumber, and the throbbing anxiety sank utterly away.

When she opened her eyes again it was in answer to her husband's voice. She awoke quite naturally to find him bending over her.

"We are at Valpré," he said.

She sat up quickly. "Why, I have been asleep!"

"Yes," he said. "And you will be the better for it. Noel has gone to secure a conveyance. The place is crammed, as you know. You are feeling all right?"

Again for a moment she felt his scrutiny, and her heart quickened under it. But she mustered a smile.

"Yes, quite. You will let me come with you, Trevor? You won't go on first?"

"I shall not leave you," he said.

He gave her his hand to descend from the train, and she clung to it while they threaded their way through the noisy, gesticulating crowd that thronged the platform.

She breathed a sigh of relief when she found herself at last in the ramshackle *fiacre* which Noel by strenuous effort had managed to commandeer. The din bewildered her. But for her husband's protecting presence she would have felt like a lost child.

As they rumbled away over the stones of Valpré he spoke.
"We are in time, Chris."

Her heart gave a great throb. "Are we? But how do you know?"

"Everyone is talking of him," he said quietly. "And I gather that he has been arrested."

"Oh, Trevor!" she breathed in dismay.

"Max is with him," he reminded her. "I don't think they would get rid of him very easily. We shall know more when we get there."

They clattered on to the *plage*, and the cold sea wind blew in upon them.

Noel snuffed it appreciatively. "Smells decent, anyway. Wonder if they're still running the same old show. I say, Chris, do you remember the Goat?"

Chris did. With her face to the dark sea and the sound of its waves in her ears, she recalled the old light-hearted days and the shrill admonitions of Mademoiselle Gautier. How often had she prophesied disaster for her charge among the rocks of Valpré! Chris smiled a little piteous smile. Ah, well!

The *fiacre* jerked and jolted over the stones. They left the *plage* behind and came to a standstill with a violent swerve.

"Now what?" said Noel.

They seemed to have come suddenly upon a crowd of people. Late though it was, all Valpré apparently was awake and abroad.

They staggered on again at a snail's pace, hearing voices all about them, now and then catching glimpses of faces in the light of the carriage-lamps.

"Feels like a funeral procession!" observed Noel jocularly.

"Shut up!" said Mordaunt curtly.

Chris squeezed his hand very hard and said nothing.

Slowly, slowly they drew near to the hotel. A glare of lights shone upon them. The whole place was a buzz of excitement.

They turned into the courtyard, passing two soldiers on guard at the gate. No one spoke to them, or attempted to delay their progress. They stopped before the swing-doors.

An obsequious official came forward to greet them as they descended, and Mordaunt entered into conversation with him. Two soldiers were on guard here also, standing like images on each side of the entrance. Noel studied them with frank interest. Chris stood and waited as one in a dream.

At last her husband turned to her. He introduced the obsequious one, who bowed very low and declared himself enchanted. And then she found herself moving through the vestibule, where a great many men of all nationalities looked at her curiously and a great babble of voices hummed like some immense machinery.

She turned to the man beside her with a touch of nervousness, and at once his hand closed upon her arm.

"Bertrand is still living," he said.

She looked up at him imploringly. "Can't we go to him?"

"Yes, we are going now. He is upstairs. They wanted to take him to the fortress, but he is too ill to be moved."

They went on together. He led her into a lift, and they passed out of reach of the staring crowd.

A familiar figure was awaiting them above, and greeted Chris deferentially as she stepped into the corridor.

"Why, Holmes!" she said, and held out her hand to him.

He took it with reverence. For the first time in her memory she detected a hint of emotion on his impassive face.

"He—hasn't gone, Holmes?" she whispered breathlessly.

"No, madam. He is waiting for you," Holmes made answer, very gently.

Waiting for her! She smiled piteously in her relief. Bertrand de Montville would be her perfect knight to the last.

As they went on down the long corridor she missed the grasp of her husband's fingers, and stopped like a child to slip her hand back into his.

He looked down at her gravely, saying nothing. And so they came at last to the door of Bertrand's room.

Two soldiers were on guard here also. The door was closed.

Holmes went quietly forward and showed a paper to one of the sentries.

Chris waited with a beating heart. Suddenly, with a sob, she turned and clung to her husband's arm. "Trevor, I—I am afraid!"

"There is no need," he said.

"I have never seen death," she whispered. "Will he seem—different?"

He looked at her for a second in such a way that her eyes fell from his.

"Would you like me to go in first?" he asked.

"No—no. Only, Trevor, hold my hand! You won't let go? Promise!"

He did not promise, but somehow without words he reassured her. The door opened before them, and they entered.

CHAPTER X
THE INDESTRUCTIBLE

Within the room all was dim.

An arm-chair piled with many pillows stood facing the open window, and as her eyes became accustomed to the twilight Chris discerned the outline of a figure that reclined in it. At the same moment there came to her the sound of a voice, husky and difficult, yet how strangely familiar.

"Ah, but the tide—the tide!" it said. "Can we not hold it back my dear Max—a little longer? It rushes up so fast—so fast. Soon all will be gone. Only a picture in the sand, you say? But no, it is more than that. See, it is greater than all the things in the world—greater than the Sphinx, *ma petite*—greater than your Cleopatra's Needle. Ah, you laugh, because you have no need of it. But yet it is your own, and so will it always be. Do you hear the tide among the rocks, *mignonne*? It is there that my heart is buried. Come with me, and I will show you the place—if the tide permit."

There came a gasp, and silence.

Some one guided Chris gently forward till she stood behind the great chair at the window, looking down upon the black head that rested against the pillow. Her fear had passed, but yet she drew no nearer. Instinctively she stood and waited.

Suddenly, and more clearly, the voice spoke again.

"We must climb, *chérie*, we must climb. We dare not stay upon these rocks. It is steep for your little feet, but to remain here is to die. *Alors*, we will say our prayers and go. *Le bon Dieu* will keep us safe. And we have been—pals—since so long."

A softer note in the last sentence made her aware that he was smiling. She bent a little above him. But still she waited.

"*Comment?*" he said. "You are afraid? But why, my bird of Paradise? Is it life that you fear—this little life of shadows? Or Death—which is the gateway to our great Reality? Listen, *mignonne*! I am a prisoner while I live, but the gate opens to me. Soon I shall be free. No, no! I cannot take you with me. I would not, *chérie*, if I could. Your place is here. But remember—always—that I love you still. And my love is stronger than death. It stretches into eternity."

He paused, and made a slight gesture of refusal. "Ah, no!" he said. "I do not want a priest. My sins are all known—and pardoned. I only want—one thing now."

"What is it, old chap?" It was Max Wyndham's voice, but pitched so low that Chris scarcely recognized it.

The head on the pillow moved, turning towards the speaker. "So, *mon ami*, you are still there?"

"What is it you are wanting?" Max said.

Bertrand drew a breath that was cut short and ended in a gasp. "*Mon ami*, I only want—to hold her little hand in mine—and to hear her say—that she is—happy."

And then it was that Chris moved forward, as if impelled by a volition not her own, and knelt down by Bertrand's side.

"Do you want me, Bertie?" she said. "I've come, dear! I've come!"

He put out his hand to her at once, but slowly, as though feeling his way. "Christine!" he said.

She took the groping hand, and held it fast pressed between her own. "Yes, dear?" she murmured.

"You are really here?" he said. "It is not—a dream?"

"No, Bertie, no! It is I myself, here with you at Valpré."

She felt his hand close within her own. "You are come—to say good-bye to me?" he said. "And Mr. Mordaunt—is he here also?"

"He brought me," whispered Chris.

"Ah!" She heard the relief in his voice. "Then—Christine, all is right between you?"

But she was silent, for she could not answer him.

He stirred. He leaned slowly forward. "Tell me," he said, very earnestly, "tell me that all is well between you."

But Chris said no word. She only bowed her head over the hand she held.

There was a brief silence. Bertrand was bending over her. He seemed to be trying to see her face. He moved at last, passed his free arm around her, and spoke. "Mr. Mordaunt—is he here?"

"Yes, I am here." Very steadily came Mordaunt's answer. Mordaunt himself took Max's place beside him.

Bertrand looked up at him. "Monsieur—" he said, and hesitated.

"Ask him what he wants," muttered Max, gripping his brother-in-law's elbow with tense insistence.

"Do you want anything?" He uttered the question at once, quite clearly, without emotion.

"Monsieur," Bertrand said again, and there was entreaty in his voice, "out of your great goodness of heart you have brought *la petite* to say adieu to me. Will you not—extend that goodness—a little farther? Will you not—now that you understand—now that you understand"—he repeated the phrase insistently—"remove the estrangement of which I have been—the so unhappy cause?"

"Bertie, no—no!" There was sharp pain in Chris's voice. She raised herself quickly. "You don't understand, dear, and I—can't explain. But you are not to ask that of him. I can't bear it."

There was a quiver of passion in the last words. It was as though they were uttered in spite of her.

Mordaunt stood motionless, in utter silence. His face was in shadow.

Bertrand turned to the kneeling girl. "Will you, then, plead for yourself, *chérie*?" he said. "He will not refuse you. He knows all."

"No, no; he doesn't," said Chris.

"But you will tell him," urged Bertrand gently. "See, I cannot leave you—my two good friends—thus. Since I have caused so much trouble between you, I must do my possible to redress the evil. *Chérie*, promise me—that you will go back to him. Not otherwise shall I die happy."

"I can't!" whispered Chris. "I can't!"

"But why not?" he said. "You love him, yes?"

But Chris was silent. She was trembling from head to foot.

"I know that you love him," Bertrand said, with confidence. "And for that—you will go back to him. You cannot live your life apart from him. You belong to him, Christine, and he—he belongs to you. Mr. Mordaunt—my dear friend—is it not so?"

But before he could answer, feverishly Chris again broke in. "Bertie, hush—hush! It isn't right! It isn't fair! Oh, forgive me for saying it! But can't you see that it isn't? He has forgiven me, and we are friends. But you mustn't ask any more than that, because—because it's no use." A sudden sob rose in her throat. She swallowed it with an immense effort. "He has been kind to me—for your sake," she said, "not my own. I have done nothing to deserve his kindness. I have never been worthy of him, and he knows it. I married him, loving you. Oh no, I didn't know it, but I ought to have known. And when I did know, I would have left him and gone with you. Nothing can ever alter that. And do you suppose he will ever forget it? Because I know—I know—that he never can!"

She ceased abruptly, and turned aside to battle with her agitation. Bertrand's hand stroked hers very tenderly, but his eyes were raised to the man who stood like a statue by his side.

He spoke after a moment very softly, almost as if to himself. "Neither will he forget," he said, "that our love was a summer idyll that came to us unawares in the days when we were young, and that though the idyll will come to an end, our love is a gift immortal—imperishable—indestructible—a flame that burns upwards and always upwards—reaching the Divine. And because he remembers this, he will understand, and think no evil. Christine," he turned to her again very persuasively, "you love him. You have need of him. I know it well. You are sad. You are lonely. Your heart cries out for him. Little Christine, will you not listen to it? Will you not go back to him?"

The man's whole soul was in the words. They quivered with the intensity of his appeal. Yet they went into silence. Chris was turned away from him. Only by the convulsive holding of her hand did he know that they had reached her heart.

The silence lengthened, became oppressive, became a burden too heavy to be borne.

"Christine!" He was becoming exhausted. His voice was no more than a whisper, but it throbbed with earnest entreaty.

Yet Chris remained silent still, for she could not speak in answer.

Several seconds passed. It seemed that the appeal would go unanswered. But at length the man who stood on Bertrand's other side made a quiet movement, bending down a little.

"You need not distress yourself, Bertrand," he said, very steadily, and as he spoke his hand was on the Frenchman's shoulder. "Chris will never leave me again."

"Ah!" Eagerly Bertrand looked up at him. He had begun to gasp again, and his words were hurried and difficult of utterance. "And you, monsieur—you will not—leave her?"

Mordaunt made no verbal answer, but their eyes must have met in the dimness and some message have passed between them, for there was a tremor of sheer relief in his voice when Bertrand spoke again.

"Oh, my friend!" he said. "My dear friend!" And, yielding to the hand that gently pressed him back, he reclined upon his pillows and became passive.

Mordaunt remained beside him for several seconds longer, but he did not speak again. When he straightened himself at length, he glanced round for Max, and motioned him away.

They went together into the adjoining room and softly closed the door.

And so Chris and her *preux chevalier* were left alone by the open window to end their summer idyll to the music of the rising tide that crooned and murmured among the rocks of Valpré that had seen its beginning.

CHAPTER XI
THE END OF THE VOYAGE

How the sun was shining on the water! What a glorious morning for a bathe! Chris laughed to herself—a happy little, inconsequent laugh.

But she must be quick or Mademoiselle Gautier would catch her and forbid her to go! Poor old Mademoiselle, who had been brought up in a convent and thought all nice things were improper!

Would Bertie be there with his boat, a white-clad, supple figure, with his handsome olive face, and his dark eyes with their friendly laugh? Surely it was the flash of his oars in the sunlight that dazzled her so! She would swim to him through the crystal water, and he would stretch out his hands to her, and she would go up to him like a bird from the sea, and perch upon the stern. He would scold her a little for swimming out so far, but what of that? She liked being scolded by Bertie!

How warmly the sun shone down upon them! And how she loved to watch the slim activity of him as he bent to his work! She wished they did not move quite so fast, even though the speed was so delicious, for they were nearing the rocks. Oh no, she was not afraid! Who could be afraid with Bertie in the boat? But when they reached the rocks, it would be the end of the voyage, and she did not want it to end.

Ah! now she could catch the sparkle of the sand, and there away in the distance a powdery whirl which was all she could see of Cinders. He was evidently digging for dear life, and again Chris laughed.

And now she stood with her back to the glittering sea, and her face to the mysterious granite of the ages. Where had he gone—her *preux chevalier*? Was he hidden in the dark recesses of the Magic Cave? She would go in search of him. He would not hide long from her, for she possessed the secret of the spell that would draw him forth.

But the rocks were slippery under her feet, and more than once she stumbled. She found herself confronted by obstacles such as had never before obstructed her path. A little tremor of distress went through her.

Why had she quitted that sunny sea? Why had she ever suffered herself to be beguiled into the boat?

It became increasingly difficult, wellnigh impossible, to go forward. She turned aside. Ah! there was Bertie, after all, out on the sand, waiting for her. He held a naked sword in his hand. Evidently he was drawing pictures. She knew what they would be before she reached him: St. George and the Dragon, that "beast enormous with eyes of fire"; the Sphinx, and Cleopatra's Needle. She saw them all; and soon the great tide would race up with a mighty roaring and wash them all away. Was it not the destiny of all things—save one?

Stay! Was it the sand on which he was expending his skill thus? Why, then, did his sword move so swiftly, like lightning-flashes, where the sun caught it? Ah, now she saw more clearly. It was a duel. He was fighting with every inch of him, steadfast, unflinching, in her cause. How splendidly he controlled himself! The clear grace of his every movement held her spellbound.

For a while she watched him, not heeding his adversary, watched the glint of the crossed swords, the pass, the thrust, and the return. And then, by some mysterious influence, her eyes were drawn upward to the face of his opponent, and it was as if one of those flashing blades had found her heart. For Bertrand de Montville was fighting the grey-eyed, level-browed Englishman who was her husband!

With a cry she sprang forward to intervene. She flung herself between them in an agony. One of them—Trevor—caught her in his arms. The other staggered backwards and fell upon the sand. She saw his dead face as he lay....

"Oh, Trevor!" she cried in anguish. "Trevor! Trevor!"

He held her closely to him. She felt his hand laid in soothing on her head. Gasping, she opened her eyes upon his face.

"That's better," he said gently. "You've had a bad dream."

"Was it a dream?" she asked him wildly. "Was it a dream?"

And then she remembered that Bertrand had fallen asleep in the very early hours of the morning, and that they had led her away to another room to rest. Worn out in mind and body, she had yielded. She marvelled now that she had been so easily persuaded.

She turned within the circle of her husband's arm. "Trevor, you promised you would call me if he waked."

His hand was still upon her head; its touch was sustaining, subtly comforting. "He did not wake, dear," he said.

The words were few, but in a flash she knew the truth. Her eyes grew wide and dark. Her clinging hands tightened upon his arm. She made no sound of any sort. She even ceased to breathe.

He drew her head down upon his shoulder, and held her fast pressed against his breast. "Don't be afraid," he said.

But she remained tense in his arms, till her rigidity and silence alarmed him. He began to rub her cold cheek.

"Chris, speak to me!"

She turned her face into his breast, and with relief he heard her begin to breathe again. But she did not speak. She only lay there dumbly in crushed stillness.

For a while he waited, but at last, as she made no movement, he spoke again. "Chris, would you like me to leave you?"

That reached her. She turned her face quickly upwards. "No, Trevor."

The wide, strained look was still in her eyes, but they did not flinch from his.

"I knew he was dead," she said, speaking very quickly, "when I woke up just now. I thought—I thought—" She broke off, as if she could not continue. "And afterwards—directly I saw you by my side—I knew it was true. Trevor"—the piteous note sounded again in her voice—"why are you not afraid of death?"

"Because I don't believe in it," he said.

"But yet—but yet—" Her words faltered away into silence.

He laid his hand again upon her head. "My dear, death is purely physical. You know it in your heart as well as I do. Death is the passing of the spirit—no more than that."

She uttered a deep sigh. "Oh, Trevor, I wish I wasn't so wicked."

His hand began to caress her hair. "I don't think you know what wickedness is, dear," he said.

"But I do—I do!" she protested. "I—I am almost terrified sometimes when I realize it. And I feel as if—as if—Bertie wouldn't have been taken away—if I hadn't loved him so." Her voice sank, she hid her face a little lower.

"But you make a mistake," he said gently. "There is no sin in love—so long as it is love and nothing else. A good many sins masquerade in the form of love, but love itself—what you and I call love—is sinless. And it is that—and that alone—that can never die." He paused a moment, and his hand ceased to stroke her bright hair and became still. "It is bad enough," he said, his voice sunk very low, "that I could ever misunderstand you; but, my dear, don't make things harder by misunderstanding yourself."

She moved at that as though it touched her very nearly, and suddenly she slipped from his arms, and knelt beside him. "Trevor," she said, with quivering lips, "don't be too kind to me! I can't bear it."

He looked down at her very sadly. "It would be a new experience for you, my Chris, if I were," he said. "No—no." She bent her face quickly, and laid it against his hand. "I've deceived you a hundred times—yes, and lied to you. You bore with me over and over again, even when you knew I wasn't being straight. You did your very utmost to keep me true. You trusted me even when you knew I was cheating. Oh, I don't wonder that I killed your love at last. The wonder was that it lived so long."

She stopped, for his hand had clenched upon itself at her words. But he said nothing. He seemed to be waiting for her to continue. She went on quickly—

"I know you feel you must be kind to me now because"—she caught her breath—"Bertie is gone, and he wished it so. But—but—I shan't expect—a great deal. I—I shall be quite grateful—if I may have—a little friendship. I don't want you to think that—that—"

"That you want my love?" he said.

"Oh, I didn't mean that!" She looked up at him in distress, but she could not see his face with any distinctness.

His elbow was on the arm of his chair, and his hand shaded it.

"I know I forfeited all that," she said. "And I want you to feel that I—understand, and shall never expect to have it again. That is what I mean when I say, don't be too kind to me. You have been that, and much more than that, already. But I won't trade on your generosity. I am not a child any longer to need support and protection. I am old enough to stand alone."

"And what of my promise to Bertrand?"

He asked the question quite quietly, as though it were of no special moment to him, but she flinched before it, and turned her face aside.

"Oh, I don't think he would want you to be kind to me for his sake—if he knew how much it hurt?"

Mordaunt was silent for a moment, then: "And you have no use for my love?" he said.

She made a movement almost convulsive. "Trevor, don't—torture me!"

"My child," he said, "I only ask because I need to know."

She laid a trembling hand on his. "If I thought—you loved me—" She stopped, battling desperately for self-control, and after a few seconds began again. "If I thought—you wanted me—"

"I do want you, Chris," he said.

She cast a startled look into his face. "Oh, but you only say that because—because—"

"Because it is the truth," he said.

"But is it the truth?" she asked, a little wildly. "Is it? Is it? Oh, Trevor, if you knew—if you knew—" Her voice failed. She began to sob. "I can't bear it," she whispered. "I can't! I can't!" And with that she broke down utterly, bowing her head upon his knee in a passion of weeping more violent than he had ever before witnessed.

"Chris! Chris!" he said.

He would have lifted her, but she sank lower, as one crushed to the earth by a burden too heavy to be borne.

For a while her weeping was the only sound in the room, but at length he spoke again over her bowed head.

"Chris—my darling—do you know—I can't bear it either if you cry like this?"

His voice was low and not very steady. It appealed to her even in the depth of her distress. She stretched up a trembling hand, and clasped his.

Gradually her sobbing grew less violent, and at length it ceased; but she remained crouched against his knee with her face hidden for many minutes.

Trevor said no more. Only at last he bent and laid his lips upon her hair.

She moved then sharply, and for a single instant she saw his face. It was enough, more than enough for her quick heart. In a moment the barrier between them was down. She raised herself and threw her arms around his neck.

"My dear! My dear!" she said.

"It's all right," he whispered back.

Her arms tightened. She clung to him passionately. "Trevor—darling, I didn't know! I didn't understand!"

"It's all right," he said again.

She pressed her face to his. "Trevor, don't fret, dear! I'm not worth it. And I—I'm coming back to you—if you will have me."

"I want you," he answered simply.

"Not just for his sake?" she pleaded. "Or even for mine?"

"For my own," he said.

She was silent for a little. Then impulsively, with something of her old, quick charm of movement, she turned her lips to his. "Trevor, I believe I should die without you."

"Poor child!" he said gently.

"No—no! Don't pity me! Love me—love me!"

He pressed her closer. "My Chris, no one ever loved you more."

"Yes," she whispered. "I know that now. And I shall never forget it. Trevor, I love you, too. You believe that?"

"I know it, dear," he said.

"And because I love you," she said, "I'm not afraid of you any more. Trevor, let us promise each other that nothing shall ever come between us again."

"Nothing ever shall," he said steadily.

"Nothing ever shall," she repeated softly. "And—and—Trevor—" She suddenly hid her face against his shoulder and became silent again.

"But you are not afraid of me?" he said.

"No, dear, no; not afraid." Her voice quivered notwithstanding. "Only foolish, you know, and—and—a little doubtful lest—lest—when I've told you—something—you shouldn't be quite—pleased."

"I am—quite pleased, dear," he said.

She raised her head. "Trevor! You know?"

He took her face between his hands. "My darling, yes."

She opened her eyes wide, searching his face. "But that—that wasn't your reason for—wanting me back?"

He looked straight down into her eyes, still holding her. "I wonder if I need answer that question," he said slowly.

She was silent for a moment, then stretched her hands to him with a gesture of complete confidence. "No, dear, you needn't. Just forgive me for asking—that's all."

He stooped at once without speaking, and the kiss that passed between them was the seal of a perfect understanding.

Not till some time later did the request he was expecting her to make find utterance. He had been giving her a few details of Bertrand's illness and death.

"He simply went in his sleep," he said, "scarcely an hour after you left him. Max and I were both with him, but he went so easily that we neither of us knew when it was. There was no suffering or distress of any sort. He just passed."

He spoke with great gentleness. He was keenly anxious to remove her fear of death. But he knew by the way her arm tightened about his neck that something of the awe of it was upon her even while he spoke.

"Trevor," she said, in a very low voice, "I almost think I would like to see him."

"Yes, dear."

"But—I can't go alone," she said. "Will you come too?"

"Of course," he said.

She rose to her feet. "Let's go now."

He rose also with her hand in his. "There is some stuff here Max gave me for you," he said. "Drink that first."

"Where is Max?" she asked.

"I sent him to bed, and Noel too."

"And you have been sitting up with me ever since?"

"It was only three hours," he said.

He gave her Max's draught with the words, as if to check all comment on his action, and Chris submissively said no more. But she held his hand very tightly as they went out together.

The dawn was just spreading golden over the sea when they entered the room where Bertrand lay asleep. The light of it poured in at the open window like a benediction. Outside, the two sentries still stood on guard. But within was no earthly presence, only the scent and sound of the sea, only the growing splendour of the day, only the quiet dead waiting for the Resurrection....

Chris's hand trembled within her husband's as she drew near. But later, when she looked upon the dear, familiar face, the awe went out of her own.

For Bertrand's sleep was very easy, serenely natural. It seemed to Chris that the man's vanished youth had come back to beautify his rest. For all the weariness she had grown accustomed to see had passed away. She even thought he smiled.

Back on a rush of memory came his words: "I know that all Love is eternal, and Death is only an incident in eternity."

Till that moment they had never recurred to her. From that moment she carried them perpetually in her heart.

She drew a little nearer. She bent above him. And it was to her as if the dead lips spoke: "Though I shall not be with you, you will know that I am loving you still. It will be as an Altar Flame that burns for ever. Believe me, Christine, Death is a very small thing compared with Love."

"I know it, I know it," whispered Chris.

When she stood up again, though her eyes were shining through tears, she was smiling also.

"Your friend and mine, Trevor," she murmured. "May I—may I kiss him just once? I never have before."

"Of course you may," he said.

She bent again, bent till her lips just touched the dead man's brow.

"I won't disturb you, *preux chevalier*," she whispered. "Only good-night, dear! Good-night!"

For a little while she stood looking down upon the dead man's rest; but at length she turned away, drawing her husband with her, and went to the open window.

Hand in hand they looked out upon a world in which "all things were made new." They spoke no word. They thought the same thoughts together, and no words were needed.

Only when they turned at length from the shimmering sunlight back into the quiet room, their eyes met. And in the silence Trevor Mordaunt bent with reverence and kissed the living, as she had kissed the dead.

CHAPTER XII
THE PROCESSION UNDER THE WINDOWS

Tramp! tramp! tramp! tramp! The procession was passing under the windows.

Bertrand de Montville, the vindicated hero, was being borne to his soldier's grave on the hill by the fortress. Soldiers preceded him. Soldiers followed him. A mixed crowd of journalists—men from all parts of Europe—came after. And from the window above, his little pal looked down.

Max Wyndham stood beside her, the corners of his mouth drawn down and a very peculiar expression in his green eyes. He had amazed his French friend by refusing to follow the *cortège*. Even Chris did not know why, for he had clothed himself in an impenetrable cloak of reserve since Bertrand's death, and he was not apparently minded to lift it even for her benefit.

Yet she was glad to have him with her, for Noel had elected to go with Mordaunt; and though she was quite willing to be left alone, she found Max's presence a help. She had seen but little of him until the moment that they stood together looking down upon the passing procession.

It was a grey day. Down on the shore the long waves rolled in to break in wide lines of surf up the rock-strewn beach. The thunder of their breaking mingled with the roll of muffled drums. The full honours of a soldier's funeral were to be accorded to the man who had died before France could make amends.

Slowly the procession wound along the *plage*, and back upon Chris's memory flashed the day when she and Cinders had waited at the garden gate to see the soldiers pass. She saw again the handsome face of the young officer marching behind his men, the sudden animation leaping into it at sight of her, the eagerness with which he turned to greet her, his momentary hesitation at her request, his smiling surrender. What would have happened, she asked herself, if he had managed to resist her that day? Had that been the beginning of his downfall? Might he otherwise have passed on unscathed?

A sudden sense of coldness assailed her. The street below was empty. She stood alone. She leaned her head against the window-frame. How grey it was!

"Sit down!" said Max practically.

She started. "Oh, Max!" she said weakly.

"Here you are," he said, and guided her down into a chair. "That's the way. Now lean back and shut your eyes."

She obeyed him, without question, as she always did. A vague sense of consolation began to steal through her. His hand, holding hers, dispelled the loneliness.

After a while she opened her eyes and found him watching her. "Oh, Max," she said, "I'm so glad you are here."

"It seems as well," he rejoined, rather grimly. "Don't you think it's time you began to behave rationally?"

"Have I been very silly?" she asked.

"Very, I should say." He sat down on the arm of her chair, and drew her head to lean against him, a very rare demonstration with him.

She relaxed with a sigh. "I can't help it," she said wistfully. "I used to think life was just splendid—it was good to be alive. And now—I sometimes wish I'd never been born."

"Which is a mistake," said Max. "There's no time for that sort of thing. Besides, it's futile. Now, don't cry! That's futile, too, when there is anything else to be done. I don't suppose Trevor will be feeling particularly jolly when he gets back from this show—though there's something rather funny about it to my mind—and you'll have to cheer him up. I suppose you won't be upset if I smoke?"

"What can you see funny in it?" questioned Chris.

He lighted his cigarette before replying. "My dear girl," he said then, "I can't endow you with a sense of humour if you don't possess one. But all this pomp and circumstance has got its funny side, I assure you. Bertrand saw that; he was a philosopher. If he were here now, he would snap his fingers and laugh."

"He might," Chris admitted. "At least, he called it a dream in the midst of a great Reality."

"Which it is," said Max. "Get outside it all. Get above it if you can. And you will see. Come, you mustn't grizzle. You don't seriously suppose you've lost anything, do you?" He looked down at her suddenly, with a smile in his shrewd eyes. "I say, you must get rid of that idea," he said. "Even I know better than that. I believe in my own way I was almost as fond of him as you were. But I knew he was going long ago, and that nothing on earth could stop him. He knew it too. Between ourselves, I don't think he much wanted to stop. But there was nothing unwholesome about him. He wasn't a shirker. He played the game. And now you're going to play it, eh? You're going to buck up. You're going to give Trevor a sample of what the Wyndhams can do. I know we're a rotten tribe, but we've got our points. In Heaven's name, let's make the most of 'em!"

He bent abruptly and kissed her.

"Life's all right," he said. "And so's the world. But you've got to get used to the idea that it's not a place to stay in. It's no good sitting down by the wayside to cry. You've got to look on ahead and keep moving. It's the only possible way. If you don't, you get buried in every sand-storm."

Chris reached up her arms and clasped him very tightly.

"Max, tell me Love doesn't die!"

"It doesn't," said Max stoutly.

"You are sure? You are sure?"

"Yes, I am sure."

"How do you know? Tell me—tell me!"

Chris's voice was piteous. Yet for a moment he was silent. Then, "I know," he said, "by the way that chap faced death."

"Because he wasn't afraid?" she whispered. "Because he died so easily?"

"Because he didn't die," said Max.

Late that night the clouds passed, and a new moon rose behind the fortress and threw a golden shimmer over the sea. The waves were washing over the rocks with a deep, mysterious murmuring. To Chris, kneeling at her window, it was as if they were trying to tell her a secret. She had knelt down to pray, but her thoughts had wandered, and somehow she could not call them back. Almost in spite of herself, she went in spirit over the rocks till she came to the Magic Cave. And here she would have entered, but could not, for the tide was rising and barred her out.

"Not there, *mignonne*," said a soft voice at her side.

She turned her head. Surely he had spoken in the stillness! Surely it was no dream!

But the action brought her back, back to the shadowy room, and the moonlit sea, and the prayer that was still little more than a vague longing in her heart.

She uttered a brief sigh, and rose. And in that moment she found herself face to face with her husband.

"Trevor!" she said, startled.

He was standing close to her, and suddenly she knew that he had been there for some time, waiting for her to rise.

Her first impulse was one of nervous irresolution, but it possessed her for a moment only. With scarcely a pause she went straight into his arms.

"I'm so glad you've come," she whispered. "Isn't the sea lovely? Have you—have you seen the new moon?"

He held her in silence, and she heard the beating of his heart, strong and steady, where she had pillowed her head. She turned her face upwards after a little.

"Trevor, do you remember, long ago, how we saw the new moon together—and you wished? Have you wished this time?"

"It is always the same wish with me," he said.

"What! Hasn't it come true yet?" She leaned her head back to see his face the better. "Trevor," she said, "are you sure it hasn't come true?"

She saw his faint smile in the moonlight. "I think I should know if it had, dear."

"I'm not so sure," said Chris. "Men are very silly. They never see anything that isn't absolutely in black and white, and not always then. Tell me what it was you wished for."

But he shook his head. "That isn't fair, is it? If the gods hear, it will be struck off the list at once."

"Never mind the gods," said Chris despotically. "I'll get it for you somehow—even if they do. Now tell me! Whisper!" She drew down his head and waited expectantly.

"What a ghastly predicament!" he said.

"Trevor! Don't laugh! I'm not laughing."

"I'm sorry," he said. "But really I can't afford to run any risks of that sort."

"Then you still think you may get it?" questioned Chris.

"I think it possible—if the gods are kind."

"My dear," she said suddenly, "let's leave off joking. If it's something you're wanting very badly, why don't you—pray for it?"

"I am praying for it, sweetheart," he said.

"Oh, Trevor, tell me! And I'll pray, too."

She wound her arms persuasively about his neck. Her face was very sweet in the moonlight. The deep-sea eyes were very tender.

He looked into them and yielded. "Chris, I am praying for the love of the woman I love."

"Oh, but, Trevor—Trevor—"

"Yes," he said, and his voice vibrated upon a deeper note—a note that was passionate. "I want more than a little, my Chris. But I will be patient. I will wait all my life long if I must. Only—O God, let me win it at last!"

He stopped. She was looking at him strangely, and there was something about her that he had never seen before—something that compelled.

"But, Trevor dearest," she said, "it was yours long—long ago. Oh, don't you understand? How shall I make you understand?"

She clasped him closer. The moonlight was shining in her eyes—the eyes of a woman who had come through suffering into peace.

"My darling," she said, "before God, I am telling you the truth. If you hadn't come back to me, I should have broken my heart."

He took her head between his hands. He bent his face to hers, looking deep into those shining, unswerving eyes.

"Won't you believe me?" she pleaded. "Dear, I couldn't lie to you if I tried. Must I put it more plainly still? Then listen! You are more to me now than Bertie ever was. I do not say more than he might have been. But we can't put back the clock. I wouldn't if I could. No—no, not even to live again those old happy days. Trevor, do you understand now, dear? For if you don't, not even Aunt Philippa could be harder to convince. I am yours. I am yours. The other was a dream that can only come true in Paradise. But this is our Reality—yours and mine. And I can't live without you. I want you so. I love you so. Trevor—my husband!"

Her lips quivered suddenly, but in that moment his found them and possessed them. She gave herself to him in complete surrender, as she had given herself on their wedding-night. Yet with a difference. For she throbbed in his arms; she thrilled to his touch. She opened to him the doors of her soul, and drew him within...

"And now you understand?" she whispered to him later.

"Yes—I understand," he said.

She laid her head again upon his breast. "To understand all is to forgive all," she said.

To which he answered softly, "But there is nothing to forgive."